Douglas G. Barron

The Court Book of the Barony of Urie

in Kincardineshire 1604-1747

Douglas G. Barron

The Court Book of the Barony of Urie
in Kincardineshire 1604-1747

ISBN/EAN: 9783337262518

Printed in Europe, USA, Canada, Australia, Japan

Cover: Foto ©Andreas Hilbeck / pixelio.de

More available books at **www.hansebooks.com**

PUBLICATIONS

OF THE

SCOTTISH HISTORY SOCIETY

VOLUME XII.

———◆———

BARON COURT BOOK OF URIE

OCTOBER 1892

THE OLD HOUSE OF URIE

(taken down in 1855)

THE COURT BOOK

OF

THE BARONY OF URIE

IN

KINCARDINESHIRE

1604-1747

Edited from the Original Manuscript with Notes

and Introduction by the

Rev. DOUGLAS GORDON BARRON

M.A.

EDINBURGH

Printed at the University Press by T. and A. Constable

for the Scottish History Society

1892

PREFATORY NOTE

THE manuscript of the Court Book of the Barony of Urie forms a small quarto volume. It has been carefully preserved, and though the writing is often slovenly and difficult to decipher, there is no part of the record which has been destroyed or rendered illegible through decay. Prior to the death of Captain Barclay-Allardice in 1854, the Court Book remained in the possession of the proprietors of Urie. It subsequently passed into the hands of its present possessor, Mr. Robert Barclay of Bury Hill, Dorking (see App. IV. p. 192), to whom the thanks of the Society are due for permitting its publication.

The manuscript has been carefully transcribed by the Rev. Walter Macleod, whose kindness in revising the proof-sheets of the text I gratefully acknowledge.

My thanks are also due to Sir Patrick Keith-Murray, Bart., of Ochtertyre, Mr. Baird of Urie, Mr. Fraser of Findrack, Mrs. Barclay-Allardice, and others, who have kindly put at my disposal materials bearing upon the history of Urie and its proprietors. To Mr. Barclay-Allardice I am indebted for notes on the pedigree of the Barclays.

The illustration of the *Old House of Urie*, which forms the frontispiece of this volume, is from an engraving by the late

William Miller, *H.R.S.A.*, Edinburgh. The signatures on
the margin are those of Colonel David Barclay and his son,
Robert Barclay, the *Apologist*.

Two maps have been introduced, in which it has been
attempted to define the original boundaries of the Baronies of
Cowie and Urie. While perfect accuracy is not claimed for
these, no trouble has been spared to render them as correct as
possible.   D. G. B.

DUNNOTTAR,
8th September 1892.

CONTENTS

———————

ILLUSTRATION—Old House of Urie, *at beginning.*

MAP of the Baronies of Cowie and of Urie, *at end of Introduction.*

CORRIGENDA

P. xxiii, l. 2, *for* James, Earl of Kinghorn, *read* John, Earl of Kinghorn

P. xliv, l. 30, *for* Baron-bailie, *read* Baron-bailiff

P. xlviii, l. 18, *for* haddocks or, *read* haddocks and

INTRODUCTION

The establishment of the Baron Court in Scotland may be regarded as an essential growth of feudalism, coincident with the spread of the tenure of land by military service, as introduced by Malcolm III. in the middle of the eleventh century, and encouraged and extended by his successors. The object of the early kings in fostering the new system of land-tenure was sufficiently apparent. Desirous to increase the influence of the Crown over their turbulent and restless subjects, they were not slow to recognise in it a ready means of bringing into subjection those who might otherwise have been the last to acknowledge their supremacy, or to seal to it the warlike tribes who followed them, and who knew no other claim to gratitude or obedience than the old 'tie of blood.'

The feudal lord, who held a charter of the king on terms of military service, acquired thereby an *imperium in imperio* which was admirably fitted to transmit through every stratum of society that hitherto unknown respect for law and discipline which it was the object of the Crown to recommend and teach. For, just as he did homage for his land, confessing himself to be the vassal of his sovereign, so those who held of him, whether as tenants or sub-vassals, were compelled to recognise a similar indebtedness on their part, and to submit themselves to his authority as their superior or over-lord. Nor did it end here. A minor proprietor, although not holding directly of the king, and being therefore the vassal of a vassal, might yet assume, in virtue of his charter, the position of an over-lord to his immediate dependants, from whom he could exact the homage he himself had rendered, and over whom he was empowered to exercise, though in a limited degree, the jurisdiction to which he was himself subject.

The machinery which controlled this complicated system was centered in the *curia baronis*, or Baron's Court. This court it was the privilege of every superior to hold within the bounds of his own lordship, provided always he had at least two vassals to sit in it as peers. A Baron Court, it will be seen, therefore, was not necessarily the Court of a Barony, unless in so far as the jurisdiction of a minor proprietor might be said to be covered by that of his superior. This principle appears to have been recognised in the right of a crown vassal to take part with his feudatory in the meetings of his private court.

The authority of our earlier barons, alike in criminal and civil matters, was practically absolute. They held their baronies not only *cum furca et fossa*, with power of pit and gallows, but even in certain instances *cum placitis quatuor punctorum coronae nostrae*, that is, with right of jurisdiction in what were termed 'the four points of the Crown'—murder, rape, robbery, and fire-raising. On one point only, that of the *crimen majestatis*, or crime of treason, did the Crown interpose its caveat to limit and restrain the jurisdiction of its immediate vassals in dealing with the rude and lawless spirit of their time.

As things progressed, or in other words, as the policy of delegating power by the State in exchange for 'homage and service' gradually brought about the change anticipated, the privileges of this dominant and ruling class were correspondingly curtailed. Their boasted right of 'pit and gallows' was tempered in the first instance by the withdrawal from their jurisdiction of the Crown Pleas, and subsequently by the limitation of their right to dispose of the homicide and thief, to cases in which the former had been caught 'red-handed,' or

the latter *infang*,—that is, with the stolen property in his
possession within the confines of the barony. But apart
altogether from this higher jurisdiction, care was taken that
the feudal lord should still possess abundant power to bring
into subjection the most refractory of his vassals, did they
venture to dispute his high prerogative and claim. Fine and
forfeiture were at all times ready and effective instruments of
discipline, while the knowledge that fines and escheats, instead
of falling to the Crown, became the lawful property of the
superior, may be supposed to have encouraged the latter in the
vindication of their just authority, even if it did not occasionally incite them to abuse its exercise through greed of gain.

As far as civil jurisdiction was concerned, the minor proprietor, who in no case possessed the power of life and death
over his vassals, and whose criminal authority was strictly
regulated by the terms of his charter, extending for the most
part to the punishment of petty thefts and the exaction of
bludwites,[1] was exactly in the same position as he who held
directly of the Crown. Both had alike the right to settle at
their court all matters of dispute concerning land and tenancy.
They were empowered to pursue for debt, to punish for neglect
or contumacy, and, generally speaking, to direct and, in no
limited or formal sense, determine the material prosperity or
its opposite of all who owed to them the feudal obligation,
and were bound by its indissoluble and jealous claim.

It was a characteristic of Feudalism that a superior in trans-
mitting power or privilege to a dependant did so, as nearly as
was possible, in the precise form in which he himself enjoyed
it. The Baron, as we have seen, exercised to all intents and
purposes the functions of a king among his vassals, and we
cannot wonder, therefore, if his court presented in its salient
features an almost literal resemblance to the sovereign courts

---

[1] Fines for shedding of blood.

of the realm. Its place of meeting was originally a hill or mound—the 'moot-hill' of an earlier period. And in the record of a Baron Court held by Sir Patrick Gray, as superior of the Barony of Longforgan, in the year 1385, we find this ancient custom still prevailing.[1]

Though interested enough to watch, and in certain circumstances, perhaps, even to influence, the judgment of the Court, the Baron did not preside, at least in later times, in person. His bailie or steward sat as preses of the Court, in this and other matters occupying a position analogous to that of the royal seneschal. Other officials were the chancellor or clerk, who was invariably a notary, and qualified, therefore, to advise on points of law and precedent ; the officer or sergeant, who acted also as bailiff to the barony ; the dempster, a functionary robbed in later times of his old power and state, and retained merely to pronounce the sentence which the bailie, in his capacity as judge, had first awarded ; and, finally, the suitors or free-tenants, who were summoned to be present, just as the Baron was himself required to sit in Parliament. Giving of 'suit and presence' at the Lord's Court was one of the imperative requirements of all feudal tenure, and no one was exempted without reasonable excuse from attending thrice yearly to perform this 'debtful service.'

The duties and responsibilities of suitors necessarily varied with the different forms of trial which obtained at different periods. Our earlier tribunals were scarcely calculated to make any very formidable demand either upon their courage or intelligence. In trials by compurgation, for example, they were probably required to assist in making up the tale of those who asserted, with no regard to evidence or fact, the

---

[1] Four separate minutes of this Court are in the possession of Sir Patrick Keith Murray, Bart., of Ochtertyre. They are described by Dr. Stuart as 'almost a solitary specimen of the proceedings of a Barony Court in Scotland in the fourteenth century.'—Third Report of Historical Manuscripts Commission, Appendix, p. 410.

inherent integrity, or the reverse, of the defendant. Where, on the other hand, 'the judgment of God' by ordeal or combat had been claimed, it doubtless sufficed that they were present as spectators, prepared if need be to bear witness that the formalities had been impartially conducted. When, however, to use the words of Mr. Cosmo Innes, 'men no longer thought it convenient that he who was accused of the theft of a cow should go free if twenty-four friends swore that they thought him incapable of stealing,'[1] and when, accordingly, the older forms of trial were gradually supplanted by the verdict of the 'good men and true' of the neighbourhood, the suitor rose to take a permanent and foremost place in the administration of justice. True, his position was still, and always would remain equivocal, in so far as he was the creature of his lord, but it was his own by universally acknowledged right and custom, and it depended on himself to maintain or to betray it. Besides serving on assize, suitors were further entitled to appear as witnesses. They were required to act as sureties for their fellow-suitors and dependants; to serve as arbiters in certain forms of dispute; to value agricultural effects; to fix the boundaries of neighbouring 'tacks,' and generally to be at the bidding of the Court in whatsoever capacity their services might be demanded.

The formalities attendant on the holding of a Baron Court are to be gathered incidentally from a variety of sources. The first step, naturally, was to apprise those interested of the place and date of meeting. This was done by written summons of the officer, who received a warrant for that purpose from the bailie. This summons he was afterwards required to read in Court, in proof that he had executed the precept of his superior. One such citation has fortunately been preserved in the record of the Court of Longforgan, previously referred to. Its terms are as follows:—

---

[1] Innes's *Scotch Legal Antiquities*, p. 218.

'I, Robyn Jobson, sergand, lauchfully made and ordanyt of
the chef part of the barony of Langforgund, throw Sir Patrick
Gray, lord of that ilk, chef part of that ilk barony in the
sheradom of Perth, somonde at the chef plaz of the tencindri
of Lytilton, and Lowranstone of Ochtyrcomane within the
Lytilton, Sir Thomas the Hay of Lowchqwhorwart, and Dam
Jonat his spouse, throw reson of his spouse, Sir William of
Cunygham, and Dam Margaret his spouse, Elizabeth of
Maxwel, Alexandir of Koeborne, and Katerin his spouse, for
reson of his spouse, and Dugal McDuel, and Eufam his spouse,
for resone of his spouse, the Wedynysday, the xvi day of the
moneth of Nouember, that thai apere lauchfolly at the
Hundhil in Langforgrond, in the sheradom of Perth, to Sir
Patrick Gray, lord of the chef part of Langforgronde, and
orlord of the lands of Lytilton and Louranzstone of Ouchtir-
comon, thys tewysday that nw ys the xvi day of this moneth of
Jenuer, to schaw how and for quat caus, throw quat charter or
ewydens thai halde or clemys to hald the landys or tenandris
of Lytiltone and Lowranzstone of Achtyrcoman of hym, and
of his chef parts of the Barony of Longforgond within the
sheradom of Perth, and to do this day efter my somonz for
yhour haldyng as the law and ordyr of law askys in yt selfe.
Yat I haf mad this somondys in this maner as I hafe recordyt
lawfully, lo here my witnez, Robyn Jonson, of Balligyrnach
and Richard of Pentland, William Scot, and Androw Yhong.'

It will be noted that the above describes the purpose of the
meeting of the Court, and also refers by name to those whose
presence was especially desired. It is just possible that a less
formal mandate may have served to cite those members of the
Court who were required to act as suitors.

Parties being assembled, the Bailie instructed his officer to
'Cry' the Court, which he did in these, or words of corresponding import—'All maner of men that have to doe here at this
day drawe near and attend to the Courte.' Proceedings were

commenced by the rehearsal of the Suit Roll of the Barony.
During its recital the names of parties absent with excuse were
notified, defaulters being summarily amerced for non-attendance.
Other preliminaries included the adjustment of the roll of
pleas, reports as to the service of distraints, and kindred
matters. Did the billet of the Court include the trial of any
criminal offence the members of assize were next declared,
and sworn. The jury of a Scottish Baron Court numbered
fifteen.[1] Of these the Chancellor or foreman was sworn first,
and by himself. The remainder took the oath in groups of
three or four together. This was followed by the recital of
the 'Charge,' during the delivery of which the assize remained
standing. This ceremony, which eventually degenerated into
a mere exhortation to defend the court, accompanied by a
threat of pain and penalty to such as should presume to trouble
or molest it, was originally a most important function.

In an anonymous volume, entitled *The Justice of the Peace*,
published in London in 1564, a copy of a Court Charge, as
used in England at that period, is printed, and although on
many points it postulates a state of things inapplicable to our
Scottish Courts, we feel that we are justified in reproducing it.
Its value will be readily admitted, not only as touching one by
one the minutiae of baronial jurisdiction, but still more as
affording in itself a picture of the social condition of the feudal
vassal at a time when feudalism might be said to be still in the
zenith of its power, the sincerity and truth of which cannot be
questioned.

THE CHARGE OF A COURT BARON.

Firste, ye good men that bene sworne, ye shall enquire and

---

[1] This statement is made on the authority of Mr. Cosmo Innes (*Legal Antiquities*, p. 59), but is not supported by the usage of the Court of Urie, where
the number of the assize varies, and appears in no instance to have reached
fifteen.

truely present al the sutoutes[1] that owe any sute unto thys courte at this day, as for theyr tenures, if they be heire or no, and presente theyr names that make defaute.

Also, if there be any tenant deade sythen the last court daye, ye shall enquyre of hym and doe us to wete[2] what he helde of this Lordeship at the day of his deathe, and what auauntage the lord shuld haue by his death, etc., as Ward, Mariage, and Reliefe or Eschete, or any other profite, and who is his next heyre, and what age he is of, and in whose keping.

Also, if there be any rent, custome, or seruice withdrawen from this lordeship that oughte of right to be done, ye shall enquire by whome it is withdrawen and what custome or seruice it is, and in what Bayliffes time, and howe it hath bene withdrawen, and where the land lieth, that we may distraine for the arrerages that are behinde.

Also, if there bee any bonde man of bloude[3] that putteth his sonne unto the scole to make him a preste or apprentice, or set him to craft, or marieth his daughter without leaue, ye shal do us to wete.

Also, if there be any bondeman that letteth his lande, that is to say, for the halfe or for the thirde shefe without leave. Or els if there be any bondeman that withdraweth his goodes or cattelles out of the lordeship without leaue, do us to wete.

Also, if the lordes common bee so charged by any tenant

---

[1] Suitors. [2] Inform us.

[3] *A bondman of blood or villein* might be either (1) *a villein in gross*, who was immediately bound to the person of his lord and his heirs; or (2) *a villein regardant to a manor*, who was bound to his lord as a member belonging and annexed to a manor whereof the lord was owner. He was properly a true *villein*, of whom the lord took redemption to marry his daughter and to make him free, and whom the lord might put out of his lands and tenements, goods and chattels at his will, and beat and chastise but not maim.—Blount's *Law Dictionary*.

A villein held his lands by *copyhold*, which means that he had nothing to show for them but the *copy* of the rolls made by the steward of the Lord's Court. He is distinguished from the *free holder*, who held in fee-simple, fee-tail, or for life. Neither of these systems of tenure was known in Scotland.

with mo beastes then he should hold after the quantitie of his tenure, ye shal do us to wete.

Also, if there be any bondman of bloud that longeth to this lordeship, that is fledde, and dwelleth withoute this lordeship without fyne or raunsome makinge, ye shal do us to wete.

Also, if there be any alienacion ouer twelve monethes and a day or lesse for terme of yeres in fee or in fee taile, ye shal do us to wete.

Also, if there be any transmutacion of possession, that is to say, copy lande for fre lande, or fre lande for copy lande, whereof the Lorde might take any dissauantage in amendinge of the one and appairing of the other, ye shal do us to wete.

Also, of all maner wast done in housinge, letting downe, or cutting the great tymbre.

Also, of al trespassours in corone or grasse, or in pastures or greanes or meades, or fychers or foulers, or hunters or haukers, within this lordeship or lordes warren, ye shall do us to wete if there be any such.

Also, if there be any tenant of copy holde, tenant at will, or tenant of bonde tenure, that suffer their tenements to bee ruinous and falle downe, or els any fermovr bounden to reparacion, repaire not as he ought to doe, do us to wete.

Also, if there be any boundemen of bloude within this lordship that purchaseth any fre lande without any leaue or licence, ye shal do us to wete what it is, and what heires he hath.

Also, of al other thinges that ye haue knowen that ought to be presented to the Lordes auayle, ye shal do us to wete thereof by the othes that ye haue made and brynge in a true presentment.

Also, if any make any rescous or breake any arest made by the baily or any other officer, or els if any man breake the lordes pounde, that is to say, a distres put in the Lords pound by an officer and taken out again without lycence, do us to wete.

Also, if ye knowe any that remoueth or pulleth up mere-stones or stactes betwene lordeship and lordship, or tenant and tenant, whether it bee fre or bonde, present theyr names.

Also, if any tenaunt giue any lande to the church, that is to say, into mortmaine, sith the statut therof was made, without licence of the king and the lord of this lordship, ye shal doe us to wete.

Also, if any man haue encroched any of the lords soile, that is to say, lande, medow, moore, pasture, or any vacant grounde without licence of the lorde, present their names.

Also, if any man holde two tenementes, and waisteth the one as if he withdraweth anye trees from the one to the other, if ye knowe any such, present their names by your forsayd othes.

Or els if ye know that any tenant hath made any strope or wast upon his bonde tenant, strope, that is to say, pulling up of trees or hedges, wast, is to saye, houses fall downe for defaut of reperacion, if there be any suche, present their names.

Also, if ye knowe any tenaunt that kepeth or withdraweth any euidence that longe to this lordshipes courtes, rolles, rentalles, customaryes, or any other euidence, ye shall present their names.

The charge delivered, or in legal phrase, 'the Court being lawfully fenced and affirmed,' the way was open for the trans-action of business. Vassals having suit against their neigh-bours were permitted to pursue in person, the superior either personally or through his chamberlain or other deputy, while in Courts of full Baronial Jurisdiction a Procurator-Fiscal was appointed to prosecute in criminal causes.

It was a peculiarity of the Court that all processes were introduced not by original writ or precept, but by *plaint*, a description of the proposed action being reduced to writing and presented to the Bailie either previous to the meeting or in open Court. This having been produced, and a true bill declared, the accused was summoned to appear against a certain day, when formal proof was led and judgment followed. Should he neglect the summons of the Court, an attachment was decreed against him and a fresh citation ordered. It being to be noted, however, that 'no defendant should be attached by his bodye, but only by his goddes,' that is to say, 'by his oxe, cowe, horse, potte, payne, or other maner of chattell.' Further, non-appearance on the part of the accused was followed by renewed distraint, till failing for the fourth time to comply with the injunction of the Court deliverance went against him by default.

Pleas to be tried were often various enough, but all passed with equal freedom through the mill of medieval justice. Here a defaulting tenant is arraigned, and promptly forfeits the choicest of his stock to pay the landlord. A farmer's horse has strayed upon his neighbour's grass, and has been expeditiously and safely poinded. No qualifying circumstance is urged or sought. The rustic Shylock claims his pound of flesh and gets it. Now an indignant Baron bitterly complains that such an one has violated the privileges of his Court by pursuing, before the Lords of Session, Sheriff, or Commissioners, a claim which ought to have been his. It is hard to realise that the great man is wounded not in pride but purse, and that his indignation centres in the fact that a presumably substantial fine has found its way into the capacious pockets of the State instead of into his, mayhap exceeding tight ones. And yet, if there be doubt upon the point, the equanimity with which he hears a further fine pronounced on his offending vassal must effectually remove it. Here a rough brawler is transferred to prison or the stocks, the distress which has been placed upon his goods increased threefold, because the blow he struck had chanced to be 'above the breath,' instead of under it. While there, a wretched thief, who has

been caught *infang*, receives short shrift from men whose only
thought is to prevent his further depredations. 'Notorious'
and 'habit and repute,' he has had both ears cropped, and
has been branded on the cheek for past delinquencies.   It
only remains—and he will not have long to wait—that he be
'whipped at a cart tail,' and 'hangit till he be ded' upon the
neighbouring gallows.

The sederunt of the Baron Court was closed by what appears
to us the curious formality of crying the Assize of Bread and
Ale.   Here, again, the authority of the Baron interposed to
fix the price of commodities which could only be produced
for sale by his express indulgence.   It may be hardly necessary
to suggest that baxter and brewer were alike required to
supply the Manor at a different price from that which they
were permitted to exact from the surrounding tenants.   The
form of conducting this Assize which was most commonly in
use has been preserved as follows :—

> In what wise the bayliffe or beddel, which scrueth the
> Courte, shall call thassyse of breade and ale whan the
> Court is ended.

The stewarde shall cause the bailiffe to take an oyes,[1] and
shall say: 'Al maner men that wyl bake breade to sell, loke
they sell foure loues for j^d. and ij loues for j ^{ob}., and loke
ye kepe thassise.   All maner of brewers that will brewe to sell
loke ye sell a galon of ale of the beste, for 1d. ob., the second
for a penye, and the worste for an ob., and kepe the assise, and
that no brewer sell out no burthen tyll the ale conoure[2] haue
assayed thereof, and sette a price thereon, upon peine of
forfayture, etc.

---

[1] A corruption of the French *oyez, hear ye*, used by the Crier of a court to
enjoin silence.

[2] The *ale conoure*, or *ale taster*, was an officer appointed to look to the assize
and quality of bread and ale, within the precinct of the lordship.

'And all maner of men that haue for to do at this day, come and you shalbe harde, or els kepe your day at the nexte Court by resonable warnynge, And God saue the kyng.'

Such, in its main outlines, was the Baron Court on which in feudal times the comfort and self-respect of the rural population in England and Scotland rested. That feudalism, at its introduction, was a power for good, cannot be questioned. No other system could so successfully have coped with the lawless spirit of the age, and brought it mercifully, as we must admit, within the pale of civil government. This task accomplished, that it eventually degenerated for the most part into an instrument of petty tyranny and greed, is equally apparent. And nowhere is this more clearly recognised than in the record of its Baron Courts, where, despite an occasional affectation of good faith, everything is so adjusted as to serve the interest of the strong against the weak, the lord against his helpless vassal and dependant. It was a red-letter day, therefore, for our country when an otherwise least thoughtful or far-seeing Prince struck a first solid and determined blow at its prerogatives.[1] The Act of Charles II. practically abolished feudalism in England, and although nominally it still survives north of the Tweed, it has long since been stripped by various Acts of its more objectionable and repellent features. Baron Courts continued to be held in Scotland till 1747, when their jurisdiction was by law curtailed to an extent which rendered them no longer a convenient source either of profit or prestige to their possessors.[2] A Baron still retains the right of holding Courts,—a privilege, however, of which he has altogether ceased to take advantage. It is still on statute that he may pursue at his own Court for feu-duties and rents, and may compel his tenants to perform their legal services. He has, besides, a jurisdiction in civil actions to the extent of 40s. A further right of punishing assault and petty theft by a fine not

---

[1] Act 12 Car. II. c. 24.   [2] Act 20 Geo. II. c. 43.

exceeding 20s., is so burdened with prohibitive restrictions as practically to preclude its exercise.

Thus far the main object of inquiry has been as to the general system of feudal laws upon which such minor judicatures as the Baron or Baron-baillie Courts of Scotland rested. To France we may look as the original source of our feudal customs and observances; but not to France directly, for it is probable that these came to Scotland through the channel of English example and practice. A Baron Court in Scotland, therefore, must have reflected in some degree the usages of both England and France, and we may take it that in all three countries, after making allowance for special national characteristics and local divergences, the main features of these Minor Courts were common to all.

The Baron Court Book of Urie, which forms the body of this volume, contains a record of the proceedings of that Court for a period extending from 1604 to 1747. These proceedings not only afford evidence that the general principles of feudalism were in full play during that period, but they preserve for us also many rural usages and customs which must have been common both to the locality of Urie and to Scotland generally. With a view to illustrating these usages and customs it will be necessary, in the first place, to give some account of the estate of Urie and its successive proprietors; and, secondly, to cite a few facts bearing upon the relations which obtained between the lairds of Urie and their tenants, more particularly in connection with the civil jurisdiction of the former as touching the occupancy of the land.

I. Urie and Monquich, which in the earlier minutes are erroneously described as the 'Barony of Urie,' are situated in

the county of Kincardine and parish of Fetteresso, and are in
the immediate vicinity of Stonehaven, the county town. They
originally formed part of the barony of Cowie. The records
of sederunt, therefore, which compose the earlier portion of
this volume, describe the doings of the court of a sub-vassal.

The early proprietors of Urie were cadets of the family of
Errol, who came into possession of the property about the
middle of the fifteenth century. Sir William Hay of Errol,
Hereditary Great Constable of Scotland, had purchased Cowie
from Sir William Fraser of Philorth in 1415. Fifteen years
later he granted to his younger son a charter of the lands of
Urie, thereby defining for the first time the extent and boundaries of the estate. He died in 1436, and was succeeded
by his grandson, also named William, who was created Earl
of Errol in 1452. To him the laird of Urie resigned his
lands, and this resignation was subsequently confirmed to his
son and successor, Nicholas, second Earl of Errol. Nicholas
thereupon conveyed Urie to his uncle, Gilbert Hay, by a
deed dated 12th April 1467. Of this Gilbert Hay, or
'Master' Gilbert Hay, as he is invariably designed, we have
successive glimpses in the records of the period. He was
educated for the law, and although he succeeded through his
wife, who was the only daughter and heiress of Sir John
Dunbar of Crimond, to very considerable estates in the shires
of Aberdeen and Elgin, he yet appears to have pursued the
practice of his profession all through his active bustling life.

From Gilbert Hay, who died in 1487, six generations in
succession held the lands of Urie. John Hay, fifth in descent
of this unbroken line, is the first who occupies the position of
proprietor in the pages of the Court Book. He succeeded to
the estates in 1588, and died in 1607. Previous to the former
date he had embarked, along with his superior, Francis, eighth
Earl of Errol, in treasonable designs against the Government
of James VI. This Earl is known in history as a leader

of the Popish faction in the North, who, after the execution of Mary Queen of Scots, entered into correspondence with the Spanish Court, then busied in preparing the *Invincible Armada* for an attack on England. In the abortive rising at Aberdeen in 1589, which was the first outcome of this ill-advised and foolishly conducted league, John Hay of Urie was involved, if not as an active participator in the fact, at least as in friendship and sympathy with the rebels. Falling henceforth under suspicion, Hay was arrested three years later on a charge of hearing Mass, and of 'resetting and intercommuning with jesuits, priests, and papists.' The indictment was in all respects a serious one enough, its gravity being proven by the circumstance that the Parliament of 1594 included 'wilful hearing of Mass' among the list of capital offences. It is evident, however, that considerable influence was brought to bear on his behalf, most probably through the initiative of his chief, whose treason, half connived at in secret by King James, was never seriously resented. He was mulcted in a fine of one thousand merks, and was required to appear in Aberdeen before a Council on Religious Doubts, there to recant and make atonement for his misdemeanours. The deliverance of the Privy Council in the case bears evidence of a deliberate attempt to shield the accused, almost at any cost, from the responsibility and weight of the arraignment. 'The king is assured,' it runs, 'that it (the offence of hearing Mass) proceeded, not of a malicious intent to contempt his Hines, but being ignorant of the tenor of the Acts and grundit in his dampnable errouris and oppinion be the crafty allurementis and persuasioun of the saidis jesuitis, he wes movit, of very simplicitie and ignorance, and upone a blind zeal borne be him towardis his professioun.'

John Hay of Urie, whose 'simplicitie and ignorance' are thus proclaimed, has failed to leave any very distinct impression of his personality on the few meetings of the Baron Court which bear to have been called by his authority. If we should venture to form any estimate of his character, as he appears before us, we would be tempted to describe him as a seemingly careless and indulgent laird who had been suddenly aroused to the necessity of economy and retrenchment. His frequent bringing to the front of obsolete or dormant statutes bears this out, and his tenants can hardly be expected to have participated in his new found admiration and respect for the 'wmquhil father of guid memorie' who is continually quoted in support of reimposed exactions.

Doubtless the revenues of Urie had been considerably overtaxed to meet the liabilities arising out of the treasonable dealings of the proprietor. These liabilities naturally tended to accumulate rather than decrease as public quarrels ripened into private enmities. William Hay, who succeeded his father in 1607, appears to have inherited, along with the estate, a countless tale of feuds and heart-burnings. Nor is it by any means apparent that the new laird was either prone to shun the entrance to a quarrel or, being in, was without stomach to maintain it. In the first year of his succession a dispute with Robert Fraser of Brachmont assumed a somewhat serious aspect; so much so, indeed, that on Fraser bringing the matter under the notice of the Privy Council, Hay was bound over, himself in a thousand pounds, his brother Alexander in five hundred, and no fewer than fifteen of their retainers (for whom Robert Irvine at the Mill of Cowie became cautioner) in three hundred merks each, to keep the peace. Six years later Robert Strauchine, M.D., complained that William Hay of Urie and Thomas Auchenleck, sometime servitor to the Earl of Orkney, being armed with various weapons, had gone to a certain dwelling-house in Stonehaven, believing him to be there, and that, to make sure of finding him and slaying him, the Laird of Urie had kept watch outside, while Auchenleck, entering the house, sword in hand, had forced the chamber doors and 'stoggit the beddis.' Disappointed in their search, and hearing that he 'had repairit to the lynkis of the said town of Stanehyve to recreat himself,' Strauchine further explains how they had followed him thither with intent to murder him, adding that they would undoubtedly have executed their purpose had he not, acting on the counsel of his friends, withdrawn himself from the links.

Such reckless conduct on the part of the laird could only eventuate in the impoverishment and ruin of his estates. The downward progress of events is shadowed forth by the Court Book in the gradual assumption of proprietary rights on the part of Francis, Earl of Errol, who, restored to royal favour in 1596, was now living in the enjoyment of his vast possessions at Slains Castle in Aberdeenshire. On 30th July 1616 the Earl's name is first inserted in the preamble of a minute of the Court, 'with special consent of the proprietor.' Such an announcement does not necessarily imply anything further than that it had pleased the Earl to exercise his prerogative of appearing at the Court in his capacity of over-lord. Two years later his name again appears, while the explanatory clause is absent. In the minute of 11th July 1620 he is associated with the laird as heritable proprietor. This continues till 5th October 1626, when the name of William Hay is abruptly dropped, and Errol is henceforth described as sole proprietor of the lordship. It is evident from the above that Hay had been gradually parting with his interest in the estates to his superior. It was not till four years after the date named, however, that a formal transfer of the property was made, following a process by 'William Hay of Wry,' to complete his title as heir to his *tritavus*, Gilbert Hay.

Francis, Earl of Errol, died in 1631 : and his son William— who during his brief tenure of the honours and estates did much to squander the resources of the earldom—in 1637. Gilbert, tenth Earl, who succeeded as a minor, is represented

at the meetings of the Court by his curators, John, Lord
Yester; James Lyon of Auldbar; and James, Earl of Kinghorn. Twice only does the Court sit during their administration, the minute of 20th November 1639 being that of their
last recorded meeting. A blank of nearly thirty years follows,
during which period the lands of Urie underwent many
changes, and passed successively through various hands. The
greater portion of Monquich was permanently alienated from
the Barony, while Urie itself was stripped of Finlayston and
Redclock, together with such minor adjuncts as the chapel
lands and crofts of Cowie. What remained of the estate
passed in the first instance, in wadset, to John Forbes of
Leslie, younger son of William Forbes of Monymusk. John
Forbes was a man of pushing and aggressive temperament,
and made himself conspicuous, not only as a purchaser of
extensive estates in the shires of Aberdeen and Kincardine,
but also as a zealous upholder of the Covenant, prepared to
do battle for his political opinions, and to maintain them
stoutly against all comers. He had acquired the lands of
Leslie in 1620 from George Leslie, last of that Ilk, and subsequent to 1637 had added to his possessions the important
estate of Banchory, in Kincardineshire. Forbes was also proprietor of the Barony of Durris, which was plundered by
the barons of the north after they had dispersed the meeting of Estates at Turriff in 1639. Five years later, Spalding
tells us, 'his girnellis in Banchorie, sic as wes left oncareit to
Urie,' were pillaged by Montrose, while, in 1645, he again
suffered at the hands of the great Marquis, who, having raided
the baronies of Dunnottar and Fetteresso, belonging to the
Earl Marischal, 'merchis to Vrie. He fyres the place, burnis
all to the voltis and haill lauche bigging, cornes and barne-
yairdis; and plunderis the haill grund.' A true type of the
hard-headed Scottish baron of the period, whether pursuing
the representatives of the broken clan Gregor through the

fastnesses of Deeside, or prosecuting his natural enemy, John
Gordon of Haddo, before the Committee of Estates of Parliament, or exchanging pistol shots with Sir Gilbert Menzies of
Pitfodels on the open highway at the entrance to the town of
Aberdeen, whereby, wounded in the leg, 'he lay wnder cure
quhill Januar 1643, and then began to walk upone ane staf
feblie and not soundlie heallit,'[1] Forbes appears to have main-
tained all through a confident and unbroken spirit, prepared
to accept with equanimity what fortune sent. He is referred
to by Spalding as 'ane gryte covenanter,' and the expression,
as descriptive of a strong man possessed of a resolutely determined will and purpose, is undoubtedly deserved.

In 1647, the affairs of the Earl of Errol having reached a
crisis, permission was granted by the Council of Estates to sell
Urie. It was purchased by the Earl Marischal at a cost, we
are told, of '2000 merks for ilk chalder of victuall and ilk
hundreth merks of silver.' Data furnished by the Court Book
enable us to estimate the number of chalders payable by the
tenants as fourteen; and it being further stated in the contract
of purchase that the money and victual rents were almost
equal, we may calculate the price paid as being roughly 56,000
merks or about £3000 sterling. Marischal, who redeemed the
wadset on the lands of Urie, resold them in the following year
to Colonel David Barclay, to whom he also disposed of a considerable part of his estates in the adjoining parish of Dunnottar, consisting of the town and mill lands of Stonehaven and
portions of each of the Baronies of Dunnottar and Uras.
Before, however, the titles to this transfer were completed, the
Earl of Marischal had been attainted by the Cromwellian
Parliament, and the subjects of the purchase were claimed as
forming part of the forfeited estate.

---

[1] Referring to this incident, Spalding remarks, 'this good cause brocht in the
beiring and weiring of gonis, quhilk bred mekill sorrow and mischeif in this
land.'—Spalding Club, *Memorialls of the Trubles in Scotland*, vol. ii. p. 205.

Colonel Barclay, who thus came into disputed possession of Urie, was the third son of David Barclay, proprietor of Mearns and Mathers. Though representative of an old and once powerful family in the district, David Barclay had become involved in pecuniary embarrassments and was soon to dispose of his possessions. Probably this circumstance was not required to induce his son, Colonel Barclay, in accordance with a custom prevalent among the junior branches of the aristocracy of the period, to proceed abroad in search of useful and congenial employment in one or other of the standing armies of the Continent. He was successful in obtaining a commission in the Swedish service under Gustavus Adolphus, and accompanied that monarch on his campaign in Germany in 1630. His splendid physique, his courage, and undoubted military aptitude soon won for him promotion, and after the death of Adolphus, on the field of Lützen in 1632, Barclay continued for some time to serve abroad. On the outbreak of the Civil War in 1638, however, he returned to this country and identifying himself with the Parliamentary Party took the field in their behalf. In 1646 we find him 'Crowner' or Colonel of a regiment of horse intrusted with the mission of punishing the Earl of Crawford, who, with a mixed band of Scots and Irish, was engaged in laying waste the northern counties. Barclay encountered his antagonist in the neighbourhood of Banff and defeated him with great slaughter. Some months later he was sent as second in command to General Middleton, to relieve the town of Inverness beleaguered by the Earl of Seaforth and the Marquis of Montrose; on which occasion, at the head of his division, he forced the crossing of the Ness in face of the opposing army, thereby raising the siege and causing the Royalist leaders to retire. Barclay continued to hold various military appointments under the Estates, and, among other services which he was the means of rendering to his party, was successful, along with General

Middleton, in repulsing the Marquis of Huntly, who, in the absence of the Parliamentary troops, had abruptly thrown himself into the town of Aberdeen, from which as a centre he proceeded to work havoc among the possessions of Presbyterian lairds. His appointment as Governor of Strathbogie followed ; and a year later, 1648, he married Catherine, eldest daughter of Sir Robert Gordon of Gordonston, second son of the Earl of Sutherland, and by his grandmother Lady Helen Stuart, cousin of King James VI.

Barclay's purchase of Urie in 1648, and the subsequent refusal of the Cromwellian Parliament to acknowledge his title to the estates, formed an important turning-point in his career. Disgusted with the treatment he had received, he determined to quit the military service, and if possible to fight a bloodless battle on his own behalf. To this end he applied himself to enter Parliament, and was returned for Sutherlandshire in 1652, and again for the united counties of Forfar and Kincardine in 1654 and 1656. He soon made his influence felt in the councils of the Commonwealth, and maintaining all through one definite and consistent purpose succeeded in securing for himself an appointment as Trustee of Confiscated Estates in Scotland. This done, infeftment in the lands of Urie followed readily, though not till 1679 did he obtain that formal charter which, combining the various subjects he had purchased from the Earl Marischal, erected them into 'Ane haill and free barony, called the Barony of Urie.' Barclay did not retire from Parliament when his own immediate object had been served. It was no part of his nature to remain indifferent while others suffered from the harsh and selfish treatment which, as applied to his own claim for justice, he had learned deeply to resent. He became henceforth the champion of the distressed and plundered Royalists, whose pleas he did not cease by every lawful effort to support. Conspicuous among those who benefited by his disinterested advocacy were the

Countess Marischal and her children, who, reduced to extremity
by the Earl's forfeiture, had so far appealed in vain to the
authorities for payment of the allowance granted them by the
Commissioners for their support. Writing to 'My verie loving
freind Patrick Rankine, advocat, dualling at the foot of the
Kirkheughe in Edinburgh,' the Countess says, 'I did not intend
to have sent this bearer untill I had heard from yow. But
having within this tuo nightes receaved a letter from Daved
Barkley showing that severall claimes on my sones estate are
cliered, and it is his advyce that I shall enter my childrines
claimes, and also that some adreses be maid to the Trusties for
alowance to my grand childrine, I resolve to send the bearer
with the best instructiones I could give him. . . . Trewlie
Colonel Barklay wrytes verie kyndlie, and promises all the
asistance that is within his reatch. Soe that I have derected
the bearer that after he hes spoken with Maister John Nisbit
and yow he shall goe to him with my letter and ask his
advyce.'[1] It might have been expected that such services,
rendered in behalf of those who had suffered on account of
their devotion to Charles I., would have assured for Colonel
Barclay at the Restoration the acknowledgment so justly
merited. On the contrary, the Colonel was seized and put in
prison, the charge against him being the singularly ungracious
one that he had acted as a Trustee under the Usurper. It was
while undergoing imprisonment for this offence in Edinburgh
Castle that Barclay came under the influence of Judge Swinton,
and, being impressed by the zeal of that remarkable enthusiast
—of whom it was said that he was more concerned to spread
the views he had adopted than to defend his own life—
was induced to become a member of the Society of Friends.
Released in 1666, he retired to Urie, where—having rebuilt the
manor-house, which, as we have seen, had been destroyed in
1645—he subsequently continued to reside. He had bid fare-

---

[1] This letter is in the possession of Sir Patrick Keith Murray, Bart.

well alike to camp and senate-house, and the remainder of
his life was spent in propagating the mystic and self-abnegat-
ing creed of Quakerism, and in striving to realise its truth and
sacredness on the practical and living side. The institution of
public meetings for the purpose of Quaker worship was one of
his first steps in this direction, and very soon the little Meeting
House at Urie was built and opened, and this continued for
more than a hundred years to be the headquarters of the
Friends in the north of Scotland. Whatever may be said of
Quakerism as a religious system, no one can impugn the honesty
of David Barclay, or fail to admire the picture which his latter
days have given us of courage and integrity, and of that mild
and cheerful and long-suffering piety which is the ideal of the
sect. The proud warrior and skilled politician of the Commonwealth has become strangely altered as we see him in the
simple garb of Quakerism, but the spirit of the old soldier of
Adolphus burns within him yet. In the face of much opposition, insult, and ill-will, he never wavers. Even renewed imprisonment at the instigation of the clergy in Aberdeen is
powerless to shake his constancy; and to one regretting the
change in his position, and the abuse to which he is subjected
on account of his religious profession, he replies, "I find more
satisfaction as well as honour in being thus insulted for my
religious principles than when, some years ago, it was usual for
the magistrates, as I passed the city of Aberdeen, to meet me
several miles, and conduct me to a public entertainment in
their Townhouse, and then convey me as far out again, in
order to gain my favour." The history of a stormy and
ungrateful period in Scottish history has preserved to us the
record of the early deeds of Colonel Barclay, but it required
the genius of Whittier to describe his latter years. That
writer's inimitable ballad, entitled 'Barclay of Urie,' is familiar
to all who are even but partially conversant with American
literature, and is a fitting tribute to the memory of one

the trial of whose manhood was not more surely made what
time

> he stood
> Ankle deep in Lützen's blood,
> With the brave Gustavus!

than when, the patient jest and scorn of an ignorant and
brutal populace,—

> Turning slow his horse's head
> Towards the Tolbooth prison,
> Where, through iron grates, he heard
> Poor disciples of the word
> Preach of Christ arisen.

In 1667, after an interval of nearly thirty years, Barclay
reconstituted the Baron Court of Urie. Among his earliest
acts in connection therewith is one which probably stands
unique in the history of such tribunals. We can easily understand how, after so long a period of practical exemption from
authority, there had grown up in the barony a race of tenants
ill-disposed to brook the will of a superior however consider-
ately and wisely it might be imposed. Accordingly on 7th
May 1669 we have the curious incident of the laird voluntarily surrendering himself as a panel at the bar of his own
court in answer to the charge of being an oppressor and
exactor. The question narrows itself to one of the rendering of certain *services*, and on the refusal of the tenants to
prosecute 'in regaird they confessed they had noe reasons soe
to doe.' Barclay himself proposes to discontinue the exaction
of service for the future on payment of a yearly money equivalent of six pounds Scots.

Yet notwithstanding this action on his part, it is not
difficult to see how, in discharging his duties as a landlord,
Barclay's religious opinions must have caused him, for a time
at all events, to be ill thought of and misjudged. In his hands
a court of legal justice is transformed, as far as may be, into a

tribunal of religious equity, and doubtless there were few so circumstanced among his vassals as rightly to appreciate the change. It upset their notions and disturbed their equanimity. It not seldom overtook with rebuke and penalty those who had not calculated to meet a moral element in the preferment of their oftentimes vexatious and ill-considered claims.

David Barclay died in 1686, and was succeeded in the barony by his son, Robert Barclay, the famous 'Apologist' of Quakers, whose name, along with that of his father, first appears in the minutes of the court in 1679.

The latter was born at Gordonston, in Morayshire, the seat of his maternal grandfather, on 28th December 1648. Here his earliest education, he tells us, 'fell among the strictest sort of Calvinists, those of this country being generally acknowledged to be the severest of that sect; in heat of zeal surpassing not only Geneva, but all other reformed churches abroad.' At an early age, however, he was withdrawn from this atmosphere of earnest and aggressive Protestantism, and transferred to Paris, where he continued till his sixteenth year a member of the Scots College, of which his uncle was then rector. Barclay's precocity soon arrested the attention of the authorities of that seminary, and no pains seem to have been spared in developing his nascent genius, and in preparing him, as doubtless his preceptors calculated, for the profession of a priest. It seemed for a time, indeed, as if their expectations would be realised, and that the Church of Rome was destined to be permanently enriched by the acquisition of the young enthusiast, who while yet a boy had practically traversed the whole field of mediæval scholarship, and whose vivacity and keenness in debate had already gained him numerous distinctions where such qualities were hard to counterfeit, just in proportion as their possession was intelligently and deeply prized. The solicitude, however, of a dying parent for her eldest born outweighed in Colonel

Barclay's mind the advantages of further residence in Paris, and accordingly he himself went thither to fulfil his wife's behest that her son might be removed from the insidious influences to which her reason told her he was being increasingly exposed. Not without regret did Barclay turn from the career which had seemed to be opening so naturally before him, but neither the promises nor expostulations of his uncle were able in the issue to prevent his sacrificing personal interest and inclination to what he felt were the imperative demands of filial duty. His return to Scotland took place in 1666, and was almost immediately followed by the arrest and imprisonment of his father in Edinburgh Castle, as above described. The subsequent conversion of the latter to Quakerism must have made a deep impression on the imagination of the youthful *savant*, who fresh, it may be, from the study of the *Augustinus* of Cornelius Jansen published under the care of Frommond in 1640, may have been already predisposed to accept the teaching of the English Quietists. Jaffray, in his *Diary*, is careful to anticipate the charge of undue influence having been brought to bear in this direction, and Barclay, speaking of himself at this period, says : ' Who, not by strength of argument, or by a particular disquisition of each doctrine, and convincement of my understanding thereby, came to receive and bear witness to the truth ; but by being secretly reached by this life. For, when I came into the silent assemblies of God's people, I felt a secret power amongst them which touched my heart ; and as I gave way unto it, I found the evil weakening in me, and the good raised up ; and so I became knit and united unto them, hungering more and more after the increase of this power and life, whereby I might find myself perfectly redeemed.'[1] Whatever may have been the impelling influence, the fact remains that in 1667 Barclay followed the example of his father, and became a member of

---

[1] *Apology for the Quakers,* Prop. xi. sect. 7.

the Society of Friends. Nothing more opportune could possibly have happened in the interest of the Quaker cause. In securing the allegiance of the younger Barclay, the fraternity had obtained the services of the one man competent, alike by education, by temperament, and by social position, to guide them safely through the troublous sea of persecution and unprincipled misrepresentation on which they had embarked. Entering with vigour upon the task which lay before him, the youthful convert gave himself for a time to the study of ecclesiastical history and the acquirement of the Greek and Hebrew languages. Thus equipped, he was ready to do battle with the adversaries of the New Evangel. Previous to engaging in the strife, however, he found time to form an alliance with the daughter of a Quaker family in Aberdeen, distinguished for zeal and piety. The letter in which he proposes to Christian Mollison is transcribed by Jaffray, and forms by no means the least interesting relic of the apologist which has been preserved. There is a delightful blending of religious mysticism and of the masterfulness of youthful passion in the following :—' Many things,' he says, ' in the natural will concur to strengthen and encourage my affection towards thee, and make thee acceptable unto me ; but that which is before all and beyond all is, that I can say in the fear of the Lord that I have received a charge from him to love thee, and for that I know his love is much towards thee, and his blessing and goodness is and shall be unto thee so long as thou abidest in a true sense of it.'

Barclay's marriage took place in 1670, and in the same year was published the first of his controversial writings, *Truth cleared of Calumnies*, being an answer to *A Dialogue between a Quaker and a stable Christian*, written by William Mitchell, catechist of St. Clement's Chapel, Aberdeen. The appearance of this work naturally occasioned no small fluttering in the dovecots of the enemy. Its language is direct and forcible,

while the boldness with which it deals with the question of the Sacraments was well calculated to terrify the orthodox, and to bring its author into sharpest conflict with the clericalism of the times. For the next ten years Barclay's pen was seldom idle, and during that period he succeeded in building up for himself a reputation, not only as a brilliant controversialist, but as a responsible and learned theologian, such as perhaps no other writer of his years has attained. His great work, and that on which his fame now chiefly rests, *An Apology for the true Christian Divinity as the same is held forth and preached by the people called in scorn Quakers*, was published in Amsterdam in 1676, when he had just completed his twenty-seventh year. It was originally composed in Latin, 'for the convenience of the learned,' but an English translation was subsequently furnished by the author. The work was prefaced by a letter addressed to Charles ii., to have written which is the best proof of Barclay's courage and sincerity, and of the unflinching candour which he dared not soften or conceal. Pleading for toleration on behalf of himself and his co-religionists he thus addresses his Majesty :—
'Thou hast tasted of prosperity and adversity ; thou knowest what it is to be banished thy native country, to be overruled as well as to rule and sit upon a throne ; and, being oppressed, thou hast reason to know how hateful the oppressor is both to God and man. If, after all these warnings and advertisements, thou dost not turn to the Lord with all thy heart, but forget Him who remembered thee in thy distress, and give up thyself to folly, lust, and vanity, surely great will be thy condemnation.' In the *Apology* itself Barclay sets forth his views in a series of fifteen propositions, the substance of which it is not necessary here to summarise. It may suffice to indicate that the main doctrine which pervades the whole treatise is, that divine truth is made known to us, not by logical investigation, but by immediate revelation to the heart of the

individual, so that the faculty by which such revelation is rendered possible is the internal light, the source of which is Christ, 'who is the true light which lighteth every man that cometh into the world.' Of Barclay's other writings the next in point of permanence to the *Apology* is his *Treatise on Universal Love,* which was composed in prison in Aberdeen in 1677. This work, which is partly biographical, has been described as ' the first of that long series of noble and gentle remonstrances against the criminality of war that has so honourably distinguished the Society of Friends.'

While in Holland, superintending the publication of the *Apology* in 1676, its author made the acquaintance of Elizabeth, Princess Palatine of the Rhine, and sister of Prince Rupert, herself a woman of sincere and earnest piety, who, if not an actual member of their Society, had much in sympathy with the doctrines of the Friends. This acquaintance, which speedily ripened into friendship, seems to have contributed in no small degree to secure for the apologist that influence he afterwards attained at the English Court, and through which he was enabled to do so much, not only to secure immunity from persecution for his own immediate friends and relatives, but to procure for Quakerism generally that sufferance and toleration it has since increasingly enjoyed.

In 1679 was published *A Vindication of the Apology,* and with this and *The Anarchy of the Ranters,* which appeared in the same year, Barclay's literary activity may be said to have entirely ceased. A new field of usefulness lay before him. The opening up of North America as a sphere of British enterprise had meanwhile been proceeding rapidly, and in 1681 the Quaker province of New Jersey, occupying a district between the Delaware and the Hudson, was formally established, chiefly through the instrumentality of William Penn. Of this province Barclay was appointed nominal life-governor, with the privilege of naming a deputy to represent him in

America, at a salary of £400 per annum. The commission
of Charles II. confirming this appointment bears that 'such
is his known fidelity and capacity that he has the government during life; but that every governor after him shall
have it for three years only.' An extensive tract of land in
the province was at the same time granted to him and to his
heirs in fee.

Henceforth it is as the advocate of the civil rights of
Quakerism, and as the indefatigable promoter of novel schemes
of emigration, that the Apologist is known. Many were the
plans devised by him to obtain settlers for the new colony,
and to secure the comfort and prosperity of those who,
whether voluntarily or by compulsion, were induced to seek a
home in the Far West. By far the greater number of his
colonists were rescued from the prisons of the mother country
—Quakers, Covenanters, Puritans—and it is interesting to
learn that among these were the famous prisoners of Dunnottar Castle, who having suffered practically within the confines of his own barony, had doubtless thereby excited his
peculiar sympathy and regard.

During this period Barclay made frequent visits to London,
where his increasing influence at Court gained for him at all
times ready access to the royal presence. These journeys
were undertaken sometimes in the interest of the Quaker
community, but more frequently on private business, a difference which had arisen between his brother-in-law, Sir Ewan
Cameron of Lochiel, and the Duke of Gordon, causing him
considerable trouble and annoyance. In November 1688
occurred his historic interview with James II., whose political
embarrassments had by that time assumed a serious com-
plexion, and who did not hesitate to make allusion to them in
conversing with one whom he had learned not only to trust
as a subject but to respect and value as a friend. They were
standing by a window in the palace when James, gazing

through the lattice, remarked, no doubt with a keen touch of bitterness, that the wind was fair to bring over the Prince of Orange. On Barclay remarking that it was hard that no expedient could be found to satisfy the people, the king replied that he was prepared to do anything becoming a gentleman except to part with liberty of conscience. Doubtless the sentiment of these words received the full approval of his Quaker confidant. Very characteristic were they too of the ill-fated monarch, of whom it has been said that 'he lost three kingdoms for a mass.'

The two remaining years of Barclay's life were spent at Urie, 'in much retirement, enjoying,' says Jaffray, 'the esteem and regard of his neighbours, the comforts of domestic society, and doubtless partaking also in good measure a soul-sustaining evidence of Divine approbation.' We are not, however, to infer from this that at forty years of age he had determined to retire from labour or anticipated giving up his share in the responsibilities and cares of life. It is possible indeed that considerations of ill-health restrained him so far, and that his death, which occurred on 3d October 1690, consequent on a cold which he had contracted at a meeting in Aberdeen some ten days previously, may not have been so altogether unexpected as it seemed. Writing to Sir David Carnegie in January 1689 he excuses himself on the ground of indisposition for having failed to keep an appointment he had made to meet him on that day. The letter is interesting as giving a hint of some new project he had been elaborating during his retirement, and in which Carnegie and others were apparently to have a part. Without attempting to offer any suggestion as to the nature of this undertaking, we venture to print the letter as an example of the apologist's epistolary style :—

$$Ury, 17th\frac{1st}{mo.}\ 1689.$$

FRIND,—I am so indisposed I could not come to Drumlithie, and hope my man will come so timously to thee as to prevent thy trouble of comeing from home.

I have here sent thee my raw project which thow may see, it being the first and only coppy I have, to receave the amendments of thy more mature judgment, which, when thow hast perused and corrected, send to Johnston, that he may transmitt to Oldbair what thow and he sees meet, that at least will let those of Angus know what is our design.

I shall expect my coppy back one the next week, and the weather being tollerable, iff in health, upon advertisement will meet thee where thow will appoint.

This would be done as I said next week, that I may communicat what may be proper to some in Aberdeen.—Mind my respects to thy lady, who am thy assured frind,

ROBERT BARCLAY.

To Sir David Carnegie.[1]

Barclay's exercise of his baronial prerogatives, if sufficiently sustained during his father's lifetime, when his name frequently appears in the pages of the Court Book, would seem in later years to have completely lapsed. It may be that he had difficulty in reconciling with his Quaker principles the assumption of his legitimate position as a feudal baron. Once only is the Court assembled during the period of his infeftment in the lands of Urie, and then for the significant and friendly purpose of adjusting the burdens put upon his tenants through the forcible quartering upon those of them whose holdings lay adjacent to the public highway ' of trouperis and souldieris' going and returning from the north. Of his character as a landlord therefore we have no materials from which to form a sufficient estimate. As scholar, controversialist, and theologian his fame has long since been so thoroughly established as to be beyond the reach of cavil or debate. According to Mosheim the

---

[1] Seventh Report of Hist. MSS. Commission, Appendix, p. 724.

'rude, confused, and ambiguous tenets of Quakerism assumed in the masterly hands of Barclay the aspect of a regular system.' To this alone is due their permanence and the spread of that peculiar phase of Christian thought and sentiment which distinguishes the teaching of the Society of Friends. The Quakerism of to-day continues to apprehend and to appreciate the doctrine of the Christ of Nazareth chiefly as deflected through the brilliant lens of his imagination, the memory of whose sterling character and broad unhindered charity is still universally cherished by the members of the Fraternity as at once their proudest ornament and worthiest boast.

Barclay was succeeded in the barony of Urie by his eldest son, also named Robert, who, like his father, was a zealous Quaker, and seems to have been appealed to by the fraternity as their natural protector in times of difficulty and dispute. Among the papers of the Family is preserved the copy of a letter by this Robert Barclay addressed to the Earl of Marr in 1713, in which he solicits his interest in regard to the 'right of affirmation,' which had already been conceded—though apparently in an unsatisfactory form—to the English Quakers, and was about to be extended to their brethren beyond the Tweed. ' Our case is this,' he argues : ' we cannot with freedom take the benefit of the solemn affirmation formerly granted to our friends in England and now under consideration of the House of Commons to be renewed and extended to us, without it be made easier and more agreeable to the simple and plain precept of our Lord and Saviour Jesus Christ. I beg of thee with all the earnestness I can, that if it come your length, thou would become our advocate for an amendment so as to make it effectual to us, thy friends in the ancient kingdom, as well as thousands of our brethren in England under the same difficulties with us, we always being willing to be subjected, upon the breach of our simple affirmation, to the same penalties by law inflicted upon perjury.'[1]

Undeterred by the apparent scruples of his predecessor, Robert Barclay, *secundus*, held frequent meetings of the Baron Court, and appears to have fulfilled the duties of proprietor with diligence and impartiality. The one obvious weakness in his administration may perhaps be best described as arising from an exaggerated estimate of his responsibility in enforcing the execution of certain statutes anent the 'destroying of wodis and dowcattis,' and the 'killing of haires, doves, partriges, moore foullis, duke and draike.' In the minute of 24th May 1698 some interesting provisions are recounted for the relief of the poor within the barony, while in a later minute the payment of 'vagabond money' is by law enforced. In dealing with criminal causes the Quaker principles of the proprietor become at once apparent. Mutilations for theft are unknown within the Court of Urie, and banishment with forfeiture of 'guidis and geyr' is the severest penalty at any time imposed. Vexatious enough perhaps were the continual restrictions with regard to the 'casting' of peats or turf within forbidden areas. But it must be remembered that the wantonness of tenants in this matter, not in Urie only but elsewhere throughout the country, had already done much to impoverish large tracts of land, which even in their own interest all parties should have been careful to protect.

Outside the pages of the Court Book, Barclay is known by his efforts to restore Urie to its original dimensions. He repurchased the lands of Finlayston and Redcloak, which, as we have seen, had been alienated during the minority of Gilbert, tenth Earl of Errol, and at the same time surrendered to the Earls Marischal, their original possessors, such detached portions of the barony as lay within the parish of Dunnottar. Dying in

---

[1] Fifth Report of Hist. MSS. Commission, Appendix, p. 632.

1747, he was succeeded by his son, who appears as 'Younger of Urie' in several minutes of the Baron Court. This laird, who was known as 'Robert the Strong,' is the first of three generations who together complete the succession of the Barclays. His son and grandson both acquired distinction; the former—whose second wife was Sarah Ann, heiress of James Allardice of Allardice—as an enlightened agriculturist; the latter, Captain Barclay-Allardice, as a pedestrian and athlete, and later as the unsuccessful claimant to no less than three dormant earldoms, to wit, those of Strathearn, Menteith, and Airth. Captain Barclay-Allardice died in 1854, when the Barony of Urie, passing from the family of Barclay, was purchased by Alexander Baird of Gartsherrie, whose nephew, Alexander Baird of Urie, is the present proprietor.

The Jurisdiction of the Court of Urie, as shown in the earlier records of sederunt, appears to have extended beyond the limits of that lordship, and to have covered certain more or less important subjects within the burgh lands of Cowie, namely, the crofts and 'chapelandrie.' The former of these had doubtless been acquired by purchase. The chapel-lands fell to the laird of Urie at the Reformation in virtue of his then position as patron of the Chapel of St. Mary and St. Nathalan, for the service of which, and for the maintenance of a permanent incumbent, they had been originally bestowed.

The town of Cowie lay to the south-east of the barony of that name, while its freehold property extended over a considerable area between the barony and the sea, embracing, among other parts and pertinents, the two Logies, which were formerly known as the lands of Logy-Cowie. Tradition tells us that the earliest charter of the burgh was granted by King David I. However this may be, we have the certain record of its re-erection into a free burgh in 1541, and there is little doubt that up to the beginning of the seventeenth century it occupied the position of a flourishing and wealthy town. It had decayed considerably before 1645, when it was plundered by the Marquis of Montrose. No vestige of the burgh now remains. The burgh lands, together with Auchorthies—at one time a portion of the lordship of Urie—form the modern estate of Cowie.

II. In turning to the consideration of the social condition and environment of the inhabitants of Urie in the seventeenth century, we are at once arrested by the marvellous change which has since then been effected in the distribution of population throughout our country districts. Many influences too complex to be safely analysed have left the modern farmer practically alone upon the land he cultivates, save, perhaps, for a couple of landless cottages, in which are housed his married servants, and the inevitable bothy whose discomforts are the common portion of the younger ploughmen. In mediæval times, however, things were different. The various sub-divisions of a feudal property were each the centre of busy populations, the individual members of which differed among themselves in rank and privilege, just as on a higher platform the minor proprietor differed from his superior, the baron from his sovereign or liege.

The Husbandmen, who came first in point of status, were the possessors each of a more or less substantial holding, ranging in extent from half a ploughgate, or fifty-two acres, upwards. They held their land of the laird by lease or 'assedation,' and this was granted, not for a limited term, but in perpetuity, or for so long at all events as they or their successors continued to fulfil the conditions of their initial contract, which could only be dissolved by formal resignation minuted at length in the proceedings of the Baron Court.

Immediately below the Husbandmen were the Cottars, who were tenants-at-will, not of the proprietor, but of the husband-

man, of whom they held in addition to their house and garden
a croft of probably an acre or a little more. For this they paid
little or no rent, either in money or in grain, but being to all
intents and purposes the vassals of the greater tenantry were
required in return for their holding to provide the latter with
a fixed number of days' labour in every year.

Lowest in the social scale were the Grassmen, Herds, etc.,
corresponding very closely to the squatters of our present croft-
ing districts. These were entirely without land, possessing merely
house and garden, which they held sometimes by service only,
though more frequently by the payment also of a moiety of
money rent. There was theoretically no provision limiting the
number of grassmen on a feudal property. Practically, however,
the laird might interfere to prevent the erection of new huts or
cottages in congested districts where the population was judged
to be already greater than the land was able to support.

In addition to the enjoyment of their private holdings,
tenants had a right of grazing over the commonalty or hill
pasturage, husbandmen being allowed to exercise this privilege
according to the acreage of the lands they tenanted, while
cottars and grassmen—the latter of whom were not prevented
from keeping cattle if they felt disposed to—were required to
pay to the laird a certain stipulated sum of money for every
sheep or ox. This rate of payment probably varied with the
poverty or richness of the season. In 1636 we find the tenants
in Urie discerned to pay for every ox sixteen shillings and eight-
pence Scots, and for every sheep a fifth of that amount.
Cattle so grazed in common would be easily distinguishable by
their owners. Sheep, however, were subjected to various
'clippings and markings,' in order to ensure their identification,
when the time came for their separation and return to their
winter quarters within the friendly shelter of the 'in haime
grass.' It was the duty of the cottars and grassmen to watch
the common-fold or cattle-pen from Rood Day till Michaelmas,

according to the number of their live stock, 'quhilk failzing,' we are told ' the contravener sall pay for ilk scheip tuelf pennies and for ilk nolt beist thre schellingis four d. for ilk nicht.'

Two or more husbandmen possessed as joint-tenants what we would now term a farm. Their rents were threefold. The major portion consisted either of *maill* or *ferme*, money or grain. But in addition to this a variety of customs were exacted, while all parties were required to give service to the laird at certain seasons; their refusal to do so, after having been duly cited by the officer of the barony, rendering them liable to punishment by fine. Husbandmen were popularly known as 'maillories' and 'fermories,' according to the form in which their rents were payable, and it is interesting to note that, notwithstanding the discontinuance of all ferme payments, the latter and not the former designation has survived. A maillor paid his rent at the terms of Whitsunday and Martinmas. A fermore's meal ferme was due at Candlemas, and his barley ferme on Rood Day. Granaries were erected by the laird for the reception of these victual payments, and a 'grinter-man' appointed to receive the grain. Arrears of rent might be recovered through the Baron Court, where a proprietor was entitled through his chamberlain to sue defaulters. A fermore's indebtedness in that case was resolved into its money equivalent, which was invariably reckoned according to the highest market values of the year.

Of the various customs payable at Urie at the date of the opening of the Court Book little need be said. A ploughgate of land carried with it in addition to the inevitable mert or store ox, to be killed at Martinmas for the winter consumption of the proprietor, two wethers, likewise intended for the provision of the manor-house, a dozen capons, and a similar number of common poultry. Somewhat later a stone of butter was added. The right of brewing entailed the payment of a stone of tallow. While for some inscrutable reason Stephen

Forbes in Cowie was held bound to furnish yearly a dozen ells of linen shirting, a commodity somewhat at a discount in the local markets, if we may judge from his repeated failures to produce it when required.

Service included the 'casting and winning' of a load of peats for the proprietor. The Urie tenants were required to stack these on the peat-hill not later than the thirty-first of July,—the tenants of Monquich, on the other hand, were allowed till the end of August to have theirs dried and properly secured. Assistance within the Mains or home farm, with men and horses, was required at seed-time and harvest; and as the chamberlain might demand attendance when it pleased him, this form of service must have frequently occasioned serious loss and inconvenience to the husbandmen in critical and backward seasons. Nor would a trip to Slains Castle in Aberdeenshire, in fulfilment of the obligation to render 'harriage and carriage,' be deemed, we may suppose, a pleasant interruption of the monotonous routine of farm labour, by the struggling tenant vexed with worries of hard times and falling markets such as he must have experienced in common with his modern representative.

There still fall to be recorded various exactions which pressed uneasily upon the feudal tenant, and aggravated the already grievous burden of his yearly rent. Among these were the payment of 'teind-silver,' where the teind of the barony, as happened in the case of Urie, was farmed at a profit by the proprietor: a tax on every ploughgate of a merk to pay the schoolmaster; a similar imposition of a boll of meal for the upkeep of the local smithy; 'officer dues' the perquisite of the baron-bailie; and last but not least the payment of 'girsome,' which is defined by Jamieson as 'a sum paid to a landlord or a superior by a tenant at the entry of a lease, or by a new heir who succeeds to a lease, or on any ground determined by the agreement of parties.' Many are the disputes arising whether from the legal or unjust exaction of this final impost which, amounting oftentimes to a whole year's rent, in the case of succession to a lease or holding, met the new tenant just at that time when naturally it was most inconvenient, if not impossible, for him to disburse.

Scarcely less grievous than the burdens which were imposed upon him by the proprietor, were the obligations which the tenant owed to the tacksman of the mill. The latter farmed the multures or mill-duties, for which he paid a yearly rent to his superior, acquiring thereby a right to pursue the tenants for the amount of their individual indebtedness as 'suckeners' within the 'thirle.' This privilege he exercised with rigorous fidelity, encouraged by the fact that every penny he was able to extort from the reluctant tenantry went to increase the profits he himself should reap from an arrangement which had been entered into not less in his own interest than for the benefit and convenience of the laird. Payments were made in kind, all *bona-fide* suckeners being required to forfeit every thirteenth peck of meal which their land was able to produce, in name of multure. A less oppressive tax appears to have been levied on the laird's tenants in the crofts and chapel-lands of Cowie, who were properly outside the thirle; while out-suckeners who were not tenants of the laird, and who probably resided chiefly on the lands of Logy-Cowie, were privileged to have their corn ground upon still easier terms, for the obvious reason that being free to convey it elsewhere they might deprive the miller of their patronage at will.

Besides paying, multure tenants were required to render frequent and vexatious services. They had to bring in water to the mill in times of storm; to keep the mill-race in repair, and free from weeds; to mend the dams; to carry home the mill-stones, and to perform a whole variety of kindred offices, such as, according to our modern ideas, ought naturally to have pertained to those who were directly interested in the sufficient maintenance of the machinery and fabric of the mill.

It is impossible not to sympathise with the mediæval agriculturist in his continued efforts to evade the claims of thirlage. Many were the expedients resorted to with this object, and seldom is the miller exempted from appearing in the capacity either of plaintiff or defendant at the meetings of the Baron Court. For the most part there is little interest in these contendings, although occasionally a specious plea is entered whose crave requires the serious consideration of the suitors and takes both time and patience to decide.

The miller did not serve the mill in person, but was represented by his servant or 'pecaman,' so called because amid a multiplicity of other duties he was required to sharpen or pick the mill stones. This official had originally for his hire a pittance known as 'loak' or 'gowpen,' the latter term meaning literally as much meal as it was possible to hold in both hands. Such a description of his fee, however, had evidently proved inadequate, and liable to be turned to his disadvantage by ill-affected parties, and accordingly a more definite scale of payment took its place in Urie, where so early as 1607 it was agreed that the pecaman should receive 'for grindeing of twente bollis gryt corne ane pek halff pek meill, and ane pek meill for the grindeing of twente boll small corne, and ane pek of meill for the metteing of twente boll meill.' In addition to grinding and measuring the grain, the pecaman was required to preserve the peace within his master's premises ; to give due precedence to customers, according to the order in which they brought in their corn to the mill ; to superintend the performance of service and report defaulters, and to prevent the mixing of 'dust and stones' with the laird's ferme, a practice so inveterate that in 1634 it was ordained that he should 'tak the haill dust and reteine the samen in his awin hous till the fermes be delyverit into the girners.' Few tasks could possibly have been more irksome than those performed by this luckless functionary, constrained on the one hand to uphold the authority and consult the interests of his master, and on the other devoted to maintain the weary feud for ever waged against him by the tenantry, who were accustomed to regard him as a common enemy, whom it was their bounden duty to harass and, if possible, out-wit. Nor does it appear that he habitually received that consideration and support to which he was entitled from those who were in authority at the Baron Court. An appeal embodied in the first minute of the Court Book to the effect that tenants should be forbidden to 'temper' or adjust the mill is promptly granted. In contrast to this, however, it seems hardly fair that the servant, not the master, should be made answerable for any damage which the corn of the tenants might sustain in the mill premises, or that on a complaint being lodged by certain parties that 'their stuf was stowyne in the miln be the puir people vnder sylence of the nycht,' the pecaman should be declared responsible, and the complainants forthwith authorised to proceed against him for the 'skaith' received.

One other class of tenants under the jurisdiction of the Court of Urie falls to be described. Mid-way between the husbandman and cottar, if not in social position at least in superiority of tenure, stood the 'skipper' of the laird's boat, who held the fisher crofts of Cowie directly of the proprietor, and was responsible for the recovery of their various proportions of rent from the individual members of his crew. The fishermen did service to the laird in carting peats and harvesting, and were to all intents and purposes *bona-fide* tillers of the soil. This, however, was only a subsidiary part of their employment, designed to occupy their leisure moments when their legitimate calling did not otherwise demand their services. The laird's boat was apparently manned by a considerable crew in addition to the skipper. The precise number cannot be ascertained. These were so completely under the control of the proprietor that he could compel them to proceed to sea in fair weather under penalty of a fine. The hull and furnishings of the boat were exclusively his property, as was also the 'hwill' or small skiff which she appears to have carried, or which may possibly have been used for work along the shore. Besides paying a monetary rent for these, the fishermen surrendered to the laird a 'boat's part' or boat's deal, as it would now be expressed, that is, a definite proportion of every catch, equivalent to that received by each individual member of the crew. This boat's part was most probably designed to meet repairs. A yearly custom of a hundred haddocks or three large cod 'to the lady,' together with a pint of oil from every fisherman, completes the record of these fisher payments.

As to the social condition of the tenantry it is obvious that it was far from perfect. Even the husbandman, though technically raised above the other members of the agricultural community, was really little in advance of them in comfort or intelligence, or in that stimulating sense of growing freedom from indebtedness which leads to both. Notions of agriculture were notoriously crude and faulty. Those lands lying nearest to the tenants' hand were subjected to some rough and ready system of rotation, and were manured with farm offal mixed with turf or 'midden feal.' The 'out-field' however was simply cropped until exhausted, and then permitted to rest for an indefinite and naturally a lengthened period till it might reasonably be expected once again to yield a harvest to the plough. 'Run-rig' lands were treated as 'in-field.' They were for the most part narrow patches disjoined from the remainder of the tenant's holding, and often situated at a considerable distance from it, their one recommendation probably being the exceptional fertility of the

soil of which they were composed. The staple crops were bere
(a rough species of barley), oats, a little wheat, and peas. Rye
is also mentioned in the minute of 9 February 1730. Tenants
were responsible for the up-keep of their farm premises, of
which the stone-work only was provided by the laird. Erections
little better than mere huts must have sufficed for dwelling-
houses, and the four bare walls of these the tenant was required,
on entering, to roof and furnish, his predecessor having stripped
them to regain the beams and rafters which he had previously
provided at his own expense. In circumstances such as these
we cannot be surprised that a tenant of Monquich, finding
himself domiciled in the mansion-house of that estate, was so
regardless of the decency and comfort it afforded him, as to
introduce his cattle to the 'hall and chalmeris,' rather than
repair the byres and stables which had been thus dismantled
and destroyed.

It is scarcely credible that this state of matters should have
continued so late as the beginning of the 18th century, and
yet in May 1705 the Court ordains that 'Noe tennant, subtennant, cottar, nor grassman, removing from ther respective
possessions within the laird of Urie's lands and heretage shall
pull doune any of there house wallis more than fries ther
timber.' Eight years later, arrangements were introduced
whereby the entering tenant should 'take over the roofs and
fittings of his house and offices at a valuation.' These were
still, however, the property of the tenant, not of the proprietor,
the latter being exempt from all responsibility to provide a
suitable and efficient covering, either for man or beast.

The guardians of the peace within the Barony were the
'birleymen' or members of the Court of Burlaw. This Neighbours Court, as it was also called, is generally described as
being popularly elected, and is further credited with having
possessed a certain jurisdiction apart from the tribunal of the
laird. Both these statements seem to be discredited by the

evidence of the Court Book. The birleymen of Urie were essentially the creatures of the proprietor. They were nominated at his Court, no doubt with his connivance and approval, and apparently with the one intention that they might assist in enforcing his authority.

Naturally enough the relations of the tenants, one towards another, were often strained and difficult. The keenness of competing interests among a class of men whose financial margins must have been of the narrowest description, and who were thrown so closely into one another's company, could scarcely have failed at times to occasion feuds and heart-burnings, which were calculated to disturb the amenity of social intercourse. To their credit be it said these quarrels seldom wore a serious aspect, and the offended cottar or defrauded husbandman was for the most part willing to accept what legal satisfaction it was in his power to compass at the Court of the Barony, whose verdict, once awarded in his favour, it was the duty of the birleyman to carry out.

Trespass and petty thefts were the most common cause of reprisals being sought before the laird's tribunal, and many are the enactments made to render the course of justice definite and smooth in dealing with such matters. It is enacted, for example, that 'Everie man that hes ane hors about the milne of Cowie, sall hauld thair horss in the stabill betuixt elevine houris at nicht and the sonne rysing in the morning; and sick as salbe fund to do in the contrair, sall pey for ilk hors that salbe fund out of the stabill opoune the nicht, xxs. *toties quoties*, to be peyit to the pairtie offendit.' And the complaisance of the Court we feel has reached a climax when on 25 August 1624 it is 'statut that ewerie ffoull that gangs amangis thair nichtbouris cornes sall pey ane peck of aits or bear quhairin thay pastur.'

Occasionally we stumble upon trials for assault and even bloodshed. Once only are the minutes of the Court marred by the record of an act of brutal and premeditated meanness. And it is satisfactory to learn that Abraham Forbes, found guilty by an assize on 30 July 1616 of cutting off the tail of a horse belonging to his neighbour, Arthur Christie, is mulcted in the substantial fine of forty pounds.

'Occupiers in stouth,' stealers of colewort, fuel, and the like, are duly fined. And the crime of cutting and pulling grass among a neighbour's corn—an offence perhaps by no means so trifling as it appears—is separately provided for and punished. Perhaps one may understand the essentially litigious spirit of the Scottish race only when he has learned, from some record such as this, how it was fostered and encouraged by the feudal masters of the soil, who through so many years possessed an absolute and unchallenged right to shape alike the character and sentiment of their dependants.

Whatever may have been their treatment of one another, it is but fair to state that the proprietor was after all the greatest sufferer from the peccadillos of his tenantry. Against him one and all made common cause, while the fines exacted by the Baron Court must in many instances have been utterly inadequate to meet his losses. It would appear to have been esteemed no felony to pilfer from the laird, no moral evil to destroy his property, and so in spite of all that he could threaten or devise his green wood fell before their thieving hatchets. They stole his peats, they trespassed in his hainings, they leapt his garden 'dykes,' to purloin, we presume, his lettuces and gooseberries, and generally they made it to be felt that however earnestly they were prepared on all occasions to defend their private rights, his were not such as were entitled in their opinion to be regarded.

There have been embodied in an Appendix to this volume various matters which it was believed might be of interest to the historical student, but which were obviously of such a character as to preclude their introduction elsewhere. These may be noticed in their order as follows:—

I. The Rentall Buik off the Barony off Wrie.

This fragment of a Rent Roll of the lands of Urie is bound up at random with the minutes of the Baron Court. It is undated. The handwriting, however, which has strongly marked peculiarities, is unmistakably that of James Davidson, who officiated as clerk at the first recorded meeting of the Court, and is thereafter superseded by John Strathauchin. We may therefore safely assign the document to a date not later than 1604. It details the various items of rent paid for certain holdings at that period, and is of value in view of the complete statement of the rentals both of Urie and Montquich given under minute of Court held on 27th June 1634. By converting the different fermes, customes, kains, etc., into their corresponding monetary equivalents (see Appendix III.), a comparison of these two rent-rolls becomes possible, and we find that the value of land has distinctly declined during the thirty odd years that have elapsed between the earlier and later valuations. This fact is borne out notwithstanding a serious clerical error in the earlier rent-roll, which describes the maill payable from Glithno as only 'sax markes.'[1] The following table shows the money values of the rents of Balnagight and Cairnton in 1604 and 1634:—

Rent in 1604.

Banageithe—ane pluche—	lb.	s.	d.	lb.	s.	d.
Ten bollis victuall,	100	00	00			
Ane custome mart,	013	06	08			
Ane vaddir,	003	06	08			
Ane dovssone of Cappounes,	004	00	00			
Ane dovssone off puttrie,	002	00	00	122	13	04

[1] See p. 32, where George Straquhan in Glithno is decerned to pay the sum of fifty merks for his Whitsunday and Martinmas maills.

Cairntoune—ane Pleuch—		lb.	s.	d.	lb.	s.	d.
Tuentie bollis victuall,	.	200	00	00			
Ane custume mart,	. .	013	06	08			
Tua vaddiris,	. .	006	13	04			
Ane dovssone off Cappounes,		004	00	00			
Dovsson off putrie,	. .	002	00	00	226	00	00

RENT IN 1634.

Bannageich—		lb.	s.	d.	lb.	s.	d.
Feftie markis,	. . .	33	06	08			
Ane custome mart,	. .	10	00	00			
Tua wadders,	. . .	06	00	00			
Ane dussone capouns, .	.	04	00	00			
Ane dussone of pultrie,	.	02	00	00			
Ane leet of peittis,		10	00	00	65	06	08
Carntoune—							
Auchteine bollis meill,	.	162	00	00			
Ane custome mart,	. .	010	00	00			
Tua wadders,	. . .	006	00	00			
Ane dussone capouns,	.	004	00	00			
Ane dussone pultrie,	.	002	00	00			
Ane leet of peitts,	. .	010	00	00	194	00	00

If we submit the rentals of all the various lands in the possession of the laird of Urie as given in the minute of 1634 to the above treatment, it appears that the money value of the entire estate, exclusive of services, teind-silver and the like, amounted at that date to 3567 02 08 pounds Scots, made up as follows :—

Chepel lands of Cowie—		lb.	s.	d.	lb.	s.	d.
Half chaplanrie in Cowie,	.	115	00	00			
Nether half chaplanrie,	.	120	00	00	0235	00	00
Crofts of Cowie—							
Smydie croft in Cowie,	.	011	09	04			
Fischers crofts,	.	006	18	08			
Tua zairdes,	.	006	13	04			
Burnesyid (1),	.	003	06	08			
„ (2),	.	003	00	00	0031	08	00

Lands of Urie—	lb.	s.	d.	lb.	s.	d.
Milne and Milne land of Cowie,	547	01	04			
Reid Cloak, . . .	108	00	00			
Walkmilne of Urie, . .	020	00	00			
Bannageich, . . .	065	06	08			
Carntoune, ...	194	00	00			
Glithnocht, . . .	100	00	00			
Woodheid—Eist syid, . .	216	00	00			
,, —West syid, .	216	00	00			
Powbair, ...	184	00	00			
Magray, ...	409	00	00			
Findlawstoune, . . .	006	13	04	2066	01	04
Lands of Monquich—						
Montquheiche — half ane pleuche, . . .	048	16	08			
,, half ane pleuche and ane croft, . .	056	13	04			
,, wther halff pleuche,	048	16	08			
,, ane pleuche, .	097	13	04			
,, ane wther pleuche,	081	13	04			
,, wther thrie pleuchs,	293	00	00			
Milne and milne croft of Montquheiche, . .	168	13	04			
Sauchinshawe, . . .	074	13	04			
Bonnagubs, . .	097	13	04			
Rothnik, . . .	141	10	00			
Quhytsyid, . . .	048	16	08			
Corsley, . . .	076	13	04	1234	13	4

II. NOTES WRITTEN ON THE FLY LEAF OF THE MS.

1. *Proclamation anent Barclay and Mathers Fairs.* These fairs appear to have been granted to Robert Barclay, son of the Apologist, by the Union Parliament, early in the eighteenth century, and subsequent, we may assume, to the surrender of the Dunnottar portion of the barony to the Earls Marischal (see page xxxix, *supra*). The right of holding fairs was a privilege at all times greatly valued by proprietors on account of the profits to be derived from customs, tolls, etc. On three

different occasions previous to this had 'free fairs' been granted
in the neighbourhood. On 11th March 1541 it was given to
the burgesses of Cowie to hold a yearly fair in their town on
the Feast of St. Nathalan (8th January). Again, on 29th
September 1663, 'Considering that the tennents, fewers, and
inhabitants of the toun of Stainhyve are much impoverished be
the late troubles, and be the ruine of the bulwarks of the said
toun, And it lying far distant from the burgh Royall, and being
a place most fit for keeping of fairs and weekly mercats, where-
vnto not only the leidges in the cuntrie adjacent may most
conveniently resort with much ease for buycing of all sorts
of commodities, if it had the freedome of some annuall fairs
and ane weekly mercat, but also the inhabitants would dayly
thereby increase in policie and tradeing,' Parliament granted to
William, Earl Marischal, and to his heirs and successors, the
right of holding a weekly market in the town of Stonehaven
every Thursday; together with two yearly fairs, to be held one
on the first Tuesday before Whitsunday, and the other on the
first Tuesday before Martinmas. In the statement of reasons
assigned for granting these fairs, it will be observed that the
Royal Burgh of Cowie, by this time no doubt sadly decayed,
is treated as if it were no longer existent. Probably Earl
Marischal in his desire to benefit Stonehaven had done his best
to minimise the importance and suitability for trading purposes
of its more ancient rival. Thirty years later, however, Sir
Thomas Burnet of Leys succeeded in obtaining from the Parliament of William I. an acknowledgment of the claims of the
latter. On 12th October 1696 he received a grant of two fairs
yearly, to be held at Cowie, which it is stated 'lyes conveniently
for faires to be keept thereat,' the first to be held upon the last
Tuesday and Wednesday of June, and the second upon the
last Tuesday and Wednesday of September. These last-men-
tioned fairs so nearly correspond in date with those referred to
in the Proclamation printed in the Appendix, as to suggest that

the two are identical, and that that document merely records the transference to the Laird of Urie of the market rights originally pertaining to Sir Thomas Burnet.

Barclay and Mathers fairs continued to be held on the hill of Megray till the present century, when they were transferred to the Market Square of the New Town of Stonehaven by Captain Barclay-Allardice. A yearly market, held in Stonehaven on the third week of October, is still popularly known as Megray Fair.

2. *Accompt of the Corne and Fodder received from the tenents of the Brae of Urie*, 1661. It is impossible to determine with certainty the precise significance of these jottings, though probably the first column may contain the amount of victual rent per acre, the second the total amount for the tenant named.

3. A form of Court Charge, evidently written down for the convenience of George Edward, the bailie therein mentioned, who presided at the final meeting of the Baron Court (see p. 171 *infra*). It is interesting not only as the last charge delivered at the Court of Urie, but as showing what form this ceremony of Charging the Court had assumed at a date immediately antecedent to the practical abolition of the baronial judicature.

III. CHRONOLOGICAL TABLE OF PRICES, CONVERTED FERMES, CUSTOMES, ETC., EXTRACTED FROM THE COURT BOOK.

This table has been compiled chiefly with a view of bringing together within convenient compass a list of the current values of the various commodities mentioned in the Court Book during the period which that record covers. The dates given are those of the Minutes of Sederunt in which the various items are referred to.

The reader will be able to glean from such a table various hints as to the social and agricultural development of Urie, especially during the period of the proprietorship of the Hays, when the Court, possessing only a minor jurisdiction, is naturally more concerned with details affecting the everyday interests of the tenantry in their several capacities as husbandmen, fishers, and the like.

IV. The Lairds of Urie—1430-1892.

This compilation in so far as it concerns the Hays of Urie is based on a MS. in the possession of Mrs. Barclay-Allardice, entitled *A Genealogy of the Barons in the Mearns of late memory deschending lenially unto the year of God* 1578. Like all genealogies of an early date it is extremely meagre, but the author appears to have been possessed of sources of reliable information, and is seldom at fault. Where we have failed to corroborate his statements by independent evidence, these have been printed within brackets.

Wood's edition of Douglas' *Peerage* has been followed without acknowledgment in treating of the Earls Errol and Marischal.

Among the various authorities consulted for the Barclays may be mentioned Jaffray's *Biography*; Robert Barclay's *Genealogical Account of the Barclays of Urie*, ed. 1812; and the inscriptions on the tombstones in the 'Houff' or burial-place of the Barclays, which is still extant, and is situated on a rising ground overlooking the mansion-house of Urie.

THE BARONY OF COWIE
(Erected 1360) Showing the lands of Urie & Monquich.

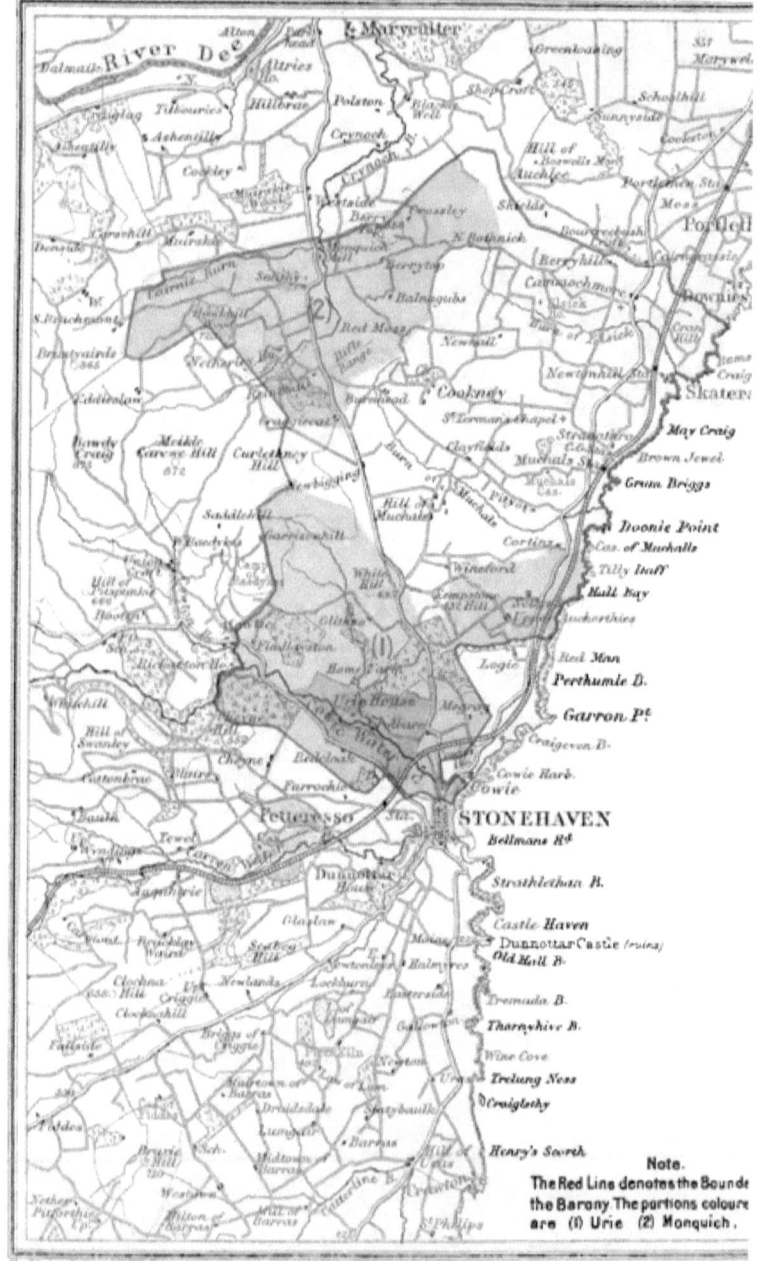

Note.
The Red Line denotes the Boundary of
the Barony. The portions coloured
are (1) Urie (2) Monquich.

THE BARONY OF URIE
(Erected 1879)

The Couirt Buik

WILLIAM HAYE OF WRY WITH MY HAND

THE COURT BOOK OF THE BARONY
OF WRIE.

The Curt of the Barroncy of Wrie,[1] *the aucht of Junij* 1604.

The said day Johne Ranney plennit in jugment,[2] alleging that thair was sum tennentis within the grund that wald nocht content thame selffis with the serwice of the Peckcaman,[3] bot tuik vpone thame to tempper[4] the Miln as thai thocht guid, without ony kynd of knawleg, and to that affect the pekaman that aucht to occuppie that office wald naways be ansorable for the miln, nor zett for the stuff: Tharfor the Lard and his Belze ordannis in all tymis cumming that na sik misordour be vsit, vnder the pane of tene punddis. Vpone the quhilkis the said Johne Ranney tuik act.

[And also it is statute that quhomsoever of the saidis tennentis mistempers the mylne in handling of hir at the grynding of thair stuf sall pay the soume of fourtie schillingis, *toties quoties.*

Continewis this Curt upon tuentie four houris warning,

Ita est Jacobus Davidson,
Notarius ac scriba.][5]

Aganis the furnissing Stanhif.[6]

The said day the Lard being in jugment allegit that thair was ane act and ordinance of Curt statuit and sett of befor

---

[1] For Rental Book of the Barony of Urie, see Appendix.

[2] Complained in court.

[3] The miller's servant, whose duty it is to keep the mill in order by *picking* the mill-stones.   [4] Regulate.

[5] The passage in brackets, which seems to be a continuation of the first minute, is written in a different hand on the reverse of the title-page of the MS.

[6] Stonehaven, the county town of Kincardineshire. Stonehaven proper is situated in the extreme corner of Dunnottar parish, towards the north and east, and adjoins the lands of Urie, over which the *New Town* of Stonehaven now extends. Until the beginning of the seventeenth century it must have occupied a

contenyng[1] sik personis as furnessis and sellis fewaill to the
Stanhyiff, within his barroney of Wrie, syik as petteis, turris, or
haidder,[2] and to that affect thair is ane pennaltie sett doun
vpone the transgressouris of the said act, To witt, tene punddis
money.   And albeit it is of werrittie that thair is ane pairt of
the said barroney sence the making of the said act fund be
sufficient tryell carriing peitteis to the Stanhyf, hierfor as off
befor, the Lard and his Belze ratifeis and apprewis the
formeyr act to contennow firme and stable, and the transgressouris thairof to be punddit preceislie as is aboun wryttin,
and euerie husbandman to be ansorable for his cotteris,[3] and
the cotteris to be compellit to releiff thair maisteris swa that
the penaltie may lycht one thame quha transgressis the act.

The Curt of the Barrony of Wrie, beginning the aucht day off Junj in anno 1604.

The Curt of the Barroney of Wrie haldyne at the Mill of
Cowie the aucht day of Junj anno ane thousand sax hundreth
and four zeiris, be ane honorable man Jhone Hay of Wry and
Maister Jhone Fullertoun his belze.   The quhilk day the
soittis callit, the Curt fensit,[4] and the memberis thairof lauchfullie sworne and admettit.

---

position little different from that of the various fishing villages which still abound
upon the coast.   In 1607, however, William, Earl Marischal, succeeded in trans-
ferring the county courts from Kincardine, the ancient capital of the county, to
Stonehaven, on the plea that suitable accommodation could not there be found
for the magistrates and their clients.   The same earl created Stonehaven a burgh
of barony in 1624, thus by these acts laying the foundation of what influence and
prosperity the town has since enjoyed.   Stonehaven and its modern suburb were
united under the Lindsay Act in 1889.   The population is returned in the census
of 1891 at 4497.

[1] *Qy.* Concernyng ; see p. 13 *infra*.   [2] Peats, turf, and heather.

[3] The *cottar* inhabited a *cot* or cottage on a farm, to which a small portion of
land was attached.   He was dependent on the *husbandman* or farmer of whom
he held his land, and to whom he paid for it in labour for a fixed number of days
in every year.

[4] Equivalent to the Latin phrase *sectis vocatis curia legitime affirmata*.   In
feudal law it was the duty of feudatories to attend the courts of their lords or
superiors.   Parties often held their land by such service, and were therefore
called suitors, or, as it is written in the text, soittis—*sectatores curiæ*.—Innes's
Legal Antiquities, p. 61.

The said day the Lard and his Belze, with consent and assent of all and haill his tennentis within the said Barroney, ratefeis and apprewis the actis and ordinance of Curt maid and sett doun be wmquhill [1] William Hay of Wrie, his father, of guid memorie, and that in speciall conserning the detfull serwice that is to be crawet of euerie tennent within the said grund according to thair sett and laboring.[2]

As also for the pennelteis sett doun for the obstraiking and withaldyng of his multeris [3] and dewitteis from his Miln, with the misordour of the destroying and cutting doun of his grene wod, togidder wyth syik wther profitable actis and ordinance of Curt to be obserwit to the vtillittie and proffeit off hym and his haill grund.

It is ordined that the pickeman shall haue for his peanes in grindeing of twente bollis [4] gryt corne, ane pek [5] halff pek meill, and ane pek meill for the grindeing of twente boll small corne, and ane peck of meill for the metteing of twente boll meill.

Aganis Stouth.[6]

The said day it is statuit and ordannit be the Lard and his Belze, wyth consent and assent of all and haill the tennentis within the Barroney, That sik personnis as beis fund onlauchfull, to wit, occupeiris in Stouth,[7] in stelying of keyll,[8] eldyng,[9] cornis, or oney wther wrangous intromessioun, sufficient tryell being had, the commeittaris of the onlauchfull delyng saill be punddit his radiest guidis and geyr,[10] extendyng to tene punddis money, and the maister of that man or woman quha is commettaris of the offenc saill at the nixt terme put thame away and discharg tham of his serwice vnder the pane of xx lib., and also tensell off his tack and roum [11] in the Larddis optioun.

---

[1] The late. [2] Lease and farm.

[3] Multure or mouter, the fee for grinding grain: properly that paid to the master of the mill.—*Jam.*

[4] *Boll:* a dry measure, the standard of which varied at different times and in different localities.

[5] The fourth part of a firlot. [6] Theft.

[7] Parties who have taken forcible possession.

[8] Colewort. [9] Fuel of any kind.

[10] *Guidis and geyr* is a common phrase signifying effects. *Guidis* occurring alone is used to denote live stock. [11] Forfeiture of his lease and holding.

For Hedrowmis.[1]

The said day, in respect of the menifald complentis that accurris frome tyme to tyme amangis nychtbouris and tennenttis within the Barroney in pasturing of thair guiddis vpone wtheris hedrowmis, in consideratioun thairof, and for pece and queitnes amangis nychtbouris, it is decernit in jugment be the Lard and his belze, with the consent of the tennentis of the grund, That eueric ane of thame saill content wyth thair awane hedrowmis, and nawayis to molest nor truble thair nycht-bouris in thair pasturag, bot to content thame selffis with thair awane bounddis, according to thair sett. And in kais that oney tennent wald appone thame selffis to transgress this act, sufficient tryell being haid, the transgressour thairof is decernit in xx lib. money, to be punddit of his radyest guidis and geyr.

The Curt contennowit to the nixt aduerttisment.

JOHANNIS STRATHAUCHIN,
Scriba dicte curie.

The Curt of the Barroney of Wric, haldyne at the Milhous of the samyne, be ane honorable man Johne Hay, lard of the grund, and Mr. Jhon Fullartoun his Belze, the 16 day of Junj 1604.

The said day Allexander Hay, officiar off the said barroney, complennit in jugment vpone the tennenttis of the grund, alleging quhat tyme the Lardis pettis was in radynes to be leyd,[2] and fra tyme that thaj war parttit, thair hes bene sik misordour in tymis paist, and that be the tennenttis serwandis that leddeis the petteis, that thaj do caist thame away in the petpotteis,[3] as also theftiouslie stowyne away and conwoyit to the Stanhyif, and to that affect desyrit the Lard and his belze, with consent and assent of the Barroney, to sett doun sik ordinance quharthrow the lyik misordour be naweyis vsit in tymis cuming. To that affect the Lard and his belze, with consent of his haill grund, statuitis and ordannis in all tymis

---

[1] The outer boundaries of a feu or toft.—*Jam.*
[2] Carted.   [3] Holes from which peats have been dug.

to cum that thair be na sik misordour, and in kais that oney be
the commetteris of the offence, it being prowyn vpone thame,
is decernit be the tennour herof to be punddit thair radiest
guiddis and geyr, extending to tene punddis money, and the
tennent to be ansorable for his serwand, and this penalttie to
be tane oup as the occacioun of the falt beis tryitt.

The said day James Miln in Cowie compeirrit in jugment,
and thair, in presence of the Lard and belze, and in audience
of the haill Curt, rennunsit all kynd of rycht, tyittill, or possessioun that he haid for the present in and to all and haill
the houssis, toift,[1] and land laist occupeit and lauborit be
James Miln his vmquhill father, and tuik hyme onlie to the
Lardis guid will as it saill pleis hym to occupie, sett, vse, and
dispone the sameyn as he thinkis guid, and quhatsumeuer
trawaill or expenssis maid be the said James thairone to be
refunddit to hym be the Lard, and that be the sicht of honest
men.   Vpone the quhilkis the Lard tuik act.

*The Curt of the Barroney of Wrie, haldyn at the Milhous of
the samyne, be ane honorable man Jhone Hay, Lard of
the grund, and Maister Jhone Fullertoun his belze, the
29 of Julie 1604.*

The said day, in consideratioun of the mennifald trublis and
molestationis that accuris amangis nychtbouris and tennentis
in the grund, the one oppressing the wther be violence, the
Lard being impaschit[2] throw thair dalie complenttis, thocht
guid to ratifie and apprewe ane act of Curt consernyng pece
and queyetnes within his grund, of the dait at the Miln of
Cowie the 16 day of October 1592 zeiris, Quhilk act and ordinance of Curt contennis in affect that quhat sum euer tennent
within the grund that happennis to inwaid[3] his nychbour, or
oney wtheris within the grund, putting hand in hym be violence, sall incur ane pennaltie, to wit, tene punddis money to

---

[1] *Toift*, or *toft*, a portion of land sufficient for a house and garden : a feu or
plot.—*Jam.*

[2] Hindered. Fr. *empécher.*   [3] Invade.

the Lard, as also to satisfie the wrang to thame to quhom thaj
haf commettit the offence.

The said day the Lard desyrit in jugment that the cutteris
of his wod sould be punddit[1] without respect of personis or
oney kind of excusis that may be allegit, and that conform to
the ordinance and decreit of Curt sett done at mair lyntht in
the days of his vmquhill father of guid memorie, Quhilk act
and ordinance contenis ane sertane pennaltie, to witt, fywe
punddis money, vpone ilk person that happennis to be fund
cutting his wod, and that for the first tyme, and gyf thaj
insist forther, saill for the secund tyme be punddit for tene
punddis money.   Vpone the quhilkis the Belze ratiffeis the
former act to contennow ferme and stable, and ordannis decreit
of Curt to pas vpone thais that ar cutteris of the Larddis wod,
and to be punddit conforme to the ordinance abone speciefeit.
Vpone the quhilkis the Lard tuik act.

The said day Stewyne Smyth, in Cowie, plennit in jugment
vpone the tennenttis in the grund, alleging that thair was ane
pairt of thame that refusit to maik hym thankfull payment of
thair zeirlie smeddie boll,[2] and alleging that the smeddie collis[3]
was risseyn to hiecher prycis and mair scant to be had thane
they war of befor, Throw the quhilkis he was vnhable to
susteyn the wark of the grund without gret loiss to hyme self.
To the quhilk allegance it was ansourit be the Lard and his
Belze that thaj wald on nawayis[4] compell the tennentis to
furnes collis, bot the said Stewane sould furnes and prowyd for
tham as he had done of befor, and euerie plucht in the grund
to pay zeirlie to the said Stewyne for thair smeddie wark ane
boll of aittis, and in kais of nonpayment the officiar to pund
for the samyne according to the wallour and prycis, and the
said Stewyne to be radie and dilligent be hym self, or ane
sufficient serwand, to be raddie at all tymis quhan occacioun
beis to serwe the grund.   Vpone the quhilkis Stewyn Smytht
tuik act.   JOHANNIS STRATHAUCHIN,
                                    Scriba dicte Curie.

---

[1] Poinded or distrained.   [2] The payment in kind due to the smith.
[3] Coals.   [4] By no means.

*The Curt of the Barroney of Wrie, haldyne at the Miln
Hous of the samyne, be ane honorable mane Johne Hay,
Lard of the grund, and Maister Robert Strathachin his
Belze, 13 of October 1604 zeiris.*

The said day Alexander Hay, the Lardis officiar, protestit
in jugment That quhatsumeuer tennent in the grund that refusit to do thair detfull serwice to the Lard in carrigis as [? or]
wtherwayis as thaj ar oblisset, saill be punddit conforme to
the ordinance statuit and sett doun in to the dayis of William
Hay of Wry, the Lardis father of guid memorie, Quhilk act
and ordinance off Curt contennis sertane pennalteis decernit to
be payit be sic tennenttis as beis fund dissobedient toward
thair detfull dewittie off serwice, quharof the tennour follouis,
viz., Of euerie hors carrige fywe punddis to Buchane, of euerie
fwit [1] carrig to Buchane xl s., of hors carrige to Aberdyne xx s.,
of fwit carrag to Aberdeyn tene schillingis, as also all wther
carrigis as thaj ar derectit be the Lard to be punddit for
dissobedience, conforme to the jurney that thaj ar to pas.

The said day the Lard protestit in jugment That quhatsumeuer tennent in the grund that ar obleist to pay hyme
custumis saill maik thame to be sufficient, and quhair thaj
haif thame nocht of thair awane, to by thame in the cunttrey
quhair thaj may be haid, or thane to pay the hiest prycis
thairfor. In consideratioun hierof the Belze, vnderstanding the
protestatioun to be altogidder resonab[le], decernis be decreit
of Curt the samyne to be fulfillit. Vpone the quhilkis the
Lard tuik act.

The said day it is decernit in jugment That the haill gress
men [2] within the Barroney, euerie ane of thame, saill help to
walk the fald, according to the nowmer off his guiddis, or to
agre with thais that walkis the fald,[3] and pay tham thairfor as
becumis his pairt.

The said day it is statuit and ordannit be the Lard and his
Belze, and be the consent of his haill Barronney, That na

---

[1] Foot.

[2] *Grass-man* : the tenant of a cottage in the country, who has no land attached
to it.—*Jam.*   [3] Watch the sheepfold.

tennent within the grund haiffing actioun of lawe aganis his
nychtbour, or oney wther tennent within the barronney, saill
nawayis be lesum to persewe thair actiounis aganis wtheris befor
the Lorddis of the Sessioun, Shireffis, or Commissionaris, bot
onlie that thair actionis to be persewit in the Larddis Curt, quha
saill be radie to do thame justice accordyng to ressoun and guid
concience. And gyff oney of the said tennentis wald purposlie transgrece the conttentis and ordinance of this former
act saill be decernit in xx lib., for the pennaltie to be payit to
the Lard.   *per me* JOHANNEM STRATHACHIN,
                                  Scriba dicte Curie.

*The Curt of the Barronney of Wrie, haldyne at the Milhous
of the samyne be ane honorable man Johne Hay, Lard
of the grund, and Maister Johne Fullertoun his Belze,
the penult day of Nouember* 1604 *zeiris.*

The said day it is decernit in jugment That na tennent
within the grund saill obstract oney kynd of multeris fra the
Lardis Mill that growis within the grund. As also it saill
nawayis be lesum to oney within the Barronney that ar malt
maikkaris to carrie the malt to oney wther miln, it being
drayit [1] in the grund, bot onlie to the Larddis miln. And in
kais that oney tennent wald purposlie transgrece this act, saill
be decernit in double multer, as also decernit for the contempt
to be punddit for xl s. money, for thair contempt to be payit
to the Lard. Vpone the quhilk Johne Ranney tuik act.

The said day ane pairt of the tennentis in the grund plennit
in jugment that thair stuf was stowyne in the miln be the
puir people vnder sylence of the nycht, and to affect it is
statuit and ordannit be the Lard and his belze That fra the
nycht cum [2] thair be nawayis fund oney sik people within the
miln, and the pekaman to be ansorable for the stuf and
wictuall [3] within the miln.

The said day the tennenttis of the grund desyrit that quhat
skaith that thaj sustennit be the pekkaman, throw his slouth
and negligence, may be refunddit vnto thame. Quhilk swit

---

[1] Dried.   [2] From nightfall.   [3] Grain of any kind.

was granttit vnto thame, according to the quantittie of the skaith sustennit. Vpone the quhilk the tennentis of the barronney tuik act.

The said day the Lard desyrit in jugment that the ordinance of Curt sett doun in the dayis of William Hay of Wrie, his vmquhill father, to be rateffeit and apprewit in this Curt consernyng the payment of his fermes be the tennenttis of his grund, To wit, that the pekcaman saill se that na dust[1] be grund amangis his ferme, and that it may be fund guid and sufficient, and that the tennenttis to haiff[2] the ferme meill in raddynes euerie zeir afor the first day of Merche, and the beir ferme aganis the Ruid day,[3] quhilk desyir was willingle granttit.

The Curt of the Barronney of Wrie, haldene at Cowie, in Stephane Smyth hous, the xxviij of May 1607, be ane honorabill man William Hay of Wry, and Dauid Grahame in Arduthie, his belze for the tyme. The quhilk day the Soittis callit the Curt fensit and the memberis thairof lauchfullie sworne and admeittit.

The said day the Lard and his Belze rateffeis and apprewis the actis of Curt sett doun in to the dayis of his guidsir and father of guid memorie to remane ferme and stable and nawayis to be alterite.

The said day the Lardis lyne men[4] that ar vpone his bott is decernit be decreit of Curt to pay the dewittie that thaj ar oblisset at the terme of Mertymes, as thaj salbe crawit conforme to the rentaill Buik.

The said day it is decernit in jugment that the fischeris vpone the Larddis boit sall nawayis ly one land in tyme of fair wetheyr, and in kais that oney of the beyttis keippeyche[5] refwis,

---

[1] The beard of the grain produced by taking off the outer rind.—*Jam.*

[2] Have.   [3] The 3rd of May; the day of the Invention of the Cross.

[4] Line, or white, fishers.

[5] The company sailing on board a ship, whether passengers or mariners. From Fr. *Equipage d'un navire.*—*Jam.* The word occurs as 'equippage' under date 1577, in a complaint before the Privy Council at the instance of John Crooke, Bernard Cartmyll, and Thomas Demaresk, merchants in Southampton, touching the seizure by Lord John Stewart, Fewar of Orkney, of their two fishing vessels, the *Michaell* and the *Mynion*, at Scalloway, in Zetland.—*Reg. of Privy Council*, vol. ii. p. 655.

the skcipper to gayng with hym to the sie salbe punddit, viz.,
xiij s. iiij d., and gif the falt be in the skeipper, he saill be
punddit for xx s., and this ordour to be keippit.

The said day the Lard and his belze ratifeis and apprewis
that actis of Curt sett doun of befor conservnyng the cutting of
his wod, and that the pennalteis that ar desernit thairvpone to
be taikkyne wp preseislie as the occaacioun of the falt beis
trayit.

The said day the tennenttis of Manquhyth desyrit in jugment to haif ane officiar creat vnto thame to do thair lauchtfull
turnis.   Quhilk swit was granttit vnto thame be the Lard and
his belze, prowyddyng that Dauid Wod, the Lardis officiar, be
nawayis prejugit of his officiar corne quhilk tennentis granttit
willinglie to pay.   Vpone the quhilk Dauid Wod tuik act.

The said day Stephane Smyth plennit in jugment that there
was ane pairt of the tennenttis in the grund that refwsit to
maik hym thankfull payment of his smeddie boll.   To that
affect the Lard and his belze decernis the said Stephane to be
thankfullie payit of his smeddie boll, conforme to the ordinance and act of Curt sett doun thairvpone be vmquhill John
Hay of Wry.   Quhilk act and ordinance of Curt desernis ane
boll of aittis to be payit zeirlie of euerie plucht to the said
Stephane.   Vpone the quhilk Stewyne tuik act.

*The Barroun Court of the Baronie of Wry, hauldin within
the duelling-hous of Stewin Forbes in Cowy, wpon the
fourt day of November 1614, in name and behalf of ane
honorabill man William Hay of Wry, Laird of the
ground, and in name of ane honorabill man Robert
Irwing at the mylne of Cowy,[1] his Bailze, James Dauidsoun, notter Clerk, Robert Duncane, officiar,*

    *Dempster.   Thre suittis callit, the Court lauchfully
fensit and affirmit.*

The said Alexander Hey creat officiar, quha hies giffin his
aithe *de fideli administratione.*

---

[1] 'Robert Irvine at the Mill of Cowie' is, in 1609, enrolled purchaser of
2000 acres of land in the Plantation of Ulster, the price—for which Edward
Johnestoun, younger, merchant in Edinburgh, is named as surety—being £400
sterling.—*Reg. of Privy Council*, vol. viii. p. 324.

The said day the haill tennentis ar ordanit to bring in thair mertis betuixt the dait present and the Fredday ewm aucht dayis, quhilk is the　of this instant.

The said day James Mancur, at the Walk-mylne [1] of Wry, and Abraham Forfar, in Monthqueche, being persewit for nocht winning and leading sufficient leitt peitts, according to the remanent of the ground,[2] viz., ilk ane of them ane leit of peittis, and in respect they hawe nocht leid nor win the sam, they are decernit be the bailze to pey for ilk leit thairof the sowm of　merkis [3] money, and the officiar ordanit to poynd for the same within terme of lawe.

The said day Abrahame Forfar, being persewit for his ferme wictuall of the cropis 1612 and 1613 zeiris, extending to four scoir tuelf bolls wictuall, half meill half beir, and in respect of his non-comperance he decernit contumassie, and to be summondit to the nixt court with certificatioun and [4] he compeir nocht the haill clame to be hauldin *pro confesso*.

Continewis this Court upone tuentie foir houris warnying.

Ita est JACOBUS DAVIDSOUN, *notarius ac scriba Curie.*

The Barrony Court of the Barrony of Ury, hauldin within the duelling hous of Robert Irwing at the mylne of Cowye, wpone the xxiij of Nouember 1614 *zeiris, be ane honorable man, Maister Williame Red, Shiref Deput of Kincardin, sedentem pro tribunali, James Davidson, notter, Clerk.*

The said day Abrahame Forfar, being persewit for his ferme wictuall of the cropis 1612-1613 zeiris, and beand oft tymis callit lauchfull tym of day biddin comperit nocht: In respect quhairof he is ordanit to be summondit to the nixt Court, and to mak just compt and reckning of the clame lybellit, with certificatioun, and he compeir nocht the haill clame to be hauldin *pro confesso.*

James Mancur decernit be his awin confessiown to pey sextein pundis for ane leitt of peittis.

---

[1] A fuller's mill.　　　　　　[2] In proportion to the other tenants.
[3] A merk is equal in value to 15s. 4d. Scots, or 1s. 1¼d. stg.　　[4] If.

The said day James Mwrray ordaneit to restoir the dour bocht be him frome Jeillis Cairncorss, and to put the samen quhair it was wnder the paine of fourtie shillingis, or elleis the sowme of tuentie shillingis, as for the pryce thairof.

The said day, the haill barrony being sufficientlye tryit to hawe leid peittis and sauld to the inhabitantis of Steinhewin, contrar the actis sett downe thairanent, In respect quhairof the bailze ordaneis ewery contrawener of the former actis sett downe thairanent to pey fourtie shillingis *toties quoties* they transgres, and to be poyndit for fywe pundis monie *pro rato* for byganes.[1]

Item, ane act to be sett down anent the grinding of the lairdis fermeis and delyuerie thairof.

The said day the haill tennentis within the Barronye of Wry, being persewit for their meirtis of the crop 1614 zeiris, quhilkis meirtis the Bailze ordaneis the saidis tennentis pey to the Laird within aucht dayis, and failzeing of delyuerie of the saidis meirtis being sufficient, the officiar to poynd for the sowme of tuenty merkis monie for ilk mert one peyit.[2]

This Court continewit upon tuenty four houris warnyng.

The Barronne Court of the Barrony of Wry, hauldin at the Mylne of Cowye upone the xxvij of October 1615, in name and behalf of ane honorabill man William Hey of Wry, and in name of honorabill men Robert Irwing and George Strathawchin, his bailzeis, James Dauidsoun, notter, Clerk, Allexander Hey, officiar, George Bery, Dempster. Thre suittis callit, the Court lauchfully fensit and affermit.

The said day James Duncane decernit to pey ane boll of aittis to the Laird be his awin confessioun.

The said day the pickman, Allexander Makie, being persewit be Stewin Forbis for spilling of certane cornis be grinding thairof, and being probablye prowin, the said Allexander is ordaneit in all tym cwming to pey ten pundis *toties quoties* he happin to fall in the lyk scair.

---

[1] Past offences.　　　[2] Unpaid.

The said day Gilbert Mathow and Allexander Middlitoun, cotter in **Wry**, decernit to pey sex peckis aittis to the Laird.

The said day Duncane Robertsoun in Findlastoun decernit to restoir to James **Manewr** his aix, borrowit be him, or elles xiij **s.** iiij d. for the same.

The said day it is statute be the Layrd and tennentis be their awin consentis that quhasoewer cwmis to the mylne first with their corneis sall keip their rowm,[1] and quhasoewir trubilis his nichtbour in the paccabill grinding of his cornis and keiping of their rowme, sall pey to the Laird the sowme of fourtie shillingis. As also it is ordaneit that quhansoewer ony of the saidis tennentis cornis beis grindand, the pickiman schelland the meill[2] to thame, and being content thairwith, the pickiman sall be frie ony skathe alledgit downe to the stuf in his default, he attendand on his serwice diligently.

The Barroun Court of the Barronye of Wry, hauldin at the mylne of Cowye, wpone the xxv day of Nouember 1615, be ane honorabill man George Strathawchin, sedentem pro tribunali, the remanent memberis of Court all present. Thre suittis callit, the Court lawfully fensit and affermit.

The said day Johne Mowet in Powbare, decernit be the depoitioun of his aithe of werity to pey to Robert Irwing sewin peckis and ane half peck beir, and absoluit of all zeiris multeris preceiding the dait heirof, in respect of his depoitioun foirsaid.

The said day the haill tennentis restand mertis ar decernit to pey sufficient mertis be the sicht of friemen,[3] or elles tuentie merkis for the peice[4] thairof, and their reddiest guidis and geir to be poyndit for the same.

James Mackie in Brunthoileis, Allexander Burnet, ordanit to sicht and compryse the mertis. Quhilkis personis ar dewly posit to that effect.

The said day Robert Duncane, be the aithe of Helein Brig, decernit to pey to Beatrix Candolin the sowme x lib. vj s. viij d.

---

[1] Retain their place, or order of coming.   [2] Taking off the husks.
[3] The term *friemen* is here used as signifying *neutral parties*.   [4] For each.

The said day Robert Wilsoun and William Brabiner decernit in ameromament of court *hinc inde*, wiz.:—to pey fourty shillingis to the Laird.

The said day Robert Wilsone decernit to pey to William Brabiner xiij s. iiij d. agane Pasche day nixt, with ane peckt of presentlye, wnder paine of poynding.

The said day James Manewr, being summondit to hawe comperit and mak peyment of threittein bollis meill for his ferme of Walkmylne, and in respect of his [non]compeirans, decernit contumase, and to pey xl s. for the same.

The Barroun Court of the Barronye of Wry, hauldin within the duelling hous of Stewin Forbes in Cowye, in name and behalf of ane honorabill man, William Hey of Wry, laird of the ground, and in name of ane honorabill man, George Straquan in Glathne, his bailze, remanent memberis of Court all present. Thre suittis callit, the Court lawfully fensit and affermit.

The said day comperit Allexander Hey of Logie, judiciallye, and maid Williame Hey of Wry, his german brother, assigney in and to ane lyfrent letter tack grantit to umquhile John Strathawchin, sumtym in Walk myln of Wry, one the towne and landis thairof, southe landis of Wry, quhilk assedatioun the said Allexander is assigney vnto, and to the uplifting of the nowmber of threttein bollis wictuall from handis of James Maneur, taxisman thairof. Quhilk assignatioun was dewlye intimat to the said James Manewr, taxisman as said is, and the said James being persewit be uertcu of the foirnamit assignatioun for peyment of the foirnamit threitein bollis wictuall the Bailze decernis the said James maik peyment thairof *pro vt in scriptis*, and the nixt Court after assignit to produce the said assignatioun for instructioun of the clame. Quhairupon the said Williame Hey desyrit act of Court.

The Barroun Court of the Barronie of Vrie, hauldin at the barn yairds thairof, vpone the penult day of July 1616, in name and behalf of ane nobill and potent Lord Franceis

Erll of Aroll,[1] *Gryt Constabill of Scotland, with speciall
consent of ane honorabill man William Hey of Vrie, proprietar of the said ground, be ane discreit man George
Straquhan, bailzie to the said William Hey, Maister
James Irwing, notter public, Clerk, Alexander Hey,
officiar, and Archibald Mwirheid, Dempster. The Court
lauchfullie fencit and affirmit, Seuttis callit, and absentis
amerciat.*

The said day Alexander Schives, Robert Duncane, Archibald
Duncane, beand accusit for away takin of the Lairdis peittis :
The saidis persones comperand and hawand deponit as follouis,
to wit, the said Alexander Schives four cartes, the said Archi-
bald Duncane and his serwandis two, and the said Robert
Duncane frie be his ayth.

The said day Abraham Forfer, perseuit be Arthour Crystie
for cutting of his hors taill, quhilk the said Abraham confessit,
and thairfoir the bailze hes put the samen to ane assyse.

The names of the Assise.

Alexander Chein.	James Downnie.
William Duthie.	Stewin Grig.
James Alardes.	Archibald Duncan.
Dauid Michell.	Rodger Skein.
Alexander Burnet.	Jhone Hutschone.
Jhone Fergusoun.	

The said day the said Abraham is conwict in ane vnlaw of
fourtie pundis money, and that be the haill assise forsaid, and
concerning the contravertit libel betuixt the said Abraham
and Arthowr, the samen is decernit to be sichtit be Alexander
Hey, James Denune, and Jhon Messour, induelleris of Man-
quheych, and quhow soever thaj decret the pairteis to stand
thairat.

The said day William Brabiner in fourtie s. for his absence
unlawit, within term of law.

The said day it is ordenit that James Duncan, in the stryp [2]

---

[1] The Earl of Errol here holds court in virtue of his position as feudal superior
of the barony.

[2] A long narrow plantation or belt of trees. —*Jam.*

of   sall pey to the Laird twa stein [1] of brew chres [2] zeirlie.

The said day Thomas Penter in Manquhiche, is decernit to be in the Lairdis will for perseuing his clame befor ane uther court, and that conforme to ane former act, and conforme to the said former act contenit.

The said day it is ordenit that ewerie ane, and quhatsumewer beis fund in tyme cuming to loip the Lairdis yaird daikis,[3] sall pey ten pundis *toties quoties.*

The said day James Boner is conuict in ane vnlaw of ten merkis for cuttin of grein wood, and thairfor ordenit to pey the samen to the Laird.

The said [day] Quhatsumewr tennentis that cummis nocht in dew tym for the Lardis serwic, being chargit be the officier fourtie aucht houris befor, the said persone sall pey aucht merkis to the Laird *toties quoties.*

The said day James Sellat confessit himself[4] to releiw George Grig of the prys, corne acclamit.

                        J. IRWING, *notar et curie scriba.*

The Barroun Court off the Baronyeis of Wrye and Mount-queiche, hauldin within the duelling hous of Stewin Forbes in Cowye, upon the auchtein day of Merche 1617, in name and behalf of ane honorable man William Hey of Wry, Lard of the ground, be Mr. Williame Reid, Sheref Deput of Kincardin, sedentem pro tribunali, James Dauid-soun, notter, Clerk, Alexander Hey, officiar, John Tail-zeour, Dempster: The suittis callit, the court lawfully fensit and affermit.

WOOD CUTTING.

The said day comperit Robert Duncane in Cairntoun and Archibald Duncane in Banageicht judicially, and ilk ane of thame became bound and oblist as cawtioner for wther and for

---

[1] A measure of weight equal to 16 lbs.—*Jam.*

[2] *Cres* or *Creischie*: tallow. *Brew cres*: the *custom* paid for the liberty of brewing. 'The *rediendo* for an alehouse and alehouse croft was often a quantity of tallow, the produce, perhaps, of the kitchen of the little inn.'—Innes's *Legal Antiquities,* p. 49, *n.* 1.

[3] Overleapt the laird's garden walls: evidently a trespass with a view to theft.

[4] Acknowledged his obligation.

their tennentis and serwandis, that they nor nane [1] of them sall cutt nor distroye ony of the Lairdis grein wood or zoung that growis within the beyndis [2] [of] the barrony of Wry, and quhow oft so ewer ather of them selffis or their tennentis beis schallangit or apprehendit in cutting thairof, obleissis thame heirby to pey to the Laird the sowm of fourtie pundis as penaltie decernit of their awin consent, but [3] modificatioun.

The said day James Mwrray, James Duncane, John Mwrray, and Dauid Murray, being persewit for cutting and distroying of the Lairdis wod, and possit thairwpon, wald nocht depone, In respect quhairof decernit all in amerciament of Court, and to pey in unlaw the sowm of ten pundis ilk ane *pro rato.*

The said day Williame Duthie and James Allardes, ilk ane, becwm cawtioneris for [other], and for their men, tennentis and serwandis, that nane of thame distroy nor cut the Lairdis wood in tym cwming, wnder paine of fourtie pundis money *toties quoties* they be apprehendit cutting ony thairof in tym cwming.

James Dewny becwm in the Lairds will foir alledgit cutting of the Lairdis woid, and decernit in amerciament of Court for the same.

James Dennie decernit in amerciament of Court for cutting and distroying of the Lairdis wood, in respect, being posit, wald nocht depone, and James Allardes becwm cawtioner for his transgressiown thairanent in tym cwming, wnder paine of fourtie pundis *toties quoties* he be apprehendit.

Archibald Siller and William Burnett ar becwm in the Lairdis will for the alledgit cutting of the Lairdis grein wood, and ilk ane of them becwm cawtioneris for wther in tym cwming wnder paine foirsaidis.

John Mwrray decernit in amerciament of Court for the alledgit cutting of the said wood, as also Archibald Mwrray decernit in amerciament, and ilk ane of thame becwme cawtioneris for wther in tym cwming wnder paine foirsaid *toties quoties* they be apprehendit thairwith.

Patrick Stewin decernit in amerciament of Court, and John Arbuthnet in Logy, becwm cawtioner for him in tyme cwming, wnder paine foirsaid.

---

[1] Nor any.   [2] Bounds.   [3] Without.

Gilbert Greig decernit in amerciament of Court, and John Arbuthnet lykwayes cawtioner for his abstinans in tym cwming, wnder paine foirsaid.

Charlie Sutter decernit in amerciament of Court, and Stewin Forbes cawtioner for his abstinand in tym cwming under paine foirsaid *toties quoties* they be apprehendit.

James Traill and John Smyth, being posit, wald nocht depone, In respect quhairof decernit in amerciament of Court, and Stewin Forbes cawtioner for their abstinans in tym cwming wnder paine foirsaid.

Allexander Traill decernit in amerciament of Court, in respect being posit wald nocht depone, and sicklyk [1] Barroun Reid, elder,[2] decernit in amerciament of Court, and ilk ane of them becwm cawtioun for wther for their abstinans in tym cwming, wnder paine foirsaid.

James Mill decernit in amerciament of Court for cutting of the said wood, and George Strathawchin in Glathno, becwm cawtioner for his abstinans thairfra in tym cwming.

Stewin Forbes decernit in amerciament of Court for cutting of the said wood. Lykas James Downye in Mounthqueiche is becwm actit judicially that the said Stewin Forbes, his men, tennentis and serwandis, sall abstein from cutting of the said wood or ony pairt thairof in tym cwming, wnder paine of fourtie pundis, specially agreit on be the said James.

Allexander Burnett decernit in amerciament of Court, and Allexander Hay becwm cawtioner for his abstinans in tym cwming.

John Arbuthnet cawtioner for James Ros abstinans fra cutting of the Lairdis wod in tym cwming.

Androw Leper decernit be his awin confessiown in amerciament of Court, and Allexander Burnett cawtioner for his abstinans in tym cwming, and the said Androw cawtioner for the said Allexander, wnder the paine foirsaid *toties quoties* ather of them be apprehendit.

James Mancur being persewit for cutting of the said wood,

---

[1] Similarly.

[2] *Senior.* 'Elder' and 'younger' were at one time used precisely as we now apply the terms *senior* and *junior*. The latter form still occurs in speaking of an heir-apparent, whom it is common to designate 'younger' of so-and-so.

and being lawfully summondit to that effect, comperit nocht,
In respect quhairof decernit contumaxed, as also William
Measoun, being summondit to the effect foirsaid, decernit
contumaxed.

James Sellett decernit in amerciament, and findis George
Strathawchin cawtioner for his abstinans in tym cwming, wnder
paine foirsaid.

Seruice.

The said day Archibald Leper and Archibald Burnett
decernit, ilk ane of thame, pey the sowme of ten pundis for
brewing but tollerans[1] of the Laird.

The said day the haill tennentis that peyis serwice within
the Barrony of Wry being present became actit of their awin
consentis, being lawfully warnit wpone tuentie four houris
warnying to enter to quhatsumewer serwice addetit be thame
or ather of thame to be dew to the Laird of **Wry**, and gyf
thaj enter nocht to ther serwice in conwenient tyme, sall pey
ten pundis money to the Laird *toties quoties* they transgress
heiranent.   *Ita est* Jacobus Dauidsoun,
                                       Notarius ac Scriba.

*The Barrone Court of the Baroneis of Wry, hauldin within
the duelling hous of Stewin Forbes in Cowy, wpone the
xij of May 1617, be ane honorabill man Maister
Williame Reid, Shiref Deput of Kincardin, sedentem pro
tribunalj, etc.   James Dauidsoun, notter publict, Clerk.*

The said day James Mancur in Walk mylne of Wry, being
persewit be George Miller, froster,[2] for cutting and distroying
of the grein woods growand within barrony of Wry, and the
said James being personall present and accusit thairwpon,
confessit the samen, In respect quhairof decernit in amerciament.

Williame Measoun, serwitour to James Mancur, decernit in
amerciament of court for cutting of the said wood, James
Mancur cawtioner for Williame Measoun, his abstinans in tym
cuming, under the pane of fourty pundis.

---

[1] Without permission.   [2] Forester.

The said day James Mancur, being desyrit [to] find cawtioun actit[1] for abstinand from cutting and distroying of the
said Wood in tym cwming, refusit to do the same, In respect
quhairof decernit *toties quoties* he be apprehendit transgres to
pey according to the act of Parliament.

John Hendersoun decernit in amerciament for cutting of
the wood, and Allexander Hey of Logy, cawtioner for his
abstinans in tym cuming, wnder paine foirsaid, as also for
Allexander Mearse, his abstinans, quha is decernit in amerciament lykwayis.

James Boner, be his awin confessioun decernit in amerciament of Court for the distroying of the Laird of Wry his wood.

Williame Duthy in Mounthqueichie becum cawtioner for
Abrahame Forfar, his abstinans frome cutting of the Lairdis
wood in tym cuming.

Thomas Sellett decernit in amerciament for cutteing of the
said wood.

SERVICE.

The said day the haill tennentis of Mountqueiche being
desyrit and requirit to enter to their serwices harrages and
carrageis within quhatsumewer meaneis[2] within the barrony of
Wrye labourit in the Lairdis name, The saidis haill tennentis
being presonally present, they and ilk ane of them became
actit of their awin frie will and consent to enter to all sort of
harrage carrage wther dew serwice within the meaneis of Wry,
or wther meaneis within the barrony thairof, labourit in the
Lairdis name wpone lawfull premonitiown and warnyng maid
be the officiar, and that conform to the remanent tennentis of
the barrony of Wry, Quhairwpone Allexander Hey, officiar and
procuratour for the Laird, tuik act and instrument.

The said day James Mancur being persewit for his reist[3]
ferme crop 1615, extending to thre bollis, quhilk the said
James confessis reistand, In respect quhairof decernit to
pey for ilk boll conform to the feir[4] of the zeir.   As also

---

[1] Entered in the court book.   [2] Common lands.

[3] That remained owing.

[4] *Feirs* or *fiars* signifies in Scotland the legally fixed prices of grain in the
different counties for the current year.   These prices are determined at a *Fiars*

~~decernit reistand the nowmber of fywe bollis meill for this present crope.~~

And being persewit for the reist ferme of this present crope 1616, comperit the said James Mancur, and offerit him prowe compleit peyment of the haill in the next court to be hauldin the xxiiij Jun nixt, except ten firlottis meill, quhilk he obleissis in caice of failze of peyment to pey for ilk boll x libis money, Quhairwpon the [said] Allexander Hey, procuratour foirsaid, tuik instrument.

The said day it is statuit be the Laird and bailze, be consent of the tennentis, that quhatsumewer cotter or geirsman within the barrony of Wry, being lauchfully chargit to his maisteris serwice, and disobeyis, sall pey sex shillingis aucht pennies for ilk day.

The Barroun Court of the Barroneis of Wry, hauldin within the duelling hous of Stewin Forbes in Cowy, vpone the xxiiij day of Jun 1617 zeiris, be ane honorabill man Maister William Reid, sedentem pro tribunalj, etc. James Dauidsoun, notter publict, Clerk.

The said day being assignit to James Mancur to prowe compleit peyment of the haill ferme for his occupatioun of Walk myl of Wry, crope 1616, lyk as he is becwm actit be ane former act to pey the sowm vij pundis money for ilk [boll] thairof that was nocht peyit, exceptand ten firlottis,[1] and being lawfully citat to that effect, lawfull executioun producit thairwpon, comperit nocht, In respect quhairof decernit contumaxed, and to pey the foirnameit sowme of ten pundis money for ilk boll he was reistand, extending in the haill to aucht bollis and ane half, at ten lib the boll.

Court, which meets in February of each year, and is presided over by the sheriff of the county. A jury is summoned, before whom the evidence of farmers, corn-dealers, and others is led as to the market values of the different grains raised in the district. The prices subsequently fixed by the opinion of the jury, and sanctioned by the sheriff, are termed the *fiars* of the year. They determine the prices of grain in all contracts where these have not been previously arranged between parties. The term *fiars* is of doubtful origin, but is probably connected with the French *affeurage,* taxation, fiars having been originally used to fix Crown rents.

[1] A corn measure, the fourth part of a boll.

The said day James Mill, being persewit be Allexander Hey, as procuratour for William Hey of Wry, for the reist of some bollis beir crop 1616, and the said James being personale present, confessit him reistand the said four bollis beir, quhilk the bailze decernit him pey within terme of law, or vij pundis for ilk boll thairoff.

The said day Abrahame Forfar, being persewit be the Laird for the nocht erecting and biging of his garding, and haill bigging[1] of Mounthquheiche possessit be him, and suffering his horss and beistis pasture within the said zaird, and inputting of his hors and guidis in the hall and chalmeris thairof, Comperit the said Abrahame and denyit the haill alledgeins[2] proponit be the Laird *ex aduerso*. The Laird, being present, offerrit him prowe the haill alledgeins in the nixt court, and to instruct the same be ane band subscryvit be the said Abrahame.

> *The Burroun Court of the Barronye of Wry, hauldin within the Wood heid, upone first day of Nouember 1617, be Maister Williame Reid, sedentem pro tribunalj, James Dauidsoun, notter publict, Clerk, remanent memberis all present. The suittis callit, the Court lawfully fensit and affermit.*

The said day it is statut and ordaneit that in all tym cwming Williame Duthie in Woodheid, Robert Duncane in Cairntown, James Allardes ther, and Archibald Duncane in Boñageicht, salbe barley men[3] for comprysing and sichting of pryce corneis, and to discern thairupone, and in Mounthqueiche William Duthie, elder, and Allexander Duthie ther, James Downy and Abrahame Forfar ther, for Mounthqueiche, and to hauld courtis, and to discerne thairwpone in all tym cwming.

---

[1] A house, properly of a large size, as opposed to a cottage.—*Jam.*

[2] Allegation.

[3] Men chosen to sit in a Court of Burlaw (A.-S. *bur*, a village). The province of this Court was to adjust disputes on minor matters between neighbours, the rights of outgoing and incoming tenants, the value of meliorations, and other questions of a similar character being referred to it for judgment. It is invariably stated in reference to the Court of Burlaw that its members were popularly elected. The above, however, seems to throw discredit on this statement, and to suggest that they were after all the mere nominees of the proprietor.

The said day James Mill in Cowy ordaineit to produce his
assedatiown in the nixt court, and to be summondit to that
effect.

The said day the haill brosteris[1] in the Barrony of Wry
ordaneit to ane stein[2] of talloun,[3] or pryce thairof, for ewery
zeir they hawe browin, fra their entry to the dait of thir presentis, except sick as produceis ane sufficient tytill.

The said day Thomas Buchan creat froster for the tor[4] and
wattersyd of Wrrye, quha hes giffin his ayth *de fidelj administratione.*

*The Barroun Courtt of the Barrony of Wrrye, haldin in
Vodheid, the auchtein day of December* 16017 *zeiris, be
Maister Williame Reid, Shireff Deput of Kincardin.
The Court lauchfullie fenssit and affirmit.*

The said day compeiritt James Millin in [Cowie], and being
persewit be Alexander Hay, officiar for brew lauche,[5] ordanitt
to pay ane stein of creischie within term of law, vnder the
paine of poinding.

Compeirit the said James Millin, and refuis in judgmentt to
pay ane stein of cris.   Quharvpone the baillye hes ordanit him
to pay within terme of law, or than to shawe his warrand in
the nixt courtt.

The said day James Mancur, in Valkmyl of Wrye, is decernit
be the Laird to pay his ferme of his tak of Walkmill, viz.
thrattine bollis, tua firlottis meill, to Maister Villiame Reid,
Shireffe Deputt of Kincardin, crope 16017.

*The Barronie Court of the Barroncy of Wry, haldin in the
bairne of Andro Alardes in Woodheid, vpoune the aucht
day of May* 1618, *in name and behalf of ane nobill and
michtie lord Franceis, erle of Eroll, lord Hay, etc., and
William Hay of Wry, heritable propriater of the grund,
and Maister William Reid in Cowy, their bailzie, James
Thomsoun, notter publict, Clerk, Alexander Hay, officiar,*

---

[1] Brewers.   [2] A measure of weight equal to 16 lbs.   [3] Tallow.
[4] A wooded hill or eminence.   [5] A tax paid for the liberty of brewing.

*John Dauidsoun, Dempster.   The suit callit, the court
lauchfullie fensit and affirmit.*

The said day James Thomesoun, notter publict, is admittit
Clark, and John Dauidsoun, Dempster, quha gave their ayth
de fideli administrationj, ay and quhill[1] thay be dischairgit.

The said day it is statuit and ordeant be cowmoune consent
of the haill tennentis of the barrony of Wry, and in speciall
the tennentis of Mountquheche, that their haill guidis sall
pastour wpoune the Mounth[2] and out boundis,[3] as thaj have
beine in vse befor, Bot it is statuit that for ilk beast, wiz.,
hors, ox, or kow, that cumes wpoun their nichtbouris in haime
gers,[4] sall pey to the pairtie interes *toties quoties* how oft thaj
sall contravein this present act the sowme of vj s. 8d., and for
ilk scheip xxxij d. *toties quoties* how oft the pairtie interest
mey prowe the contraventioune of this act, and the officiar
ordeanit to poynd thairfor, quhairanent this present act salbe
ane sufficient warrand.

The said day the haill tennentis of Montquheye is decernit
be the bailzie to cum and do their service be the Manse[5] of
Wry the morne,[6] the nynt of May instant, wnder the paine
contenit in the former actis, and the officiar ordenit to poynd
thairfor.

The said day it statuit and ordeanit that quhasoeuer within
the barrouny off Wry salbe fund to lowp the gairdine dyik of
Wry, ather Maister or servand, sall pey tuentie schillingis
money to the Laird, and the Maister to be comptable for his
servand, and the officiar ordeanit to poynd thairfor.

The said day James Miln in Cowie, being chargit to this
court be Alexander Hay, officiar, quhairon he gave his aith to
produce his assedatioune annent his brew talloune, conforme to
the ordinance of the last courtt, and in respect the said James,
his nocht compeirance, according to the will of the former act,

---

[1] Until.

[2] The name given to the district covered by the eastern extremity of the
Grampians.   [3] Common pasturage.

[4] *In haime gers* : that which belonged to the private holdings of the tenants,
in opposition to the grass of the ' Mounth and out boundis.'

[5] Mains.   [6] To-morrow.

the said James is decernit to pey ane staine of Talloun within terme of law, or than four merkis for the price thairof.

Ita est Jacobus Thomesoun,
notarius publicus ac scriba Curie.

The Barrowne Courtt off the Barronny of Wry, haldin in the barne of Andro Allardes in Woodheid, wpoune the xvij day of Jun 1618, in name of ane nobill and potent lord Frances, erle of Erroll, Lord Hay, etc., and William Hay of Wry, heritabill propriator of the said landis, Mr. William Reid, thair bailzie, James Thomesoun, notter publict, court clerk, Alexander Hay, officiar. Thrie suitis calit, the court laufullie fensit and affirmit. Andro Tullo, Dempster.

The said day Archebald Burnet is decernit to pey four merkis for ane zeiris brew Talloun, within terme of law, wnder pain of poynding within terme of law.

Peats.

The said day it is statuit and ordeanit, with cowmoun consent of the haill tennentis of the barroney of Wry, baith husbandis and cotters convenit for the tyme, that nane of tham sall sell, dispone, or away put any peitt or fewall to any man in ony tym cumming without leave of the erle of Erroll and the laird of Wry be wryt,[1] wnder the paine of tene pundis money, to be peyit be the contraveiner to the laird of Wry, and the officiar ordenit to poynd for the same.

The said day the haill tennents of Wry and Mountquheiche is decernit, sick as ar astrickit to service, to cum in on Mononday nixt, ilk pleuche with tua hors, and leid sick peittis as the laird hed causit cast, and that by and attour[2] ordinar leitt peitts baithe of Wry and Montquheiche respective, quhair thaj aucht to leid the same, wnder the pain of xl s. ilk pleuche, and the tennents of Mountquheiche ordenit to cast, win, and leid thrie leitt of peittis to the hall of Montquheiche, wnder pain of x merkis for ilk leitt wneastin win and led in maner foirsaid.

The said day the haill tennentis of the Burnesyd and the

---

[1] By written permission.   [2] Over and above.

fisharis in Cowie are decernit and ordenit to pey to the laird
sick service in sheiring [1] and leading of cornis and in leiding of
peitts as thaj war in vse to pey to his wmquhile father, and it
is ordeanit that Archibald Murreys tak be sichtit and maid
equall with the rest.

The said day compeirit James Milne in Cowij, and confessit
him self to be restand awand to the laird of Wry four bollis bear,
and to Maister Andro Milne,[2] Minister, tua bollis ane firlott
bear of his occupatioun of the Chapelandrie of Cowy [3] for the
crope 1617 zeiris, and in respect of the said James confessioun
the bailzie decernis the said James to pey the same to the said
Laird and Minister respectiue ilk ane for their awin pairtis,
and in caice of failzie Alexander Hey, procuratour for the laird,
and the persoune for him self, protestit for the heichest pryss.

The said day the haill tennentis of the barrony of Wry ar
decernit to pey ilk pleuche xiij s. iiij d. to the school maister
zeirlie, and the officiar ordenit to poynd for the sam.

The said day Archibald Leaper, John Smyth, Ninian Robertson, and John Foull is decernit to pey sextein merkis money for
their maill for tua zeiris bygane befor Witsonday last, wnder
paine of poynding, together with ilk ane of thame ane pynt of
oylly zeirlie for ilk zeir of the said tua zeiris.[4]

      J. Thomesoune, *notarius publicus ac scriba Curiæ.*

---

[1] Reaping.

[2] Mr. Andrew Milne was admitted minister of Fetteresso in 1605. He was a
member of the General Assemblies of 1638, '39, and died 12th October 1640 in
his fifty-eighth year.—Scott's *Fasti Ecclesiæ Scoticanæ*, vol. iii. Part II. p. 869.

[3] Chapel lands of Cowie. The Chapel of Cowie was dedicated by William
Wishart, Bishop of St. Andrews, as a subsidiary place of worship for the
parishioners of Fetteresso, in June 1276, *ita quod nullam prejudicium generetur
matrici ecclesie de Fethyressach* (Fetteresso).—*Statuta Ecclesiæ Scoticanæ*, vol. i.
p. 303. This chapel was originally possessed of a considerable endowment in
lands and otherwise, the value of the benefice being estimated at the time of the
Reformation at 24 bolls of bear. In 1601, the then minister of Fetteresso, also
named Andrew Milne, received from the King, in appreciation of his 'gude,
trew, and thankfull seruices, etc.,' a grant of one-third of the Chaplainrie of
Cowie, to be held during his lifetime. From the above it would appear that
this grant had been continued to his successor.

[4] The above parties were evidently fishermen (see p. 32, where Smith and
Robertson are described as such). The *reddendo* exacted was oil manufactured
from fish livers, to be used for burning in the open lamps or *cruisies* common all
over Scotland a generation ago.

The Barroun Court of the Barronny of Wry, haldin in the dueling hous of Andro Alardys in Woodheid, wpoun the xxiiij of July 1618 zeiris, in name and behalf of ane nobill and potent lord Francis, erle of Erroll, and William Hay of Wry, and Robert Irving at Miln of Cowie, their bailzie deput for the tyme, James Thomesoun, notter publict, Clerk, Alexander Hay, officiar.
Andro Tullo, Dempster.
The suits callit, the Court laufullie fensit and afirmit.

The said day compeirit Duncan Robertsoun in Findlastoun, and is decernit to pey to Alexander Blak, maltman, burges of Aberde[en], the soum of aucht merkis iij s. iiij d. for the price of ane boll malt restand be him to the said Alexander In respect refuisit to give his ayth in the contrair.[1]

The said day it is statuit and ordeanit be the **Laird** and his bailzie that John Miln at the milne of Montqueiche and Alexander Maky, miler at the milne of Cowie, salbe officiar to thame selffis, and be thir presents givis thame power to poynd for all dissobedience thair miln service.

J. THOMESOUNE, *notarius publicus ac scriba Curiæ.*

The Barroun Court of the Barrouny of Wrye, haldin in the Scholhous off Wrie, wpoune the tuentie fyve day of Marche 1620 zeiris, in name and behalf of ane nobill and potent lord Francis, erle of Erroll, Lord Hay, etc., and William Hay of Wrie, heritable propriater off the said barrouny off Wrie, and in name of ane discreit gentilmane Georg Mowatt in Reidcloak, thair bailzie deput for the tyme. James Thomsoune, notter publict, Court Clark, Alexander Hay, officiar, James Spark, Dempster. The suits calet, the Court laufullie fensit and affirmit.

The said day Georg Mowatt in Reidcloak is admitit greatt bailzie, James Wyshart and James Spark, Dempster, quha gave their aithe *de fideli administrationj*, ay and quhill thay be dischairgeit.

---

[1] Refused to deny his indebtedness on oath.

The said day John Tailzeour in Reidcloak being persewit be
Thomas Durart, his nichtbour, and James Wyshart, procuratour fiscall, for the erle of Erroll and the laird of Wrie for his
entres, for hurting, wounding, and bluid-drawing off the said
Thomas Durart in the back syid off the heid, and the samen
being sufficientlie provin be Alexander Mowat and William
Blindscheall, admitit witness be the said John Tailzeour his
consent, the said John Tailzeour is decernit to pey to the erle
off Erroll and the Laird the sowme of tene pundis money
within terme of law vnder paine of poynding.

J. THOMESOUNE, *notarius scriba.*

The Barroune Court of the Barrouny of Wrie, haldin in
James Alardes barne in Woodhead, vpoune the xxj day
of Julij 1620, in name and behalf of ane nobill and potent
erle Francis, erle of Erroll, Lord Hay, etc., and William
Hay of Wrie, heritable propriaters of the saids landis,
and in name of ane honourable man John Hay of
Crimoundmogit[1] *their bailzie. James Thomsoune, notter,*
Clark, Alexander Hay, officiar, William Gicht, Dempster.
The suits calit, the Court lawfullie fensit and affirmit.

The said day William Gicht was creat Dempster, quha gave
his ayth *de fideij administrationj,* ay and quhill he be dischargit.

The said day the haill tennentis efter specifeit ar decernit be
thair awin consentis to pay ilk ane for their awine pairtis the
particular quantaties of wictuall customes and sowmes of money
wnder writtin to John Mowatt, in Powbair, as chalmerlane and
factour to my lord of Erroll, wiz.—Nynteine bollis meill and
nyne bollis of bear restand be Gilbert Barclay of his ferme of
Magray, crop 1619, with thrie dussane of caponis, or than

---

[1] Cousin of the Laird of Urie. He succeeded his father, designed William
Hay of Little Arnage, in 1614.—Retours, *Aberdeenshire,* 135. Crimonmogate,
in the Buchan district of Aberdeenshire, formed part of the barony of Crimond,
which was acquired by the lairds of Urie in the latter part of the fifteenth century, through the marriage of Gilbert Hay of Urie to Beatrix, daughter of Sir
John Dunbar of Crimond. Crimonmogate is now in the possession of the Ban-
nermans, formerly of Elrick, to whom it was bequeathed by Mr. Patrick Milne.—
Smith's *New Hist. of Aberdeenshire,* vol. ii. p. 942.

vj s. 8 d. for the peice thairoff, with thrie custome wadders
wnder the woll,[1] or thane fyve merk for the peice thairoff, for
his customes crope forsaid 1619. Margarat Cheine, spous to
Robert Irving at the milne of Cowie, ane boll and thrie pecks
bear of hir ferme off the milne of Cowie, crope 1619, with ane
custome mert, or than tene punds money for the price thairoff,
crope forsaid, with auchtein caponis, or than vj s. 8 d. for the
peice thairof, crope forsaid. William Duthie and James and
Andro Alardess is decernit to pey their haill fermes, dewties,
and wther customes for their seuerall occupationis of Woodheid,
for the crope 1619 zeiris, in caice they produce nocht sufficient
acquittances vpoune the recept thairoff. Robert Duncane, in
Cairntoune, decernit for his haill dewitie of the said crope
in lyk manner, in caice he produce nocht ane sufficient dischairge thairvpoune. James Milne, in Cowie, is decernit be
his awin confessioun to pey to the said chalmerlane thrie bollis
thrie firlottis bear, in peyment of his ferme bear for the crope
1619 zeiris, with 1 dozen of pultrie foullis, or than iii s. iiij d.
for the peice thairof, crope forsaid. Stephane Forbes in Cowie
is decernit to pey the sowme of sex pundis money for ilk dozen
off fourtein dozen elnis[2] of sarking lining clayth[3] restand be
him this fourtein zeiris bygaine, in caice the said Stephane
produce nocht his assedatioune within terme of law bearand
that he aucht nocht to pey the same. Archebald Duncan in
Bannageith is decernit to pey feftie merkis money for his
Mertimes maill, in j m. vj c. and nynteine, and Witsonday in
1620. George Milne in Corsley ane quarter of butter and
four pultrie foullis. Alexander Duthie in Montquhiche the
sowme off feftie merkis money for his Witsonday maill in
1620. Abrahame Forfar, elevine merkis money in compleit
peyment of his Mertimes maill in 1619, with feftie merkis
money for his Witsonday maill, 1620. Alexander Wyshart
in Montquhiche feftie merkis money for his Witsonday maill,

---

[1] *Under the woll:* unshorn.

[2] The Scotch ell contains 37·0598 imperial inches. The *Plaiding ell*, by
which some coarse stuffs were measured, was somewhat longer, that in the
custody of the Dean of Guild of Aberdeen containing 38·416 imperial inches.—
Elgen's *Tables*, p. 21.

[3] *Sarking lining clayth:* linen cloth suitable for making shirts.

in this instant zeir of God 1620 zeiris. Dauid Dunbar in Rothnik and Georg Schiphird in Bannagubs, is decernit to pey to the said John Mowatt, factour forsaid, the sowme off ane hundreth pundis money for the Witsonday maill of the saidis landis, in this instant zeir of God 1620 zeiris. Georg Straquhan in Glithno is decernit to pey the soume of fiftie merkis for his Witsonday and Mertimes maillis, in anno 1619, with tuentie fyve merkis for his Witsonday maill, in this instant zeir of God 1620 zeiris. Alexander Hey of Findlaw- stoune is decernit to pey to John Mowatt, chalmerlane, the sowme of tuentie merkis money for his Mertimes maill of Find- lawstoune in 1619 and Witsonday in 1620. John Foullar is decernit to pey xxxiij s. iiij d. for his maill for ilk zeir, thir thrie zeiris bygaine extendis to fyve pundis. John Smyth, fischer in Cowie, is decernit in lyk maner to pey fyve pundis for his maill thir thrie zeiris bygane, with ane pynt of oylie, or than viij s. Ninian Robertsoune, fischer, is decernit in lyk manner to pey the sowme of fyve pundis money for his maill thir thrie zeiris bigaine. The quhilkis haill personis aboun wreittin are ilk decernit respectiue for thair awine pairtis to content and pey the haill nowmber and quantatie of wictuall, meill, and bear befor mentionat, with the haill customes or prisses thairoff befor wreittin, and haill particular sowmes befor specifeitt to the said John Mowatt, chalmerlane, within terme of law, wnder the paine of poynding of ilk ane of their rediest guidis and geir respectiue for their awine pairts, wnder the paine of poyinding within terme of law.

The said day it is statut and ordeainet be the bailzie that quhatsumeiuer persone or personis that happine to brew and sell within the barrouny of Wrie, or my lordis landis in Cowie, sall pey zeirlie ane staine of brew tallowne, or thane fyve merkis for ilk staine thairof.

The said day it is statut and ordeanit be the bailzie that ewerie pleuche in Montquhiche and Corsley sall cast, wine, leid, and stak zeirlie ane sufficient leitt of peittis in dew tyme, and in caice of failzie to pey fyve pundis money for the price of ilk halff leitt, and the officiar ordeanit to poynd thairfor.

The said day it is statut and ordeanit, with consent of the haill tennentis within the barrouny of Wrie, that quhatsumeuer persone or personis salbe fund and tryit to steill or away taik ony off their nichtbouris peittis in tyme cuming, sall pey for ewerie burding of peitts xx s. for ilk laid of peits on hors with creillis,[1] xl s. for ilk kairt full of peitts, thrie pundis money, and the officiar ordeanit to poynd for the same.

The said day it is statut and ordeanit be the bailzie, with cowmoune consent of the haill tennentis within the barrouny, that quhatsumeuer persone or personis beis fund to steill, pull, or away tak ony off their nichtbouris peis,[2] sall pey for ewerie tyme, toties quoties how oft soeuer they be chalengit, the sowme off fourtie shilings money, and the maisteris to be comptable for their bairnis and servandis.

The said day it is statut and ordeanit be the bailzie that quhatsumeuer persoune or personis in tymes cuming sall leid peittis furth of the barrouny of Wrie, and sell to the indualars of Stanehevine without ane speciall lycence and libertie haid and obtenit be thame of my lord of Erroll, sall pey the sowme of tene pundis money to the said nobill erle, and the officiar ordeanit to poynd for the sam.

The said day James Dewinny in Montquhiche, William Duthie there, Robert Duncane in Cairntoune, and William Duthie thair, is electit, nominat, and chossin barlaw men within the barrouny of Montquhiche and Wrie in tyme cuming, quha gave their aithe de fidelj administrationj ay and quhill they be dischairgit.

The said day compeirit John Mowat, procuratour for the erle of Erroll, and protestit for the heighest priss for sick bollis of wictuall as sall happin to be restand be ony of the tennents efter the terme of Lambes [3] nixt.

The said day it is statut and ordeanit be the bailzie, with consent of the haill tennentis of the barrouny of Wrie that ar obleist to cast and win leitt peitis, sall cast, win, leid, and stack, ilk ane of thame, ane sufficient leit off peittis, as thaj ar obleist, wpoune the peithill of Wrie, zeirly befoir the last of Julij, wnder the pain of ten pundis money for ilk leitt thairoff, and the officiar ordeanit to poynd for the same.

The said day the personis following is convenit and aggriet

---

[1] Baskets made of osiers.   [2] Peas.
[3] Lammas, the 1st of August.

C

with Margarat Cheine, spous to Robert Irving, for their
bygane multeris befor [1] the crope on the grund in this instant
zeir of God 1620, in manner wnder wreittin, to wit, William
Duthie in Woidheid j firlott malt, Andro and James Alardes
j firlot malt, John Hendersoune j peck of schilingis,[2] Archebald
Duncane ij pecks meill, quhilk they ar decernit to pey to hir
within terme of law.   J. Thomesoune, *notarius publicus,*
ac scriba Curie.

> *The Barroune Court of the Barrouny of Wry, haldin in*
> *William Duthies barne in Woidheid, vpoune the xvj*
> *daye of Junij 1621 zeiris, in name and behalf of ane*
> *nobill and potent lord Francis, erle of Erroll, Lord Hay,*
> *etc., and in name of the richt honorable William Hay of*
> *Wry, propriater of the said landis, Maister William*
> *Reid in Cowy thair bailzie, Alexander Hay, officiar*
> *deput for the tyme, James Thomsoun, notter, Clark,*
> *Archibald Murray, Dempster.   The suitis calit, the*
> *court laufullie fensit and affirmit.*

The said day Archebald Murray in Cowij was creat, constitut, and ordeainet dempster, qua gave ayth *de fidelj admini-*
strationj ay and quhill he be dischairgit.

The said day compeirit James Alardes, elder in Woodheid,
tennent and taksman of the halff thairof, and voluntarlie,
frielie, and of his awin guid will, with his blissing and kyndnes,
rennuncit, resignit, dischairgit, quytclamet and *simpliciter* over
gaiwe his haill occupatioune off the toune and landis of Woodheid, with housses, bigings, zairds, toftis, crofts, pairtis, pen-
diculs,[3] and pertinents of the same, lyand within the barrony
of Wrie, parochine of Fethereschawe,[4] and sherefdome of Kincardine, to and in favouris of ane nobill and potent lord

---

[1] For.

[2] Grain that has passed through the mill and been freed from the husk.—*Jam.*

[3] A *pendicle* is a small piece of ground either depending on a larger farm, or
let separately by the owner.—*Jam.*

[4] *Fetteresso.* The anomalous termination *schawe* occurs in Gordon of Straloch's
Map of Scotland in 1654, where the name of the parish is printed *Fethirschaw.*
Earlier authorities give the forms *Fodresach, Fethyressach, Fetheressow,* and the
like, and from these must necessarily be traced the modern spelling.

Francis, erle of Erroll, Lord Hay, etc., and William Hay of
Wry, heritable propriater thairoff, with libertie and licens to
the said nobill lord and William Hay of Wry, or ather of
thame, be thame selffis, thir servandis, or vtheris in thir names,
presentlie to enter thairwith, jois, occupie, labour, and manure
the samen at their plessour in all tyme cuming, but actioun of
ejectioune, interusioun, spoyliatioun, or deid of wrang in ony
sort, to be mowet, suitit, or persewit be him thairanent, and
be the tennour heirof grantis him selff to be als ordourlie
remowet thairfra at the terme of Witsonday last bypast, in
this instant zeir of God abovne writtin, as iff the said nobill
lord and William Hay of Wry haid obtenit ane decreit off
remowing against him befor the lordis of Counsall and Sessioun,
or Shereff of Kincardine, decernand and ordeanand him to
remowe thairfra, Quhairwpoune the said William Hay of Wry
him self, and John Mowat in Powbair, as procuratour for the
said nobill lord, tuik act of Court and instrument, and the
said James is content, and consentis that this present renun-
ciatioun be insert and registrat in the Shereff Court buikis of
Kincardyne, that executioun may pas thairon.

MILL SERUICE.

The said day it is statut and ordeainet, be consent of the
Laird and bailzie, that the four men following, to wit, James
Dewiny in Montquheiche, Gilbert Grig in Schauchinschaw,
John Main there, and Robert Duncane in Cairntoune, sall pas
and try the marches[1] betuixt Abrahame Forfar in Montquheiche and Alexander Duthie thair, and sick as the saidis
four men sall find efter dew tryall to haue bein propertie in
tymes past sall remaine propertie, and sick as hes bein in vse
off Cowmountie sall remain in cowmontie, and ather of the
saidis tua that salbe tryit to be ane malicious and ewill nichtbour thairefter, sall pey to the laird the soume of tene pundis
Scotis money.

The said day it is statut and ordeanit, with consent of the
haill tennentis in the Nether barrouny,[2] that ewerie maister of

---

[1] *Pas and try the marches*: measure (*lit.* pace) and legally determine the
boundaries.

[2] Urie as distinguished from Monquich, which is repeatedly referred to elsewhere as the Over Barony.

ane pleuche sall pas, vpoune tuentie four houris warning, to
the dame of the milne of Cowij, and thair be thame selffis,
thair servantis, hors, and kairtis, sall mend and repair the
haill milne dame, and mak the same sufficient, wnder the paine
of fourtie shilling money, to be peyit be ewerie ane that sall
happin to dissobey quhen they salbe requyirit as said is, and to
be gewin to theas that sall obey and mend the said dame, and
the officiar ordeanit to poynd for the same.

The said day it is statut and ordeanit that ewerie man that
hes ane hors about the milne of Cowij sall hauld thair horss in
the stabill betuixt elevine houris at nicht and the sonne rysing
in the morning, and sick as salbe fund to do in the contrair
sall pey for ilk hors that salbe fund out of the stabill vpoune
the nicht sall pey for ilk hors xx s. *toties quoties*, to be peyit
to the pairtie offendit.[1]

The said day James Milne in Cowij is decernit be his awin
confessioun to pay to the Laird fywe bollis thrie firlots bear
betuixt the dait heirof and the sext day off Julij nixt, or than
to pey the soume off fywe pundis money for ilk boll thairoff,
with thrie dozen of pultrie foullis, or than fourtie schilings for
ilk dozen thairof, within terme of law.

The said day Stephane Forbes in Cowij is decernit to pey to
the Ladie Wry ane dozen elnis of sufficient sarking lyning for
this zeir to Mertimes nixt, or thane sex pund for the price
thairof.

The said day the haill tennentis of the our and nether
barrony is decernit be thair awine consent that ilk occupiar off
ane plewche of the saidis landis sall zeirlie cast, wine, and leid
ane leitt of peits, and the tennentis of Montquheiche to stak
the same on the peithill of Montquheiche, and the tennentis of
Wry to stack thair leits on the peithill of Wry zeirlie befor
the xxiiij of August, and in caice of failzie, to pey for ilk leit
that sall happin to be wnstackit in manner forsaid to pey the
soume off tene pundis.

The said day it is decernit and ordeanit that the haill tennentis in Montquheiche sall pas and teill and rywe out[2] new

---

[1] Injured, viz., by the trespass of the horse upon their lands.

[2] To plough. Spoken of ground that has either long lain in lea, or has never
been ploughed before.—*Jam.*

landis be thame selflis, thair servandis, and plewches wpoune
the boundis nixt adjacent to the laird of Petfoddellis merchs [1]
within the clame, and ewerie man that sall happin to refuis
and dissobey to go himself, als weill as his servandis and
pleuchs, sall pey the soume of tuentie pundis *toties quoties* how
oft they sall dissobey.

The said day the haill tennentis in Montquheiche is decernit
and ordeanit to repair the lairdis zaird dyik in Montquheiche,
wnder the pain of fourtie shillings money, to be peyit be ilk
dissobedient.   J. THOMESOUNE, *notarius publicus,*
                                ac scriba Curie.

*The Barrowne Court of Wrie, hauldin in Stephane Forbes
dualing hous in Cowy, on the penult day of August
1621, in name and behalf of ane nobill lord Francis, erle
of Erroll, Lord Hay, etc., and William Hay of Wry
heritable propriater of the said land, and in name of ane
honorable manc Maister William Reid in Cowy, thair
bailzie, James Thomsoun, notter, Clark, Alexander Hay,
officiar, Robert Crystie, Dempster. The suits calit, the
Court laufullie fensit and affirmit.*

The said day the bailzie ordeanis the four barlaw men to pas
presentlie and visie the leit peittis, bothe vpoune the peithill
of Wrie and Mountquheiche, and quhair it salbe fund that
ewerie persoune that is obleist to stak ane leit of peits wpoune
ather of the said peithillis, and the same be nocht fund sufficient, ilk persone is decernit for thair awin pairtis to pey x lib.
money for ilk leit, conforme to ane former act.

The said day the haill tennentis of the barrouny of Wry and
Montquheiche is decernit and ordeanit be thair awine consentis
to pay to the laird zeirlie and ilk zeir in tyme cuming sufficient

---

[1] The boundaries of the lands of Blairs in the neighbouring parish of Banchory-Devenick are here referred to.   Blairs was then in the possession of Sir
Gilbert Menzies of Pitfodels.   Sir Gilbert was a devoted Royalist, and greatly
distinguished himself in the north during the Civil Wars.   He is referred to in
the following lines :

' Gilbert Menzies of Pitfodels
Did for King Charles wear the blue.'
Old Ballad.

wictuall at the termes of peyment vsit and wount of the wictuall
that growis on thair awin possessioune.

SERUICE MILL OF MONQUHEICH.

The said day it is statuit and ordeaniet be the Laird and
bailzie, with consent of the haill tennents and sub-tennents,
cotteris, greas men, and wtheris quhatsumeur, that wha soeuer
sall disobey to cum to any cowmoune actioun in tym cuming
perteining to my lord, or the lairds weill, vtilitie, profeit, or
honour, sall pey tene pundis.

The said day it is statuit and ordeanit be the Laird and
bailzie, with consent of the haill tennents, cotteris, and greas
men, that whatsumeuer persone or personis salbe tryit at ony
tyme heirefter to cut or pull[1] any greas amangs thair maisters
[or] nichtbouris cornis in tyme cuming sall pey fourtie shilings
to the pairtie offendit *toties quoties* how oft thaj sall be tryit
to contravein this present act. Quhairon Maister Androw
Leslie, Gilbert Barclay, George Milne, for thame selffis, and in
name of the rest of the tennents tuik act.

The said day it is statuit and ordeanit be the Laird and
bailzie, with consent of the haill tennentis in the our barrouny,
that ewerie tennent and subtennent, cotters, and greasmen, sall
answer and obey John Milne, milner at the milne of Montquhciche, as they salbe requyrit to cast the laids,[2] fens the
damis,[3] and bring watter to the milne in stormes, and at wther
tymes as they salbe requyrit, as said is sall pey ewerie man
xl s. *toties quoties* how oft they sall be fund to dissobey, and the
said John ordeanit to be officiar in that pairt.

*The Barroune Court of Wry, hauldin in Woodheid on the
sevint day of November* 1621 *zeir, in nam and behalf of
ane nobill and potent lord Francis, erle of Erroll, Lord*

---

[1] For cutting or pulling.

[2] Cut the mill-races. The meaning probably is that they were required to
keep them clear by cutting or digging out the weeds, etc., by which they were
liable to be become choked.

[3] To fence, in the sense of keeping them water-tight. Should they be broken
through in time of storms, it was the duty of the tenants to repair them, and so
keep the mill supplied with water.

Hay, etc., and William Hay of Wry, heritable propriaters
of the saidis landis, and in name of ane honorable man
Maister William Reid in Cowy, thair bailzie, James
Thomsoune, notter, Clark, Alexander Hay, officiar, Dauid
Mitchell, Dempster. The suits calit, the Court fensit
and affirmit.

Absentis.

James Dewiny in Montquhciche.
Maister Andro Leslie thair.
George Dewny thair.
William Duthie thair.
Alexander Duthie thair.
Archibald Duncane thair.
George Milne in Corsley.
Robert Duncane in Cairntoune.
John Hendersoun in Bannageiche.
Gilbert Barclay in Magray.
Stephane Forbes in Cowy.
~~Alexander McKay at the milm of Cowy.~~[1]
Archibald Murray thair.
Alexander Burnett thair.

The said day the haill absents aboun wreitten ar decernit to pey the sowme of fyve pundis for thair absence, and the officiar ordeanit to poynd for the same.

The said day George Straquhan decernit be his awin confessioun to pey to Thomas Cruikshank liii s. 4 d. for ane eln broun fleming, xxj s. for ane eln bred lyning,[2] x s. for ane vther eln of thrie quarter bred, xviij s. for ane vnce edgit frenzies,[3] with xxv s. monie.

The said day James Milne in Cowy is decernit to pey to the Laird ane boll malt restand be him of the crop 1620 zeirs, withine terme of law, wnder the pain of poynding.

---

[1] The clerk has drawn his pen over this entry in the MS., from which we may infer that while M'Kay was absent when the 'suits' were called he had appeared later, and in time to take his part in the business of the Court. The usage is a common one in old records of sederunt.

[2] A particular kind of soft woollen cloth, so called from the *Flemings*, who introduced its manufacture into Scotland.

[3] Pointed fringe. It was evidently sold by weight.

The said day compeirit Alexander McKey, millar at the milne of Cowie, and gave his ayth that he sall nocht suffer dust nor staines to [be] put amang the lairdis fermes, and that the sam sall be milnt as effeirs.

The said day the haill browsters, within the barrouny of Wry, ar decernit to pey thair brew talloun within terme of law, or four punds for the staine thairof.

The said day the haill tennents that peyes maillis is decernit to pey thair Mertimes mailles to John Mowatt, chalmerlane, befor the terme of Mertimes nixt, wnder the pain of poynding.

GIRSOMES.[1]

The said day compeirit John Mowatt, chalmerlane, and persewit Georg Straquhan in Glithno for peyment of the sowme of ane hundreth markis monie for the greassum of Glithno, alledgeit promeist be him to the guidman[2] of Crimmondmogit *ex aduersso* compeirit the said George, and alledget he was na enterit tennent, and that he never promeist gersum and siclyk, being persewit for all byrune maillis sence the said John his entres to the said office of chalmerlanrie, and the said George alledgeit he haid peyit the same to the laird, and haid his in acquittancis thairupoun, quhilk the bailzie ordeanis him to produce befor the laird, bailzie, and clark within terme of law, wtherways to pey the saidis byrune maillis to the chalmerlane, wnder paine of poynding.   J. THOMESOUNE, *scriba.*

The said dey

> *The Barroune Court of the barrouny of Wry, haldin at the milne of Cowj, on the nynteine day of Januar 1622 zeiris, in nam and behalf of ane nobill and potent lord Francis, erle of Erroll, Lord Hay, etc., and William Hay of Wry, heritabill propriaters of the grund, Maister William Reid*

---

[1] *Girsome*, or *grassum*: a sum of money paid by the tenant to the landlord on entering into possession of his farm.—*Jam.* It may also mean a fine paid for a lease of land during a term of years.—Bell's *Law of Scotland*, p. 411.

[2] A small proprietor who farms his own land, a bonnet-laird.

in Cowy, their bailzie, James Thomsoun, notter, thair
Clark, Alexander Hay, officiar, Archibald Murrey,
Dempster. The suitis calit, the court lawfully fenssit
and affirmit.

The said day the haill tennents within the barrouny of Wry
and Monquheiche, without exceptioun, ar decernit and ordeanit
ilk ane for thair awin pairte to carye the lairdis letters to
Slaines,[1] or els quhair as thej sall occur, ewerie pleuche thair
tyme about as it sall fall to thame, and whasoeuer sall dissobey
to pey the sowme of xl s. for ilk dissobedience *toties quoties*.

Girsomes.

The said day compeirit John Mowatt, chalmerlane, and persewit Abrahame Forfar, for the sowme of ane hundreth merkis
of gressam, for fyve zeirs tak of his rowme in Montquhiche, fra
Witsonday last by past in j^m vj^c tuentie ane zeiris, with ane
hundreth merkis money for his Witsonday and Mertimes maill
of the zeir of God 1621 zeirs, togither with twentie sevin
merkis for his customes of the said zeir, quhilk the bailzie
decernit the said Abrahame to pey within terme of law, wnder
the paine of poynding, or thane to obteine my lord Erroll his
discharge thair wpoun.

The said day James Milne is decernit be his awin confessioun
to pey to the laird twalff bollis ferme bear for his occupatioun
of the chapleurie of Cowij for the zeir of God 1621 zeiris within
terme of law, wnder the pain of poynding, or than the sowme
of tene pundis money, conforme to ane protestatioun takin be
John Mowat, chalmerlane.

The said day compeirit John Mowatt, chalmerlane, and persewit Robert Irving, at the miln of Cowy, for sex bollis tene
pecks bear, and nynteine bollis tua firlotis ferme meill, for his
ferme of miln of Cowie, for this instant zeir of God 1621 zeiris.
Compeirit the said Robert Irving, and confest he was restand
the said bear and meill respectiue aboun wreittin. In respect
quhairof the bailzie forsaid decernit the said Robert to mak
peyment thairoff within terme of law, wnder the pain of
poynding.

---

[1] Slains Castle in Aberdeenshire, the seat of the Earls of Errol.

The said day James Alardes in Woodheid is decernit be his awin confessioun to pey tene bollis meill and tua bollis bear for the rest of his ferme for the wast syid of Wodheid for the zeir of God 1621 zeiris within terme of law, wnder pain of poynding.   J. THOMESOUNE.

The Barroune Court of the Barrouny of Wrie, haldin in Bannagubis wpoun the sewint day of May 1622 zeiris, in name and behalff of ane nobill and potent lord Francis, erle of Erroll, Lord Hay, etc., and William Hay of Wry, heritable proprietars of the saidis landis, Maister William Reid in Cowy, bailzie, James Thomsoun, notter, Court Clark, Alexander Hay, officiar, John Tailzeour, Dempster. The suitis calit, the Court laufullie fensit and affirmit.

The said day compeirit Alexander Bannerman of Elsick,[1] as procuratour for John Bannermane, his brother, and protestit that the haulding of this court wpoun the toune and landis of Bannagubis be nawayis preiudiciall to the said John Bannermane his letter of tak, quhilk he hes of my lord of Erroll and William Hay of Wry wpoun the saidis landis of Bannacubis and Rothuik for the spaice of sevin zeir nixt efter the redemptioun of the saidis landis, at the leist of sua mony of the saidis sevin zeirs as ar zit to rune. Quhairwpoun the said Alexander tuik act of Court and instrument.

The said dey the haill tennents that peyis maill and customs to the laird ar decernit to pey the same at the terme of Witsonday nixt to cum, wnder pain of poynding.

The said day William Duthie in Montquheiche, James Dewiny thair, Archibald Duncane thair, and Georg Dewiny thair, ar nominat, electit, and chossin be mutual consent of the laird and Abrahame Forfar to mett, messour, and designe als meikle land to the laird furth of Abrahame Forffar his occupatioun in Montquheiche as the said Abrahame hes gottin designit

---

[1] Alexander Bannerman, burgess of Aberdeen, had a charter in 1387 from Sir Alexander Fraser of Cowie of the lands of Elsick, which continued to be the seat of the family for three hundred and seventy years.—Stodart's *Arms of Scotland*, vol. ii. p. 396.

to him furth of the rest of the lands of Montquheiche, and the
saidis four men being personallie present, war ordeanit to do
the same before the fyiftein days nixt to cum, ilk ane of thame,
wnder the paine of x lib., and the officiar ordeanit to poynd
thairfoir.   J. THOMESOUNE, *scriba*.

> *The Barroune Court of the Barrouny off Wrie hauddin in
> the dualing hous of Maister William Reid in Cowy,
> wpoun the secund day off July 1622 zeiris, in name and
> behalff of ane nobill and potent lord Francis, erle of Erroll,
> etc., and William Hay of Wrie, heritable propriators of
> the saidis landis, Maister William Reid thair bailzie,
> James Thomesoun, notter, Clark, Alexander Hay, officiar,
> Archibald Murrey, Dempster.   The suitis calit, the
> court laufully fenssit and affirmit.*

The said day James Milne in Cowy being laufullie summondit
to this court, was decernit to pey to the laird four bollis
threttein pecks bear for the rest of his ferme bear of the crop
1621 zeirs, quhilk the Judge forthwith decernit him to pey
within terme of law or thane the heigest pryss conforme to the
lairds protestatioun, and siclyk the said James is decernit to
pey xl s. for his contumacie, being laufullie warnit within
terme of law wnder paine of poynding.

The said day Andro and Archibald Leapperis, John Fowllar,
and Niniane Robertsounes ar decernit to redelyuer back the
saill of the boit bak to the laird, als sufficient as they receauit
the same, or than fourtie merkis for the price thairoff, within
terme of law, wnder paine of poynding.

                                               J. THOMESOUNE, *scriba*.

> *The Barroune Court of the Barrouny of Wrie, haldin in the
> dualing hous off Stephane Forbes, alies Smyth in Cowie,
> wpoun the first day of August 1622 zeirs, in name and
> behalff of ane nobill and potent lord Francis, erle of
> Erroll, Lord Hay, etc., William Hay of Wry, heritable
> propriators of the said barrouny, Maister William Reid
> in Cowie thair bailzie, James Thomesoun, notter, Clark,*

Alexander Hay, officiar, Archibald Murrey, Dempster.
The suits calit, the court fenssit and affirmit.

This day Archibald Duncane in Montquheiche is decernit be his awin confessioune to pay to John Mowatt, chalmerlane, the sowme off tuentie sewine merkis Scotis money, and that for his customes of his occupatioun of Montquheiche, quhilk suld hawe beine peyit at Mertinmes last by past in j^m vj^c tuentie ane zeirs, togidder with feftie merkis monie for his Witsonday maill in this instant zeir of God j^m vj^c xxij zeirs, and siclyk Alexander Duthie in Montquheiche is decernit be his awin confessioun to pay to the said John Mowatt, chalmerlane, feftie merkis monie for his Witsonday maill in this instant zeir of God 1622, and that within fyfteine days nixt efter they be requyirit thairto, wnder the paine of poynding, and the officiar ordeanit to poynd for the sam. J. Thomesoune, *scriba.*

The Barroune Court off the Barrouny off Wry, hauldin in
the dualing hous off Stephane Forbes in Cowie, wpoun
the tuentie tua day off November 1622 zeirs, in name and
behalff off ane nobill and potent lord Francis, erle of
Erroll, Lord Hay, etc., and William Hay off Wry,
heritable propriators of the said barrouny, George Mowatt
thair bailzie, James Thomesoun, notter publict, clark,
Alexander Hay, officiar, James Neilson, Dempster. The
suitis calit, the court laufullie fenssit and affirmit.

The said day the haill tennents underwritten are decernit, ilk ane for thair awin pairtis, to pey to John Mowat, chalmerlane, the sowmes of money efter specifeit, wiz.: Archibald Duncane in Montquheiche for his Mertimes maill and customes of this instant zeir of God 1622 zeirs, and of all termes and zeirs preceiding, the sowme off sewine scoir fourteine merkis; Alexander Duthie thair for his Martimes terms maill and customes in this instant zeir of God 1622 zeirs, and for all termes preceiding, sex scoir sevin merkis; George Milne in Corsley tuentie pundis money for his Mertinmes maile, 1622 zeires, with auchteine pundis for his customes the said crope; James Dewinny in Montquheiche feftie merkis for his Mertimes maill 1622, with xviij lib. for his customes; Maister Andro

Leslie feftie merkis for his Mertimes maill 1622, with xviij lib.
for his customes, within terme of law, wnder pain of poynding.

The said day James Milne in Cowie, Stephane Forbes thair,
Archibald Burnett at Cowie milne, Alexander Maky thair,
James Cumming, James Duncan in Strype, ar ilk ane decernit
to pey ane staine of brew talloun or than fyve merkis to the
laird, within terme of law wnder pain of poynding.

The said dey compeirit Robert Irving at the milne of Cowie,
and being persewit for peyment off the fermes off milne of
Cowy restand be him for the crope 1622 zeirs, the bailzie forsaid decernis the said Robert Irving to mak peyment to John
Mowatt, chalmerlane, of all fermes, meill, and bear, and quhyt,[1]
and with all wther customes, capouns, milne swyne,[2] and
moull[3] for the crop forsaid, at the leist to find sufficient
cautioun for the peyment thairoff, within terme of law, or
wther ways to mell and intromett with the milne clap[4] and
wptake the multers thairoff conforme to the decreit of remoweing obtenit against the said Robert.

The said dey the haill fischers ar decernit ilk lyneman to pey
ane hundreth haddox zeirlie and thrie keilling thir thrie
zeiris bygane promitit be thame to the Lady, or wtherways to
produce the Ladys acquittance thairwpoun.

The said day it is statut and ordained that ilk husbandman
within this barrouny that hes ather cotter, greasman, or woman
that is thocht be thair honest nichtbouris nocht to be laufull
nichtbouris, and wantis keall or peitts, that thair maister sall
remowe thame within aucht dayis nixt following the dait heirof,
or thane to pey tene pundis money, the ane half thairof to the
laird and the other half to the pairtie skaythit.

The said day in respect off the great abuse that is enterit in
amangs the cowmond[5] people in steilling, thairfor it is statut
and ordeainet be the laird and bailzie that Georg Dewiny and
Alexander Duthie in Montquheiche sall gang throwe the haill

---

[1] Wheat.

[2] Swine fed at the mill.   A mill even in modern rentals, often gives the
reddendo of a fat pig.—Innes's *Legal Antiquities*, p. 49.

[3] The refuse of the meal, commonly used for swine-feeding.—*Jam.*

[4] A piece of wood that strikes and shakes the hopper of the mill during grinding. The symbol for giving sasine in a mill is the clap and hopper.—Bell's *Law
of Scotland*, p. 567.   [5] Common.

ower barrouny as officiars conjunctlie and seueraly, with the
assistance of thair nichtbouris, and dacker,[1] searche, and seik all
stowin guidis, as they salbe requirit thairto.

The said day it is statut and ordeaned that ewerie man
within the nether barrouny of Wry, als weill husbandmen,
cotters, as greasmen, salbe thirlit[2] to wirk thair haill irne wark
with Stephane Forbes, smyth in Cowie, as he and they cane
agyrie, ilk ane for thair awin pairtis, and that iff they or ather
of thame pass by and cumes nocht to wirk with him as saidis,
they sall pey him smydie boll as iff they haid wrocht with him.
Lykas also the said Stephane Forbes bindis and obleidges him
to giwe ilk ane of thame in thair awin rowmes as they sall cum
and crave the samen, or wtherways in caice of failzie and nocht
tymous service, in that caice to pey to ilk man that is nocht
thankfullie and tymouslie servit the dowble of ane zeirs boll.
Quhairon the saidis tennents and Stewin Forbes tuik act.

The said day the haill tennentis ar decernit and ordeanit ilk
ane to gang thair ordinar cairadge, thair tyme about as thaj
salbe warnit thairto, wnder the pain of xx s., and the officiar
to poynd thairfor.   J. THOMESOUNE.

*The Barroune Court of the Barrouny of Wry, hauldin [in]
Wodheid the fyft day of December 1622 zeirs, in name
and behalff of ane nobill and potent lord Francis, erle of
Erroll, Lord Hay, etc., and William Hay of Wry, heritable propriaters thairoff, and in name of ane honorable
man John Hay of Crimondmogit, thair bailzie, Dauid
Burnett, officiar, Georg Walcar, Dempster. The suits
calit, the Court lanfullie fenssit and affirmit.*

ABSENTIS.

Archibald Murrey.
Archibald Burnet.
~~John Hendersoune in Bannageiche.~~
~~Andro Arbuthnot in Findlawstoune.~~
John Hendersoune thair.

---

[1] To search for stolen goods.
[2] Bound by lease or otherwise.—*Jam.*

Alexander Hay of Logy.
George Straquin in Glithno.
James Kewiny in Montquheiche.
Georg Milne in Corsley.
~~Georg Gairdyne in Rothuik.~~
Georg Shiphird in Bannagubs.

The said Dauid Burnet was creat, constitut, and ordeant officiar within the barrouny of Wry and Montquheiche, quha gaiue his aithe *de fidelj administratione*, ay and quhill he be dischairget.

The said day Archibald Duncane in Montequheiche is decernit be his awin confessioun to pey to John Mowatt, chalmerlane, the sowme off sewin scoir fourteine merkis money for his Mertimes maill and customes in this instant zeir of God 1622 zeirs, and for all bygane maillis and customes preceiding the said terme [quhairin he was decernit alredy], within terme of law, wnder pain of poynding.

The said dey Alexander Duthie in Montquheiche is decernit be his awin confessioun to pey to John Mowatt, chalmerlan, of the sowme off sex scoir sewin merkis for his Mertimes maill and customes in this instant zeir of God 1622 zeirs, and for all bygane dewties preceiding the said terme, within terme of law, wnder pain of poynding.

The said day Abrahame Forfar is decernit be his awin confessioun to pey to John Mowatt, chalmerlaine, the sowme off ane hundreth merkis for fyve zeirs gressam, tuo hundreth and feftie merkis money for his Whitsonday and Mertimes maill in 1622 zeirs, and for all bygaine maillis restand be him preceiding the said terme, togither with feftie four merkis for his customes of Montquheiche for the crope 1622 zeirs instant and the crope to cum in 1623 zeirs, makand in the haill four hundreth and four merkis money, within terme of law, wnder pain of poynding.

The said dey Maister Andro Leslie in Montquheiche is decernit be his awin confessioun to pey to John Mowatt, chalmerlane, feftie merkis money for his Mertimes maill 1622 zeirs, with auchteine pundis for his customes for the crop 1623 zeirs, within terme of law, *vt supra*.

The said day Georg Milne in Corsley is decernit to pey to

the chalmerlane auchteine pundis money for his customes for
the crop 1623.

The said day Georg Straquhan in Glithno is decernit to pey
to the chalmerlane fourtie fyve merkis money for his Witsonday
and Mertimes maill 1622 zeirs.

The said day John Hendersoune in Bannageiche is decernit
be his awin confessioune to pey to John Mowatt, chalmerlane,
tuentie merkis money for the rest of his Mertimes maill in this
instant zeir of God 1622 zeirs.

The said dey James Milne in Cowy is decernit to pey to
John Mowatt, chalmerlane, fywe merkis money for ilk staine
off thrie staine of brew talloun for the zeirs of God j^m vj^c and
tuentie ane and tuentie tua zeirs. Stephane Forbes in Cowy
is decernit to pey ane staine of brew talloune zeirlie in tyme
cuming be his awin confessioun. Alexander Maky is decernit
to pey to the chalmerlane ane staine of brew talloun for the
zeir 1622 zeirs, or thane fyve merkis money. James Cuming
ane staine of talloune, or thane fyve merkis, for the zeir
1622. And James Duncane ane staine of brew talloun for the
crop 1622, or thane fyve merkis, within terme of law, wnder
the pain of poynding.

The said dey the haill tennents within the barrouny of Wrie
that peys ferme, ar decernit and ordeanit to lay in thair meill
ferme into the girners [1] befor Candlemes nixt to cum, or thane
to pey tene pundis monie for ilk boll thairoff, and thair haill
bear ferme befor Ruid day nixt, or thane tualff pundis money,
for ilk boll thairoff.

The said dey the haill tennents within the barrouny of Wry,
that set nocht thair leitt peitts wpoun the peit hill of Wry
this zeir instant 1622 zeirs, sall pey to the chalmerlane fywe
merkis money for ilk leitt thairoff.

The said day compeirit Robert Irving at the milne off Cowy,
and being persewit be John Mowatt, chalmerlaine, for peyment
off his fermes for this instant crop and zeir of God j^m vj^c tuentie
tua zeirs, compeirit the said Robert Irving, and wilinglie off
his awin guid will band and obleist him selff to cum to the

---

[1] Granaries. These were the storehouses of the laird, to which the tenants
were held bound to bring their payments in kind.

said John Mowatt befor the fourteine day off December, and find ane sufficient and responssall cautiouner to the said John Mowatt for peyment off the said dewitieis at the termes of peyment vsit and wount, and in caice of failzie and nocht finding of the said cautioun, thane and in that caice, the said Robert Irving, be tennour heiroff obleidges him to pey his haill bear ferme befor the said day aboun wreittin, and for peyment of the meill ferme rennuncis quytclames, and dischairges the haill multers of the barrouny of Wrie and out suckin[1] whatsumeuer in fauouris of the said John Mowatt, to be collectit and ingatherit be the said John Mowatt and his deputis quhom he sall appoynt, ay and quhill the haill meill ferme be compleitlee peyit, and to that effect obleidges him selff to delyuer to the laird the milne clap,[2] to be delyuerit to the said John Mowatt the said fourtein day of December nixt; and in caice of absence of the said Robert the said day, to delyuer the said clap, and to put the said John in possessioun, the said John Mowatt to have power be thir presents to enter with the said clap milne and multers thairoff, knawshipe[3] and sequells of the said milne, the day forsaid, but actioun of ejectioun, intrusioun, wrangous intromissioun, or ony deid of wrang whatsumeuer.

Roᵀ. Irving.

J. Thomesoune, *scriba*.

The Barrounie Court off the Barrouny of Wrie, hauldin in the dualing hous of James Thomsoune, in Woodheid, wpoun the 17 *of Appryll* 1623 *zeirs, in name and behalf off ane nobill and potent erle Francis, erle off Erroll, etc., and*

---

[1] *Sucken* is the jurisdiction attached to a mill; or that extent of ground, the tenants of which were bound to bring their grain thither. *Out-sucken*, on the contrary, means the freedom from bondage to a mill; or the liberty which a tenant may enjoy, by his lease, of taking his grain to be ground where he pleases.—*Jam.*

[2] See p. 45 n. 4, *supra.*

[3] One of the sequels of thirlage. Sequels, as distinguished from multure, which was paid to the proprietor or tacksman of the mill, were payments of grain made to the mill servants for grinding. These sequels differed according to the particular usage of the mill, and were known as ' knaveship,' ' hannock,' and ' lock ' or ' gowpen.'

William Hay of Wrry, heritable propriators thairoff,
Georg Mowat, in Reidcloak, thair bailzie, James Thome-
soun, notter publict, court Clark, Dauid Burnet, officiar,
Archibald Murray, Dempster. The suits calit, the court
laufullie fenssit and affirmit.

The said day the haill tennentis wnder wreittin ar decernit
be thair awin confessioun to pay the particular bollis of ferme
victuall, wiz., meill and bear restand be ilk ane of thame for thair
awin pairts for the crope last by past 1622 zeirs, within terme
off law, or thane the prysses following, wiz., Robert Duncane in
Cairntoune aucht bollis meill; Dauid Grahame for the walk-
mylne of Wry four bollis thrie firlotis meill; William Duthie
in Woodheid four bollis thrie firlotis meill, with four bollis
bear; James Thomesoune tua bollis thrie firlotis thrie pecks
bear; John Mowatt, for his occupatioun of milne off Cowy,
four bollis bear; James Miln in Cowy sevine bollis sevine
pecks bear. Quhilikis haill personis ar ilk ane decernit to mak
peyment for awin pairts of the haill bollis of wictuall aboun
specifeit within terme off law, or thane tene pundis of money
for ilk boll thairof, wnder the paine of poynding.

The said day Stephane Forbes is decernit to pey to the Ladie
Wrry ane dozen elnis off sarking lyneing for the zeir of God
1622 zeirs, within terme of law, or thane viij s. for ilk elne
thairoff, wnder paine of poynding.

The said day Alexander McKy, at the milne off Cowie, is
decernit to pey to the Laird tene merkis money, within terme
of law, for his milne swyne, wnder pain of poynding, with
aucht capounis, or thane vjs. 8d. for ilk peice thairoff.

The said day compeirit John Midltoun, being warnit to this
court at the instance of James Murrey, and the said James
nocht compeirand to persew him, protestit for his expenssis
befor the said James be hard to persewet him.

J. THOMESOUNE, *scriba.*

The Barroune Court of the Barrouny of Wrie, haldin at the
eist syid of the gairdyne of Montquheiche, the nynt of
Junj 1623 zeirs, be ane honorable man John Hay of
Crimondmogit, bailzie to ane nobill and potent erle

Francis, erle of Erroll, etc., and William Hay of Wry,
heritable propriaters off the saidis landis, James Thom-
soun, notter, clark, Dauid Burnet, officiar, James Lich-
toun, Dempster. The suits calit, the court laufully fenssit
and affirmit.

The said day the haill tennents of Montquheiche, Corsley,
Bannagubs, and Rothnik, is decernit to pay thair Witsondays
maill in this instant zeir of God 1623 to John Mowatt, chalmer-
lain, within terme off law, wnder pain of poynding.

The said day John Smyth, skipper, is ordeanit to sit xxiiij
houris in the stokis, for abussing off John Mowat in lawage.

The said day the haill tennents in Montquheiche ar ordeanit
and decernit to pay thair haill customes to the laird within
terme of law.

The said day James Lichtoune is constitut, creat, and
ordeanit pundlar in the milne off Cowy, and be the tennour
heiroff the said James sall hawe power to tak and poynd all
and quhatsunneuer guides that sall happin to cum wpoun the
greas thairoff, wiz.: ilk hors or nolt vj s. 8d., ilk scheip ij s. 8d.,
toties quoties how oft they be apprehendit.

The Barroune Court off the Barrounie off Wrie, hauldin in
Woodheid, wpoune the xxv. day of October 1623 zeirs, in
name and behalff off ane nobill and potent erle Francis,
erle off Erroll, etc., and William Hay off Wry, heritable
propriaters off the saidis landis, and in nam and behalff
off ane honorable man John Hay off Crimoundmogatt,
thair bailzie, James Thomsone, notter publict, court clark,
Dauid Burnett, officiar, Richard Gilbert, Dempster. The
suitis calit, the court laufully fenssit and affirmit.

The said day compt and rakning being haid withe Alexander
Duthie in Montquheiche, it is fund that he is restand for his
Witsonday maill feftie markis money last by past in this
instant zeir of God 1623, with xviij lib. for his custumes the
said yeir, quhilk he is decernit to pay to John Mowatt, chalmerlan, within terme off law, wnder pain off poynding.

The said day Abrahame Forfar is decernit be his awin confes-

sioun to pay to John Mowatt, chalmerlane, feftie markis money
for his Witsonday of Montquheiche last by past in this instant
zeir of God 1622 zeirs, within terme of law, etc.

The said day Robert Duncan is decernit to pey to the Laird
the sowme off   money for ilk boll off aucht bollis meill
restand be him for his occupatioune of Carntoun off the crope
1622 zeirs ; and iff it salbe fund, efter compt and rakning with
the Lady, that he hes peyit ony thairoff, the samen to be
allouit to him.

> *The Barroune Court of Wry, hauldin in Wodheid vpoun the*
> *aucht day of November 1623, in name and behalff off*
> *ane nobill and potent erle Francis, erle off Erroll, etc.,*
> *and William Hay of Wry, heritable propriators of the*
> *saidis landis, Georg Mowatt in Reidcloak, bailzie, James*
> *Thomsoun, notter, clark, Dauid Burnet, officiar, Archi-*
> *bald Murrey, Dempster. The suits calit, the court lau-*
> *fully fensit and affirmit.*

The said day in the actioun of blood persewit be Edward
Irving *contra* Alexander Maky being refferit to the said Alex-
ander, his ayth of weritie the said Alexander tuik the xv. of
November to depone with certificatioun *pro confesso.*

J. THOMSONE, Scriba.

> *The Barroune Court of the Barrouny of Wrie, hauldin in the*
> *dualing hous of James Thomsone in Wodheid, vpoun the*
> *tuentie day of Merche 1624 zeirs, in name and behalf of*
> *ane nobill and potent erle Francis, erle of Erroll, lord*
> *Hay, etc., and William Hay of Wry, heritable pro-*
> *priators of the saidis landis, Maister William Reid in*
> *Cowy, and George Mowatt in Reidcloak, thair conjunct*
> *bailzies, James Thomsone, notter publict, Court Clark,*
> *Dauid Burnet, officiar, John Cathnes, Dempster. The*
> *suits calit, the court laufullie fenssit and affirmit.*

The said day James Milne in Cowy being persewit be the
Laird, compeirit Jean Fullartoun his spous, and confessit that
hir said husband is justlie restand to the laird ane firlot bear
of the rest of thair ferme of the crope 1623 zeirs, togidder

with aucht bollis bear for his ferme of the chaplanrie in Cowie
for the crop last by past 1623 zeirs, quhilk the bailzies forsaid
decernit the said James Mylne to pay within terme off law
wnder pain of poynding.   J. Thomsone, *Scriba.*

> *The Barroune Court of the Barrouny of Wry, hauldin in the*
> *dualing hous of James Thomsone in Wodheid the secund*
> *of Junij* 1624 *zeirs, be ane discreit gentilman Andro*
> *Hay, bailzie for the tyme to ane nobill and potent erle*
> *Francis, erle of Erroll, etc., and William Hay of Wry,*
> *heritable propriators of the saidis lands, James Thom-*
> *sone, notter, Clark, Dauid Burnet, officiar, Archibald*
> *Murrey, Dempster. The suitis calit, the court laufullie*
> *fenssit and affirmitt.*

The said day compeirit Maister Androw Lesly in Montquheiche and confest that his sone John Leslie strak and dang
John Fergussone in Montquheiche, for the quhilk said Maister
Androw become in the lairdis will, and thairfor the bailzie
forsaid decernit the said Maister Androw to pay tene pundis
money to the laird within fyftein dayis wnder paine of
poynding.   J. Thomsone, *Scriba.*

> *The Barroune Court of the Barrouny off Wry, hauldin in the*
> *dualing hous of James Thomsone in Wodheid wpoun the*
> *xcv day of Junij* 1624 *zeirs, in nam and behalf of ane*
> *noble and potent erle Francis, erle of Erroll, etc., and*
> *William Hay of Wry, heritable propriators thairof, and*
> *in nam of ane honorable man John Hay of Crimond-*
> *mograt thair bailzie, James Thomsone, notter publict*
> *court Clark, Dauid Burnet, officiar, Archibald Murrey,*
> *Dempster, etc. The suitis calit, the court laufullie fenssit*
> *and affirmit.*

The said day compeirit William Duthie in Woodheid, and
grantit him selff restand to the laird four bollis ferme bear for
his ferme bear of the crope 1623 zeirs, with tua bollis thrie
firlots meill for the rest of his ferme meill of the said crope
1623, thrie capouns and ane custome wadder, quhilk suld have
bein peyit at Witsonday last, in this instant zeir of God 1624

zeirs.   Robert Duncane in Cairntoune is decernit be his awin
confessioun to pay to the laird fywe bollis, thrie firlotis, tua
pecks meill, for the rest of his ferme of Cairntoun for the
crope 1623, with aucht capouns for the crope forsaid.   Archibald Duncane in Bannageiche, tuentie fywe merkis money for
his Witsonday maill of Bannageiche in this instant zeir of
God 1624 zeirs.   Jean Fullartoun, relict of vmquhile James
Mylne in Cowie, fywe bollis ane peck bear for the rest of hir
ferme of the half chaplanrie of Cowij, for the crope forsaid
1623 zeirs.   Quhilkis haill personis respective aboun specifeit
ar ordeanit ilk ane for thair awin parts to pay to the laird
within terme of law, wnder pain of poynding.

The said day the haill tennents within the suckin of the
milne of Cowij ar, ilk ane for thair awin pairts, decernit and
ordeanit to gang wpoun dew and laufull warning of tualff
houris warning and dyik in hauld [1] the watter to the milne in
the dames thairoff, and quhasoeuer sall happin to failzie sall
pay xl s. to the remanent that wphauldis and wirkis the samen,
and the officiar ordeanit to poynd for the samen.

The said day the Judge forsaid decernis and ordeanis Andro
Leapper to aggrie with John Law, skipper, and pay his dewtie
for his hous, yaird, and land to the said John Law, or thane to
remowe thairfra, and leave the samen woid, red and patent to
the said John Law, conforme to his set thairoff.

J. THOMSONE.

*The Barroune Court of Wry, hauldin in the Hall thairoff be
ane honorable man Maister William Reid in Cowy, bailzie
be ane nobill and potent erle Francis, erle of Erroll, etc.,
and William Hay of Wry, Jamis Thomsone, notter
publict, Clark, David Burnet, officiar, John Fergussone,
Dempster.   The suits calit, etc.*

The said day Alexander Annand, elder of Ochterallane,[2]

---

[1] To enclose with walls or ramparts.

[2] Alexander Annand succeeded his father in the lands of Auchterellon, in
Aberdeenshire, in July 1601.   He married Margaret, daughter of Cheyne of
Esslemont.—Pratt's *Buchan*, p. 264.   Annand evidently resided in Wrie at this
period, as he is subsequently designed ' Alexander Annand, Elder, in Findlawstoun,' see p. 59, *infra.*

was constitut, creat, and ordeanit bailzie of the barrouny of
Wry, wha gie his ayth *de fidelj administratione* ay and quhill
he be dischargit.

Secunda Curia.

The said day Alexander Fraser was admitit officiar, wha
gaive his ayth *de fidelj administrationj*.

The said day it is statuit and ordeanit that all cornes that
thoill fyir and watter[1] within the grund sall pas to the mylne,
or wtherways salbe obleisit to pay dowbill multer.

The said day Gilbert Barclay is decernit to pay sex bollis
nyne pecks sufficient malt for the rest of his ferme bear of the
crop 1623, betuixt the dait heirof and the xxiv day of August
nixt to cum, or thane the heighest pryss.

The said day the haill tennents ar ordeanit to cast the peitts
befor the fyftein day of May, to leid the samen befor Lambes,
or thane to pay tene lib. for ilk leitt thairoff.

*The Barroune Court of Wry, haldin in Woodheid wpoun the
xxv day of August 1624 zeirs, be ane honorable man
John Hay of Crimundmogat, bailzie to ane nobill erle
Francis, erle of Erroll, etc., James Thomsoun, notter,
clark, Alexander Fraser, officiar, Archibald Murrey,
Dempster.*

The said day Stephane Forbes in Cowij is decernit to pay to
my lord or his factouris tene merkis money for his maill of the
zeir of God 1623 zeirs, with aucht shilings money for ilk elne of
i dozen ellis of lyning.

The said day Georg Straquhan in Glithno is decernit be his
awin confessioun to pay the soum of tuentie fyve merkis money

---

[1] This phrase is descriptive of one of the forms of thirlage. These were (1)
omnia grana crescentia, which included, with the exception of certain duties,
such as farm rent, teinds, etc., all grains grown within the thirle or sucken;
(2) *grana molibilia*, restricted to so much only of the grain grown within the
thirle as the vassal had occasion to grind for his own use; and (3) *omnia grana
invecta et illata*, or all grain brought within the thirle that 'tholes fire and water,'
i.e. that has not been ground before being brought in. 'Tholes [or suffers] fire
and water' refers to the *cobling* and *kilning* (steeping and firing) to which the
grain was subjected in preparing it for the mill.—Erskine's *Institutes*, p. 424.

for his Witsonday maill in 1624, within terme of law, wnder pain of poynding.

The said day Gilbert Barclay is decernit to pay to the laird tene pundis money for ilk boll of fyve bollis nyne pecks malt restand be him of the crope 1623 zeirs, within terme of law, wnder pain of poynding.

The said day it being refferit to Robert and Archibald Duncanes, Abrahame Forfar, and William Duthie, what suld be allowit to Jeane Fullartoune, relict of James Mylne, for the want of the castellhead of Cowij, quhilk was ewictit fra hir be law be the erle Merschall,[1] wha deponit that they thoct the said peice land worthe tuo firlots bear zeirlie, and thairfor thair is deducit be the laird and bailzie to hir tua bollis bear of that quhilk scho is restand for the crope 1623 zeirs, quhilk payis hir of all lose and interest sustenit be hir preceiding the crop in this instant 1624 zeirs.

The said day William Duthie is decernit to pay to the laird tene pundis for cuting of the lairdis wood.

The said day Alexander Fraser is admitit grinter man[2] to receawe the fermes of the barrouny of Wry in my lords name, etc.

The said day it is statuit and ordeanit that the officiar sall poynd xx s. for ewerie dissobedient, and iff they wha is poyndit releive nocht, thair poynd be peyit within fyifteine days, the officiar to dispone thairwpoune.

The said day it is statuit that ewerie ffoull that gangs amangis thair nichtbouris cornes sall pey ane peck of aits or bear quhairin thay pastur, etc.   J. THOMSONE.

The Barroune Court off the Barrouny of Wry, haldin wpoune the xvij day of Novimber 1624, in the dualing hous of James Thomsone in Wodheid, in name of ane nobill and potent erle Francis, erle of Erroll, etc., and William Hay of Wry, be ane honorable man John Hay of Crimondmogat, thair bailzie, James Thomsone, notter, court clark, Alexander Fraser, officiar, Archibald Raitt, Dempster,

---

[1] William, sixth Earl Marischal, is here referred to. He succeeded his father, George, fifth Earl, the founder of Marischal College, Aberdeen, in April 1623.

[2] The keeper of the laird's granary.

etc.   The suits calit, the court laufully fenssit and affirmit.

The said day Georg Straquhan in Glithnocht is decernit be the bailzie forsaid be his awin confessioun to pay to the laird the sowme of tuentie fywe markis money for his Mertimes maill of Glithnocht, for this instant zeir of God 1624, with tuentie fywe markis for his Witsonday maill of the said zeir within terme of law, etc.

Secunda Curia, laufullie fenssit and affirmit.

The said day John Mowatt at the milne of Cowy is constitut, creat, and ordeainit bailzie deput in John Hay of Crimond-mogat his veice and plaice, quha gaive his ayth *de fidelij administrationj* ay and quhill he be dischairgit.

The said day the haill tennentis, husbandis, cotters, and greas men, within the barrouny of Wry and Montquheiche, ar decernit ilk ane for thair awin pairts respective to mak payment of thair officiar cornes to Alexander Fraser, officiar, as they war in vse abefor to pay to vmquhile Alexander Hay, or ony wther officiars within the said barrouny, and the said Alexander Fraser to poynd thairfor as neid beis.

JOHN THOMSONE.

The Barrony Court of Wry, haldin in the Hall thairoff, wpoun the xxv day of Maij 1625 zeirs, be ane honorable man John Hay of Crimondmogat, bailzie to ane nobill and potent erle Francis, erle of Erroll, and William Hay of Wry; James Thomsone, notter publict, clark, Alexander Fraser, officiar, Archibald Murrey, Dempster.   The suits calit, etc.

The said day compt and rakning being laid betuixt the laird and the tennents, it is fund that James Thomsone hes maid compleit payment and satisfactioun off all maills, customes, and fermes, and wther dewties preceiding the crope to cum in this instant zeir of God 1625 zeirs, quhairon he hes the laird his acquittance.   Jeane Fullartoun is decernit be hir awin con-fessioun to pay thrie bollis bear for the rest of hir ferme off the crope j^m vj^c tuentie and four zeirs.   John Mowatt is decernit to

mak payment to the laird four bollis meill, with
                    bear for the rest off his ferme of Powbair and
mylne of Cowij for the crop 1624 zeirs. Georg Mowatt, for
the ferme off Walkmylne of the crope 1624 zeirs, thretteine
bollis meill with thrie bollis malt for the rest of his ferme off
Reidcloak for the crope forsaid. Stephane Forbes is decernit
to pay tene markis money for his Witsonday and Mertimes
maill 1624 zeirs, with ane clne of lyneing for the crop forsaid,
with fywe markis for his Witsonday maill to cum in this instant
zeir 1625. Gilbert Barclay is decernit be his awin confessioune
to pay to the laird tene bollis meill for the crope 1624 zeirs,
with   bear for the crope forsaid, with
xx s. for the rest of his capouns of the crope 1625. Quhilkis
haill personis, ilk ane for thair awin pairts respective, ar decernit
to mak payment of the particular wictuall and sowmes respective as is aboun dewyidit within terme of law, wnder pain of
poynding. Mair, William Duthie is decernit to pay to the
laird sex bollis tua peckis les of bear, viz., tua bollis for the rest
of his ferme 1623, tua bollis tua pecks les, and four bollis for
the crop 1624 zeirs.

The said day John Lawe, skipper, is decernit to pay aucht
shillings money for ane pynt of oylie for the crope 1624.
Archibald Leapper   .   .   .   .   .   .

The said day compeirit Georg Mowatt in Reidcloak, and
voluntarlie of his awin guid vill, with his guid and kyndnes,
Remuncit, resignit, dischairgit, and quhytclamet all and whatsumeuer richt, tytill of richt, clame, entres, or possessioun,
baythe petitour[1] and possessour that he hes haid, or ony ways
may pretend to have, in and to that pairt and pendicull of
milne off Cowy, calit Thomas Haining,[2] lyand on the southe
syid of the watter of Cowie, to and in favouris of John Mowatt,
present possessour of the mylne and milne landis of Cowij, with
power to the said John to enter thairwith at the terme off

---

[1] One entitled to raise a petitory action, *i.e.* an action by which something is
sought to be decreed by the judge, in consequence of a right of property in the
pursuer.—Bell's *Law of Scotland*, p. 632.

[2] *Haining* is the term applied to an enclosed portion of pasture-land from
which the tenants cut their hay.—Innes's *Legal Antiquities*, p. 242.

Witsonday nixt to cum in this instant zeir of God 1625, but
actioun of ejectioun, intervussioun, or any deid off wrang,[1]
quhairon the saids George and John tuik instruments.

GEORGE MOWAT.

The said day it is statuit and ordeanit that all and whatsumeuer persones, puir or riche, within the suckin of the milne off
Cowie, sall have meit grund to thame at the milne scheilling
off thair awin cornes, and also John Mowatt sall [have] libertie
to met all malt heirefter in the milne fluir befoir it be grund,
and sall have halff ane peck malt ower ilk boll malt.

The said day the haill tennents within the barrouny of Wry
and Montquheiche that payis maill is decernit to pay thair
Witsonday maills for this instant zeir of God 1625 zeirs, within
terme off law, wnder pain of poynding.

J. THOMSONE, *Scriba.*

*The Barrouny Court off Wry, haldin in the dualing hous of
James Thomsone, notter publict, in Woodheid the last of
Novr. 1625, in nam and behalf of ane nobill and potent
erle Francis, erle off Erroll, Lord Hay, etc., and William
Hay of Wry, heritable propriaters of the saidis landis, be
ane honorable man Allexander Annand, elder in Findlawstoun, bailzie, James Thomsone forsaid, clark, Alexander
Frasser, officiar, Archibald Murrey, Dempster. The
suits calit, the court laufullie fenssit and affirmit.*

The said day the haill tennents wnder writtin ar decernit ilk
ane for thair awin pairtis to pay to John Mowatt, chalmerlan,
the sowmes off money efter specifeitt, wiz., Maister Andro Leslie,
the sowme off ane hundrethe merkis money for his Witsonday
and Mertimes maill, in this instant zeir of God $j^m v^c$ tuentie and
fywe zeirs. Georg Dewiny, ane hundrethe merkis money for his
Witsonday and Mertimes of Netherley, in the zeir off God forsaid. James Dewiny, feftie marks money for his Mertimes maill
last by past, in the zeir of God aboun wrettin. Georg Milne, in
Corsley, tuentie pundis money for his Mertimes maill forsaid.
Johnne Bannerman, thrie hundrethe markis for the Witsonday

---

[1] An unlawful act.

and Mertimes maill, in the zeir forsaid, for Rothnik and Bannagubs, and that the officiar is ordeanit to poynd presentlie for the samen, in respect terme of law is alredy expyirit efter the terme.

The said day Georg Straquhan, in Glithnocht, is decernit to pey to the laird tuentie fywe markis money for his Mertimes maill last by past, in this instant zeir 1625.

The said day the tennents wnder wreittin ar decernit ilk ane for thair awin pairts respective to pay to John Mowatt, chalmerlan, the sowmes wnder wreittin for the rest of thair teynd siluer[1] for the crops $j^m vj^c$ tuentie tua, xxiij, and xxiiij zeirs. Georg Straquhane tualff pundis money for the said thrie zeirs teynd siluer of Glithnocht.

.   .   .   .

The said day Stephane Forbes, in Cowie, is decernit to pay tuentie markis money for his maill of the zeirs of God 1624 and 1625 zeirs, with ij dozen clnes of sarking lyneing for the said zeirs, or vj s. 8 d. for ilk clne thairoff, within terme of law, wnder pain of poynding.

The said day Stephane Forbes is decernit to pay to the laird fyve markis money for ilk stane of tua staine of brew talloun for the zeirs of God 1623 and 1624. As also Alexander Maky, at Cowie milne, is decernit to pay fyve markis for ilk staine of sex quarters brew talloun for the zeirs forsaid, within terme of law, wnder pain of poynding.

The said day the haill tennents within the barrouny of Wry that addetit and restand any fermes for the crope 1625, ar ordeanit to hawe the samen in redines, and to pay the samen at the termes of payment vsit and wcount.

The said day Archebald Murrey is decernit to pay to the laird xl s. money for the maill of ane peice fischerland, with xx s. for thrie capounes restand be him that he become debtour ffor John Mowatt for 1624 zeirs, within terme off law, under pain of poynding.   J. THOMSONE, *Scriba.*

---

[1] A proprietor might have a tack of teinds, conveying to him the whole parsonage and vicarage teinds of his estate at a fixed rent, and he levied the amount, no doubt, somewhat increased from the tenants, but commuted or fixed.—Innes's *Legal Antiquities,* p. 261.

The Baroun Court of the Baronie of Vrie, haldin at Wodheid vpon the aucht day of August 1626 zeirs, James Thomsoun, bailzie, Alexander Fraser, officiar, Archibald Murray, Dempster. The court laufullie fensit and affiermit.

The tennentis efter nominat being calit for payment of thair byrun dewties restand be tham cropis 1625, 1626, quhairof the terms of payment is bypast, viz., George Myln, in Corsley, crop 1625, fyve pultrie foullis.   George Schiphird, for Rothnik and Bannagubis, for the crop 1627, sex wedders or iij lib. for the pece, within term of law, wnder the pain of poynding.

The said Stephane Forbes is decernit to pay five markis male for Mertimes term 1625, and fyve markis for Witsondayis term 1626, with tuelff ellis lyning, or viij s. for ilk ell, for the crop 1625, within term of law, wnder the pane of poynding.

The quhilk day George Gordoun is decernit to pay to [1] the customes and service of his occupatioun of Megra restand sen Witsonday last and in all tyme cuming, and that within term of law, wnder pane of poynding.

The quhilk day the haill fremen[2] are decernit to pay thair ulie of this zeir, or the pryces thairof, within term of law, wnder the pane of poynding.

The quhilk day Maister Andro Leslie is decernit to pay his Witsondayis male last by past, viz., fiftie markis, within term of law, wnder the pane of poynding.

The quhilk day the said Maister Andro Leslie Stephan Forbes and John Aberdein ar ilk ane decernit to pay tuentie shillingis money for thair non comperans to this court this day, within term of law, wnder the pane of poynding.

---

[1] Pay up.

[2] *Fremen* is obviously used to denote the fishing population, they being the only parties who paid customs in oil.   If we could assume that a popular notion, still occasionally advanced, prevailed at this period, to the effect that the fishermen along the coast of Kincardineshire were originally 'incomers' who had settled there from foreign parts, we might refer the term *fremen* to the root *frem,* signifying strange or foreign.   It may possibly, however, be akin to the Orcadian *fram* the sea, *by fram* seaward, in which case *framen* or *fremen* would mean seamen.

The Baroun Court of Vrie, haldin at Wodheid vpon the fyift day of October 1626 be James Thomsoun, bailzie, to Frances, earle of Erroll, heritable proprietar of the saidis landis. The suittis callit, the court laufullie fensit. Alexander Fraser, officiar, John Murray, Dempster.

The quhilk day Thomas Sellat is decernit he his awin confessioun to pay to James Deviny, in Montquheiche, ten markis hous male, with ten shillingis for thrie pultrie, and four pundis sevin shillingis sex pennies horrrowit money, within term of law, wnder the pane of poynding.

The quhilk day the bailzie ratefeis and approves all former actis maid anent the payment of the fermes and vther deuties to the said Maister of ground, viz., the earle of Erroll and his chalmerlane of all croftis bygane and to cum, viz., the fermes to Alexander Fraser, and the remanent deuties to John Mowat. The haill tennentis convenit assentis, and ar becum actit thairfoir according to thair assedatiounes and former actis maid thairanent. Quhairvpon the chalmerlanes tuik act.

The quhilk day the haill tennentis that payis martis ar ordanit to pay thame befoir Halumes, or ten pundis for the pece thairof.

The Court of the Barrounie of Wrie, haldin in the Woodheid of Wrie, the sevinteine day of July 1627 zeirs, in name and behalff of ane nobill and potent erle, Francis erle of Erroll, Lord Hay, etc., Heiche Constabill of Scotland, and heritable propriater of the saidis landis, be Maister Andro Leslie, bailzie for the tyme. James Thomsone, notter publict, clark, Alexander Fraser, officiar, John Murrey, Dempster. The suits calit, the court laufullie fenssit and affeirmit.

The said day Maister Andro Leslie is admitit and creat bailzie for the tyme, wha gaive his ayth *de fidelij administrationj*, ay and quhill he be dischairgit.

The said day John Law, skipper, Archibald Leapper, Niniane Robertsone, Magnus Fowllar, and the remanent fremen in Cowy, ar decernit to pas to sie ilk day that vther boitis in the

cost syid in sick schoiris gois to sie, or thane to pay ane boits
pairt of fischss for ilk day thay ly on land, quhen thay may
convenientlie go to sie.

The said day Georg Gordoune is decernit be his awin confessioun to pay to my Lord thrie sufficient custome wedderis
with thair woll for his custome wadderis, quhilk suld beine
payit at Ruid day last by past. Archebald Duncane, twa
customes wadders with the woll that suld beine payit at the
terme forsaid, or thane the ordinar prycis, wnder pain of
poynding.

The said day compeirit Alexander Fraser as procuratour for
my lord, and protestit for the heighest prycis of all sick fermes,
meill and bear, as sall happin to be restand efter the terme of
Lambes nixt, within the barrouny of Vrie, Quhairon the procuratour forsaid tuik act of court and instrument.

The said day Stephane Forbes is decernit be his awin confessioun to pay to my lord ane dozen elns lyning, quhilk suld bein
peyit at Witsonday last in this instant zeir 1627 zeirs, or thane
aucht shillings for ilk elne thairoff, within terme of law, wnder
pain of poynding.   J. THOMSONE, *Scriba*.

The Baroun Court of the Baronie of Vrie, haldin at Woodheid
vpone the tent day of November 1627, James Thomson,
bailzie, Alexander Fraser, officiar, John Murray, Demp-
ster. The suttis callit, the court laufullie fensit and
affiermit.

The quhilk day Maister Andro Leslie, George Schiphird,
and Archibald Duncan ar decernit ilk ane of thame to pay to
the Maister of the grund ane sufficient mart, or ten pundis
money, within term of law, wnder the pain of poynding.

The quhilk day George Gordoun and William Duthie ar
decernit in the pryces contenit in ane former act for ilk leit of
peitis restand be thame, crop 1627.

The quhilk day George Myln in Findlastoun, is decernit to
pay to the Maister of the ground ane steane brew creische, or
four markis, preceiding the dait hereof, viz., for the brewing,
tyme forsaid, and that within terme of law, wnder the paine of
poynding.

The quhilk day James Duncan is decernit to pay to Thomas Measoun tua markis borruit money with four shillings expenses, within term of law, wnder the pane of poynding.

PATRIK LAISHAN.

The Baroun Court of the Baronie of Vrie, haldin at Woodheid vpon the ellevint day of December 1627 be George Mowat and James Thomsoun, bailzies, to ane potent erle Frances, erle of Erroll, etc., Alexander Fraser, officiar, John Murray, Dempster.

The quhilk day Jeane Fullertoun is decernit to pay to William Duthie four markis iij s. viij d., within term of law, wnder the pain of poynding.

The quhilk day the haill sucken is ordanit to keip the myln, wnder the pane of paying dubill multer for thair abstractit multeris, and poynding to follow thairvpon, and the malt to be groundin vpon the sheiling.[1]

The quhilk day the haill tennentis ar obleist to gif in thair ferm beir in sufficient holsum stuff to his maltmen, to the effect the malt may be sufficient to serue his hous.

The quhilk day James Allardes is decernit be his awin confessioun to pay to James Thomsoun tuentie tua merkis x s. viijd. byrun male, within term of law, wnder the pain of poynding.

The Baroun Court of the Baronie of Vrie, haldin at Woodheid vpone the sevint day of Maij 1628 be James Thomsoun, bailzie, to ane potent earle Frances, earle of Erroll, etc., heritable proprietar of the forsaid baronie. The suittis callit, the court laufullie fensit. Alexander Fraser, officiar, James Murray, Dempster.

The quhilk day the haill tennentis ar decernit and ordanit to cast thair leit peatis in dew tyme, conform to the former act maid thairanent, and wnder the failzie thairin mentionat.

---

[1] *Sheiling* here stands for *sheiling-mill.* According to modern usage malt is crushed by being passed through iron rollers in a separate mill provided for the purpose. Formerly, however, the sheiling-mill was used, or that by which in the ordinary process of meal-making the husk and dust are detached from the grain previous to its being ground.

The quhilk day the haill tennentis that ar obleist to pay wedderis, ar ordanit to gif in thair wedderis wnder woll worth thrie pundis be the sicht of John Mowat and George Davenie betuix, befoir the fyiftein of this instant Maij, or ellis the pryce forsaid.

The quhilk day the haill tennentis ar decernit to pay thair Witsonday male preceislie at the term, wnder the pane of poynding.

The quhilk day all cotteris ar decernit to keip[1] thair maisteris fauld, with their guidis maistlie betuix rud day and Michelmes, quhilk failzeing the contravener sall pay for ilk scheip tuelf pennies, and for ilk nolt beist thre schillingis four d. for ilk nicht, and that to be extended in all tyme cuming, and poynding to follow thairvpon.

The quhilk day Alexander Syret is decernit to pay to the laird of the ground ten pundis for selling peatis without the lairdis consent, and refusit to sell to the laird him self, and that within term of law, wnder the pane of poynding.

The quhilk day it is ordanit, be consent of the haill tennentis convenit for the tyme, that quhoseuir takis away ony of thair nichtbouris peitis thaj sall pay tuentie schillingis thairfoir *toties quoties*.   Quhairvpon thaj tuik act.

The Barroune Court of Wrie, haldin in Wodheid the penult day of January 1629, be ane honorable man John Hay of Cremoundmogat, bailzie to ane nobill erle Francis, erle of Erroll, Lord Hay, etc., heritable propriater of the saidis landis, James Thomsone, notter publict, Clark, Alexander Fraser, officiar, James Murrey, Dempster, etc.

The said day Maister Andro Leslie in Montquheiche is decernit to pay to John Mowatt feftie merkis for his Mertimes maill in j^m vj^e tuentie aucht zeirs.   Abrahame Forfar tuentie fyve merkis, and James Forfar tuentie fyve markis, for thair Mertimes maillis the zeir forsaidis within terme of law wnder paine of poynding.

The said day Maister Andro Leslie is decernit to pay to the

---

[1] Watch. 'Keip the fauld' is equivalent to the expression 'walk the fald' on p. 9.

laird xx lib. for his custome mairte for 1627 and 1628 zeirs.
Abrahame Forfar and James Forfar x lib. for thair mairt 1628
zeirs, within terme of law, etc.

The said day it is statuit that ilk tennent addebtit in payment of ferme meill within the barrouny sall mak at least ane
chalder[1] aitis at ane tyme in ferme, to the effect the millar
may keip the ferme frie of dust.   J. THOMSONE, *Scriba.*

> *The Barroune Court of Wry, haldin in Woodheid vpone the*
> *aucht day of Maij 1629 zeirs, be ane honorable man*
> *John Hay of Crimoundmogat, bailzie to ane nobill and*
> *potent erle Francis, erle of Erroll, etc., heritable pro-*
> *priater of the said barrouny, James Thomsone, notter*
> *publict, Court Clark, Alexander Fraser, officiar, Robert*
> *Syrie, Dempster. The suits calit, etc.*

The said [day] the haill tennents of Montquheiche, Rothnik,
Bannagubs, and Corsley, is decernit to cast and leid thair leitt
peitts this instant zeir in the ordinar moss of Wrie, and leid
the samen to the peithill of Wrie in dew tyme, conforme to
the former actis.

The said day Allexander Fraser is ordeanit to receave the
fermes and customes of the Bray of Wrie, and to give dischairges thairwpone, quhilk salbe sufficient to the tennentis,
Quhairon George Mowatt in name of the remanent tuik act.

The said day the haill tennents within the barrouny of
Wrie that ar restand ony of thair fermes for the crope 1629
zeiris, ar decernit to pay the samen to the girner in Wrie
within terme of law, or thane tualff pundis money for ilk
thairof, meill and bear respectively, wnder paine of poynding.
        J. THOMSONE, *Scriba.*

> *The Barroune Court of Wrie, haldin in Wodheid wpone the*
> *xj day of Nouember 1629 zeiris, be ane honorable man*
> *John Douglas of Wast Barras,[2] bailzie constitut ay and*

---

[1] A measure consisting of sixteen bolls.

[2] John Douglas of Wester Barras was fourth son of Sir William Douglas of
Glenbervie, who succeeded to the earldom of Angus on the death of Archibald,
eighth earl, in 1588. John Douglas received the lands of Wester Barras, which
had previously formed part of the Barony of Glenbervie, in portion from his

quhill he be dischairgit be ane nobill and potent lord
William Hay, etc., heritable propriater of the saidis
landis, James Thomsone, notter publict, Clark, Allexander
Fraser, officiar, Robert Syrie, Dempster. The suits
calit, the court laufullie fensit and affirmit.

The said day James Forfar is decernit to pay to the laird of
Wrie fywe pundis money for halff ane leit of peits, quhilk suld
have beine set vpone the peithill of Montquheiche this instant
zeir 1629, with fyve pundis for his half mairt 1629, and xx s.
for sex pultrie foullis, within terme of law, wnder paine of
poynding.

The said day William Duthie in Wodheid is decernit be his
awin confessioun to pay to the laird ane sufficient custome
mairt, or thane tene pundis money for the pryce thairoff, within
terme of law, wnder pain of poynding.

The said day the haill tennentis within the barrouny of
Wrie ar decernit be the bailzie forsaidis to pay in thair fermes
to Alexander Fraser, to wit the meill ferme befor Candlmes nixt
to cum in 1630, and the bear ferme befor ruid day thairefter.

The said day Georg Milne in Corsley is decernit be the
judge forsaid to pay to John Mowatt, chalmerlane, ane hundrethe markis money for his Witsonday and Mertimes maillis
of Crosley last by past in this instant zeir 1629 zeiris, with ane
vther hundrethe markis for his Witsonday and Mertimes maill
of ane pleuche of Montquheiche last occupiet be Maister
Andro Leslie, and now occupiet be him for this instant zeir
1629, Quhairwnto the said Georg objectit and alledgit he suld
nocht pay bot onlie thrie scoir sextein markis zeirlie, conforme to ane conditione maid be him with the laird of Wrie.
[Nochtwithstanding of the quhilk objectioun the bailzie forsaid decernit the said George to mak payment of the sowme of
ane hundrethe markis zeirlie for the said pleuche in Montquheiche, within terme of law, wnder paine of poynding].[1]

---

father. He married Jean, daughter of Fraser of Durris. His son, John Douglas,
sold Wester Barras, in 1640, to his brother-in-law, George Ogilvie, who so nobly
defended the castle of Dunottar against the forces of the Commonwealth in
1651-2.—Nisbet's *Heraldry*, Appendix, p. 222.

[1] The passage printed within brackets has marks of erasure drawn over it in
the original MS.

Quhairwpone he gave his ayth and thairfor was decernit to pay bot onlie the said soum of thrie scoir sextein markis for the said tua termes.

The said day Georg Moscrope alies Shiphird is decernit to mak payment to John Mowatt, chalmerlan, of the soume of tua hundrethe markis for his Witsonday and Mertimes maill of Rothnik, in this instant zeir 1629 zeirs. William Maine is decernit to pay to the chalmerlane ane hundrethe markis for his Witsonday and Mertimes [maill] of ane pleuche in Mont-quheiche, occupiet be him in this instant zeir 1629. Abraham Forfar is decernit to pay to the chalmerlane fourtie markis in compleit payment of his Witsonday and Mertimes maill of half ane pleuche in Montquheiche in this instant zeir 1629, within terme of law. George Straquhan is decernit to pay feftie pundis for his Mertimes maill of Glithnocht in this instant zeir 1629, within terme of law, wnder pain of poynding.

The said day William Murray and Alexander Munzie ar decernit to pay to the laird of Wrie tuentie markis money equalie betuix thame for thair Mertimes maill 1629. John Maissone in Montquheiche tene pundis for his Mertimes maill, and Archebald Duncane tuentie ffyve markis for his Mertimes maill of Bannageiche, in this instant zeir 1629. Stephane Forbes in Cowie tene markis for his Witsonday and Mertimes maill of the smydie croft in this instant zeir, with aucht shil-ings for ilk elne of ane dozen elnes of lyning restand be him for the said zeir, within terme of law, wnder paine of poynding.

The said day Abrahame Forfar, being persewit be Alexander Fraser, officiar, for deforcing him in taking ane plaid frome him quhilk he had poyndit from the said Abrahame for his dissobedience, being warnit to have cariet corne frome Mont-quheiche to Wrie. Compeirit the said Abrahame, and refferit the samen to the said Allexander, his ayth of weritie, wha being sworne deponit the said Abrahame deforcit him in taking back the said plaid. Quhairfor the judge forsaid decernit the said Abrahame in ane amerciament of tene pundis, quhilk he is decernit to pay to the laird within terme of law, wnder paine of poynding.

The said day Stephane Forbes in Cowie is decernit to pay to Georg Johnstoun, burges of Aberdein, fyve markis money

restand be him to the said Georg of byrun compts, within
terme of law.   J. Thomsone, *Scriba.*

The Barroune Court of Wrie, haldin in the Hall thairoff
wpone the sexteine day of Junij 1630 zeirs, in name and
behalf of ane nobill and potent lord William, Lord Hay,
etc., and ane honorable man John Hay of Crimound-
mogat, his lordship's bailzie, James Thomsone, notter
publiet, court clark, Alexander Fraser, officiar, Robert
Syrie, Dempster. The suits calit, etc., the court laufullie
fenssit and affirmit.

The said day the haill tennentis within the barrouny of Wrie
and Montquheiche that ar restand thair Witsonday maill in
this instant zeir 1630 zeirs, ar decernit ilk ane for thair awin
pairtis respective to mak payment thairof to John Mowatt,
chalmerlane, within terme of law, wnder paine of poynding.

The said day the tennentis efter specifeit ar decernit ilk ane
for thair awin pairts respective to pay to the laird of Wrie the
particular bollis of bear and meill wnder written, wiz. : William
Duthie four bollis bear for the crope 1629.   Jeane Fullartoun
ffyve bollis bear.   Georg Gordoune tua bollis thrie firlots
bear and four bollis meill.   Robert Duncane ane boll thrie
pecks meill, within terme of law, or thane tene pundis for ilk
boll thairoff, wnder paine of poynding.

The said day George Gordoune is decernit to pay four libs.
for ilk dussone of thrie dozen caponis restand be him for the
crope 1629 zeirs, within terme of law, wnder pain of poynding.

The said day the haill tennents within the barrouny of Wrie
that sall happin in any tyme heirefter to reais fyir and burne
mwir within any pairte of the said barrouny efter the tent day
of Marche zeirlie, sall pay tene pundis *toties quoties* to the laird
for ilk mwir burne [1] to be reaisit be thame efter the said day
abone mentionat.

The said day Stephane Forbes in Cowie is decernit be his
awin confessioun to pay tuentie markis for his maill of the
smydie croft in Cowie for the Witsonday terme last by past in
this instant zeir 1630, and [for] all termes preceeding, togidder

---

[1] The act of burning moors or heath.—*Jam.*

with ane dozen elnes lyning clayth, or thane aucht shilingis
for ilk elne thairof for the said Witsonday terme abone wreittin,
within terme of law, wnder paine of poynding.

The said day it is statuit and ordeanit that ewerie cotter
and greas man within the barrouny of Wrie that is hird to his
awin guidis in the day tyme, sall watche and waird for thame
in the fauld or the aucht tyme,[1] conforme to the number of
guids that he hes, and iff any skayth sall happin in thair default,
to be comptable for the samen and pay the skayth.

The said day it is statuit and ordeanit that the haill tennents
within the nether barrouny of Wrie that ar thirlit to the milne
of Cowie sall keip the said milne in all tyme cuminge, and pay
the ordinar multers of thair corns, conforme as thaj war in vse
in vmquhile John Hays tyme, of sick corn as growis within
the grund, and all vther that is coft and brocht in and tholis
flyir and watter within the grund sall pay out suckin[2] to the
said mylne.

*The Barroune Court of Wrie, haldin in the Woodheid wpoune
the sextein day of Maij, be ane honorable man Johnne
Hay of Crimoundmogat, bailzie to ane nobill and potent
erle Francis, erle of Erroll, and William Lord Hay, heritable propriaters thairof, James Thomsoune, notter publict, clark, Allexander Fraser, officiar, Dauid Mitchell,
Dempster. The suits calit, the court laufullie fenssit and
affirmit.*

Note.—The
Laird has gotten
x li. of this
soume.
The said day the haill tennents wnder wreittin ar decernit to
pay to John Mowatt in Powbair the sowmes efter specifeit,
restand be ilk ane of thame for thair awin pairt respectiue for
thair Mertimes maillis last by past in j^m vj^c and threttie zeirs,
wiz.: George Milne in Corsley feftie merkis, with the ordinar
annuel-rent thairof since the said terme. Georg Moscrope in
Bannagubis foir his Mertimes maill of Rothnik and Quhytsyid
the zeir forsaid four scoir sevinteine markis sex sh[ilings]
viiij d., with the ordinar annuel-rent thairof since the terme

---

[1] Up till eight times.

[2] *Out-suckin* here signifies the remuneration which the 'out-suckeners' paid
to the miller for grinding their grain.

forsaid. Allexander Mengzeis in Montquheiche threttie aucht markis for his Mertimes maill 1630. Dauid Craig tuentie fyve markis for his Mertimes maill the zeir forsaid, with the ordinar annuel-rent thairoff. Georg Straquhane in Glithnocht feftie pundis for his Mertimes maill the zeir forsaid, with the ordinar annuel-rent since the said terme, within terme of law, wnder paine of [poynding], as also the haill tenents addebtit in payment of siluer maill ar decernit ilk ane for thair awin pairts respectiue to mak payment of thair Witsonday maillis in this instant zeir j^m vj^c threttie ane zeirs preceislie at the terme of Witsonday, wnder paine of poynding.

The said day the haill tennents within the barrouny of Wrie that ar restand any of thair fermes for the crope j^m vj^c and threttie zeiris ar ilk ane for thair awine pairtis respectiue sua far as is restand be thame, and ilk ane of thame ar decernit to mak payment thairof to the laird of Wrie, within terme of law, or thane tene pundis money for ilk vndelyuerit boll thairof meill and bear respectiue, wnder paine of poynding, and the officiar ordeanit to poynd for the samen.

The said day the haill tennents that ar restand any customes wadders, capouns, and pultrie ar decernit ilk ane for thair awine pairtis at the termes of payment vsit and wount, or thane the ordinar prycis thairoff, wnder paine of poynding.

The said day Stephane Forbes in Cowie is decernit to pay to the laird fyve markis money for his Witsonday maill in this instant zeir 1631, with ane dozen elnes of lyning clayth quhilk suld beine payit oniday last by past, or thane aucht shilings money for ilk elne thairof, wnder paine of poynding.

The said day the bailzie forsaid decernis and ordeanis Georg Milne in Corsley tene pundis money for ane leit of peittis quhilk he suld have castin for that pleuche in Montquheiche occupiet be him in j^m vj^c and threttie zeiris, within terme of law, wnder paine of poynding.			J. THOMSONE, Scriba.

The said day Thomas Sellatt in Montquheiche is decernit to pay to John Midltoune in Findlawstoun tene pundis for ane kow, etc.

The Barroun Court of the Barrouny of Wrie, haldin in Woodheid wpoun the xj day of September 1632 zeiris, be

John Mowatt in Powbair, bailzie to ane nobill and potent erle William, erle of Erroll, Lord Hay, etc., heritable propriater of the saidis landis, James Thomsone, notter publict, court clark, Alexander Fraser, officiar, Rob. Syrie, Dempster. The suits calit, etc.

The said day compeirit William Reid, scruitor to John Mowatt in Rothnik, and complenit wpoun Agnes Duncan, dochter to William Duncane thair, that the said Agnes hade dung, strukin, and bled the said William. Compeirit the said Agnes and denyit the samen, in respect quhairof the forsaid referrit the samen to the knawledge of ane assyse, wha be the mouth of George Straquhane, chosin chanceler,[1] convict the said Agnes in the blood, in respect of her awin confessioun. Quhairfor the Judge forsaid decernis the said Agnes to pay ffyve pundis to Alexander Fraser, procuratour fiscall, within terme of law, wnder pain of poynding.

The said day compeirit William Duncane in Rothnik, and being persewit for contravening of ane former act quhairin the haill tennents ar obleidgit naine of thame to persew wtheris befor the Shereff, and the said William haweing persewit Allexander Munzie befor the Shereff, he refferit himself in William Hay of Wrie his will. Quhairon Allexander Fraser tuik act.   J. THOMSONE, *Scriba.*

The Barroune Court of the barrouny of Wrie, haldin in the dualing hous of James Thomsone in Woodheid wpoun the twentie aucht day of Januar 1634, be John Hay of Ardlethine,[2] bailzie to ane nobill and potent erle William, erle of Erroll, Lord Hay, Heiche Constable of Scotland, heretable propriater of the saidis landis, James Thomsone, notter publict, clark, Allexander Fraser, officiar, Robert Syrie, Dempster. The suits calit, the court laufullie fenssit and affirmit.

The said day compeirit John Ramsay in Magray and con-

---

[1] The Chancellor of a jury is the preses or foreman, who announces the verdict. —Bell's *Law of Scotland*, p. 151.

[2] The lands of Ardlethen are situated in the parish of Ellon in Aberdeenshire. John Hay succeeded his father, George, third son of George, sixth Earl of Errol, in these lands subsequent to 1612.—*Reg. Priv. Coun.* vol. ix. p. 417.

fessit himself to be restand aucht bollis bear of his ferme crop
1632 zeiris, in respect quhairof the bailzie forsaid decernis and
ordeanis the said John Ramsay to pay nyne pundis money for
ilk boll thairof to John Mowatt, chalmerlane, within terme of
law, wnder pain of poynding.

The said day compeirit Abrahame Forfar in Montquheiche
and confessit himselff to be restand ane hundrethe and ffywe
markis money for his Mertimes termes maill of his occupatioun
of Montquheiche last by past in 1633, and in compleit payment
of his haill maillis of all zeirs and termes bygain preceiding the
said terme of Mertimes. Quhilk sowme the said Abrahame is
decernit to pay to the said John Mowatt, chalmerlane, within
terme of law, wnder paine of poynding, as also the said
Abrahame is fund restand ane custome mairt pryce tene pundis
with sex pundis money for the pryce of tua custome wadders,
and that for his customes of Montquheiche for the crope 1633,
and for the crope to cum in this instant zeir 1634 zeirs, quhilk
he is decernit to pay to the chalmerlane forsaid, within term
of law, wnder pain of poynding.

The said day compeirit Allexander Menzeis in Montquheiche
and confest him selff to be restand ane hundrethe and fourteine
markis for his Mertimes maill last by past in 1633, and all zeirs
and termes preceiding, quhilk sowme he is decernit to pay to
John Mowatt, chalmerlane, within terme of law, wnder pain of
poynding.

The said day Georg Straquhane in Glithnocht is decernit be
his awine confessioun to pay feftie pundis money to John
Mowat, chalmerlane, for his Mertimes termes maill 1633,
within terme of law, wnder pain of poynding.

The said day James Gordoun and John Mowatt in Rothnik
is decernit be thair awin confessioun to pay to John Mowatt,
chalmerlane, feftie pundis for their Mertimes maill 1633, within
terme of law, wnder pain of poynding.

The said day Allexander Munzie in Quhytsyid is decernit to
pay tuentie fywe markis for his Mertimes maill 1633, with fyve
pundis for half ane mairt to the chalmerlane forsaid, within
terme of law, wnder the pain of poynding.

The said day the haill tennents within the barrouny of Wrie
ar decernit to mak payment of thair haill fermes meill and bear

restand be thame for the crope 1633, to John Mowatt in Powbair into the girners of Wrie, in sufficient wictuall cleane but dust or steanes (except James Thomsone, wha hes producit ane dischairge of the said zeirs ferme alredie), the meill ferme befor the first of Marche, or thane nyne pundis for the boll thairof, and the bear befor the thrid day of Maij nixt to cum, or thane tene pundis for ilk boll thairof.

The said day it is statuit and ordeanit be the bailzie forsaid that whosoeuer within this barouny salbe tryit to cut or distroy any of the planting of Wrie sall pay tene pundis money to my lord efter dew tryall.

Note.—Abra-hame suld have sex bollis of the tene bollis 3 firlots for £4, 3s. 4d. the boll.

The said day the bailzie forsaid decernis and ordeanis Abrahame Forfar to pay tene bollis ane firlot of his meill ferme of Findlawstoun for the crope 1632, with his haill ferme, meill, and bear for the crope 1633, into the girners in Wrie, to John Mowatt to be keipit and preservit be the said John to the weill and profeit of Allexander Annand of Findlawstoun, or any wther who salbe fund to have best richt thairto. And in caice of failzie to pay my lordis prycis. As also the said Abrahame is decernit to pay his customes or prycis thairof to the said John, within terme of law.

The said day Magnus Milne at the milne of Cowie is ordeanit to sie the ferme cleine sheilit, and that thair be nather dust nor staines put amangis the samen, and to that effect he sall tak the haill dust and retcine the samen in his awin hous till the fermes be delyuerit into the girners, quhairwpoun he hes given his ayth.

The said [day] John Irving in Corsley is decernit to pay feftie markis for his Mertimes maill 1633, to John Mowatt, within terme of law, wnder pain of poynding.

> *The Barroune Court of Wrie, haldin in Woodheid wpoune the 27 of Junij 1634 zeirs, be ane honorable man John Hay of Ardlethin, bailzie to ane nobill and michtie erle William, erle of Erroll, Lord Hay, Heiche Constable of Scotland, etc., heritable propriator of the saidis landis; James Thomson, notter clark, Allexander Fraser, officiar, Dauid Syrie, Dempster. The suit calit, etc.*

The said day compeiret the haill tennents wnder writtin, per-

sonallie, and confessit that ilk ane of thame ar in vse to pay for
thair seuerall occupatiounis efter specifeit the particular maillis,
fermes, and dewties respectiue efter mentionat, wiz. : Jeane
Fullartoune, for the half chaplanrie in Cowie, elevine bollis tua
firlots bear. And Patrik Austiane, Shereff Clerk of Kincardyne,
being necessarlie absent from this court, in respect he was at
ane Shereff Court, declairit to the bailzie forsaid this morning
that he payis for the nether half chaplanrie tualf bollis bear.
Stewine Forbes payit for the smydie croft in Cowie tene markis,
ane dussone of lyning clayth, and vphaldis ane pleuchs smyth
wark in the mainse of Wrie. John Law, skipper, Magnus
Falconner, Archibald Leapper, and Edward Robertsone,
fischers in Cowie, pays aucht markis tua quartis of oylie, the
boits pairt being drawin.[1] Thomas Maine payis for tua
zairdis thair tene markis. Dauid Burnet at the burnesyid of
Cowie payis fyive markis. George Quhyt thair payis thrie
pundis. Magnus Milne payis for the milne dozen[2] of Covie
tuentie four bollis meill, and for the milne land thairoff threttie
bollis bear, four dussoun capouns, ane milne swyne, ane
custome mairt, fourtie shilings of maill, ane leitt of peittis.
Georg Mowatt payis for Reidcloak tuentie pundis of maill,
four bollis malt, thrie bollis hors corne, four wadders, auchteine
capons, auchteine pultrie. Item, mair he payis for Walkmilne
of Wrie ffourtie pundis money. Archibald Duncane payis for
Bannageich feftie markis, ane custome mart, tua wadders, ane
dussone capouns, ane dussone of pultrie, ane leit of peittis.
Robert Duncane payis for Carntoune auchteine bollis meill,
ane custome mart, tua wadders, ane dussone capouns and ane
dussone pultrie, ane leitt of peitts. Georg Straquhane pay[is]
for Glithnocht ane hundrethe pundis money. William Duthie
pays for the cist syid of Woodheid sexteine bollis meill, and
four bollis bear, ane custome mart, tua wadders, ane dussone
capons, ane dussone pultrie, ane leitt of peitts. James
Thomsone pays for the wast half thairoff the lyik dewtie,
except sick he hade doun[3] for his seruice. John Mowatt pays
for Powbair sexteine bollis meill and four bollis bear.

---

[1] Withdrawn or passed.—*Jam.* (Supplement).
[2] See p. 79 n. 2, *infra.*
[3] What he had done.

Abrahame Forfar payis for half ane pleuche in Montquheiche feftie markis, half ane mart, ane wadder, half ane staine of butter, sex pultrie, half ane leitt peittis. Gilbert Menzies payis for half ane pleuche and ane croft thrie scoir sexteine markis, with sex pundis for customes. John Mowatt payis for ane wther halff pleuche thair feftie markis, half ane mart, ane wadder, half ane staine butter, sex pultrie, and half ane leitt of peittis. William Maine pays for ane pleuche thair ane hundrethe markis, ane mart, tua wadders, ane staine of butter, ane dussone of pultrie, ane leitt of peittis. Alexander Menzies pays for ane wther pleuche thair thrie scoir sexteine markis, ane mart, tua wadders, ane staine of butter, ane dussone of pultrie, and ane leitt of peittis. The wther thrie pleuchs in Montquheiche wodset to George Dewinny, and pays to him, ilk pleuche, ane hundrethe markis, ane mart, tua wadders, ane staine of butter, ane dossone pultrie and leidis ane leit of peits, ilk pleuche, to the peithill in Montquheiche. John Milne payis for the milne and milne croft of Montquheiche tuentie bollis meill, aucht pundis of maill, ane mylne swyne, ane dussone capouns. Sauchinshawe, wodset to Georg Dewinny, pas to him ane hundrethe markis, ane wadder, ane staine of butter, ane dussone pultrie. Bonnagubs, wodset to Georg Shiphird, *alies* Moscrope, pays ane hundrethe markis, ane mart, tua wadders, ane staine butter, ane dussone pultrie, and ane leit of peittis.

James Gordoune and John Mowatt pays for Rothnik ane hundrethe pundis of maill, ane mart, half mart, thrie wadders, ane staine, half staine of butter, auchteine pultrie, ane leitt of peitis. Quhytsyid being the quarter of Rothnik, and now waist, payis feftie markis, half ane mart, ane wadder, half ane staine of butter, sex pultrie, and half ane leitt of peittis. Corsley being now waist and tennentlese, in respect John Irvings remowing thairfra, payit ane hundrethe markis and ane leit of peittis onlie. In respect vmquhile John Ramsey, wha was tennent in Magray, is laitlie depairtit this present lyff, and his relict being vnable to compeir this day, it is declairit be John Mowatt, chalmerlane, and wthers that knawis the rentall, that Magray payis fourtie bollis wictuall, half meill, half bear, thrie wadders, tua dussone capouns, ane dussone

pultrie, tua leitt of peittis.   In respect Allexander Annand in
Findlawstoune was not present, it is declairit be William Hay
of Wrie and the chalmerlane that Findlawstoune payis onlie
tene markis of maill, Quhilkis haill tennents particularlie
abowe namet are ilk ane for thair awine pairtis respective
decernit, except the wodset landis abowe specifeit, be the bailzie
forsaid, to mak payment of the particular maillis, fermes, and
dewties addebtit be ilk ane of thame for thair seueral occupa-
tiones respective abowe specifeit, wiz: the fermes for crope
instantlie presentlie wpoun the ground in this present zeir of
God j^m vj^c threttie four zeiris, and thair maillis and customes
for the crope to cum in zeir of God j^m vj^c threttie ffyve zeirs
to the said nobill erle and his chalmerlane in his name, wiz.,
John Mowatt in Powbair, at the termes of payment vsit and
wount, wnder the paine of poynding.

The said day Androw Duncane is decernit to pay to Allexander Maine xx tb. be his awin confessioun, wnder paine of
poynding, within terme of law.

The Barrouny Court of Wrie, haldin in Woodheid, the 26
of Februar 1635, *be John Hay of Ardlethine, bailzie to
ane nobill and potent erle William, eroll of Erroll, Lord
Hay, etc., Heiche Constable of Scotland, heritable propriator of the saidis landis, James Thomsone, notter clerk,
Dauid Burnet, officiar, Allexander Murray, Dempster.
The suits calit, the court laufullie fenssit and affirmit.*

The said day the haill tennents within the barrouny of
Wrie ar, ilk ane for thair awin pairts respective, decernit to pay
in thair fermes of the crope j^m vj^c threttie four zeirs, to John
Mowatt, chalmerlane, into the girners in Wrie, befor Pashe
nixt, or thane tene pundis for ilk boll meill and twalff pundis
for ilk boll bear, wnder pain of poynding.

The said day the haill tennents that payis siluer maill
within the said barrouny (except Georg Mowatt, wha alleges
he hes ane dischairge of the laird of Wrie) are decernit, ilk ane
for thair awin pairts respective, to mak payment to the
chalmerlane forsaid of thair Mertimes maillis last by past in
the zeir of God j^m vj^c threttie ffour zeiris, Togidder with the

ordiner pryces of thair customes marts, wadders, pultric, and
capones for the crope to cum in this instant zeir jm vj° threttie
ffyve zeirs, within terme of law, wnder pain of poynding.

The said day Georg Dewinny in Montquheiche, William
Maine thair, Georg Shiphird in Bannagubis, William Duthie
in Woodheid, and Archebald Duncane and Magnus Milne in
Bannageiche, ar admitit to be barlawe men within the barrouny
of Wrie, wha gave thair aithes *de fidelj administratione* ay and
quhill they be dischairgit.

The said day Patrik Makie in Glithnocht is decernit be his
awin confessioun to pay to Maister Thomas Blakhall in
Aberdein aucht pundis for the pryce of ane boll meill, coft and
receauit be him fra the said Maister Thomas, within terme of
law, under pain of poynding.

> *The Barroune Court of the Barrouny of Wrie, haldin at
> Wrie, the elevint day off September j^m vj° threttie ffyve
> zeiris, be John Hay of Ardlethine, bailzie to ane nobill
> and potent erle William, erle of Erroll, lord Hay, Heiche
> Constable off Scotland, heretable propriator thairoff,
> James Thomsone, notter publict, court clark, Dauid
> Burnet, officier, Allexander Murray, Dempster. The
> suits calit, the court laufullie fenssit and affirmit.*

The said day the haill tennents within the barrouny of Wrie
that payis siluer maill are ilk ane decernit for thair awin
pairtis respective to mak peyment of thair Witsonday maillis
last by past in this instant zeir of God 1635 zeirs, within
terme of law, wnder the pain of poynding.

The said day it is statuit and ordeanit that the barlawmen
sall go and sicht Gilbert Menzeis, Abrahame Forfar, and
William Murray's rowmes in Montqueithe, and wha ewer salbe
fund to hawe the halff pleuche and the croft in Montquheithe
that suld be amang them, salbe obleist to pay the rentall
thairoff.

The said day compeirit . . .

> *The Barroune Court of Wrie, haldin in the Woodheid
> thairoff, wpone the nynt day off Januar 1636 zeirs, be*

John Hay of Ardlethine, bailzie to ane nobill and potent erle William, erle of Erroll, lord Hay, Heiche Constable of Scotland, heretable propriater thairoff. James Thomsone, notter publict, court clark, Dauid Burnet, officiar, Allexander Murray, Dempster. The suits calit, the court laufullie fenssit and affirmit.

The said day the haill tennents within the barrouny of Wrie that are addebtit in payment of siluer maill ar decernit ilk ane for their awin pairtis respective to mak payment to John Mowatt, chalmerlane, of their Mertimes maillis last by past in the zeir of God j^m vj^c threttie ffyve zeiris, within terme of law, wnder pain of poynding thair rediest guidis and geir.

The said day the haill tennents within the barrouny of Wrie ar ordeanit to conveine and pairt the mainse of Wrie, and reid[1] the samen equalie amongest thame, conforme to thair promeis maid to my lord for this zeir.

The said day the haill tennents within the said barrouny that ar addebtit in payment of ferme victuall, meill, and bear ar decernit to pay thair meill ferme before Candlmes nixt and thair bear ferme befoir the thrid of May nixt to cum to Georg Pattoun of Ferrochie or his vnder receaver, my lordis mil dozen,[2] or thane tene pund for ilk boll meill and xij tib. for ilk boll bear.

The said day it is statuit and ordeanit that the barlaw men sall visseit and compryse that hous that perteinet to vmquhile Issobell Gilaspie, and what it is furthe to be worthe[3] at hir deceas. John Gairdyne, wha is fund to have melit thairwith and demolished the samen, is decernit and ordeanit to reidifie the samen and mak it alse guid as it was the tyme he medlit

---

[1] To put in order, to clear.—*Jam.*

[2] *My lordis mil dozen* signifies the multure payable to the laird by those using the mill. Parties grinding their corn were held bound to render him every *thirteenth peck* in virtue of his position as proprietor. This scale of payment is of very ancient origin. In an Act of Alexander III., of date 1284, and intended to discourage the use of Querns, as prejudicial to the intercsts of those landlords who had erected water-mills for the accommodation of their tenants, it is provided that 'na man sall presume to grind quheit, maisblock, or rye, with hand mylne, except he be compelled by storm, or be in lack of mills quhilk sould grinde the samen. And in this case, gif a man grindes at hand mylnes, he sall gif the *threttein measure as multer,* and gif any man contraveins this our prohibition, he sall tine his hand mylnes perpetuallie.'—Blount's *Ancient Tenures,* p. 614.

[3] *Furthe to be worthe,* manifestly worth.

with it, or thane to pay the pryce of it, as salbe comprysit be
the barlaw men, within terme of law, wnder pain of poynding.

The said day John Law, Skipper, Archebald Leapper,
Magnus Falconner, and Edward Robertsone, lyne men in the
boit of Cowie, ar decernit and ordeanit to pay thair boits pairt
to thease wha hes richt to receave the samen dewlie and
trewlie, conforme as the boits of Muchallis[1] and Elsick payis,
and the officiar ordeanit to poynd for the samen.

The said day the cotteris in Wrie, wiz., John Murray,
Richard Smyth, and Georg Walcar, ar decernit to pay to the
chalmerlane for the grease of thair guidis as follows to John
Murray :—

> . . .[2] for ane mear ; sextein shilings aucht pennes for ilk
> beist of thrie nolt, 3s. 4d. for ilk sheip of   heidis
> of sheip.   Richard Smyth,   for ane staig, with sex-
> tein shilings aucht pennes for ilk beast of four nolt, 3s. 4d.
> for ilk sheipe of sixtein heidis.   Archebald Walcar, 16s. 8d.
> for ilk nolt beist of thrie, with 3s. 4d. for ilk sheip of
> aucht sheip.

The said day the haill tennentis sick as are mailleris within
the barrony of Wrie ar decernit and ordeneit to content and
[pay] the haill rest maillis, Witsounday and Mertimes termes,
within terme of law, wnder pain of poynding, and sick of the
saidis tennentis, mailloris allenerlie as saidis, that ar resting
thair saidis maillis and fealyieis in payment within fyiftein
dayis nixt efter the expyiring of the said fyiftein deyis, ar
decernit, sic thairof as peyis ane hundreth markis or fyiftie
markis ar decernit, ilk persone conforme to his mailling, *pro
rato*, to content and pey the soume of ten pundis money for ilk
termes failzie to the chalmerleane, Viz., ten pundis for ilk
hundreth markis fealzie, and sua furth, conforme to thair
maillingis.

The said day it is decernit that sick of the fermoreis[3] within
the said barrony of Vrie as fealzeis in tymeous peyment mack-

---

[1] Alexander Burnett of Leys had a charter of the lands of Muchals, which
formed part of the barony of Cowie—with fishings, mills, etc.—on the resignation of Francis, Earl of Errol, granted at Edinburgh, 24th June 1606.—*Reg.
Mag. Sig.* (1593-1608) 1764.

[2] Blank in MS.   [3] Payers of ferme, *i.e.* farmers.

ing of thair fermeis ar decernit to content and pey for ilk boll
vnpeyit bear the soume of aucht pundis money, and for ilk
vnsatisfeit boll of meall the soume of sex pundis fyve shillingis
money.

The said day the haill tennentis within the said barrony ar
decerneit and ordeneit to pay ther haill keains,[1] customes, and
vther dewteis, sick thairof as ar restand the samen to pey the
samen to the chalmerleane, within terme of law, vnder pain of
poynding.

The said dey ilk persone inhabeiting within the barrony of
Vrie, or any of thair guidis that salbe apprehendit passing or
pastouring throw the zaird or hainingis of Vrie, ilk persone
passing or gaiting[2] throw the zaird, or possessour off any beast
pastouring in the haining as said is, ar decernit to pey to the
gairdner the soume of fourtie shillingis.

*The Baroun Court of the Baronie of Vrie, haldin in the
Maner place thairof, vpon the aucht day of November
1638, be Johnne Hay of Ardlethin, bailzie to John, Lord
Zester,[3] and James Lyon of Auldbar,[4] with consent of
John, eirle of Kinghorn, Lord Lyon, etc.[5] Dauid Burnet,
officiar, George Quheit, Dempster. The suittis callit, the
court laufullie affermit.*

The quhilk day the haill tennentis of the said barronie
restand fermis customes or male of thair cropt 1637, and Witsondayis term 1638, ar decernit all and ilk ane of thame,
conform to thair rest comptis, to pay the samen to John Mowat,
chalmerlane, within xv dayis, wnder the pain of poynding.

The quhilk day Archebald Duncan in Bannageiche is

---

[1] Customes paid in poultry, eggs, etc.

[2] Making their way.

[3] John Hay, 8th Lord Yester, succeeded his father in 1600. He was created
Earl of Tweeddale, 1st December 1646, and died 1653.—Douglas' *Peerage*, vol. ii.
p. 607.

[4] James Lyon of Auldbar, second son of Patrick, 11th Lord Glammis and 1st
Earl of Kinghorn.—*Ibid.* p. 561.

[5] John, Earl of Kinghorn, elder brother of James Lyon of Auldbar. He
succeeded his father as 2d Earl of Kinghorn in 1615. Auldbar and Kinghorn
were uncles of Gilbert, 10th Earl of Errol, whose father, William, 9th Earl,
married their sister, Lady Ann Lyon.—*Ibid.* p. 565.

decernit be his awin confessioun to pay to Stephin Lichtoun in
Glithno fyve markis, within term of law.

> *The Court of the Barony of Wry, haldin in the Hall thairoff,*
> *vpon the xx day of November* 1639, *be James Hay of*
> *Muryfaldis,[1] bailye to ane noble erlle Gilbert, erlle of*
> *Erroll, and be ane noble erlle John, erlle of Kinghorne,*
> *his lordship's tutour, gydar, and administrator. John*
> *Wishart, notter clark, Dauid Burnet, officiar, William*
> *Quhyte, Dempster. The suitts callit, and the court lau-*
> *fullie fencit and affirmit.*

It is ordaned be the bailie, with consent of the haill grund,
that at quhat tyme they be chargit for helping of the dame of
the myln of Cowie, ilk man salbe, with his horss and kairttes
and serwandis, wpon the first advirteisment, vnder the pane of
twante schillings, vnlaw *toties quoties* they contravein the
premissis.

It is ordaned that the Maister of the myln and his servandis
sall haue his myln redy pickit be fair day licht at all occasionis
for grinding or sheiling, and the maister of the myln sall haue
onle four bollis malt betuixt the grinding and sheiling, vnder
the pane foirsaid.

It is ordaned that the pikkeman sall haue for his panes in
grinding everie twantie bollis great aittis ane pek and half pek
meall, and ane pek meall for ilk twintie bollis small aittis, and
ane pek meall for metting of ilk twantie bollis meall, etc.

Lyk as it is ordaned that at the grinding of the tennentis
fermes the chalmerlen salbe advertesit at thair entre thairto,
and the dust sett in the millars house thair to remane wntill
the ferms be delyuerit.

The quhilk day the haill tennentis of the said barony
addettit in thair maillis, customes, and dewties for the
Mertimes terme last by past 1639, and all yeires and termes

---

[1] James Hay of Muriefauld in Aberdeenshire was a cadet of the house of Errol.
Adopting the policy of his chief, he appears as a supporter of the Covenant, and
is intrusted with the command of ‘the Erll of Errollis men in Buchane,’ at the
hosting of the shires of Aberdeen, Kincardine, and Banff, held at Aberdeen, by
order of Committee, in September 1644.—Spalding's *Memorialls of the Trubles
in Scotland,* vol. ii. p. 401.

preceiding, are decernit to mak payment thairof within fyftene dayis nixt heirefter to John Mowat, chalmerlen, wtherveyes the birla men appointit to poynd and distrenzie for the thrid peny mair nor the just debt.

ABRAHAME FORFFAR, with my hand.

The quhilk day it is statuite and ordaned that ilk person within the said barony that salbe fund using pastour quhair[1] wayes or gaittes throw the yeardis and hanynges of the yeardis of Wry, the contravenars heirof sall pay *toties quoties*, it be qualifyit that they haue transgressit, sall pay of wnlaw to my lord and his chalmerlene, *totics quoties*, the sowme of fourtie shilling money and remane in the stokis for the space of fourtie aucht houris.

It is appoyntit and aggreit betuixt John Mowat, chalmerlen, on the ane pairt, and the fisheris of Cowie on the other pairt in manner following, viz.: That for the present he sall caus beit[2] the hwill[3] and boit they have sufficientlie. For the quhilk boit they sall pey twante four lib. till Witsonday nixt, and at the said terme he sall caus build ane sufficient boitt, and they sall pay for the samen sic sowmes as the laird of Leyes resaues for his boit, and they to haue land and houssis as his fisheres hes in possessione.

[The long blank between this and the following Minute may be accounted for partly by reference to the unsettled state of the district during the Revolution period, and partly to peculiar cir- cumstances in connection with the proprietorship of the lands, which are explained in the Introduction.]

The Court of the Barronie of Wrie, haldine within the hous of Johne Auchinleck in Cowie, the 23 Maij 1667 zeires, in name and behalfe of Dawid Barclay, heritable pro- priater of the landis of Wrie, and in name and behalfe of Alexander Mowat in Reidcloake, his bailzie. Johne Auch- inleck, notar publict, Clerke to the court, Androw Mancur, officier, Dawid Mitchell, Dempster. The suitts callitt, the court laufullie fenssit and affirmett.

ANDROW MANCUR, *officier.*

DA. MITCHELL, *dempster.*

---

[1] Where are.   [2] Repair.
[3] *Hwill* or *whill*, equivalent to the Shetland *whilly*, a small skiff.

The said day the tenants within the landis off Wrie and
Manquith belanging to Collonel Barclay, conveined thes that
ar found restand off mailles dewties ar ordainet to pey in ther
severall proportiones as they ar found heir restand within terme
off law. Lykwayes thes that ar found restand ther fermes,
is ordainet to pey in ther fermes betuixt the dait heiroff and
the day aucht dayes, or else to bring money therfor.

The said day John Mowat in Rothnick is found restand
for his maill and silver dewtie sevine pundes and thretteine
schillinge Scottis, James Gordoune ther is found restand four
lïb. nynteinth schillinge Scottis, George Mowat is found
restand four merkis Scottis, Margrat Cadonheid at the milne
off Manquith aucht merkis Scottis, John Duncane in Bannageith tuentie sex pundis Scottis and sex schillinge, George
and Androw Farfare tuentie aucht lïb. sexteine schillinge
Scottis, and tuentie bollis and ane halfe boll meill, Androw
Mancurr in Wodheid is found restand tuentie sex boll and
ane half of meill and three bollis fywe peckes bear, Magnus
Broune in Magra sevine merkis Scottis money, fywe bollis
and ane halfe bear, William Wilsone and Alexander Falkoner
restes eleven pund fyfteine schillinge four d. money, and ten
bollis and ane halfe meill and tuelfe bollis bear, and that for
the cropsis and zeiris of God j^{m}vj^c sextie fywe and sextie sext
yeires, and ar ordainet the abowreittin silver and ferme dewtie,
within terme of law.

The said day the pickieman is ordainet to hawe for ilk
chalder off meill grinding within the milne of Cowie, or the
meill off two chalder small oates, ane peck off meill, and ane
peck off meill for the metting off ilk tuentie bollis, and lykwayes the pickeman off the mill off Manquith.

The said day Androw Mancurr in Wodheid constitute and
appoyntit ground officer, and heirby the heall tennents ar
ordainet to obey him, and pey in the officer dewties to him
wsed and wount.

Jon. Auchinleck, Scriba Curiæ.

*The Court of the Barronie of Wrie, haldine within the hous
of Androw Mancurr in Woodheid, the 2de day off
November 1667, in name and behalfe [of] Collonel*

*Dawid Barclay, heritable propriater of the landis of Vrie,
and in name and behalfe of Alexander Mowat, his bailzie.
Johne Auchinleck, Clerk to the said Court, Andrew Mancurr, officier, Robert Spairke, Dempster. The Suitts
callit, the court lawfullie fenssit and affirmet.*

ANDROW MANCURR, *officier.*
ROBERT SPAIRKE, *dempster.*

The quhilk day William Duthie inactis himselfe to pey his
heall bygone restes mailles preceiding Mertimes nixt to come
within ten dayes after the terme.

Margrat Cadoneheid inactis hir selfe to pey hir rests within
ten dayes after the terme.

Walter Wilsone inactis to pay his heall bygone restis within
ten dayes after the terme.

Alexander Falkoner and William Wilsone inactis themselwes
to pey ther heall bygane restis preceiding Mertimes nixt, and
the Mertimes maill, within ten dayes after the terme.

Johne Duncan inactis himselfe to pey his bygone restis within
ten dayes after the terme.

.   .   .   .

Magnus Broune hes peyed fourteine pundes for his Witsonday customes 1667.

The haill tennantis off Irvie and Manquith ar ordained to
keipe themselwes from goeing throug the yeard and plantine
of Irvie, and whosumewer sall cut any green timber wpon the
water syd or Williesbog ar inacted to pey ten punds Scottis,
toties quoties, And this present Act is to be intimat be the
tennantis to ther subtennantis, that they pretend no ignorance.

It is inacted that the tennantis who suffers any in Staine-
hywe to cast or vinne turwes or peites within ther heid rowme,
or within the mairch off the land, that they sall imediatlie
make wse off them, wtherwayes if they suffer,[1] they ar to pey
ten punds Scottis, *toties quoties*, for ilk fault.

The said day Alexander Murry in Powbair is ordainet to
pey to Stevin Broune ane firlot off oates for pryze corne, wnder
the paine of poynding, within terme of law.

JON. AUCHINLECK, *Scriba Curiæ.*

---

[1] Delay.

*The Barrone Court off the Barronie of Wrie, haldine vithin
the hous of Androw Mancurr in Woodheid, the 7th day
of December 1667, in name of Collonel Dawid Barclay, off
Wrie, heritable propriater off the saidis landes, and Alexander Mowat in Reidcloake, his bailzie. Johne Auchinleck, Clerk to the said Court, Androw Mancurr, his officier,
Robert Sparke, Dempster. The suitts callit, the court
lawfullie fenssit and affirmet.*

ANDROW MANCUR, *officer.*
ROBERT SPARKE, *dempster.*

The said day compeiret Androw Mancurr, officier, who, in
name of his maister, did goe lawfullie and dacker the ground
for severalls thinges wanted about the hous of Wrie and wther
places on the ground.

The said day the officier produced some plucked wooll[1] and
fishes and wthers thinges found within the hous of Dawid
Watt in Woodheid. Quhilk wes referred to ane assysse whither
they found lawfull or not.

THE ASSYSSES NAMES.

Georg Carmock.	William Wilsone.
Walter Wilsone.	Magnus Broune.
George Lyell.	Robert Lyon.
George Mackinzie.	
Johne Mancurr.	
Johne Erskine.	

The abowwreitin assysse findes the abow wreittin thinges
found within the hous off the said Dawid Watt to be wnlawfull
and not to be his oune. Wherwpon the Judge ordaines him to
remowe with his wyfe and children from his hous and without
the ground, betuixt this and the 10th off this instant, and John
Mancurr, his master, inactis himselfe to put him from the
hous and off the toune, at or beffor the said day, wnder the
paine off ane hundreth pundes, and it is ordained that Androw
Mancurr sall be peyed off ten merkes Scottis off the first and
off the rediest goodes and gear belonging now to the said

---

[1] The system of plucking the fleece, or pulling it from the sheep, instead of
clipping it, still maintains in Shetland; the advantage being that the wool thus
obtained is longer in fibre than if it had been shorn.

Dawid, and it is ordained that the servant that shore for the said Dawid in harvest sall be peyit, and the officer is ordained to poynd for hir fie.

The said day George Lyell inactis himselfe to remowe from the ground of Wrie at Witsonday nixt, and inactis himself that his heall guides and gear sall be confiscatt to the Laird in caice he doe not behawe himselfe honestlie during the said tyme, and ffor not remoweing at the said terme.

The said day Johne Brabner inactis himselfe to remowe from the ground of Vrie at Witsonday nixt, and in caice any wnlikely be found off thift or disobedience ether to his maister or the officer off the ground, his haill guides and gear is to be confiscat.

Johne Jamiesone in Glithno is ordainet to pey to George Carnock in Cowie ane yeirs culse maill [1] and ten libs. Scottis, in caice the said George sall prowe his hors ever to be teathert on his grasse. And the said George inactis himselfe in the contrair, and this at the nixt court day.

Jon. AUCHINLECK, No^r: Publicus Scriba Curiæ.

The Barrone Court off the Barronie off Vrie, holdine att the
Manor place theiroff, vpon the sevint day off May j^mvj^c
sextie nyne yeirs, be Alexander Keith of Cowtoune[2],

---

[1] *Causeway-mail*: road dues. This probably refers to the tax imposed by Parliament in 1634, and renewed on 22d Feb. 1661, for the upkeep of the 'Kingis Calsay in Cowiemont.' We find that previous to 1630 the highway from Stonehaven to Aberdeen had fallen into such serious disrepair that various representations had been made to the King and his Council concerning it. The Act of 1661 gives power, during a period of nineteen years, to the Bailies of Aberdeen and others to uplift the following duties: 'Of everie footman two pennies, of everie horseman eight pennies, of everie horseload of whatsumever commoditie eight pennies, of everie ten sheep eight pennies, of everie cow or ox four pennies, and of everie Pairt of whatsumever commodities two shilling, to be applied for the beiting, mending, and upholding of the saids Calsayes, with power to collectors to poind for payment, and to close the port of the saids Calsayes, and suffer non to have passage that way bot such as shall pay the forsaid duetie.'—*Acta Parl.* vol. vii. c. 61, p. 42.

[2] Alexander Keith of Cowton was the lineal descendant of Alexander, fourth son of William third Earl Marischal, who obtained the lands of Pittendrum in Aberdeenshire, on resignation of his brother Gilbert in 1513. Alexander Keith married, in 1659, Marjory, daughter of Robert Arbuthnot of Little Fiddes. He sold Cowton in 1672, and purchased in its stead the wadset of Uras, in the parish of Dunnottar, becoming thereby the founder of the family of Keith of Uras, to which the famous Bishop Robert Keith belonged.—*MS. Pedigree of Family of Marischal*, in possession of Sir Patrick Keith Murray, Bart. of Ochtertyre.

bailzie to Colonell David Barclay of Vrie. Georg
Thomson, nottar publict, Clerk, George Forfar, officer,
and William King, Dempster.

Scetis vocatis.   *Curia legittime affirmata.*

The said day the tennentis off Vrie and Montwhich belonging to Colonel David Barclay being present, and it being
presented to the Judge by the said Colonell David Barclay
that he was informed some off his tennentis did calumniate him
as ane opressor and exactor. This being farr from his mynd
as he professed he was willing that all his tennentis might be
heard as to their just and laufull complaints, and willinglie
removed himselff till these compleaintis might be given in.
Wherupon the tennentis being called and present to give in
their complaintis, they refused to doe itt in regaird they confessed they had noe reasons soe to doe.

And as to tyme cumeing that cleanes[1] might be betwixt
maister and tennent as to the mater of seruice, it was frielie
offered by the maister that it should be in the tennentis
optione aither to pey hariadge, cariadge, and dew service as
they should be requyred, or wtherways to pay tenne merkis
yeirlie for the said service. The tennentis haveing considdered
the propositione, they all with one accord and consent agrie to
their giveing of dew service as they shall be requyred. And in
caice they failie, or any of them being so lawfullie requyred,
the Judge ordeanes them of their owne consent twente sex
shillinges eight pennies for ilk dayes failyie. From this act is
excepted the tennentis of Rothnick, Corsley, Tries, and Burne-
hauch, who are onlie to pey the tenne merkis of service siller
and four pundis for their — and ilk ane of their leitt of peittis
and swa to be frie of all wther service. The rest of the
tennentis in the nether barronie are obleidged for their service
casting and winning of their leittes of peittis, conform to their
assedatiounes, Powbaire onlie excepted, who is to pey money
for their service. And it is declaired that the Montwhich
men their peyment of the four pundis for the leitt of peittis
is in the first end of the yeirlie dewties conteaned in their
assedationes.

It is statute and ordeaned that the haill tennentis macke

---

[1] A clear understanding.

peyment of their Witsonday maillis and silver dewties preceislie
against the terme of Witsonday nixt, vnder the paine of
poynding, etc.

It is statute that the tennentis of the nether barronie shall
keip the smiddie att Cransacker with Charles Robb, smith
ther, and work their haill iron work with him—they getting
good service to pey such proportiones of oattis or meill as the
maister, with the tennentis advyse, sall agrie wpone.

The said sevint day off Maij 1669 it is statute and ordeaned
by the Judge foirsaid that the haill tennentis of the nether
barronie of Wrie, immediatlie efter darseing[1] of their bear seid,
ilk pleuch vpon advertisement furnish two men, with ane hors
and cairt, to work att the milne daime of Cowie till the samen
be sufficientlie repaired.   And the pickieman is constituite
officer for chargeing the tennentis, and vpon refusall or
deficiencie and not observaince efter charge lawfullie given to
poynd for thrie pundis Scottis from ilk pleuch swa deficient in
ther dewtie.

It is ordeaned that the haill tennentis that ar deficient in
peyment of the Scholemaisteris ordinare dewtie macke peyment to him of the samen, within terme of law.

The said day Georg Hunter in Tries being called for his
contumacious disobedience to the maisteris commandis in
laboring ane peice of contraverted ground betuixt Tries and
Brachmount, which was ordained to ly vnlabored.

The said George pleading ignorance, and it being found by
the Judge to have beine done vpon wther sinister grounds,
wherwpon the judge haveing tacken the mater to consideratione,
he ordeanes the said ground to ly vnlaboreit in tyme cumeing
till setting of marches, conforme to mutual condescendance,
and for his former disobedience and contempt of his maisteris
commandis decernes him in the sowme of fortie pundis, to be
peyit to the maister, within terme of law, wnder pane of
poynding.   GEO. THOMSON, Scriba.

---

[1] We have been unable to identify this term, which does not occur in *Jamieson*,
nor in any of the various vocabularies we have had the opportunity of consulting.
It was probably a local expression; but if so, its use has long since been aban-
doned in the district, where it is now absolutely unknown.   Fortunately the
context renders the meaning of the term unmistakable.   The tenants are summoned to do service 'immediatlie efter darseing (or *sowing*) of their bear seid.'

*The Barone Court of Dawid Barcley of Wrie, haldine within
the plaice of Wrie, the 15th day of Januarij the yeir of
God j^m^vj^c^ and sevintie yeires, by Alexander Keith of
Cowtoune, bailzie to the said Dawid. Johne Auchinleck,
notar publict, clerk, George Farfur, officier.
The suittes called and the court laufullie affermit.*

The said day the Judge ordaines and constitutes that ilk
plugh within the nether barronie is to send tuo sufficient men
and tuo horse for home-draweing off the milne stones off the
milne of Cowie at whatsoewer time they ar to be brought home
for the use of the said milne, and sicklyk they ar ordained to
send tuo horse and tuo men for helpeing wp the milne dame,
ilk plughe of the said nether barronie, wpon lawfullie premoni-
tione by the pickieman off the said milne, constitute officier for
that effect, wnder the failzie off sex pundes Scottis, *toties quoties*,
for ilk plugh, and this besyd the cottars and girseman if they
any haw.[1] And the cottars and girseman is to pey ilk on of
them the soum off fourtie schillinge Scottis for their deficiencie
in all tyme comeing. And the pickieman is ordained to giwe
notice to the master off the ground off the severall absenters
imediatlie vnder the failzie off ffourtie schillinge Scottis for ilk
persone that he concealls or giwe no notice therof to his said
master.

It is statute and ordainet that no tennant within the
barronie off Wrie sall at [any] time heirafter cast wp any
suard ground or meddow ground for midding feall[2] or wtherwayes, wnder the paines conteaned in the act off parlament at
ilk tyme they failzie. And in caice any off them pretend they
hawe non, they ar to come to ther master or his factor, who is
to showe them wher they ar to cast in[3] ther severall toumes.[4]
And if any sall brack to advertise ther master and wiolentlie
brack the forsaid act, they are imediatlie to be punished
accordinglie.

Foralsmuch it hes beine the custome off the former actis off

---

[1] Have any.
[2] Turf that is mixed with manure to form a dung heap.—*Jam.*
[3] To make or construct, as in *casting ditches.*
[4] Places into which rubbish or manure is emptied.—*Ibid.*

the courts of this land dischairging all selling off peittes, therffor the said Judge statutes and ordaines that no tennant, cottar, nor grasman, sall presume to sell any peittes off the land in all tyme comeing, without leaw askit and gewen by ther master, wnder the failzie of ten pundes Scottis, *toties quoties*, for ilk fault how oft they sall be fownd to transgress.

The act insert in the former courtis ratified anent the smith that ilk tennant sall keipe the smiddie, providing they gett sufficient service and pey the ordinar dewties thereto, vnder failzie off the dowble off ther dewties to the said smiddie. And in caice the smith sall feall to giwe readie service, the smith, wpon complent maid by the tennant, is to [be] punished by his master.

It is inactit (ewerie tennant being present) that they ar to come and resawe in ther severall proportiones off the land off the haugh [1] and buttes,[2] presentlie in ther masters hand, and ear and labour the samen tymouslie to all farres.[3]

It is inactit that ewerie tennant lyable for leitt peittes sall cast and lead ther severall leitt peittes, halfe leitt or heall leitt, in optione of ther said master, and that tymouslie, ther master aloweing them, according to wse and wont, for ther casting and leading, and peying them, conforme quhich is four pund for ilk leitt off peittes and ane firlott off meill.

It is ordainet that ilk persone within the ground off Wrie being lawfullie sumondit to come to the Barrone Court within the ground, and does failzie to come after they being lawfullie warned, sall pey for ther contumacie the soume off fourtie schillinge Scottis, without they instruct [4] relevant excuses.

Jon. Auchinleck, *Scriba Curiæ*.

The Barroun Court of the Barronie of Vrie perteaneing heritablie to David Barclay of Vrie, holdin within the manour place therof, vpon the tuentie thrid day of Agust j^{m}vj^c sevintie two, by Alexander Keith of Cowtoune,

---

[1] Low-lying flat ground, properly on the border of a river, and such as is sometimes overflowed.—*Jam.*

[2] Small piece of ground disjoined from the adjacent lands.—*Ibid.*

[3] Boundaries; properly ridges marked out by the plough.—*Ibid.*

[4] To prove clearly.—*Ibid.*

bailȝie, Georg Thomson, nottar Clerk, Thomas Kergie,
officer, James Melvall, Dempster.

The which day David and James Wyes in Woodheid, Walter
Wilson at Milne of Cowie, Alexander and James Lyell in
Cairnetonne and maines of Vrie, being personallie present,
Alexander Wyllie in Powbair, Issobell Wyllie in Magray,
Janet Rollock, relict of John Auchenleck, for the said rowme
of Magray, being lawfullie warned to ther dyet, and it being
holdin furth be the said David Barclay to the said Alexander
Keith, bailyie, that he haveing requyred and desyred his
tennentis afoirsaid tymeouslie to have peyit in their meill and
bear ferme for the crope jᵐvjᶜ sevintie one last past, and had
promised to have helped them who soe peyit in their bollis
with victuall in sarins[1] at the merchantis pryce.   Notwithstanding quherof the foirnamed persones, and ilk ane of them, wer
resting seuerall bollis of beare and meill for the said crope, and
therfor craveing they might be decerned to pey such pryces
therfoir as he haid receaved for the rest of his ferme victuall
crope foirsaid, Viz.: Tenne merkis for ilk boll of beare and
sex pundis for ilk boll of meill, and that preceislie befor or at
the terme of Martimes nixt to come.

Which desyre being by the foirsaid bailyie considdered and
found reasonable, and the tennentis present haveing noething
to object in the contrair, he decerned and decernes ilk ane of
saidis tennentis for ther awine pairtis to satisfie and pey to
their said maister the foirsaid sowme of tenne merkis Scotts for
ilk rest boll of beare and sex pundis money foirsaid for ilk rest
boll of meill dew be them for the crope forsaid, and that preceislie at or befoir the said terme of Martimes nixt to come,
vnder the pane of poynding of their readiest goodis and geir.

Sicklyke, complaint being maid by the gardner that some
people within the ground did break the orchard dykes and
steall furth therof turnepes and carrottis and wther rootis; It
is therfor inacted by the Judge foirsaid that whoever shall be
found guiltie of the cryme forsaid and convict therof sall be
punished and fyned, conforme to the acts of parliament, and
the ground officer to poynd therfor.   AL. KEITH,

GEO. THOMSON, *Scriba Curiæ.*

---

[1] Services of food for a man or beast.—*Jam.*

The Barronie Court of the lands and barronie of Urie, belong-
ing heretablie to David Barclay, holdine within the
Manour place of Urie vpone the eightene day of Maij
j^mvj^c sevintie four yeires, be Alexander Keith of Cowtoune,
bailyie, George Thomsone, nottar Clerk, Thomas Kergie,
officiar, William Carnegie, Dempster.
Sectis vocatis Curia legittima affirmata.

The whilk day compt and reckoning being maid betwixt the
said David Barclay and Walter Wilsone, his tennent at the
milne of Cowie, for his bygone rest dewtie 1673, And it is
found by Walter, his awine confessione, that he is resting eight
bollis beare, thrie firlottis and tuo pecks meill, and thrie scoir
pundis money, wherof the Judge foirsaid ordeanes the said
Walter to mack peyment to his master within fyifteine dayes,
vnder the paine of poynding of his readiest guidis and geir,
and failyieng of peyment at the day foirsaid decernes him to
pey sex pundis fyve shillinge for ilk boll of beare, and such
pryce for the meill as he gettis from wtheris to whome he sellis
the same.

Sicklyke, compt and reckoning being maid with Alexander
Wyis in Woodheid. The said Alexander acknowledges he is
resting four bollis meill crope 1673, wherof the bailzie ordeanes
him to make peyment to his master within fyifteine dayes,
vnder paine off poynding, at such rate and pryce as the said
David Barclay, his said maister, gettis for the rest of his meil.

James Presho in Magray haveing beine lawfullie summoned
to this dyet of court oft tymes called and not compeirand, the
said David Barclay declaired to the judge foirsaid that he had
set vp accompt with the said James sincerlie, and he was
trewlie resting thrie bollis beare of the crope 1672 and
eighteine bollis beare for the crop 1673, wherof the bailyie
ordeanes the said James Preschoe to make peyment to his said
maister within fyifteine dayes, vnder paine of poynding, and
failyieing of peyment at the day foirsaid sex pundis fyve
shillinges for ilk boll of the said beare, both cropes.

The said day Walter Wilsone, David and Alexander Wyiss,
being removeing tennentis, are with their awine consentis
ordeaned to cast and wine the leit peittis for this yeir 1674,

and the incumeing tennent ordeaned to lead the samen, for
which the caster and winner is to have the ordinar allowance of
meill and the leader of the peittis the money, and this forme
is ordeaned to be keiped amongst the tennentis of the saidis
landis as to outgoer and incomer in tyme comeing.

The said day the ground maister, considdering the trouble
the tennentis ar at in vpholding the milne dame, moved to [1]
these that wer present befor the judge what they wer willing
to give yeirlie to the miller to wphold their proportiones of the
said milne dame, and they frielie offered ane firlot of meill
yeirlie for ilk pleuch, and theirfor the judge decernes ilk pleuch
to pey the said miller yeirlie ane firlot of meill for wpholding
their proportione of the said dame. And the cotter and grasmen
to be lyable in halff ane peck ilk ane of them theirof.

The said day it is, with consent of the tennentis present and
William Gibbon, entring tennent at the milne of Cowie,
ordeaned by the judge foirsaid that the pickieman at the said
milne shall have ane cogill [2] of meill for grinding fyve peckis of
shilling or malt, keiping the peck as formerlie, and this by and
attour the tennentis guidwill at their owne pleassour to the
pickieman, his servant, for such service as he sall doe to them.

The said day the tennentis present, of their awine consent,
are ordeaned ilk pleuch to pay tenne merkis yeirlie for their
service as formerlie in caice they satisfie nocht the laird with
corne and fodder for the same.   AL. KEITH,

GEO. THOMSON, *Scriba Curiæ.*

14 *March* 1679.

*Court of the landes and baronie of Wrie, belonging heritablie
to David and Robert Barclayes, holdine be the said Robert,
personallie present, by Johne Erskine in Glithnoe, bailzie,
within George Selbie, fuller at the manor place. George
Thomsone, notter publict, Clerke of Court, Thomas
Ke[rgie], offi[ciar], and   , Dempster.*
The Court being laufullie affirmed.

The said day the Judge forsaid ordaines the heall tennentis

---

[1] Asked.

[2] A measure used at mills containing the fourth part of a peck.—*Jam.*

of the barrony of Wrie to lead and carrie to the mill of Cowie ilke plewch ffour wyises[1] of strae for thatching of the said mill, and that betwixt and the last of March instant, wnder the failzie of tuelff pennies ilk wyise, and ordaines the saids tennentis, wpon William Gibones advertisement, to carie to the said mill the trees that lye at Reedcloake for the wse of the said mill, and that wnder the failzie of tuentie shilling Scotes to be peyed by the refuseris wpon the said adverticement.

Jo. Erskine, bealie.
Geo. Thomsone, <i>N.P., Clericus Curiæ.</i></div>

24 March 1679.

The said day ane compleant being given in by Thomas Kergie, plentive, for and in name of James Baginet in Muchallis, and gave in the said compleant against James Melvine, servitor to George Selbie, fuller, at the walke mill of Wrie, showing wheras ther being some wordes passing betwixt the saids parties, they bothe straike and bett ilke ane another within the said George Selbie his house. And the said James Melvine, compeiring personallie, acknowledged the stricking of the said James Baginet, in respecte wherof the said John Erskine amerciat the said James Melvine in ane wnlaw of ten pounds and in the assythment of 40 shilling to the said James Baginet for the wrong sustained by him, and peyment to be maid therof within terme of law, and executione to pas heirone in forme as effieris.

Jo. Erskine, bealie.
Geo. Thomsone, <i>N.P., Cls. Curiæ.</i></div>

24 Martij 1679.

The said day compeired Thomas Kergie, procurator for Robert Murray, residenter in Newcastell, and gave in ane clame at the instance of the said Robert against the said James Melvine for peyment macking to him of the soume of tenn merkis Scotis money. The said James compeiring, acknouleidgit the forsaid clame, in respect quherof the said John Erskine, bailzie, decernet the said James Melvine to pey and satisffie the samen, And lyikwayes decerned the said

---

[1] Trusses.

George Selbie, who compeiring lykways and confessing to be
debiter to the said Robert Murray therof at the said George
his terme of peyment, wherto the said James assented, and
whervpone the said Judge interpones his authoritie.

Jo. Erskine, *bealie*,

Geo. Thomsone, *Clericus Curiæ*.

Wrie, 29 *July* 1682.

The haill tennenties of Montquheich being conveined, they
and everie one of them amicablie concord and condiscend to
lead this instant yeir ane leit of peates out of the latch of
Glithnoe and moss of Cairntoune, quhich are castine by the
laird, and to carrie the same to the peat hill of Wrie betwixt
and the eight day of Agust nixt, and everie plewch condiscend
to furnish three horss till the said leit beis ledd, For quhich the
laird is to furnish mans meat and hors meat, and this noewayes
to infer any preparative of yeirlie service of such nature.

Da. Barclay.

Alexr. Mowatt, *bcyclie*.

Curia terrarum et Baroniæ de Wrie, tenta in Manericj loco
ejusdem vigesimo nono die mensis Julij millesimo sexcen-
tesimo octuagesimo secundo per Allexandrum Mowat in
Reedcloake, ballivum honorabilium virorum Davidis et
Robertj Barclayes de Wrie, Georgium Thomsone, notarium
publicum, Scribam curiæ, Thomam Kergie, officiarium, et
Jacobum Sinclair, Dempsterum. Sectis vocatis Curia
legittime affirmata.

The said [day] in presence of the said David Barclay and
his said balzie and als the heall tennentis of the baronies of
Wrie and Montwheich being personallie present, the Laird
and balzie ordained the heall tennentis of both baronies to set
and plant trees yeirlie in their respective yeardes, to wit, ashes,
plaines, birkes, fir or rountrie, geintrie, To wit everie husband-
mane yeirlie sex trees, every cottar three, and everie grasman
two trees yeirlie, and that wnder the failzie of eight poundis
everie husbandman, everie cottar ffourtie shilling, and every
grasman twentie shilling, whilkis trees, of the qualities for-

saidis, the saidis tennentis are ordained to come and receive from the Laird or his gairdner yeirlie at Michalmas and March, begining at Michalmas nixt, in the yeire of God above wreittin, and swa to continue during the tacks, wherof the heall tennentis acceptes.

DA. BARCLAY.

ALEXR. MOWATT, *beylie.*

GEO. THOMSON, *Scriba Curiæ.*

At Wrie the twentie nynt day of Julij j^m vj^c eightie two yeires.

The said day John Mowat in Rothnicke, being persewed at the instance of Alexander Thom in Balnagight for the alleadged wrongous clipping and marking of ane wedder[1] belonging to the said Alexander, which, being exameined, the said Alexander Thom declaired the said wedder was strayed and away from the rest of his sheep the speace of eight dayes, and he, macking inquerie therfor, ffound his said sheep pasturing promiscuouslie amongest the said John Mowates sheepe and otheris in the hill, and that his sheep was clipped and marked with the said John Mowat his sheepes marke, but wold not imput the same to be done aither be the said John nor his servantes. The said John Mowat compeiring judicieallie and interrogat annent the premisses, the bailzie, instead of ane farder probatione, remitted the same to his oath of veritie simpliciter, who deponed solemnlie that he, his wyff, bairnes, nor servantis, to his knowledge, never clipped nor marked the said sheep directlie nor indirectlie. Wherwpon the bailzie absolves the said John Mowat from the forsaid alleadged cryme, and ordaines Thom to intromet with his awine sheep, and to dispone theirone at his pleassour.

ALEXR. MOWATT, *beyelie.*

GEO. THOMSONE, *Scriba Curiæ.*

Court of the lands and Barony of Wrie and Montgwheich pertaining to Collonell Dawid Barcklay of Wrie and Robert Barclay, fiar[2] therof, holdine at Wrie in presence

---

[1] It is still the custom in certain districts for owners to distinguish sheep which are fed on common pasturage by cutting or 'clipping' each his private mark upon the ears of those which belong to him.

[2] One who has the reversion of property.—*Jam.*

of the said Robert Barcklay, upon the twentie eight day
of Januarij j^m vj^c eightie four yeires, by John Erskine
in Glithnoe, balzie, George Thomsone, notar publict,
Clerke of Court, Ja. Sinclair, Phiscull, Thomas Kergie,
officiar, and   Dempster, Ja. Sinclair,
Fiscall.   Sectis vocatis curie legittime affirmata.

The which day the judge forsaid, taiking to consideratione
ane compleant given in befor him be the said James Sinclair,
procurator fiscall, against William Gibons at mill of Cowie,
William Gibons younger ther, John Cruishanke ther, William
Mowat in Trees, Allexander Wylie in Powbair, William
Mowat in Rothnicke, Hugh Mowat at Mill of Monthqwheich,
James Gordoune in Rothnicke, James Broune in Magray,
William Falconar in Glithnoe, and Allexander Mowat in
Crosley, ffor ilke ane of the foirnamed persones ther transgressing his Majesties actis of parliament in carrying of gunes,
pistoless, and other fyre ingynes, and for killing of hares,
doves, partriges, duke and draike, and otheris forbidden be
the saids, and particularlie the fyifteint parliament of King
James the Sext, cap. 248, and the other actes maid against
the saids forbidden ffoullis, Ilke ane of the foirnamed persones
compeiring personallie acknowledged ther having off gunnes,
and that they had killed ffoullis and haires and otheris prohibited be the actes of parliament.   The saids Hugh Mowat
and James Gordoune acknowledged having off gunnes and
grewhound dogs wherwith they had killed haires, etc.

The said balzie, taiking the fforsaids confessiones to his
consideratione, and efter revising the saids actes of parliament,
Decerned and decernes ilke ane of the foirnamed persones in
ane wnlaw of ten pounds Scotes money, and ordaines the saids
actes to be put to executione, conform to the tenor theroff,
and to delyver wp ther severall gunes, pistolets, or other ffire
ingynes they have in ther custodyes to the saids Collonell
David and Robert Barclayes immediatlie, and this present act
to be put in executione in forme as effieris, and ilke ane of
them to flind cautione conform to the actes off parliament.

R. BARCLAY.   Jo. ERSKINE, *baylie.*
                                     GEO. THOMSONE, *N.P.,*
                                          Cls. Curiæ.

28 *January* 1684.

Ordaines the heall tennents that they doe not in any tyme heirefter carry with horss or otherwayes any peats to Stonhyve, wnder the falzie off **tenn** pounds, without libertie of the master.   Jo. Erskine, *Baily.*

*Court of the lands and Barony of Wrie and Montqwheich, belonging to Robert Barclay of Wrie, holdine within the Manor place of Wrie be John Erskine in Glithnoc, bailzie, George Thomson, notar publict, Clerke of Court, Thomas Kergie, officiar, and   Dempster, this threttie day of December j*m* vj*c eightie nyne yeires. The suitis called and the Court laufullie fenced and affirmed.*

The said day the said Robert Barclay of Wrie and his said bailzie taiking to ther consideratione the great burdence of quartering of trouperis and souldieris wpon the lands of Mill of Cowie, Magray, Powbair, Woodhead, and Glithnoe, in ther transeunt quarteris, and that the tounes and lands of Crossley, Rothnike, Mill of Montqwheich, Burnhauch, Trees, and Balnagight are frie of the saids transeunt quarterings, therfor that the saids laigh roumes above mentioned mey be eased of ther burdeine of furnishing baggadge horss to souldieris and trouperis when quartering occurres in tyme comeing, it is statute, apoynted, and ordained that the saids wpper toones and lands furnish for transporting baggadge tenn horss, To wit, Crossley one horss, Rothnik thre hors, Mill of Montqwheich one hors, Trees and Burnhaugh three horss, Glithnoe and Balnagight two horss, and ordaines William Durie, Wm. Knollis, and Alexander Lyell, wpon adverticement from William Gibons or Allexander Wylie, to goe imediatly efter adverticement as said is to the saids wpper roumes wpon night or day, and to order the saids lands to bring furth ther horss proportionallie as they are appoynted to Stonhyve against the particular hour wherto they are adverticed, with such furniture as shall be ordained, begining first at Rothnik and Crossley, nixt Mill of Montqwheich, Burnhaugh, and Trees, and lastly Glithnoe and Balnagight, and swa furth circuitlie

by turnes, that non mey be burdeined be otheris;[1] and in caice
of the recusantis or not tymeus comeing wp to Stonhyve
against the hour appoynted, the failzieris are heirby enacted
and decerned in ane wnlaw of ten merkis *toties quoties* they
faill in ther respective obedience and performances, and ordaines
poynding to pas heirone as effieris, and in respect Glithmoe is
sometimes burdened with quartering, therfor ordaines the
saids premonisheris to ease the said toune (when quartered
wpon) of anie hors at that tyme.

R. BARCLAY.

JON. ERSKIN, *Bealyie.*

GEO. THOMSONE, *N.P., Scriba Curie.*

Octavo February 1692.

*Court of the lands and Barrony of Wry, perteining heritably
to Robert Barclay of Wry, holdin within the said
Manour place, in presence of the said Robert, by William
Gibone at Mill of Cowie, Balzie, chosen to the said court,
Alexander Wylie in Powbair, procuratour Fiscall,
George Thomsone, nottar publict, Clerke of Court,
Thomas Kergie, officiar, and   Dempster.
The suittis called and the court laufullie affenced.*

The which day the said Balzie taiking to his serius consideratione and compleant givein in befor him at the instance
of the said procuratour fiscall against George Mowat in Trees,
William Mowat in Rothnicke, James Broune in Magray,
Alexander Broune in Woodhead, James Haig, gairdner at Wry,
George Knoullis in Kairntoune, James Lightoune in Woodhead, Andro Melvine in Maines of Wrie, Johne Melvine ther,
William Binnie ther, who being all sumoned and personallie
apprehended and sicklyike compeirand to answer to the poyntis
of the said procuratour fiscall his said compleant given in this
day and plaice—That is to say, for transgressing the severall
lawes and actis of parliament, and particularlie the fifteint
parliament of King James the Sext, capt. 248, wherby the
killing of haires, doves, partriges, moorefoullis, duke and
draike, and otheris therein specifeit, are expresslie prohibited

---

[1] More than others.

to be killed with gunns, pistollis, stamps, girnes, or such other ingynes, wnder the paines and penalties expresslie therin set doune, and the heall foirnamed persoines, personallie present, being by the said judge interrogat anent the premisses, they and ilke ane of them acknowledged and confessit the killing of hairis with gunes and other ingynes. The saids **George Mowat,** James Broune, Andro Melvine, William Mowat, James Haig, sicklyike acknouledged ther killing of moore foullis and par- triges with gunnes, which poyntis of dittay the said balzie haveing advyised and being therwith reaplie informed be the heall foirnamed persones ther above written confessiones, finds ther heall moveablis to become escheat in respect of the carry- ing of gunns, ordaining the saids gunns to be delyvered up to ther said **master,** and decernes ilke ane of them in the soume of twentie merkis less or more, appoynted to be peyed be ilke ane of them for killing of the saids haires and wild foullis, and therfor decerned and ordained, and heirby decernes and ordaines peyment of the saids fynes to be made within terme of law, with certificatione as effieris, and ordaines the clerke of Court to extract precepts for the causses forsaids in forme as effieris. In testimonie wherof the said balzie hes heirto inter- poned his autoritie and subscryvit thir presentis with the said Robert Barclay and clerke of court, etc.

R. BARCLAY.

WILL. GIBON, *baillzie.*

GEO. THOMSONE, *N.P., Clericus Curie.*

Court of the lands and baronie of Wrie, holdine within the manor place therof wpon the nynt day of Apryll j^m vj^c nyntie two yeiris, by William Gibone at Mill of Cowie, balzie to ane honorable gentleman Robert Barclay of Wry, George Thomsone, nottar publict, clerke of Court, Allexander Wylie in Powbair, procurator Fiscall, Thomas Kairgie, officiar, and   Dempster. Sectis vocatis Curia legittime affirmata.

The whilke day the said Allexander Wylie, procurator fiscall, gave in ane Indytment against John Buchane, in Magray, for his stealing and away taiking of certaine peattis furth of the

peat stackis of Allexander Burnet, in Cowie, some tymes bygane. The said John Buchane, being cited to this day and
place, compeiring personallie and interrogat annent the said
thift and cryme, he judiciallie acknowledged that he helped
and assisted his wyf to carrie away ane backe burdeine of the
said Allexander Burnet his peattis, and that he carried away
ane burdeine of some person's peatis furth of the moss himself,
but knew not to whom the same pertained, and that he hade
severall tymes carried away gathrings of lairis[1] of peatis of
other persones furth of the moss, but never anie more belonging to Allexander Burnet. The said bailzie taiking the said
John his confessione to consideratione, he fyns and amerciatis
the said John Buchane in ane wnlaw of twentie pounds Scotis,
and to give satisfactione to the said Allexander Burnet at the
said Robert Barclay or his said balzie's arbitrement, and
ordanis precepts to be direct heirone as effieris. In witnes
wherof the said balzie and clerke have subscrivit thir presentis,
and inacts and statutes, in caice any such ryotis shall heirefter be done in the ground, that the persons found guyltie
shall be imediatly removed fra ther possessions, and put in the
Shereff's hands for ther ffynes.

> WILL. GIBON, *balzie.*
> GEO. THOMSONE, *N.P. Clericus Curie.*

*Barrone Court of the lands and baronie of Wrie, pertaineing
heretablie to ane honorable gentleman Robert Barclay of
Wrie, heretable proprietar therof, holden within the great
hall of Urie, upon the tuentie fourth day of May $j^m vj^c$
nyntie eight yearis, in presence of the said Robert Barclay, by James Thomsone in Stonhyve, balzie. George
Thomsone, nottar publict, clerk of court. John Buchan,
officer. William Gibone at Mill of Stonhive, procurator
Fiscall, and   Dempster. Sectis
vocatis curia legittime affirmata.*

The which day the said Robert Barclay, in obedience to the
Councillis proclamatione emitted for mantaineing of the poor
within this kingdom, ordaineing and appoynting the heritors,

---

[1] Places for spreading peats to dry.—*Jam.*

ministers, and kirk-sessione of the respective parishes within
the samen, to appoynt provisione for the severall poore within
ther particular parishes, as the said act bearis. In obedience
to which the haill heritoris within the parish of Fetteresso
haveing unanimouslie, with concourse of the minister, elders,
and kirksessione of the said parish, aggreed wpon and condi-
scended that ilk ane of them shall maintaine the poor within
thair particular lands by themselfes and thair tenents, and to
give badges [1] to such as are travelling within ther own grounds.
Therfor the said Robert Barclay and his said balzie appoynts
and ordans ane peck and ane half peck of meall to be given
weekly to Rachel Lightoune, in Glithno, blind woman, and
ane servant to attend her. Sicklyke appoynts half ane peck
of meall weekly to be given to Alexander Burnet, in Powbair,
his children, and ordains badges to be given to the persones
following, Viz'., Isobell Murray in Glithno, Marioun Ritchie
thair, tuo children of Alexander Burnetis thair, Margaret
Boys in Magro, and George Mill at Mill of Montwheich, and
ordainis half ane peck of meall weekly to Margaret Lyell and
her children, which quantity of victuall to be given out to
beddells,[2] extends to weekly two peckis half peck meall, and
ordains the saids beddalls to begin at William Giboue at Mill
of Cowie, and receave from him the saids tuo pecks half peck
meall, commenseing upon the tuentie thrid of May instant,
which compleits his peyment to them for fyftine weekis nixt
therafter; 2dly, appoynts them to goe to James Brown in
Maigroe, and ther to receave the like quantity for the subsequent week, which compleitis his payment for the space
forsaid; 3dly, appoyntis them to goe to Powbair, and ther
to receave fyve peckis meall, which compleitis Janet Mowat
ther her payment for tuo weeks, for the space of fyftine weeks
therafter; 4tly, to goe to the Mains of Urie to the laird
himself, and ther to receave the like fyve pecks, which com-

---

[1] The 'beggar's badge' conferred the right to solicit alms within a certain
district. It was generally made of pewter, and bore, in addition to the name of
the parish from which it was issued, a number corresponding to that which the
recipient held in the parish alms-book. The Fetteresso badges are of copper.
They are oval in form, and measure 3 inches by 4½ inches.

[2] Licensed beggars.

pleits his payment for tuo weeks to them for the said space of
fyftine weeks; 5tly, to goe to Balnagight, ther to receave 2
pecks half peck meall, which compleits his payment for one
week to him for the said space; 6tly, to Glithno 2 pecks half
peck meall for the said space; 7tly, Rothnike 5 pecks for tuo
weeks, compleiting as afforsaid; 8tly, Crossley 2 pecks half
peck meall for one week, compleiting as said is, includeing
Mill of Montwheich; 9tly, Burnhaugh 2 pecks half peck for
one week, compleiting as said is; 10tly, Trees 2 pecks half
peck for one week, compleiting as said is; 11^{ly}, Woodheads a
2 pecks half peck for one week, which compleits as afforsaid.
The said balzie ordains the said method and order to be keept
in tyme comeing, aye and till the counsell shall rescind ther forsaid act; and whoever shall be deficient or disobedient to give in
thair forsaides contributiones weekly, in maner above appoynted,
amerciatis the deficient in the double of the quantity, and
executione to pass heiron as effeiris, wherunto the said bailzie
interpones his authority.   JA. THOMSONE, *baylie.*

GEO. THOMSONE, *Clericus.*

Urie the tuentie fourth day of May 1698 *years.*

The said day anent ane complent given in by William
Gibone, at Mill of Cowie, against the haill tennents within the
sucken of the said Mill, for ther abstracting of ane great
quantity of ther grindable grane of the said Mill. The said
balzie enacts and ordains ilk ane of the saids tennents to compone and aggree with the said William Gibone within fyftine
days after this date, otherwayes decernitur conforme to his
clame; and als statuts and ordains that noe persone nor persons within the said Mill sucken, shall abstract any of ther
grindable grane from the said mill in tyme comeing, under the
pain of the double of the quantity and quality of the said
grane suae abstracted, and shall be oblidged to make faith
theranent, otherwayes decerniture,[1] wherto the said balzie
interpones his authority.

JA. THOMSONE, *baylie.*

GEO. THOMSONE, *Cls.*

---

[1] A decree or sentence of a court, sometimes as enforcing payment of a debt.
—*Jam.*

The said day Hugh Mowat, at Mill of Montwheich, gave in
the like complent against the tennentis within the sucken of
the Mill. The said balzie considering the samen statuts,
enacts, decerns, and ordains, in maner and conforme the forsaid
decernitur past in favours of the forsaid William Gibone, and
ordains executioune to pass heiron as effeirs, wherunto the said
balzie interpones his authority.

JA. THOMSON, <i>Baylie.</i>
GEO. THOMSONE, <i>Cls.</i>

Urie, the 24 May 1698 yearis.

The said day the said balzie statuts, enacts, and ordains that
non of the subtenentis of the toune and lands of Glithnoe shall
cast, won, lead, transport, or away carie, or sell, any peats furth
of the latch of Glithnoe, moss or banks therof, in any tyme
comeing, and particularlie from putting of any peatis in stackis
or selling any to the toune of Stonhive, or any other persone
or place whatsomever, under the penaltie of ten pounds, <i>toties
quoties</i> any person shall be found guilty therof, permitting and
excaipting alwayes James Smith, cotterman in Glithnoe, to
cast such peatis therin as may serve him in fire allenerly, without selling any peatis, and ordains executione to pass heiron as
effeiris, whereunto the said balzie interpones his authority.

JA. THOMSONE, <i>baylie.</i>
GEO. THOMSONE, <i>Cls.</i>

Urie, 24 May 1698 yearis.

JAMES THOMSONE, <i>balzie.</i>

The whilk day, anent the actione and cause intented and
perseued at the instance of William Gibone at Mill of Stonhyve, Procuratour Fiscall, of the said Robert his Barone Court
against the persones after mentioned, makeing mentione that
wher by the 6 Act of 6 Session of His Majestie King William
his first parliament it is expresslie statute and ordained that,
from and after the first day of January then next to come all
sorts of meall bought and sold within this kingdome shall be
sold and delivered be weight at 8 ston Troys weight in place

of the boll of Lithgo measure,[1] and soe proportionallie, and
that under the pains contained in the said tack [? Act], And
sicklyke be the 37 Act of the said parliament it is statute and
ordained that in tyme comeing all malt that is sold and
bought within the kingdome shall be delivered with the heap
measure[2] according to the bear firlot of the place wher it is
delivered, certifieing the leiges[3] and under the amerciaments
contained in the saids acts. Nevertheless true it is and of
verity William Gibon at Mill of Cowie and otheris, the
persones underwryttin, within the saids lands and baronie of
Wrie, are guilty of the saids acts made both anent meall and
malt since the saids acts of parliament had prohibit the samen,
the quantities wherof they cannot particularlie condiscend on
at the tyme nor make faith theranent, and therfor the said
William Gibone, Alexander Mackie, his pikieman, Alexander
Broun in Maigroe, Janet Mowat in Powbair, Elizabeth
Douglas in Glithnoe, Alexander Broun and James Edward in
Woodhead, William Mowat in Rothnick, Margaret Wylie
ther, John Wylie in Crossley, Hugh Mowat at Mill of Montwheich, William Thomsone ther, William Duthie in Burnhaugh, George Mowat in Trees, George Troup in Cramsaker,
are not only guilty themselves, but also ther wifes, in selling
particular quantities of the said prohibited victuall, and in
respect the saids persones could not condiscend upon the samen
particular quantities sua sold be them or ther wifes in maner
lybelled be the said procuratour fiscall, the quantities and

---

[1] The Act of King William above referred to aimed at bringing about a
uniform standard of Dry Measures such as had not hitherto prevailed in Scotland.
The nominal standard for meal was the Linlithgow boll, but the capacity of the
actual measures used in the various counties only approximated to the Linlithgow
measure, and hence it was only by discarding these altogether, and substituting
weight for measurement, that an absolute uniformity could be obtained. Eight
stone Troy was therefore constituted the standard boll. A stone Scots Troy, or
Dutch weight, as it was also termed, consisted of 17½ pounds avoirdupois.—
Elgin's *Tables*, p. 16.

[2] *Heap measure* is that in which the measure is *heaped* with the hand till it
can hold no more. It is opposed to *sleaks* or *streeks*, where the measure is only
filled up to the edge of the wood or a little higher.

[3] *Certifieing the leiges*, warning the vassals. Certification means the assurance
given to a party of the course to be pursued in case he disobeys the order of the
court.—Bell's *Law of Scotland*, p. 148.

qualities wherof are more particularlie mentioned and set
doune in the said lybell and indictment: Therefor the said
balzies, takeing ther saids confessions of ther said guilt,
decerned and ordained, and heirby decernes and ordaines them
to make payment to the said procuratour fiscall, informer, of
the double of the value of ilk quantity of the samen suae sold
be them contrar to the saids acts of parliament, and ordains
incarceratione of ther persones at the said Robert Barclay his
pleasure, and ordains all executione to pass against them in
forme as effeiris, wherunto the said judge and ballzie hes
interponed, and heirby interpones, ther authority, and which
act is subscryvit be the said Robert Barclay.

R. BARCLAY.

JA. THOMSONE, *baylie*.

GEO. THOMSONE, *Cls.*

Court of the lands and baronie of Urie, holden within the
manor place therof, upon the tuentie seventh day of May
1698 yearis, by James Thomsone in Stonhive, balzie to
Robert Barclay of Urie, heritable proprietar of the said
lands and baronie therof, in his personall presence;
George Thomsone, nottar publict, Clerk of Court, Johne
Davine in Stonhyve, Procuratour Fiscall, John Buchan,
officer and Dempster.
The Sutes being called, the Court laufullie affirmed.

The quhilk day, in presence of the said Robert Barclay of
Urie, the said John Davin, procurator fiscall, gave in ane
lybell and indictment against John Knows, servitor to William
Knows in Urie, mentioneing wheras the said John Knows was
ane commune and notour thieff by stealing certane cloaths and
other particulars furth of the house of Springhall, and particularly ane pair of sheets and several clews of yearne[1] furth
of the said house, and being laufully summoned be the said
ground officer to have compeared this day and place to have
answered befor the said judge at the instance of the said
procurator fiscall to underly the law for the forsaid crime of
thift, the said John Knows being oft tymes called and not

---

[1] Balls of thread.

compeirand, the said judge and balzie fund him guilty of thift,
and declares him fugitive and outlaw, and ordains his haill
moveable goods and gear to be escheat and inbrought to the
said fiscall his use for the said John his contempt and disobedience, and ordains his persone to be apprehended in caice
he shall be found within the said baronie of Urie and brought
to condigne punishment for the said crime, and ordains all
executioun necessar to pass heiron as effeiris.

R. Barclay.
Ja. Thomsone, baylie.
Geo. Thomsone, Cls.

> *Barone Court of the lands and Baronie of Urie pertenning
> heritablie to Robert Barclay of Urie, holden within the
> great hall of the manor place therof, in the personall pre-
> sence of the said Robert Barclay, wpon the tuentie two
> day of March j^mvj^c nyntie nyne yearis, by James
> Thomsone in Stonhyve, Balzie, George Thomsone, notar
> publict, Clerke of Court, William Gibone at Mill of
> Cowie, Procurator Fiscall, William Gray, Officer and
> Dempster.*

The suits called and Court affirmed.

The which day the judge and balzie, haveing heard ane
compleant given in be the said procurator fiscall and Helen
Buchane in Glithnoe against Allexander Duncane in Glithnoe
ffor the said Allexander his stealling of cornes with the fodder
off from the goodwyif of Glithnoes land last harvest. The
said Allexander, compeiring personally, denyed the samen, and
creaved witnesses might be adduced in the said mater. The
said Helen Buchane alleadgit that Margaret Findlay, servant
to the said Allexander Duncan sayd that he had taiken the
saids cornes above uryttin, which alleadgeance being taiken to
the balzies consideratione, amerciats the said Helen in ten
pounds Scots money.

R. Barclay,
Ja. Thomsone.
Geo. Thomsone, Cls.

The said day being the tuentie secund day of March j^m vj^c
nyntie nyne, in presence of the said James Thomson, balzie,

the said Allexander Duncane being conveined for alleadgeing
that Helen Buchane and her sister had plucked his keall and
wer guyiltie of the stealling of two ewes he then wanted. The
said Allexander confessed he had sayd they had stollen his
keall, but could not approve the samen. Wherfor the said
balzie amerciats him in ten pounds for his forsaid alleadgeance,
and failzieing to approve the same. And as to the woole of the
ewes, compeired George Troup in Cransaker, examined theranent, declaired that Allexander Duncane did say that he
suspected none for the thift of his ewes but Helen Buchane,
Marjory Richie, her mother, and her sister. The said Allexander being interrogat whither he could approve the samen or
not, he declaired he could not, and therfor amerciat him in
other ten pounds. And in the mean tyme the said laird of
Ury and his balzie ordaines the said Marjory Richie and her
daughteris to flit and remove themselffs furth of the lands of
Ury within tuentie four houris, otherways the laird wold
ordaine them to be carryed to the theefs hole[1] at Stonhyve,
besyd what other punishment he should inflict.

R. Barclay.
Ja. Thomsone.
Geo. Thomsone, <i>Cls.</i>

The said day Allexander Duncane within designed being
conveined for stealing of grass and pasturaig with his horss
within the lairds Hainings and deikis in sumer last, he compeired and acknouleidged the samen, wherfor the balzie
amerciats and fynes him in the soume of ten pounds Scotis
money, and statutis and ordaines in caice the said Allexander
shall at any tyme comeing be found with his bestiall, or that it
cane be approven against him that he shall distroy the lairds
grass, or the goodwyf of Glithnoes, but wher he is or may be
privieledged be her, he shall pey the soume of ten pounds
toties quoties he shall be found guyltie.   R. Barclay.

Ja. Thomsone.

The said day amerciats William Gray at the mill of Cowie
in the soume of ffourtie shilling for killing of dooves within

---

[1] The common prison. It was popularly known all over Scotland by this
designation.

the bounds of the lairds ducat. And also amerciats James
Edward in Woodhead and James Walker in Magray in the
soume of ten pounds the peece[1] for killing of salmon and
smoutis within his wateris this winter, and ordaines them to
bring in ther spearis[2] to the laird. And in caice any persone
shall be found guyltie of killing of dooves or fishes within his
wateris in tyme comeing, they are heirby fyned ilke persone
guyltie in the soume of ten pounds *toties quoties* without
libertie grantet.   R. BARCLAY.
                                      JA. THOMSONE.

The said day the balzie prohibits all tennentis, cottaris,
grassmen, and otheris within the lands of Ury not to harbour
or recept within ther houssis any beggeris whatsomever over
one night, wnder the penaltie of fourtie shilling Scotis *toties
quoties*. And in caice any persone shall be found to have in
ther custodie anie suspect goodes, wherannent they cannot
prove the buying of the said goodes by honest witnesses who
saw them buy the samen, the persone soe guiltie shall be holden
and repute as theefs, and punished according to law, and proceeded against therfor as accords. And whatever goodes shall
be offered to [? by] any person that may be suspect infamous,
the persone who shall get the goods offered to them are heirby
enacted to bring the same to the laird, wnder the penalty of
ffour pounds *toties quoties*.
                R. BARCLAY.   JA. THOMSONE.
                                   GEO. THOMSONE, *Cls.*

22 *March* 1699.—Allexander Duncane requyred to make
peyment of his amerciamentis, etc.

*Court of the lands and Barony of Ury, pertaining heretablie
    to Robert Barclay of Ury, holden at the Manor place
    theroff the tenth day of May one thousand seven hundreth*

---

[1] Each.

[2] The above tenants had evidently been guilty of *leistering*. This sport, which
was very popular in many districts of Scotland till a recent date, and which was
known in the Lowland counties as 'burning the water,' was usually engaged in
under cover of night. A torch was held above the pool where the salmon were
supposed to be lying, and the fish running towards the light, were struck with
spears or *leisters*. Scott, in *Guy Mannering*, chap. xxvi., describes the sport.

*and one yeiris, by James Thomsone, Balzie, George
Thomsone, notar publict, Clerke of Court, William
Gibone, Procurator Fiscall, Thomas Scott, officer, and
Dempster. Sectis vocatis Curia
legittime affirmata.*

The said day the said Robert Barclay, considering his leet
peats, as they are now peyable and built on the stacke hill of
Ury doe not sufficiently winne and dry, creaved that the
tenentis might condiscend to build ther leitis in the terms
following, viz.: That ilke leet of peats shall consist of ten
ellis and ane half of length and three ellis of breadth. The
heall tenentis present condiscend to build ther respective leitis
proportionally to ten ellis of length and three ellis of breadth,
and to cover the same sufficiently with turff within fourteine
dayes, as weather serves, after building of the saids leitis,
wherwith the laird, tennentis, and balzie are content, and
ordaines this present act to continue in tyme coming.

R. BARCLAY.
JA. THOMSONE, *baylie.*

The said day the said balzie statutes enacts and ordaines
that considering the laird of Ury hath beine at a considerable
charge and expensse in building of deikis and inclosuris for
preservatione of grass and trees planted therin, amerciats ilke
persone whose sheepe shall hapin to leape the saids inclosuris,
except in tyme of snowie wreathes, shall pey fourtie penies for
ilke sheepe *toties quoties*, the deike being sufficiently coped
with stons, and als amerciatis ilke tennent, cottar, grasman,
and servant within the ground shall happine to leape the
inclosuris at any tyme coming, shall pey fourty pennies *toties
quoties*, the master being alwayes lyable for the servantis dilict,
retaining allwayes off the servantis fie the fynes wherin the
servant is culpable, wherinto the balzie interpones his authority.

R. BARCLAY.
JA. THOMSONE, *baylie.*

Ury, 10*th May* 1701.

Statuts inactis and ordaines that noe tennentis whatsomever,
nor subtennentis, shall cast any ley or sward meadow ground

within ther respective possessions, wnder the penalty of
twenty pounds ilke tennent, and ten pound ilke persone
inferior to a tennentis degrie.   R. BARCLAY.

JA. THOMSONE, *baylie.*

The said day amerciatis ilke tennent, cottar, and grassman
who shall happine to cast potts[1] within any of the laird of
Wryes propertie or comountie betwixt him and the Earle
Marischall and the laird of Leyes, shall pey ffour pounds for
ilke pott made by them in any of the saids mosses, property,
or comountie, but what peats they cast therin shall be made
wpe with ane face of ane moss without potting.

R. BARCLAY.

JA. THOMSONE, *baylie.*

GEO. THOMSONE, *Cls. Curie.*

Urie, 10th May 1701.

The said day amerciatis John Mauld in Glithnoe, and
Allexander Duncane ther, ilke ane of them in fyftie poundis
Scotis for mutuall beating and striking of otheris, and ordains
peyment to be made heiroff within fiftein dayes, and precepts
to be direct heirone.   R. BARCLAY.

JA. THOMSONE, *baylie.*

GEO. THOMSONE, *Cls. Curie.*

*Baronie Court of the lands and Baronie of Ury, pertaining
heretablie to Robert Barclay, proprietar of the saids
lands, in his owen presence, holden by Mr. James Keith
of Aqwhorske,[2] Shereff Deput of Kincardyne, balzie,*

---

[1] Moss-holes whence peats have been dug.—*Jam.*

[2] The lands of Aquhorsk formed part of the barony of Kintore in Aberdeenshire, and their possessors, who had held the lands for a very considerable period,
were probably a younger branch of the Keith Mareschal family.   On 1st Nov.
1601, James Keith of Aquhorsk is summoned, under caution of 100 merks, to
answer before the Lords of Secret Council to the challenge made against him by
George, Earl of Marshall, for 'invading certain persons with pistolets.'—*Reg.
Privy Council,* vol. vi. p. 697.   In all likelihood this act of violence on his part
may have been intended to avenge the death of his father, Alexander Keith of
Aquhorsk, who was slain in Aberdeen, 7th June 1584, by the Guidman of
Babithan, Arthur Anderson, burgess in Aberdeen, and Walter Leslie, all of
whom we find obtained a free pardon by deed of Council dated 7th June 1596,
on the ground that the murder of Keith was 'accidental.'—Spalding Club
Miscellany, vol. ii. p. 56 ; *Reg. Privy Council,* vol. v. p. 397.

George Thomsone, notar publict, Clerk of Court,
William Melvine, Procurator Fiscall, Thomas Scott,
officer, and   Dempster. Holden this
twentie second day of May j^m vij^c and five yeiris.
Sectis vocatis Curea legittime affirmata.

The said day the said balzie statutis, enactis, and ordains
that noe tennent, subtennent, cottar, nor grassmen, removeing
from ther respective possessiones within the laird of Uries
lands and heretage, shall pull doune any of ther house wallis
more then fries ther timber, neither pull doune anie of ther
yeard deikis, wnder the penaltie off fourtie pound ilke tennent,
and ten pound ilke subtennent, cottar, and grassmen, by and
attour peyment of the expensses of reparatione.   J. KEITH.

The said day the said balzie statutis, enactis, and ordaines
that the haill tennentis lyable in peyment of leet peatts shall
cast their respective proportions of leets in such moss yeirly as
the laird shall appoynt and ordor, wnder the penalty of fourtie
pound Scots ilk tennent transgressing *toties quoties.*

J. KEITH.

22 May 1705.

The said day the said Balzie enacts and ordains that noe
tennent lead ther leet peets in the night tyme, and that ilke
tennent keepe ther owen larache[1] and wnder moss dry and
levell, under the penaltie of ten pounds *toties quoties*, and that
if any cottaris, grassmen, subtennent, or heardis,[2] or any
otheris, transgress the premisses, whither wnder pretence of
command from the masteris, or any other wayes whatsomever,
without particular order from the laird, ilke cottar, grassman,
heard, or hyreman[3] shall be lyable in fyve pound to the laird
toties quoties, and which fynes are to be made furthcoming by
the masteris out of ther readiest of the hyremen transgressoris
fies, and if cottaris or grasmen, ilke ane of them to be immediatly poynded for the said fyve pound.   J. KEITH.

---

[1] The site of a building.—*Jam.* *Larache* is obviously used in the text to
signify the sole of the ground from which peats have been cut.

[2] Parties whose duty it is to tend cattle.—*Jam.*

[3] A male servant who works for wages.—*Jam.*

The said day the said balzie ordaines ilke tennent within the lards nether baronie of Urie to keep the entering smith his smidie with ther heall iron work and pey ther ordinarie boll, he, the said smith, giveing allwayes good and readie service to the ground, excepting furth heiroff[1] the mill of Cowie, in caice the smith cannot work the mill irons, and that wnder the penaltie of tuentic pounds attour performance.

J. KEITH.

22 May 1705.

The said day the said Balzie amerciats and fynes ilke persone found cutting of wands in willies bog, shall pay fourtie shilling Scots *toties quoties*, ilke master comptable for his servants, and ilke parent for ther childreine.

J. KEITH.

The said day the said Balzie statutis, enactis, and ordaines that ilke tennent within the ground lyable in payment of ferme meall shall pay in to William Gibone, grintall man, ther respective ferme mealls yearly, good and sufficient merchand stuff, and that at eight stone four pound weight ilke boll, and that William Gibone give recepts to the tennentis of the said weight, conforme to eight stone four pound the boll yeirlie in tyme comeing, Wherwnto the said balzie interpones his authoritie, and wherto the heall tennentis consentes.

J. KEITH.
GEO. THOMSONE, Cls.

Barone Court of the lands and Baronie of Urie, comprehend-ing the lands of Montqwheich, pertaining heritablie to Robert Barclay of Urie, holden at Urie the nynteinth day of July j^m vij^c and twelve yeiris, by ane discreet gentleman Master John Raitt of Findlawstoune, Balzie, George Thomsone, notar publict, Clerk of Court, James Thomsone in Stonhyve, Procurator Fiscall, Thomas Scot, officer, and   Dempster.

Sectis vocatis Curea legittime affirmata.

The said day annent ane complaint given in befor the said Balzie at the instance of the procurator ffiscall, who hade

---

[1] *Excepting furth heiroff :* excluding from the above.

advyce from certaine people of the countrie complain to the
laird of Urie that the tennentis, subtennentis, cottaris, grasmen and servantis of the saids lands of Ury this yeire, in tyme
of leading their leit peatts to the peatt hill of Urie, had not
only wrongouslie intrometted with and away tacken severall
other persones peatts, casten in the moss of Cowie neir adjacent
to the saids leit peatts, and carried the samen to mack wp
their leit peattis at Wry, but also it is the forsaids persons
their yeirlie custome and practize soe to do these severall
yeires bygone, and lyikwayes to make comoune roads throw
otheris persones peatts, to the great prejudice of the owneris
therof, and the persones guiltie ought and should be amerchiat
therfor, and the damnadges repaired at the balzies discretion.

Urie, the nynteint day of Julij 1712.

The said day the haill tennentis, subtennentis, cottaris,
grasmen, and servantis being conveined befor the Balzie within
designed for the caussis within expressit, ther was noe persone
found guiltie in stealling of peatts except George Whyt, servant to William Duthie in Burnehaugh, who, after deponing,
confessed, and is fyned in four pound Scots money, and the
said four pound is ordained to lye in his masteris hands of his
fie till the samen be peyed, quherof intimatione is made to
the said William Duthie *apud acta*.   As also amerciats John
Blaber in the soume of ffourtie shilling Scots as guiltie of the
lyik fault, and the same is ordained to be made furthcomand
by Hugh Mowat at mill of Montqwheich, his master, wherof
he was warned at the barr, and sicklyike Robert Spark, servant to William Mowat in Rothnick, is fyned in twentie shilling for the lyike fault, and the same is ordained to be made
furthcomand out of his fie.   Wherwnto the balzie interpones
his authoritie, and ordaines precepts to be direct heiron as
effieris.   Jo. Raitt.

The said day the balzie of new enactis and ordaines that the
heall tennentis lyable in peyment of leitis shall not at any
tyme heirafter lead any leat peatts in the night tyme, and
befor any persone lift his first draught, without his principall

servant present with his horss, for whom the master shall be
answerable, the master shall be fyned and amerciat in twentie
pounds Scots money, how soone any compleant of stealling of
peats is dilated to the laird.   Jo. RAITT.

> GEO. THOMSONE, *Cls.*

19 *July* 1712.

The said day the said balzie statutis, enactis, and ordaines
that noe cottar nor grass man within the land, who shall heirafter
remove from ther respective possessions, shall not hinder nor
impead the entering tennent to labour the emptie ground of
ther kaill yeards at Pasch yeirlie, without doeing prejudice to
the tennent then removeing, and any persone contraveening
the premisses is heirby amerciat in fourtie shilling Scots.

> Jo. RAITT.
>
> GEO. THOMSONE, *Cls.*

The said day the said Balzie statuts, enacts, and ordains that
noe cottar nor grassmen shall at any tyme comeing taike doune
any of the timber of ther office housses, such as barne, byre, or
cott, without first offering the same to the entering tennent for
sale, and that they shall not pull doune the thatch nor walls
therof, wnder the penaltie of ten pound. And in caice the
removeing and the entering tennent cannot agrie betwixt them-
selffis as to the pryces of the timber of the saids housses, it is
heirby ordained that both shall choise two honest men for
maiking the pryce therof, wnder the penaltie above written.

> Jo. RAITT.
>
> GEO. THOMSONE, *Cls., N.P.*

Sward and ley groundis allreadie enacted, 10 May 1701.[1]

Court of the lands and Baronie of Ury pertaining heretablie
to the much honored Robert Barclay of Ury, holden
within the Maner house therof, wpon the second day of
Maij one thousand seven hundred and tuentie yeirs

---

[1] See p. 111, *supra.*

(the said Robert Barclay being personallie present) be
George *Thomson, notar publict in Stonhyve, Bailie,
James Milne, notar publict, Clerk*, **John Souter, Fiscall,**
Thomas Scot, officer, and ,
Dempster.
　　Sectis vocatis Curia legitime affirmata.

The which day compeared John Edward in Munboys, and
gave in ane complaint against John Donald in Springhall,
representing that the said John had medled with and crav'd
right and title to a wedder hog[1] pertaining to him, the said
John Edward. The action being called, both parties personallie present, the said John Edward offered to prove the samen
by witnesses, and having adduced such witnesses as were
summoned for that effect, they declined to give their oaths of
veritie theranent, and Elspeth Donald, sister to the said John
Donald, compeiring personallie (and owning the hog to be hers),
the veritie quherof was admitted be the said John Edward to
her oath, quheranent she depon'd affirmative, and that the hog
was lambed of ane of her own ews, and that the same was hers.
The Bailie having considered the petitioners complaint, and
his failing to prove his allegiance, with the said Elspet Donald
her deposition, ordains the hog to belong to her allannerllie,
and amerciats John Edward in fourtie shillings Scots, to be
peyed to the fiscall of Court for his medling therwith, within
term of law.　　　　　　　　　　GEO. THOMSONE, *Balie.*
　　　　　　　　　　　　JA. MILNE, *N.P. Clk.*

The said day compeared the said John Edward, and gave in
ane other complaint against the said John Donald, alleadging
that yesterday, being the Sabboth day, Donald's bestiall were
pastureing upon his grass and propertie, and that Donald had
beat and struck the said John Edward with stones, and chased
him in the time he was turning the bestiall, and, for proveing
of Donald's bestiall pasturing upon Edwards propertie, adduced
Marjorie Tailour, spouse to Andrew Masson in Glithno. Shee
compearing declared shee knew nocht the propertie pertaining

---

[1] A sheep of a year old.

to either partie, but was willing to goe to the particular parcell of ground with the laird, and show him where the bestiall were pastureing. Which being considered be the bailie that in caice it shall be found be the laird that Donald's bestiall were pastureing wpon John Edward's propertie, he amerciats Donald in ten punds Scots to be peyed to the Fiscall of Court. And further the said complaint bears that the forsaid day, and in that meantime, when John Edward was indeavouring to drive off Donald's bestiall off the forsaid propertie, he, the said Donald, threw stones at the said Edward and beat him therwith, which Donald did not deny, at least would not depon theranent. Wherefore the Bailie holds him as confest, and amerciats him in tuentie punds Scots, especiallie seeing the same was done upon the Saboth day. And amerciats the said John Edward in ten punds Scots for his beating and stricking of John Donald the mean time with a stick which he confest.

GEO. THOMSONE, *Balie.*

JA. MILNE, *N.P. Clk.*

The said day amerciats Jean Barclay in Springhall in ten pund Scots for her cursing of John Edward in face of court.

GEO. THOMSONE, *Balie.*

JA. MILNE, *N.P. Clk.*

Court of the lands and Baronie of Urye pertaining heretablie to the much honored Robert Barclay of Ury, holden within the Maner house therof, upon the tuentie eight day of Februarij one thousand seven hundred tuentie one years, in presence of the said Robert Barclay, be George Thomson, notar publict, in Stonhyve, Bailie, James Milne, notar publict, Clerk, John Souter, Phiscall, Thomas Scot, officer, and   , Dempster.

The which day the persons under writen being laufullie summoned to this day and place to answer at the instance of the said Phiscall of Court, for transgressing the severall laws and acts of parliament, and particularlie the fifteent parliament of King James 6, cap. 248, wherby the killing of hares, doves, partridges, moor foullis, duke, draick, and others therin specifeit are expressly prohibited to be killed with guns, pistollis, stampts, girns, or other ingines, under the pains and penalties therin exprest. Compeard Alexander Gibbon at miln of Cowie, and confest he had kill'd only one pair of partridges three years past, and no other foulls dureing that time, and declared this to be of truth, as he shall answer to God.

> ALEXR. GIBBONE.
> GEO. THOMSONE, *Balie.*
> JA. MILNE, *N.P., Clk.*

Compeared Robert Wyllie in Powbair and deny'd the haill clame, which is of truth, as he shall answer to God.

> ROT. WYLLIE.
> GEO. THOMSONE, *Balie.*
> JA. MILNE, *N.P., Clk.*

Alexander Gibbon, milner at miln of Cowie, compeared and deponed negative, and declard this to be of truth, as he shall answer to God. ALEXR. GIBON.

> GEO. THOMSONE, *Balie.*
> JA. MILNE, *N.P., Clk.*

James Strachan, masson ther, compeard and depond negative, and declar'd he could not writ. GEO. THOMSONE, *Balie.*

> JA. MILNE, *N.P., Clk.*

James Wyss in Glithno compeard and acknowledged he killd only one pair of partridges these three years bypast, and this was of truth, as he shall answer to God, and declard he could not writ. GEO. THOMSONE, *Bailie.*

Compeard Alexander Mowat in Rothnick and confest guilty.

> ALEXR. MOWAT.
> GEO. THOMSONE, *Balie.*
> JA. MILNE, *N.P., Clk.*

Compeard James Mowat at miln of Montquheich and depon'd negative. JAMES MOWAT.

> GEO. THOMSONE, *Balie.*
> JA. MILNE, *N.P., Clk.*

Compeard William Duthie in Burnhaugh and depond negative, but owns he keeps a gun.　　WILLIAM DUTHIE.

GEO. THOMSONE, *Balie.*
JA. MILNE, *N.P., Clk.*

Compeard John Lyon in Cransacre and depond negative, and declares he cannot writ.　　GEO. THOMSONE, *Balie.*
JA. MILNE, *N.P., Clk.*

William Duthie in Trees compeard be Alexander Duncan his servant, and depond, his master being sick and not able to come to this Court this day, that his master bid him acknowledge that he was guilty of killing of hares.

GEO. THOMSONE, *Balie.*
JA. MILNE, *N.P., Clk.*

Compeard Alexander Duthie in Crosley and confesses the killing of three hares these three years bygon, and no other beast nor foull prohibited by law.　　ALEXR. DUTHIE.

GEO. THOMSONE, *Balie.*
JA. MILNE, *N.P., Clk.*

Compeard James Milne in Mains of Ury and depon'd he had only killd one dove these three years bygon, and this was of truth, as he shall answer to God, and declares he has a gun.　　JAMES MILNE.

GEO. THOMSONE, *Balie.*
JA. MILNE, *N.P., Cl.*

Compeard James Broun in Maigray and ownd he keeps a gun, and had only shot a dove, and no other foulls nor hares these three years bypast, and this he declar'd to be of truth, as he shall answer to God.　　I. B.

GEO. THOMSONE, *Balie.*
JA. MILNE, *N.P., Clk.*

Compeard Alexander Broun in Maigray and confesses he killd some doves, but nothing els these three years past.

ALEXR. BROWN.
GEO. THOMSONE, *Balie.*
JA. MILNE, *N.P., Clk.*

Compeard **James Edward** ther, and ownd he had only killd one dove this year, with ane borrowd gun, which is of truth as he shall answer to God.   JAMES EDWARD.

GEO. THOMSONE, *Balie.*

JA. MILNE, *N.P., Clk.*

The said day the said Bailie having taken to his consideration the confessants, their severall acknowledgments of their guilt as is mentioned in their depositions wpon the preceeding pages in this act of Court, amerciats each one of them in the penalties prescribed by acts of parliament, and ordains each one of the havers of the guns to bring in the same to the laird to be disposed upon be him as he shall think fitt, and ordains precepts to be issued out to the effect forsaid.

GEO. THOMSONE, *Balie.*

JA. MILNE, *N.P., Clk.*

Barron Court off the lands and barronie off Urie pertaining heretably to the much honoured **Robert Barclay,** *younger thereof, holden within the* **Manor** *place thereof, by* **Robert Wyllie** *in Polbair, Balie, qualified in the terms of law. Georg Thomson, noter publick, Clerk of Court, John Sutor, Procurator Fiscall, John Hunter, offisier and Dempster.*

Sectis vocatis curia legittime affirmata.

The which day, in presence of the said herctor and balie forsaid, anent ane complaint given in befor them against James Wise in Glithno, att the instance of the said procurator fiscall, makeing mention that wher, in ane publick mercat holden wpon the hill called Magrie hill, wpon the eightenth day of June instant, the said James Wise was found in handie grips[1] with one George Caddell, fisherman in Couie, and they strugling on with another, by which it came to earnest, and that the said James Wise did hurt and blood drew of the said Georg Caddell.

The said James Wise being laufully summoned by the said ground offischer to compeir befor the Balie forsaid in ane

---

[1] Close grappling.

barron court to be holden within the Manor place of Urie this
day, compeired the said James Wise, and being called to
answer at the instance of the said procurator fiscall to hear and
see himself deserned be decreet of Court order of law and
justice, and to heir and see the said indictment sufficientlie
verefied and proven, and the samen being suae verefied, himself to underly the law in the pains and penaltes thereof.

Compeired the said James Wise, and being examined and interrogat anent the points of the said indictment, confessed and
acknolidged that he, being appointed by his said master to go
as one of the guard with others of the said merket, it hapned
their fell a plee betuixt the said Georg Caddel and one Grig,
sone to John Grig, smith in Stonhyve, by which the merket
was disturbed, and he the said James Wise endeauouring
campesce and setle them, he the said George Caddel, out of
his fury and rage becaus he could not gett his will of Grig,
invaded and pursued the said James Wise, so that he could not
be ridd of the said Caddel, who fell wpon him most inhumanely
by dragging him by the brest, and in his oun defence bleed
Caddel with the butt of his gun, by which both parties wer
seized by Uries servants and dispached [1] the merket. The
procurator fiscall alledged their wer witneses to the said ryot,
and creaved they might be examined. And accordingly compeired John Mouat, younger in Wodhead, James Kaird,
younger their, Robert Cruikshank in Mountboy, and John
Youngson in Balnagight, all lawfully summoned to this day
and place, who, being publickly called, compeiring and
solemnly suoren, interrogat ilk ane of them deponed in maner
wnder writen. To witt, the said John Mouat, younger, of the
age of twentie three or thereby, witnes, cited, solemnly suoren,
purged of partiall counsel, examined, deponed that he did see
James Wise and Georg Caddel in handie grips together, and
did hear and see the said Wise desireing Caddell to stand of
from him, and did hear and see the said Caddel invad Wise
two severall times, and being thus prouoked and pursued by
Caddel, he did see James Wise give him two stroaks with the
butt of a gun to the effusion of Caddels blood, which is all he

---

[1] Driven out of.

did heir and see, and which is a truth, as he shall answer to God, *causa scientie patet* he wes present all the time.

JOHN MOWAT.
ROT. WYLLIE, *balie*.

The said day compeired James Kaird in Woodhead, of the age of twentie three years or thereby, witnes, cited, solemnly suoren, purged of partiall counscel, examined, deponed that he did see Georg Caddel invade James Wise by takeing him by the breast, and did hear Wise severall times desireing him to stand off, which Caddel would not, and att last did see James Wise give Caddel two stroaks to the effusion of his blood, which was all that he did see or heir, as he shall answer to God, *causa scientie patet* he wes present all the time.

JA. CAIRD.
RT. WYLLIE, *ballie*.

The said day compeired **Robert Crukshank** in Mountboy, aged thertie years or thereby, a maried man, witnes cited, admitted, purged of partiall counscel, examined, deponed *in omnibus* conform to James Caird, which is a truth, as he shall answer to God, *causa scientie patet*, he was present all the time.

R. C.
ROT. WYLLIE, *balie*.

The said day compeired John Youngson in Balnagight, unmaried, of the age of twentie four years or thereby, witnes cited, solemnly suorn, purged of partiall counscel, examined, interrogat, depones that he wes within a litle distance off Georg Caddel, he did see James Wise come touards Georg Caddell, desireing him to be at pase and not disturb the merket. The deponent did see James Wise draw a stroak att Caddel, but depons he did not see the stroak given, but did see Caddels blood when he was brought to the tent, which is all he did see or hear, as he shall answer to God, and declares he cannot write.

ROT. WYLLIE, *balie*.
GEO. THOMSONE, *Clk*.

Urie, 20th June 1724.

Robert Wyllie, balie within mentioned, haveing heard and

considered the within written indictment, the defender his judiciall confession and witneses depositions, and being reaply aduised, he fines and amerciats the said James Wise in the soume of fiftie pound Scots money, to be payed within term of law to the fiscall of Court, and ordains the ground offischer to require him to make payment thereof, within term of law, and ordains precepts to be direct hereupon.

Rot. WYLLIE, balie.

The said day the Balie deserns and ordains the said James Wise to pay to the said George Caddel the soume of ten pounds Scots of assythment for cureing his wound, and ordains precepts to be direct hereupon, in form as effeirs.

R. BARCLAY, Junr.
Rot. WYLLIE, balie.
GEO. THOMSONE, Clk.

The said day, in presence of the said Robert Wyllie, balie, it is enacted and ordained that no tennent, cottar, nor grase man within the barronie of Urie shall presume nor take wpon hand to cast, ween, led, sell, nor away put any peats, turf, or feuell furth of the moss and latch of Glithno, nor cast foot peatis[1] in the hill of Glithno or Alachie, under the penaltie of fourtie shilling Scots toties quoties, they shall be found guiltie in con-traveening this present act.   Rot. WYLLIE, balie.

The said day, in presence of Robert Wyllie, balie, it is statute, enacted, and ordained that ilk tennent of one plough lauboring or above it shall sow yearely ane firlot of pise or beans wpon their possession ; betuixt a pleugh and fiftie merks pay two pecks yearely, and inferior to fiftie merks pay to ane acre of land ane peck, and under that half peck, and in cace of contravention of this present act, the contraveeners shall pay four pound Scots gradually from the highest to louest that

---

[1] Foot peats are peats cast by the digger standing on the surface and pressing in the peat spade with his foot. They are distinguished from breast peats, which are cast from a perpendicular face of moss, the digger standing on the level of the bottom, and driving in the spade horizontally. The former manner of work-ing would naturally maintain where the turf was shallow and least suitable for casting, and this may explain the prohibition of the text. See p. 133, infra.

should sow half a peck, and ordains the ground offischer to go and inspect yearly the tennents and subtennents within the barronie of Urie, and report the samen to the heretor.

Rot. Wyllie, balie.

The said day, in presence of Robert Wyllie, balie, it is statute and ordained that, begining within the barronie of Urie, that two men shall attend the two mercets of Magray yearely, begining at the one end of the land to the other, under the penaltie of three pound ilk defiscient man, he being in health or [not] giveing a lawfull excuse, and ordains the ground offischer yearely befor each merket to give due intimation to the persons that should attend the saids merkets.[1]

Rot. Wyllie, balie.

The said day, in presenc of Robert Wyllie, balie, it is statute, enacted, and ordained that no tennent within the said barronie shall att any time hereafter outlabour[2] any outfield[3] or ley ground within their possesions att their removel theirfrae in prejudice of the entring tennent, under the penaltie of one hundred pound Scots.

Rot. Wyllie, balie.

The said day, in presenc of Robert Wyllie, balie, it is statute, enacted, and ordained that no tennent, cotter, nor grase man, their servents, themselves, nor their children, shall att ony time hereafter burn any mosses or moores within the said barronie, under the penaltie of twentie pound Scots toties quoties, and the master to be ansuerable for their children and servants.

R. Barclay, Jr.
Rot. Wyllie, balie.
Geo. Thomson, Clk.

Barron Court off the lands and Barn mie of Urie perteincing heretably to the much honoured Robert Barclay of Urie, junier thereof, heretor thereof, holden at Cransacre, by Robert Wyllie, balie, qualified in terms of law. Alex-

---

[1] These were probably required to act as guard ; see p. 122, supra.

[2] To exhaust by too much tillage.—Jam.

[3] A term applied to arable land, which is not manured, but cropped till it is worn out, so as to be unfit for bearing corn for some years.—Jam.

ander Gibbon at Mill of Cowie, Clerk of Court, John
Souter, Procurator Fiscall, John Hunter, Officer, and
, Dempster.

April the 22, 1725.

Sectis vocatis curia legittime affirmata.

The whilk day, in presence of the said heretor and balie,
anent ane complent at the instance of the said procurator
fiscall, showing that William White and his wife Agnes Heriat
in Woodhead, had wounded and beatt William Walker in the
said toun of Woodhead, in a cruel maner, therefor desired they
might be prosecute according to law. The said William White
and his said wife being lawfully summonsed and compeiring,
being interogat thereupon, they both confessed that in the
hight of their passion they wer guilty of invading and beatting
the said William Walker. The forsaid balie, takeing their
said confessions into his consideration and being ripely advised
thereupon, ammerciats each of the said persons in the soume
of ten pound Scots, to be payed to the fiscal of court, within
term of law, and ordains precepts to be direct hereupon in
form as effiers, and requisitions to be made by the ground
offischer to the effect above mentioned.

> R. BARCLAY, Jr.
> ROT. WYLLIE, *balie.*
> ALEXR. GIBBON, *scriba curie.*

Barron Court of the lands and barronie of Urie pertaineing
heritably to the much honoured Robert Barclay of Urie,
junier, holden at Cransacre, by Robert Wyllie, Balie,
quallified in terms of law, Alexander Gibbon, Clerk of
Court, Robert Eduard, Fiscal, and John Hunter, offiser,
and , Dempster.

June the 4th, 1726.

Sectis vocatis [curia] legittime affirmata.

Cransacre, June the 4th, 1726.

The which day, in presenc of the heretor and balie forsaid,
compeared John Fergison, servant to Alexander Gibbon att

mill of Cowie, being lawfully summoned to this day att the
instance of the said procurator fiscall to answer to the balie of
the said court, according to law and justice, for his beatting
and whipeing of James Laurie, servant to   Duthie
in Craigwalls, att the hous of James Strachan, brewer in mill
of Cowie, wpon the second day of June seventeen hundred and
twentie six, about the midle of the said day, the said John
Fargeson, being about his lawfull occasions in serving his
master at Polbair, wes personaly summonsed ther as aforsaid
befor lawfull witnesses, Robert Millne and James Burnes, servants their, by the afforsaid ground officeer, and the said John
Fergeson comperand accordingly, being interrogat declared and
confessed that the said Lawrie haveing his whip in his custodie
among his masters empty secks, the said Fergeson presumeing
that Laurie had stol it from him, or malisiously taken it away,
and he haveing found the same confessed he gave the said
Laurie severall stroaks with it. Which judiciall confession the
afforsaid balie haveing taken to his consideration, amerciats
the said Fergison in the soume of ten pound Scots to be payed
to the fiscall of court within term of law, and ordains precepts
to be direct thereon in form as effeirs.

R. BARCLAY, Junr.

ROT. WYLLIE, balie.

ALER. GIBBON, scriba curie.

Cransacre, June the 4th, 1726.

The said day the afforsaid fiscall made a complent against
John Suiter, gardner att Urie, did graple and disturb in a
rietous maner Alexander Keith alies Craig in Invercarren, for
which he ought to be summoned according to law. The said
John Souter being lawfully summonsed and interrogat their-
anent, accnoledged that in drinking with Alexander Keith in
ane ale hous in Invercarren he wes guilty of throwing doun and
grapling with the said Alexander Keith, they being both
inebriat, for which the balie fyns him in ten pound Scots, and
ordains the same to be payed within term of law.

R. BARCLAY, Junr.   ALER. GIBBON, Clk.

ROT. WYLLIE, bailie.

Court of the lands and baronie of Urie pertaining heretablie to
the much honourd Robert Barclay, younger of Urie, holden
within the Manner place theroff (he himself being present
personallie) upon the last day of December one thousand
seven hundred and twenty six years, be Robert Wyllie
in Powbair, Ballie, James Millne, notar publick, Clerk,
John Souter, gardiner of Urie, Fischall, John Hunter,
Officer, and   , Dempster.

The which day anent the action and riot intented and pursued at the instance of the said procurator fischall against the
haill persons after named and designed, tennants and possessors
of the forsaid lands and baronie, for their killing, shooting, and
destroying of hares, partridges, and other wild fowls, and keeping, caryeing, and useing of guns contrair to law.

Compeard Alexander Brown in Mains of Urie, James Wyse
there, Robert Young there, Alexander Beatie there, William
Clark there, Robert Beattie there, Alexander Duncan there,
and   and   Duncans his
sons there, and John Strachan there, and all being interrogate
annent the forsaid riot denyed the lybell, and the fischall offers
to prove.   JA. MILNE, *N.P., Clk.*

Compeard also Alexander Youngson in Bannagight, William
Thomson there, and William Murray there, and being interrogate *ut supra* denyed the hail lybell, and the fischall offered
to prove.   JA. MILNE, *N.P., Clk.*

Compeard likeways John Steivenson in Kairntown, John
Jack there, and John Laurance there, and deny'd the hail
lybell, except the said John Laurance, who owns the keeping
and caryeing of a gun.   JA. MILNE, *N.P., Clk.*

Compeard also Robert Cruckshank, George Mowat, and
John Pypper in Munboy, Andrew Mason in Glithnow, Alexander Wobster there, James Wobster there, Andrew Mason
younger there, John Strachan there, and Andrew Morgan
there, and all denyed the lybell, and the fischall offered to
prove.   JA. MILNE, *N.P., Clk.*

Compeard lykeways John Lyon in Cransaire, John Youngson there, Robert Mason there, John Smith there, Thomas Forester there, and John Hunter there, and all denyed. The fischall offers to prove against them, excepting the said John Lyon, who owens the keeping of a gun.   JA. MILNE, N.P., Clk.

Compeard also James Kairds elder and younger in Woodhead, John Mowats elder and younger there, William Kaird there, Robert Selbie there, John Sutor there, and Robert Pypper there, and all denyed, an the fischall offers to prove against them, except the saids John Mowat and Robert Selbie, who owend the keeping of a gun each.
                                        JA. MILNE, N.P., Clk.

Compeard lykways Alexander Cruikshank in Powbair, David Walker there, William Walker there, Andrew Melvill there, Robert Wyllie there, and   and
                his servants, and denyed, and the fischall offers to prove against them, except the said Andrew Melvill, who confessed the keeping of a gun.
                                        JA. MILNE, N.P., Clk.

Compeard also James Brown in Megrey, William Main there, James Edward there, George Scot there, George Allan there, John Ferguson there, and all denyed, except the said John Ferguson confesses the keeping and useing of a gun and shooting of hares and fowls contrair to law.
                                        JA. MILNE, N.P., Clk.

Compeard, lastly, Allexander Gibbon att Milln of Cowie, Allexander Gibbon, miller there, John Ferquhar there, James Ker there, James Strachan there, and Allexander Deans there, and the said James Ker and Allexander Deans denyed the lybell, and the fischall offered to prove against them, and the said Allexander Gibbon, tenent, and John Farquhar owend the shooting ut supra, and the said Allexander Gibbon, miller, and James Strachan owend the keeping of a gun each.
                                        JA. MILNE, N.P., Clk.
                                        ROT. WYLLIE, balie.

I

The day within writen and year forsaid the ballie, haveing considered the severall confessions of the persons summoned to this court anent the facts libelled; fines and amerciats each one of the confessants in the penalties prescribed by acts of Parliament, and ordains each one of the havers and users of their guns and pistols to bring up the same to the said laird of Urie, their master, to be disposed upon be him as he shall think fit, and ordains precepts and other executorialls needfull, to be issued out and direct heiron in form as effeirs.

Rot. Wyllie, *balie.*
Ja. Milne, *N.P., Clk.*

The ballie forsaid heirby enacts and ordains that no person within this Baronie shall cast turffs for seale, excepting upon the commontie, under the penalltie of fourty shilling Scots, *toties quoties,* and that none, under the said penalltie and payeing and makeing up the damnages, shall pot[1] the fisher myres, or any other mosses within the barronie, excepting the smith for his coals. And sicklike that no person shall cast turffs or earth whatsoever upon the ground contiguous to his neighbours corns, if his neighbours incline to improve the same for corn ground. And, lastly, the ballie ordains that no tenent or inhabitant whatsoever within the baronie shall pull down any of their houses at their removeall, after the inventar of the biggings is fullfilled and satisfied, without offering the same for sale to the master or entring tenent, under the penalltie of ten pounds Scots, and, in caice they shall not agree one the price, that they shall chuse and call ane honest man or two for decideing the difference and adhere thereto.

Rot. Wyllie, *balie.*
Ja. Milne, *N.P., Clk.*

Barron Court of the lands and Barrony of Urie, holden within the Mannour place of Urie upon the twenty fourth day of January one thousand seven hundreth and thirty years (in presence of Robert Barclay, younger of Urie, heritable proprietar of the saids lands) be Robert

---

[1] Cast peats upon.

*Wyllie in Pollbair, Barron Baillie, **John Maule**,[1] nottar*
publick and Clerk of Court, John Souter, Fiscall, William
Thomson, officer,   **Dempster.**
Sectis vocatis Curia legitime afirmata.

The said day the fiscall haveing given in a complaint that
the pasturage, muirs, meadow, and sward ground within the
said lands and barrony of Ury were so cast up and destroyed
that in a short time it would be quite wore out and rendred
useless unless timously prevented.   And the same being
seriously considered by the said baillie, he enacts, statutes, and
ordains that for the better preserving of the said ground,
pasturage, and muirs from being destroyed in time coming,
and for assertaining a certain piece of hill for pasturage to

---

[1] John Maule, writer, Stonehaven, was a cadet of the house of Panmure. He
appears to have been a man of considerable force of character, and his name is
still remembered in the district as that of a prominent adherent of the Stuart
cause.   Previous to the Rebellion of 1745, Maule held the responsible position
of Procurator-Fiscal for the county of Kincardine, in which capacity he distinguished himself by the energy and zeal with which he entered into the discharge of his official duties.   Many are the stories illustrative of his harsh treatment of offenders, which were still current in the neighbourhood a generation
ago.   It is told of him, for example, that a woman guilty of theft having been
sentenced to be branded with a red-hot iron, he not only superintended the
execution of her sentence, but subjected to the same barbarous cruelty the infant
whom she carried at her breast.   On another occasion one Farnie was con-
demned to be whipped through the town for sheep-stealing, and so effectually
was this chastisement administered under his direction that it became a saying
in the district, as applied to any act of seemingly gratuitous severity,—' It 's
weel whuppit, quo' Farnie.'   Maule joined the Stuart faction in '45, and having
obtained a commission as an ensign in the rebel army, soon made himself conspicuous in the enlistment of recruits.   He himself proclaimed the Pretender in
the market-place of Stonehaven, going through the ceremony of drawing a flag
over the Cross in token of allegiance to King James.   In the official list of rebels
presented to the Commissioners of Assize, in May 1746, Maule is reported ' dead.'
But this statement is inaccurate, and the mistake may in all probability
have been less the result of accident than of design.   Maule survived the battle
of Culloden, and, escaping southwards, seems to have contemplated returning to
Stonehaven.   He was recognised, however, lurking in the vicinity of the town,
and narrowly escaped capture at the hands of the soldiers of the Duke of Cum-
berland, by one of whom he was shot in the leg.   Badly wounded though he was,
Maule contrived to baffle his pursuers, and pressing towards Dundee obtained
a safe asylum in the neighbourhood of that city.   There he remained for several
years in hiding, but eventually obtained a free pardon from the Government,
through the influence of his kinsman, Lord Panmure.   The remaining years of
his life were spent in Stonehaven, in the practice of his profession as a lawyer.

each toun within the said barrony, it is hereby enacted, statute, and ordained, that no person or persons whatsomever shall, at any time hereafter, cast any turf, faill, or other fewell whatsomever for firring or other uses upon the plans following, Viz.: To the westward of the high road from the foord to the toun of Megray upon the said hill, upon the northward of the den called the Den of Woodhead, and westward of the new and present cart road of the hill of Glithno to the place called the Heathery Bridges upon north side of Bruxden, and eastward of the high road betwixt Bruxden and Montboys of the hill of the Mains, and upon the north side of the hill of Cairntoun and Balnagight from the water draught[1] of the loch of Balnagight, including the binty[2] ground along to the edge of the uppermost part of Bruxden, presently possessed by John Steinson.   Also that non cast up any ground for what occasion soever within the wards[3] called the Wards of Megray and Pollbair, as the samen is bounded by the vistage of an old faill dyke round the same, nor that no ground upon what occasion soever shall be cast upon any part of the grass meadow or corne ground of the whole touns and lands of Megray and miln of Cowie, excepting upon the ground that lyes betwixt the aboun ward of Megray and George Allans croft, for a moderate use of midden faill allenarly, and upon the common brea or bogg betwixt the said toun of Megray and miln of Cowie.   And likeways that no other person upon any other part of the said barrony of Ury cast up any faill or land quhatsomever upon any lands or meadow ground, nor upon any other part of their possessions, except for a moderate use of midden faill in ground not particularly excepted by this or former acts of Court, in those places they have been in use of casting for severall years bygon.   And the contravenners of any of these acts to be fynd and ammerciat in the sum of twenty pound Scots money so often as they shall be found guilty of incurring the said penalty, by and attour makeing up the dammages the lands incurrs, and forfaulture of the truf, faill, divott[4] or others whatsomever so casten contrary to this act.

---

[1] The outlet for the water.   [2] Covered with bent grass.

[3] Small pieces of pasture ground, enclosed on all sides.—*Jam.*

[4] A thin flat turf, generally of an oblong form, used for covering cottages and also for fuel.—*Jam.*

As also it is ordain'd that no person upon the west side of the
burn of Glithno shall cast aboun one days casting of truf,
excepting on the west and north sides of the lands of Montboy and Balnagight belonging to George Mouat and William
Murray, and that under the forsaid penalty so often as the
samin is incurrd, and ordains the said penalty to be payed so
often as the same is incurrd to the said fiscall, and the said
turf or divot so cast contrary to this act to be forfeit, as said
is, for the use of the said Robert Barclay, who may lead or
destroy the same *brevi manu*. And likways it is ordained that
the casting of any fewell for fire whatsomever with the foot
spade is by this act intirly abolishd for ever under the above
written penalty, to be applyed as above mentioned, and forfaulture likeways. To all and sundry the premisses the baillie
forsaid interpons his authority.   Rot. WYLLIE, *Balie.*
                                    JOHN MAULE, *Clk.*

24th *January* 1730, *presentia* Robert Wyllie.

Anent the complaint given in at the procurator fiscalls instance, against John Piper and John Jack in Cairntown and
Montboys, for their illegal and unwarrantable cutting and
letting out of the water out of the water furr[1] belonging to
the said Robert Barclay.

Compeard the said John Piper and John Jack, and judicially
confessd the same, which, being considerd by the said baille,
he fynd and amerciate ilk one of them in the sum of one pound
ten shilling Scots, and ordained the same to be instantly payed
in to the said fiscall for the use of the said Robert Barclay, or
to go to prison till the same be payed. Rot. WYLLIE, *Balie.*
                                    JOHN MAULE, *Clk.*

Barron Court of the lands and barrony of Urie pertaining to
the honourable Robert Barclay, younger of Urie, heritable
proprietor therof, holden, in his own presence, within the
Mannour place therof, upon the ninth day of February
one thousand seven hundreth and thirty years, be Robert

---

[1] A furrow formed by the plough for draining off surface water.—*Jam.*

Wyllie in Polbair, Baillie, John Maule, nottar publick,
Clerk, John Souter in Whinnidelf, Procurator Fiscall,
William Thomson, Officer, and   ,
Demster.
Sectis vocatis Curieque legitime afirmata.

The said day compeard Alexander Gibbon, tacksman of miln
of Cowie, and produced ane Execution, together with ane
Lybelld Summons, at his instance against the haill tennents,
subtennents, cotters, and others, not only within the said lands
and barrony of Urie, but also those within the lands of Reid
Cloak, Findlaystoun, and toun of Cowie, all lyable in multure
and thirld to the said miln of Cowie, as the said execution,
under the hand of the said William Thomson, officer, bearing
and containing the names and designations of the said haill
tennents, and others, within the said sucken of miln of Cowie,
and that he had personally summond them, and ilk one of
them, to this day and place (and who were all accordingly personally present and answerd to their severall names), and in the
said lybell craveing from them, and ilk one of them, the number
and quantity of ten bolls of oats or eight merks for ilk boll
thereof, eight bolls of bear or six pound Scots as the price of
ilk boll therof, six bolls of peas or six pound Scots for
ilk boll therof, six bolls of white or nine pound Scots for ilk
boll therof, and six bolls of rey or five pound mony forsaid for
ilk boll therof, all due by them, and ilk one of them, for
abstracted multurs abstracted from the miln of Cowie be them,
and ilk one of them, of their severall grundable grains above
mentioned, for these five years bygone preceding this date, and
for which the said Alexander Gibbon had good and undoubted
right to pursue as taxman forsaid, as the said lybell and
execution forsaid, on a paper apart, more fully bear.   And this
same being again called,

Compeard Alexander Roger in Reid Cloack, and confess'd
that he was only due for the multure of two bolls of bear and
no more.   Item, James Dounie there, and confess'd that he
was due for the multure of half a boll of bear.   Item, Andrew
Melvin there, and confess'd that he was due to the pursuer for
five pecks of bear of abstracted multures.   Item, compeard
Thomas Walker in Findlaystoun, and being solemnly sworn,

depon'd that he was due to the pursuer the multure of two
bolls of bear and one boll of corn, and no more, and this he
declair'd to be truth, as he shall answer to God, and declair'd
he could not write.

Item, Alexander Lighton in Pollbair confessd that he was
due the multure of two pecks of bear, and no more. Item,
James Edward in Myre confessd that he was due to the pursuer
a firlot of bear, and William Main there depond *ut supra* that
he was due three firlots of bear to the pursuer, abstracted as
said is. Item, Robert Edward in Cowie confessd that he was
due for the multure of seven bolls of bear at the one and
twentieth current.[1] And further, it is agreed on, betwixt the
said Robert Edward in Bridgeston of Cowie and Alexander
Gibbon, that, in regard a part of the said Robert Edwards
lands payd the seventeenth current and another part the
twenty-fifth current, therfor they both judicially agree that, as
a medium 'twixt the two, the said Robert Edward shall pay in
time comeing the one and twentieth current of multure, as was
formerly payed, seed and farm bear excepted, and that within
the haill tack of Bridgeston as possessed be him and his pre-
dicessors, and in testimony wherof they have subscrived the
same.   R. E.
                                         ALEXR. GIBBON.

And the Baillie decernd against the haill forenamed persons,
conform to their severall depositions and confessions mentioned
in the two preceding pages. And also decern'd, and hereby
decerns, against John Main in Cowie for the multure of four
bolls and a half of bear yearly for the space of five years
bygone preceding this date, and decernd, and hereby decerns,
against George Mouat in Mains of Urie, Andrew Measson in
Glithno, Alexander Webster there, and James Kaird in
Woodhead, conform to the claim, in respect of their compearing

---

[1] While parties thirled to a mill had, as a general rule, to pay every thirteenth
peck as multure (see p. 79, *supra*), it might so happen that in certain circumstances a smaller duty was demanded. It was probably on account of his land
lying within the precinct of the town of Cowie that Robert Edward was taxed
at the one and twentieth current, or, in other words, was only required to pay
every twenty-first peck.

and refusing to depon. And ordaind, and hereby ordains, all
execution to pass hereon in terms of law, and to which the
baillie forsaid interpons his authority. And assollzied, and
hereby assollzies, the haill other persons contain'd in the said
execution and lybell for the reasons therin mentioned.

Rot. Wyllie, *balie.*
John Maule, *Clk.*

The said ninth day of February 1730, in presence forsaid,
compeard William Duthie, tennent in Reid Cloak, and gave in
ane representation and petition subscrived with his hand, mentioning that the tacks of Bruntholls and Lachdewis were not
lyable in the payment of miln multures for twelve bolls of bear
allenarly, and that the above multures had not been payed be
the tennents thereof nor regularly required or obtain'd for the
space of fourty years backward, and therfor presumd that gave
a right to the possessing of twelve bolls of bear multure free in
all time coming, and creaved that he might be assignd a day
for proveing the same be witnesses. To whom the baillie forsaid assign'd the first lawfull day of August next for that
effect as on the said paper apart bears.

Rot. Wyllie, *balie.*
John Maule, *Clk.*

The said ninth day of February, in presence forsaid, anent
ane complaint given in by the whole above mentioned tennents
within the said sucken, petitioning the knavships and loak or
bannock belonging to the miller may be regulate, and that
they are willing to pay full knawship, which before to the
goodman of the miln was only ane lippie[1] meall for grinding
five pecks of shillin, the other fifth being applyed for making
the millers luk and goodwill the better. But now they are
content and creave that they may pay the whole knawship to
the goodman, which is one lippie for the four pecks of shillin
grinding, and instead of the dues commonly called luk and
goodwill, they condisend to pay half of the said knaveship,
which is half a lippie for the grinding of four pecks of shillin.

---

[1] The fourth part of a peck.

Which petition the said heritor and baillie refer'd the consideration therof to the next court to be holden place forsaid.

> R. BARCLAY, Jr.
> ROT. WYLLIE, *balie.*
> JOHN MAULE, *Clk.*

*Mannor place of Urie the first day of August j^mvij^c and thirty.
In presence of Robert Wyllie in Polbair, Baillie, of the
lands and barrony of Ury.*

The said day, in the term assign'd to William Duthie in
Reid Cloack for proveing, in terms of the petition and representation given in by him upon the ninth day of February last
by past, anent the miln multures of Lochdews and Bruntholes,
Compear'd the said William Duthie, and aduiced as witnesses
for proveing therof James Lighton in Smiddiemuir, John
Craig in Clofrickdyke of Muchells, and Andrew Melvin in
Mosshead of Reid Cloack, and Katherin Hunter in the Hillhead therof, and the saids witnesses being called, compeard the
said James Lighton in Smiddiemuir, married man, aged sixty
nine years or thereby, witness, admitted, received, purged of
partiall councill, and interrogate, depon'd that, about thirty
four years since, he possessd, as subtennent to the taxman of
Reid Cloack, the said town of Bruntholes and Lochdews, and
that during the time he possessd the same, which was about
fourteen years or thereby, He had allowed to him twelve bolls
of bear free of multure from his master, which was then
possessd be Robert Keith, taxman therof, and that he payed
the said twelve bolls of bear yearly to his said master, and that
Lochdews, which payed eight bolls therof, was only cottar
crofts before that time. Depons that he knows not whether
the said twelve bolls of bear payed multure, or not, since his
removall from the said taks. And also depons that he was
required to pay multures for the said bear by William Gibbon,
tennent of Mill of Cowie, for the saids years during his possession, but the liferentrix of Reid Cloack and Ury common'd [1]
about it, but does not know what agreement they made. And
also remembers that the multures therof was pursued for before

---

[1] Had dealings.

the Sherrif Court before that time. And this he declairs to be truth, as he shall answer to God, and that he cannot write.

ROT. WYLLIE, *balie.*

JOHN MAULE, *Clk.*

The said first of August 1730.

Presentia forsaid Baillie.

Compeard John Craig in Clofrickdykes above named, married man, aged sixty years or thereby, witness, admitted, received, purged of partiall councill, and interrogate, depon'd That, about thirty years or thereby since, he was servant to Robert Keith in Reid Cloack, who was taxman therof, and that the sub-tennents that possess'd the saids Lochdews and Bruntholes payed to the said taxman twelve bolls of fearm bear, and that the said Robert Keith told him that he payed no multure for the same to the tennent of Miln of Cowie. And likeways depons that before that time, when he was servant there, that there was a cotter man upon Lochdews who wrought for his croft and payed no fearm bear. And this is the truth, as he shall answer to God, and declairs he cannot write.

ROT. WYLLIE, *balie.*

JOHN MAULE, *Clk.*

The said first of August 1730.

Presentia forsaid Baillie.

Compeard the said Andrew Melvin in Mosshead of Reid Cloack, married man, aged fifty years or thereby, witness, admitted, received, purged of partiall counceli, and interrogate, depon'd that, about thirty nine years since or thereby, his father in law, John Duthie, possessd, as subtennent to the said Robert Keith, and Alexander Mouat, taxmen of Reid Cloack, the said place called Lochdews, and that he payed eight bolls of farm bear therfore, but that the said eight bolls of bear payed no multure to the tennent of Miln of Cowie for ought that he, the deponent, knew. But that he knows William Gibbon, then tennent in Miln of Cowie, frequently demanded the multure thereof. And likeways that he knows that for the space of twenty four years by past the said touns have payed

no fearm bear, but only money, to the principal tennent, and payed full multure for the haill grouth therof to the tennent of Miln of Cowie of what they carried to the said miln. Also depons that, befor his father in law dwelled on the said Lochdewes, he knew one cotter man dwell theron, and that he pay'd no farm bear, but wrought for his said possession. And this he declair'd to be truth, as he shall answer to God, and declairs he cannot write.   Ror. WYLLIE, *balie.*
                                   JOHN MAULE, *Clk.*

Compeard Katherin Hunter in Hillhead of Reid Cloack, aged seventy three years or thereby, witness, admitted, received, purged of partiall councill, and interrogate *ut supra,* depon'd that, about sixty years or thereby, she knew the said Lochdewes four cottar crofts, and that it then payed no farm bear, and that one John Roy afterwards payed money rent as it doth just now, and has done for above this eighteen years past. And also depons that immediatly after the said John Roy, the said Lochdews was possessd by John Duthie, and Bruntholls be William Hunter, the deponents father, and that the said John Duthie payed eight bolls of farm bear, and that William Hunter payed four bolls of farm bear. And this is the truth, as she shall answer to God, and declares she cannot write. And further depons that it is fifty one years since her father possess'd the said tack.   Ror. WYLLIE, *balie.*

Therafter compeard the said William Duthie, and renounced any further probation, but alledged that by the above proof adduced and witnesses depositions, that it was proven that for betwixt this fourty and fifty years by past, that it was in custom, till within this eighteen years past, that the said Lochdews and Bruntholes payed twelve bolls of fearm bear and no mony, and payed no multure for the said twelve bolls, and since the conversion of that bear into mony. Therfor creaves that the said two tacks may be assolzied from payment of any multure for the saids quantity of bear in time comeing, in regard they have never payed any multure for what bear they have sold in that place since that date.   Ror. WYLLIE, *balie.*
                                   JOHN MAULE, *Clk.*

To which it was answerd be the said heritor and tennent of Miln of Cowie, That 1ᵐᵒ, The generall thirlage of the haill toun of Reid Cloak being proven (and what they doe not pretend to deny) in all the said heritors dispositions and charters ratified in Parliament, and even the heritors of Reid-cloaks charters is burthen'd with the same, being formerly part of the barrony of Ury, no part therof is free of multure but what can be proven *scripto*.

2d. That some of these subtacks were antiently the cottar crofts of the toun of Reidcloak, as is proven be the evidence adduced be the said William Duthie, and afterwards [were paid for] in mony rent, before that ever they were sett for farm bear. And seeing likeways the said two tacks of Bruntholes and Lochdewes have for these eighteen years and upwards payed mony rent and full multure at the miln, as they formerly did when they were cottar crofts, according to the witnesses depositions, there only remains thirty two or thirty three years that ever they payed fearm bear, which is so far from proveing that it payed fourty years farm bear, as the said William Duthie asserts, that it clearly demonstrates the contrary.

3ᵗⁱᵒ. That if it were otherways, yet it is not in the power of ane heritor, much less a tennent, to constitute a farm bear at pleasure after he is thirled, in order to evade the payment of multurs. Since, if it were, ane heritor might constitute as much farm bear as would exhaust all the grain upon the lands thirl'd, and afterwards, colluding with their tennents, convert it into mony rent for the ease of the tennents, and so evade the payment of multurs, the just property of another person, which is clearly the case hereof. In regard it cannot be proven that ever there grew so much as twelve bolls of bear upon the said two tacks *communibus annis* above [1] the seed, so they constituted that extraordinary farm bear purposly to evade paying of multurs, because they immediatly turnd it into mony rent, by reason it never grew to the said quantity, and so creaved it to be free of so much multure. And likeways the deponents swears that they were always pursued before the Sherrif Court and requir'd be the taxman of the miln, even in the time of

---

[1] In addition to.

the payment of farm bear, for the multurs therof, another evidence of its not being fourty years proscrived.

Lastly, as to that of their not paying dry multure[1] for these eighteen years bygone for what bear they have sold, is an argument what the greatest part of this sucken, yea, the whole kingdom, may pretend to. Which only shows the negligence or lenity of the taxman of the miln, and their defrauding the taxman of his just right, but can never infringe the lawful property of the proprietar, and dues of the tennent, and therfore creaves they may be found lyable in manner acclaim'd.

1st August 1730.

Presentia Robert Wyllie, Baillie forsaid.

The Baillie forsaid haveing consider'd fully the witnesses depositions, William Duthies alleadgances therupon, together with the answers therto, Finds the thirlage of the whole toun of Reidcloak relevant to include the multurs of the saids two subtacks of Lochdews and Bruntholls, and that the prescription pretended by virtue of farm bear are not suficient to take off payment of multures. In regard it is proven that they were formerly and prior to their payment of farm bear cottar crofts, and payed full multure, and since for these eighteen years bygone they were and presently are sett for mony rent which pays the same full dues. And likewise finds that no tennent bound to the miln can at his pleasure subsett a tack for farm bear, so as to defraud the heritor or taxman of the said miln of his just dues. And lastly, that their not paying dry multure these severall years past is also irrelivant, in so farr as it was only done by the negligence of the taxmans not requiring it for some years, it being proven that they were always pursued before the Judge competent for and required to make payment of the same. In respect wherof, Finds the defenders lyable, and Decerns against them in manner acclaim'd.

Rot. Wyllie, balie.
John Maule, Clk.

---

[1] *Dry multure:* a yearly payment paid in money or grain, whether the tenant grind his grain at the mill or not. —Bell's *Law of Scotland*, p. 824.

Barron Court of the land and Barrony of Urie pertaining
heritably to the honourable Robert Barclay, younger of
Urie, holden at the mannor place therof, in the place
where the said Court usually sitts, upon the sixteenth day
of November one thousand seven hundred and thirty
years, in presence of the said Robert Barclay, by James
Edward in Maigro, Baillie, Alexander Brown in Mains
of Ury, Procurator Fiscall, and John Maule, nottar
publick, Clerk therto, William Thomson, officer, and
Dempster.

Sectis vocatis Curia legittime affirmata.

The said day anent the complaint given in at the instance
of the said procurator fiscall against Alexander Gibbon in
Miln of Cowie, mentioning that the said Alexander Gibbon,
notwithstanding by the nature of all tacks every tenement is
obliged to keep the ground he has in possession in good order,
and defend it from any accidentall dammage of water and
otherways, and by law is restrain'd from wasting and destroying their possessions, which they only have for their lawfull use
and advantage, and likeways the said Alexander Gibbon is
expressly bound in his assedation, herewith produced, to defend
his ground from the incursions of the water of Cowie, and also
there are severall acts of this Court against casting of faill or
divot, ather in sward, ley, or grass ground, etc., and particularly
the toun of miln of Cowie is not to be cast up, except upon
the common breas therof allenarly, as by ane act of this court,
dated the twenty fourth day of January last by past more fully
bears, and that under the penalty of twenty pound Scots mony,
by and attour the dammages incurr'd by the heritors there
thorrow, Yet nevertheless the said Alexander Gibbon has negli-
gently or willfully allowed the water of Cowie to break in upon
the ground of the lands of the Miln of Cowie, and destroyed
the same with utter ruin therof, and also allowed a burn that
runs betwixt the said lands and that of Polbair, whereby the
saids ground is likeways destroyed, all extending to the value
of fifty merks Scots of dammages, the property therof being
forever rendred useless; and also the said Alexander Gibbon
has by himself or servants, since the term of Whitsunday last

by past, cast up faill and divott upon the balks of the lands
called the Craighouse of the Miln of Cowie, which was the best
grass of the haill lands on the said toun, and therby forever
rendred useless, and therfore the said Alexander Gibbon ought
and should be decern'd and ordained to pay and deliver to the
said procurator Fiscall, for the use and behoof of the said
Robert Barclay, not only the said sum of fifty merks Scots of
damnage, but also the said sum of twenty pound Scots mony
of penalty incurrd as above, and otherways enacted, fynd, and
amerciate in terms of law, to the terror of others from com-
mitting the like in time comeing.

Whereupon compeard the said Alexander Gibbon, and being
interrogate in terms of the above complaint, acknowledged that
the water of Cowie had incroached upon the said lands and
done some damnage therto, but that the same was but small
and inconsiderate, and also confessd the casting up of feall on
the said balks of the Craighouse.   ALEXR. GIBBON.

The Baillie forsaid haveing considerd the above complaint,
togither with the said Alexander Gibbon his judiciall confession, fyns and amerciates the said Alexander Gibbon in the
sum of twenty pound Scots for his casting up of the said faill
on the Craighouse, and also fyns and amerciates him in the
like sum of twenty pound Scots for the damnage done to the
saids lands by the water of Cowie, and decerns against him
therfor, and ordains all execution to pass hereon for the saids
sums in term of law.   JAMES EDVARD, Ba.
                                       JOHN MAULE, Clk.

The said day the Baillie forsaid enacts and ordains that,
within three days next of this, the said Alexander Gibbon shall
repair, by bullwarks or other such fences, the lands he possess
that are adjacent or lyable to the incursions of the said water
of Cowie and burn betwixt Polbairs lands and his, which if the
said Alexander Gibbon faill to doe, then it shall be lawfull for,
and in the power of the said Robert Barclay to employ workmen for securing the saids lands from the incroachments or
damnage of the said waters, upon the proper charge and
expence of the said Alexander Gibbon, and not only from what

damnage is done just now, but likeways in time comeing, to
which the said Alexander Gibbon consents, and therto the
Baillie forsaid interpons his authority.

ALEXR. GIBBON.
JAMES EDARD, *Ba.*
JOHN MAULE, *Clk.*

The forsaid day the said Baillie enacts that no person shall
cast any faill or turf quhatsumever upon the muir and hill
lying upon the eastward of the high road that goes betwixt
Bruxden and the place called the Sandiehillock, and that under
the penalty of twenty pound Scots mony, to be payed in to the
use of the said heritor, *toties quoties* they are found guilty
therof, and forfaulting of the faill or turf so cast up, wherunto
the Baillie forsaid interpons his authority.

JAMES EDWARD, *Ba.*
JOHN MAULE, *Clk.*

> *Court of the lands and Baronie of Urie pertaining heretably*
> *to the honorable Robert Barclay, younger therof, holden*
> *att the manor place therof, upon the thretteint day of*
> *February one thousand seven hundred and threttie one*
> *years, be Alexander Broun in Mains, Bailie James Milne,*
> *notar publict, Clerk, John Souter, Fiscall, and William*
> *Kairn, Dempster, and William Thomson, officer, in*
> *presence of the Laird.*

The which day anent the action and ryot pursued at the
instance of the said procurator fiscall against John Smith,
servitor to the said laird of Urie, for hurting, wounding, and
blood drawing of John and James Davidsons, brothers, in
Muchollis, and Alexander Davidson and William Henderson,
all at the lands of Muchollis, and that in and about the house
of Cransacre, upon the third, fourt, or fift days of February
last, or one or other of the saids days, and the said phiscall
craved one assythment to be decernd in favours of the said
Alexander Davidson (if the ryot shall be proven) or any other
persons wounded, and to underly the law therfore, and to be
amerciat conform to law.

Compeard the said John Smith, and said that upon one or

other of the forsaids days he was mightily provock'd and insulted by the above named Davidsons and Henderson in
Mucholls, being first abusd in the house of Cransacre, and then
went out to shun their company, they folloued him armed with
staffs and other weapons, and pursued him for his life, so that
he was necessarly obliged to beat them in his oun defence.
The fiscall to confirm and fortifie the forsaid confession craved
the witnesses cited for proveing the said lybell might be
examined.   JA. MILNE, *N.P.*, *Clk*.

Compeard Robert Measson in Cransacre, witnes cited,
solemnly suorn, purgd of partiall counsell, and examined and
interrogat, depons, That upon one or other of the saids days
he heard Alexander Davidson abuse James Burne in Powbair
to a great degree, and threatne to beat him; to prevent which
John Lyon remov'd them all out of his house, But they afterwards came back and abusd and insulted the said John Smith,
threatning him with his staff. Afterwards he saw the said
John Smith goe out of the house, and thereafter the said
Alexander Davidson, and the other above persons in Mucholls,
folloued him armed as above, and then the said deponent went
out and saw the said John Smith give the forsaid Alexander
Davidsone one stroak to the effusion of his bloud. And this
is truth, as he shall answer to God, and declares he can sign
no otherwise than his initial letters. R. M.
                               ALEXR. BROVN, *balie.*
                               JA. MILNE, *N.P.*, *Clk*.

Compeard Robert Milne in Powbair, witnes cited, solemnly
sworn, purgd of partiall Counsell, and examined and interogat,
depons, That upon one or other of the forsaids days he was in
Cransacre, and saw John Lyon put out the above Davidsons
and Henderson furth of his house becaus of their making
abuse and disturbance therin, and therafter they returned again
and insulted, provocked, and abused John Smith: after that
they and he went out of the house together, and then the
deponent following, saw the forsaid John Smith beat the said
Alexander Davidson to the effusion of his bloud, and further
depons that the other tuo Davidsons came and pursue[d] the

said John Smith as he thought, whom he turned back. And
this is truth, as he shall answer to God, and declares he cannot
writ.

*De mandato dicti Roberti Milne Scribere nescientis ut asseruit
ego Jacobus Milne notarius publicus subscribo.*

ALEXR. BROVN, baile.
JA. MILNE, <i>N.P., Clk.</i></div>

Eodem die, The Bailie forsaid having considered the said
John Smith, his judiciall confession, and the witnesses depositions, amerciat the within named John Smith in Fiftie punds
Scots, to be paid to the fiscall of Court within term of law,
and ordains precepts to be issued out in form as effeirs for that
effect. But finds no assythment due to the said Alexander
Davidson, in regard by the above depositions he was provocked
to doe what he did in his oun defence, and therefore absolves
the said John Smith therfrom in all time coming.

R. BARCLAY, JR.   ALEXR. BROVN, *bailie.*
                         JA. MILNF, *N.P., Clk.*

*Court of the lands and Baronie of Ury pertaining heritably
to Robert Barclay, younger therof, holden att his Manor
house upon the tuentie first day of July one thousand
seven hundred threttie tuo years, be William Duthie in
Reid Cloake, his honour's Bailie, James Milne, notar
publict, Clerk, John Souter, Fiscall, William Edward,
officer, and   Dempster.*

Will. Duthie, Bailie.

The which day anent the action and ryot intented and pur-
sued at the instance of the said fiscall of Court against John
Cassie and Robert Laurence, servitors to William Ronald in
Stonhyve, George Lightoun, sone to James Lightoun in
Smiddie moor, and Robert Chalmer, servitor to John Young,
Shirreff Clerk of Kincardine,[1] for their ryotous destroying of

---

[1] John Young, Sheriff-Clerk of Kincardine, was proprietor of the lands of
Stank (now Bellfield), in the parish of Kinneff, having acquired the same by
purchase from Mr. Isaac Fullerton. He died in 1750. His son, William Young
of Fawside, sold Stank to Mr. Charles Abercromby, writer, Edinburgh. The
lands are now in the possession of the trustees of the late William Harvie.

the corns and grass of Robert Wyllie in Powbair, with horss
and carts going through the same this day, and severall other
days of the last moneth, to the outter ruin therof, and the
said Robert Wyllie his great detriment and loss, contrair to
all laws, equitie, and justice, and for which ryot, when proven,
the above named defenders ought to be fynd and amerciat and
decernd in such damages to the partie forsaid as the Bailie
shall think fitt.

Compeared the haill forenamed defenders, and being interrogat anent the forsaid ryot, they all and each of them plainly
confessd and acknowledgd the same as lybelld, and all of them
gave the Clerk of Court power to sign this their said judiciall
confession, except the said Robert Chalmer, who signd himself.

*De mandato prefati Joannis Cassie Robertj Laurence et
Georgij Lightoun scribere nescientium ut asseruere ego
Jacobus Milne, notarius publicus, subscribo.*

WILL. DUTHIE, *Balie.*
JA. MILNE, *N.P., Clk.*

The Bailie within named and designd having considered the
defenders within named their within confession, fyns and amerciats each one of them in six punds Scots, to be paid to the
fiscall of Court within term of law.

WILL. DUTHIE, *Bailie.*
JA. MILNE, *N.P., Clk.*

*Court of the lands and Baronie of Ury, pertaining heretably
to Robert Barclay, younger therof, holden at his Manor
place upon the tuentie first day of July one thousand
seven hundred threttie tuo years, be William Duthie in
Reidcloak, Bailie, James Milne, notar publict, clerk, John
Souter, Fiscall, William Thomson, officer, and
Dempster.*

The which day anent the action and ryot intented and pursued at the instance of the said fiscall of Court against Robert
Edward, servitor to the said laird of Ury, for hurting, wounding, and bloud draueing of David Smith and   Hamptoun, servitors to John Falconer at miln of Stonhyve, who
craved assythments off the said Robert Edward.

Compear'd the said Robert Edward and declar'd and acknowledged that being ordered by his said Master to endeavour
to apprehend the persons who were willfully and masterfully
destroying Robert Wyllie in Powbair, his corns and grass, the
saids David Smith and   Hamptoun gave him very
abusive and provocking language, and impudently own'd that
they had destroyed the saids corns and grass, and would doe it
again; and they still persisting in doing therof, and the said
Robert endeavouring to apprehend them and stop them therfrom, they violently attempted to throw him down.   For which
cause and reason he in his own defence owns he did beat them
severall times to the effusion of their bloud, and one of them
trying to catch a mercat halbert from him, which he had in
his hand, run his hand theron and bled him.   And the said
Robert does not deny but that in the strugle and grapling he
might have drawen bloud of one or both of them.

The Bailie forsaid having considered the above confession,
finds that the said Robert, endeavouring to apprehend the
forenamed persons, who were actually upon the said Robert
Wyllies grass and corns, sufficient to liberat and free him from
all assythment, especiallie since what he did was in his own
defence as said is, and that the wounds they had receaved
were occasioned by their own foollish and willfull trying to
take the halbert from him, but owns his beating and stricking
of them with his hands and otherwise, which was contrair to
all law.   Therefore the said Bailie fyns and amerciats the said
Robert Edward in the sum of fiftie punds Scots, to be paid to
the fiscall of Court within term of law under the pain of
poinding.   WILL. DUTHIE, *Bailie.*
                          JA. MILNE, *N.P., Clk.*

Barron Court of the lands and Barrony of Ury pertaining
  heritably to Robert Barclay, younger of Ury, holden at
  the Mannor place thereof, in the place where the said
  Court usually sitts, upon the thirteenth day of February
  one thousand seven hundreth and thirty three years, in
  presence of the said Robert Barclay, by William Duthie,
  in Reid Cloak, Baillie, Robert Wyllie, in Pollbair, Pro-
  curator Fiscall, and John Maule, nottar publick, Clerk

thereto, William Thomson, officer, and   Dempster.
The suits called and the Court lawfully fenced and
affirmed.

The which day the Baillie forsaid takeing in to his serious
consideration, at the desire of the said proprietar, that many
laudable laws and acts of parliament have been made to cause
their tennants and others plant trees in their yeards and possessions, and that the whole Barrony of Ury is now inteirly
destitute of planting notwithstanding thereof and severall acts
of Court made for that effect, to the great loss of the heritor
and improvement and ornament of the country in generall,
hereby ordains the present gairdner of Ury, or any other
gairdner or person that the said heritor shall appoynt, to plant
trees in the respective yeards of the whole Barrony, as well
that of Montqueich as the Nether Barrony of Ury, and that
with all convenient speed. And in regard some trees formerly
planted have been intirly spoylled in the grouth, not only by
cutting and breaking thereof, but likeways by digging and
cutting the roots of the trees so planted with their spades,
therfore it is hereby statute and ordained that each tennant,
subtenant, and other within the said Barrony shall hereafter
leave unlaboured a strip of ground round their respective
yeard dykes, not under two feet and ane half of measure, for
preserving the said trees, and that no person nor persons in
time comeing digg, break, or cutt the roots, or any part of the
said trees, under the penalty of ten pound Scots for each tree
so broak, cutt, or otherways defaced or abused, to be payed
to the said heritor for each tree under ten years growth,
and twenty pound Scots for each tree so broak or defaced
above ten years growth ; and each tennent, cottar, grassmen,
and others to be lyable for all their wifes, bairns, servants, and
others within their severall housses who shall be guilty of
breaking or destroying the saids trees, according to the 16th
Act of the 7th Session of King Williams first parliament, etc.,
for preservation of planting. And likeways each tennent and
subtennent to clear their several yeards of all sauchs or shrubs
whatsumever, betwixt this and the fifteent day of March next
to come, that the trees so to be planted may receive no prejudice thereby, and that under the penalty of ten pound Scots,

to be payed by the contravener to the said heritor, with power
to him to employ workmen to clear the same, and that at the
expence and charge of the contraveener.

WILL. DUTHIE, *Balie.*
JOHN MAULE, *Clk.*

13 *February* 1733.

Presentia William Duthie, Baillie forsaid.

Anent the complaint given in by the ground officer, with
concurse of the said heritor, anent the loss of the said ground
officers dues for some time past by tennents casting on the
burthen of their officers corn on their subtenents, afterwards
turning out their subtennents and taking their crofts in their
own hand. Then they neglect to pay their officers corn and
services, not only to their loss but also the loss of others, who
are obliged to come to harriage and carriage the oftner upon
that account, and particularly condescends upon Andrew
Meason and Alexander Wobster in Glithno, John Lyon in
Cransacher, and Alexander Youngson in Balnagight, who have
been deficient therof. To remieding wherof the Baillie forsaid
ordains each toun to pay what they were in use and custom to
pay, either of officer dues or services, and when the subtennent
is putt out the principall tennent shall pay and uphold officer
dues and services for each subtennent so putt out of their
respective possessions in all time comeing. And for the more
effectual clearing thereof the following quotas are found due
and ordained to be payed by each tennent within the touns of
the lands of Ury aftermentioned : *videlicet*, for Balnagight as
possessed by Alexander Youngson, three firlots and two pecks
of corn and services for five familys ; John Lounann in Cairntoun, two pecks and service effeiring to his possession. Item,
Robert Cruikshank in Montboy, one firlot and service for two
familys. Item, George Mouat in Mosstoun, two pecks and
service conform. Item, Andrew Meason in Glithno, one firlot
of corn and service for two familys. Item, Alexander Webster,
one firlot and service for two familys. Item, John Strachan
there, six pecks of corn and service for two familys. Item,
John Lyon in Cransaicker, ten pecks of corn and service for

four familys.   Item, James Kaird and William Kaird in Woodhead, each of them two pecks of corn and usuall service. Item, John Mouat there, one firlot and service for two familys. Item, Robert Wyllie in Polbair, seventeen pecks of corn and service used by himself and for six familys.   Item, Alexander Brown in Maigro, four pecks of corn and services for two familys.   Item, James Edward there, one firlot of corn and services for two familys; William Main there, two pecks and services conform.   Item, John Main in Cowic, services conform to neighbours and others.   Alexander Gibbon, in Miln of Cowie, one firlot and usuall services, and ordains all the above to be performed yearly, and ilk year in time comeing, under the pain of poynding and other execution needfull to pas hereon in form as effeirs.   WILL. DUTHIE, *Balie.*

JOHN MAULE, *Clk.*

Court of the lands and Baronie of Urie pertaining heretably to the much honored **Robert Barclay**, *younger therof, holden at the Manor place of Urie, upon the sixteent day of June one thousand seven hundred threttie three years, be William Duthie in* **Reidcloak**, *Bailie, James Milne, notar publict, Clerk,* **John Souter**, *Phiscall, William Thomson, Officer, and*

Dempster.

The which day, anent the action and ryot intented and pursued at the instance of the said phiscall, with concourse of the heritor of the said lands and baronie, against the persons particularly afternamed, for their kindling of mureburn,[1] fire raising, and burning the mosses and mures within the said baronie, and priviledges thereof, particularly within the fisher Myres and bounds adjacent therto, which, if proven, the persons guilty and convict ought to be fyn'd and amerciated in the pains and penalties prescribed be law.

Compear'd William White in Woodhead, aged fiftie three years or therby, lawfull cited, solemnly sworn, and examined,

---

[1] The practice of *mureburn* was resorted to for the purpose of producing turfs. The grass and heath were set fire to about Midsummer, and the surface of the ground so burned was subsequently raised to be used as fuel or otherwise.

and interrogat annent the forsaid ryot, who depon'd negative
theranent, and was absolved, and declar'd he could not writ.

WILL. DUTHIE, *Balie.*
JA. MILNE, *N.P., Clk.*

Compear'd William White, younger there, cited, sworn,
and examined, and interogat *ut supra*, acknowledges himself
guilty of the said ryot, and referred himself to the Bailie, and
declares he cannot writ.   WILL. DUTHIE, *Balie.*
JA. MILNE, *N.P., Clk.*

Compear'd David Walker in Woodhead, lawfullie cited,
solemnly sworn, and examined and interogat, depon'd that he
rais'd fire in the moss, but that he extinguished the same
before he left it, and declares he cannot write.

WILL. DUTHIE, *Balie.*
JA. MILNE, *N.P., Clk.*

The Judge and Bailie forsaid having considered the confessions of the above named William White, younger, and David
Walker, fyns and amerciats each of them in fyve punds Scots,
to be paid in to the Fiscall of Court, within term of law, who
were required to make payment *apud acta* for that effect.

WILL. DUTHIE, *Balie.*
JA. MILNE, *N.P., Clk.*

The said day and place the Bailie forsaid, for the more
effectual preventing the fyreing of mosses and mures in time
coming, ordains that no person whatsoever shall give out fire
out of his or their houses, or allow the same to be taken out,
or know of the same, without stopping of it; otherwise the
contraveeners shall be deem'd as guilty of [? as] the raiseris of
fire, and suffer the pains and penalties of law accordingly, and
pay the damages thereof.   WILL. DUTHIE, *Balie.*
JA. MILNE, *N.P., Clk.*

Also, the said Bailie ordains that every person within the
Baronie keep his bank and lairs, both upper and under, level
and not hollow the same beneath to the splitting or falling

doun of the upper survice of the bank, but that the faces of
the bank shall be made intirely even, otherwise the person or
persons convict for controveening this act each shall be lyable
in a penaltie of ten pundis to the Fiscall of Court *toties quoties*.
And further, ordains the ground officer, or any other person
the laird shall appoint, to inspect the . mosses yearly at
Lambmas, beginning this present year, and so on yearly thereafter, and to levell, smooth, and make right any of the mosses
that shall be casten contrair to this act.   And the said ground
officer or other person so imploy'd shall be paid for his pains
att the rate of half ane merk each day, to be paid be the
person convict, besides the penaltie above exprest, all which
the Bailie ordains to be paid, within term of law, under pain
of poinding.   WILL. DUTHIE, *Balie*.

Barron Court of the lands and Barrony of Urie pertaining
heritably to the honourable Robert Barclay, younger of
Urie, holden at the Mannour place thereof, where the
said court usually sitts, upon the twenty eight day of
Jully j^mvij^c and thirty five years, in presence of the said
Robert Barclay, by James Gordon in Rothnick, Barron
Baillie, Robert Wyllie in Polbair, Fiscall, John Maule,
nottar publick, Clerk, William Thomson, Officer,
*   , Dempster.*
The suits called, and the court lawfully fenced and affirmed.

The said day, in presence forsaid, compeard the said
Robert Barclay, and gave in the following complaint against
the haill tennents within the said Barrony, mentioning that,
notwithstanding of the many and former acts of this Court
made against weasting of ground within the barrony of Urie,
yet the lands continue to be ruined to the irreparrable loss both
of the heritor and tennents, and that it is pretended the same
is much occasioned by the tennents not being more particularly
regulated in their labouring and casting up of meadow sward,
moss, or other ground whatsoever.   And which being considered by the Baillie forsaid, he not only ratifies, homologates,
approves, and confirms all former acts of Court already made in
this barrony against the casting up of any meadow, sward,

moss, or other ground in the haill articles, heads, and contents
thereof, but also in corroboration thereof, and for further re-
meeding of the same, hereby enacts, statutes, and ordains that
in all time coming from and after this date, all the saids
former acts shall be expressly kept and obeyed under the
severall penaltys therin contained, and for further clearing the
same that no ground upon the toun of Trees shall be cast
up upon any account to the eastward of the east-most hous in
Curbigg and the hill of Trees in a straight line, nor below the
nether Cassie upon the west side of the said hill, nor upon any
of the bentis or green ground below the ridge of the hill, nor
for fireing to the eastward of the mosses and Bruntland of
Carbigg in a straight line to the new Bruntland upon the west
side of Trees, nor upon any place of the toun of Burnhaugh,
except upon the Haulk hill, nor upon the lands of milne of
Montqueich except for peats where they presently cast, and
for mending the damm, and that only in proper ground sett
apart by the heritor, and noways detrimentall to the grass or
corn land of the said toun, nor upon the toun of Crossley
except in ditches and near the present sheep rive,[1] and only on
ground where the surface is already cast up, nor upon the
toun of Rothnick, but where they are or shall be licensed by
the heritor upon certain places where the surface is already
cast up, not exceeding the half of the quantity usually casten,
nor upon the toun of Balnagight, Cairntoun, Montboy, and
Woodhead, except in the mains thereof that are not prohibited,
nor upon Glithno nor Crans Aicker, except upon the north east
of the Newfolds above Andrew Measons house, and to the
northward of the northmost corn lands of Alexander Webster,
John Straiton, and John Lyon, nor upon the toun of Polbair,
but upon the ground where the surface is already cast up lying
betwixt the corn yeard thereof and the corn land to the northward of the same for a moderate use allenarly, nor upon
Megray except in the muir thereof, James Edward being to
cast in the Mercatt stance and non else, and in the common
breas betwixt that and milne of Cowie where the tennents of
Milne of Cowie are priviledged to cast allenarly and no where

---

[1] *Sheep rive*, pasturage for sheep.

else. And likways it is enacted and ordained that all mosses be
regularly and even cast up without underminding the moss,
and the under lair levelled, and where the surface of the moss
happens to be green or bent, or anything else but black ground
wholly, they shall first cast the surface of the ground with a
flaughter spade[1] and carefully lay the same upon the bottom of
the moss so cast up, that the same may grow green again. As
also that all who possess land upon the banks of waters or
stripes fortifie the same against the incurtions of the water, and
non labour ground within the waterflood marks. That no
ground be brunt until after the first of Jully yearly, and non
brunt at all except what is ribb'd[2] and above two foot deep of
black or moss ground, and that non be over brunt. And in
case any of the saids acts shall happen to be contraveen'd, the
Baillie ordains the ground officer to cause any two honest men
whom the heritor shall appoynt to view the trespass committed
and legally report the damnage at the first Barron Court then
next after, when the contravenner or contravenners of any of
the above acts shall, for each offence so committed by him or
them, and found guilty of, shall, for each offence, incurr the
penalty of twenty pound Scots money to the heritor by and
attour the damnage committed by him or them at the modi-
fication of the Baillie then sitting in judgement. And also
ordains that, for the better preservation of planting and in-
closures, that no person either in their persons, or with their
bestiall, pastureng within the parks of the said barrony for the
future, nor be found traveling therin or leaping over the dykes
and fences thereof, under the penalty of five pound Scots money
toties quoties. To all which the Baillie forsaid interpon'd his
authority.   JAMES GORDON, *balie.*
                                    JOHN MAULE, *Clk.*

28th Jully 1735.

Presentia said Baillie; anent the Complaint given in by the
Fiscall against Alexander Youngson, younger in Balnagight,

---

[1] A long two-handed instrument used for casting turfs.—*Jam.*

[2] Half ploughed. In *ribbing* land the furrow raised by the plough is turned
over upon an equal superficies of land left firm.—Agricultural Survey, *Peebles-
shire,* p. 137.

and Robert Cruikshank, younger in Montboys, for their
mutuall beating, bruising, and blooding of one another,
grapling with each other, and throwing one another to the
ground, and that upon the twenty fourth day of June last.
Compeared the said defenders, and denyed the lybell, and the
fiscall offered to prove the same by witnesses.   Wherupon
compeard Andrew Meason, younger in Glithno, unmarried
man, aged twenty five years or thereby, witness, addmitted,
sworn, purged of partiall concill, and interrogate, depon'd that
at the time lybelled he saw the defenders throw a dogg [1] at each
other, and then grapple with one another, that the said Alexander Youngson did throw Robert Cruikshank violently to the
ground, that he saw them both blooding when they were
parted.   And this is the truth, as he shall answer to God.

ANDREW MEASON.
JAMES GORDON.

Compear'd John Glenny in Montboy, unmarried man, aged
twenty years or thereby, witness, admitted *ut supra*, and
solemnly sworn, depon'd *conformis presidente in omnibus*, only
with this variation, that he saw no blood upon Alexander
Youngson when he and Robert Cruikshank were parted from
other.   And this is truth, as he shall answer to God.

JOHN GLENNIE.
JAMES GORDON, bailie.
JOHN MAUIE, Clk.

28th Jully 1735, *Presentia* Baillie forsaid.

The Baillie forsaid haveing consider'd the forsaid lybell with
the witnesses depositions, finds both the blooding and beating
proven against the said Alexander Youngson, younger, and the
beating proven against the said Robert Cruikshank, and therfor
ammerciates the said Alexander Youngson in the sum of fifty
pound Scots, and the said Robert Cruikshank in ten pound, to
be payed to the fiscall for the heritors behoof, and ordains
them to goe to prison until the same be payed.

JAMES GORDON, balie.
JOHN MAULF, Clk.

---

[1] A lever used by blacksmiths in hooping cart-wheels.—*Jam.*

*Barron Court of the lands and Barrony of Urie, pertaining
heritably to the honourable **Robert Barclay**, younger of
Urie, holden at the Manour place therof where the said
Court usually sitts, upon the thirteenth day of January
jᵐvijᶜ and thirty eight years, in presence of the said
Robert Barclay, by **John** Somervell, merchant in **Aberdeen**, Baillie, **Robert** Wyllie, Fiscall, John Maule, nottar
publick, **Clerk**, William Thomson, Officer,
Dempster.*

The suitts called, and the court lawfully fenced and affirmed.

The said day, in presence forsaid, compear'd the said Robert
Barclay, and gave in to the said Baillie the Decreet Arbitrall
pronounced by Master Robert Dundas of Arnistoun,[1] advocate,
now Lord Arniston, in the submission entered into betwixt him
the said Robert Barclay and John Fullertoun of Cowie, creave-
ing the Baillie forsaid might ordain his clerk to read and publish
the same in presence of the haill **tennents** and subtennents of
the haill lands and barrony of **Urie**, which desire the Baillie
found reasonable, and accordingly the said Decreet was publickly read and published that non of the tennents and others
forsaid might pretend ignorance.   Whereupon the Baillie
ordained the contents of the said Decreet to be punctually
observed by the haill tennents forsaid, under the highest pains
of law, by and attour the performance thereof.

Jo. SOMERVEL, *Bailie.*

JOHN MAULE, *Clk.*

13 *January* 1738, *Presentia* Baillie Somervell.

It being represented the loss the tennents of this barrony are
at for want of legall sworn barly men for deciding anent eaten
corns[2] and other controversies that may arise 'twixt master

---

[1] Robert Dundas of Arniston was born 9th December 1685. He was called
to the Bar in 1709, and appointed Solicitor-General for Scotland in 1717.
In 1720 he became Lord Advocate, and two years later was elected Member of
Parliament for the county of Edinburgh. In June 1737 Mr. Dundas was raised
to the bench as Lord Arniston, and on 10th September 1748 he succeeded
Duncan Forbes of Culloden as Lord President of the Court of Session. He died
26th August 1753.—Anderson's *Scottish Nation*, vol. ii. p. 95.

[2] *Eaten corns* probably corns that had been destroyed by the trespass of cattle
belonging to the tenants of neighbouring holdings.

and tennent, or betwixt tennent and subtennents themselves,
or 'twixt tennent and tennent, and for appryzing houses, and
doeing every other thing pertaining to legall sworn barlymen.
And John Lyon in Cransaicker, James Edward in Megray,
Robert Edward in Mill of Cowie, John Strachan in Glithno,
James Gordon in Rothnick, John Airth in Trees, and James
Murray in Corsley being named, with the consent of the
heritors and haill tenents, they compeard, and being solemnly
sworn, gave their oath *de fideli* as barly men forsaid, and
accepted as such by their respective subscriptions. To which
the Baillie interpon'd his authority, and ordain'd any one or
more of them when called to act as a sworn barly man in
maner forsaid, the Baillie and Clerk of Court haveing subscrived for such of them as cannot write.

> JAMES EDWARD.
> JAMES GORDON.
> JOHN AIRTH.
> Jo. SOMERVEL, *Bailie*.
> JOHN MAULE, *Clk*.

13th *January* 1738, *Presentia* Baillie Somervell.

Compear'd Robert Barclay, elder of Urie, and the said
Barclay, younger thereof, and gave in a joynt complaint not
only against the tennents and subtennents of the nether part
of the Barrony of Urie, but also against the tennents of that
part of the said Barrony of Urie called Montqueich, representing the greatt damnage done to the proper mosses and muirs of
the said barrony in and thorrow the said haill tennents and
their subtennents casting up, wasting, selling, and destroying
thereof. Which complaint haveing been seriously considered by
the said Baillie, he enacted, decerned, and ordain'd, and hereby
enacts, decerns, and ordains that in all time comeing from and
after this date, that no tennent, subtennent, or other possessor
within the lands and Barrony of Urie shall not cast up any
truf or other fewell to the west and south west of the road
that leads from the Lonn of Shigyhead to the foord of
Auchanyark, and from the said foord to the Katherie Bridges,
and that no peats, turf, or other fewell be sold by any tenent,

subtennent, or other possessor within the said barrony out of
the moss called the Coall Moss and mosses of Montqueich, or
any other of the proper mosses or muirs within any part of the
haill barrony of Urie, under the penalty of half a crown for
each load of turf or peats that shall so happen to be sold
toties quoties by and attour confiscation of all such peats or
other fewell.   And further, the Baillie forsaid enacts and
ordains that Andrew Meason in Glithno and his subtennents
shall in all time comeing cast his haill fireing, whether turf or
peats, where the other tennents of Glithno presently cast their
peats and other fewell, and no where else, under the above
pennalty of half a crown for each load, and confiscation of the
haill to the heritor.   And that no turf be cast and sold off of
the Hill called the Blairs, and this but prejudice of all former
acts of court; all which, togither with this present act, the
Baillie forsaid ordains to be punctually observed, under the
respective penaltys therin contain'd, and hereto interpons his
authority.   Jo. SOMERVEL, *Bailie.*
                                    JOHN MAULE, *Clk.*

13*th January* 1738.—*Presentia* Baillie Somervell.

The Baillie forsaid ordained the principall tennent of each
plough within this Barrony to pay in yearly four shilling and
six pennies Scots for each plough of vagabond mony [1] as long
as the same shall be continued as a cess upon the shyre, and
that to Robert Wyllie in Powbair, collector appoynted for that
effect, under the pain of poynding.   To which the haill
tennents present consented, and the Baillie interpon'd his
authority thereto.   Jo. SOMERVEL, *Bailie.*
                                    JOHN MAULE, *Clk.*

The said day a complaint being enter'd by the said heritor
and fiscall against Alexander Burnet, subtennent in Glithno,
for his casting up ground upon the commonty without liberty,
and he compearing and being interrogate, judicially confest the

---

[1] *Vagabond money* was a tax levied one half from the heritors and one half
from the tenants, according to their means and substance, to meet such weekly
charges as might be sufficient to sustain the poor.—*Acta Parl.* c. 52, vii.
p. 485.

same.   Wherfor the Baillie amerciate him in six pound Scots,
to be payed to the fiscall for the heritors behoof, within term
of law, and ordained precepts of poynding in common form.
Therafter compear'd the said Alexander Burnet, and judicially
enacted himself to flitt, redd, and remove himself, his wife,
bairns, family, servants, goods, and gear furth and from the
occupation of his said possession, and that within forty eight
hours after the term of Whitsunday next to come, under the
penalty of twenty pound Scots, besides being ejected by the
ground officer of this Barrony.   And declaired he could not write,
and therfor the Baillie interpon'd his authority thereto, and
subscrived for him, as did also the Clerk, having gott power
from him for that effect.   Jo. SOMERVEL, *Bailie.*
                                             JOHN MAULE, *Clk.*

The said day anent a Complaint given in by John Lyon,
ground smith of the said Barrony, that the most of tennents
and subtennents had abstracted themselves from his smiddy,
therfor creaves that they may be all bound and pay their dues
for the futher,[1] in terms of a former act of this Court, dated
anno j^{m}vij^{c} and five,[2] which desire the Baillie forsaid found
reasonable, and therfor revived and herby ordain'd the said act
to be keep'd in all time coming, under the penaltys therin contain'd, as oft as the same is contraven'd by and attour performance.   The said John Lyon being always obliged to give true,
ready, and sufficient service and work, in terms of the said act.
To which the Baillie forsaid interpons his authority.
                                             Jo. SOMERVEL, *Bailie.*
                                             JOHN MAULE, *Clk.*

Barron Court of the lands and Barrony of Urie, pertaining
   heritably to the honourable Robert Barclay, younger of
   Urie, holden at the mannour place thereof, where the said
   Court usually sits, upon this fourth day of November
   j^{m}vij^{c} and thirty eight years, in presence of the said
   Robert Barclay, by Alexander Walker[3] *in Auquhirie,*

---

[1] For the time coming.   [2] See p. 114, *supra.*

[3] Alexander Walker, who farmed the lands of Auquhirie, in the parish of
Dunnottar, was a prominent agriculturist in his time.   He was succeeded in the

Baillie, James Lighton, Fiscall, John Maule, nottar
publick, Clerk, Alexander Edward, officer,
Dempster.
The suits called, and the court lawfully fenced and affirmed.

The said day, in presence forsaid, compear'd the said heritor
and fiscall, and gave in a complaint against William Kaird in
Woodhead, representing that the said William Kaird had in a
most contentious and vitious manner cast up water furrs, and
carried the said water from that of his own possession upon the
lands also belonging to the said heritor possess'd by the said
James Lighton, wherby the same was damnaged to a considerable value, and that after the said William Kaird was duely
interpell'd from acting or doeing the same. Whereupon compear'd the said William Kaird, and judicially confess'd that he
had fill'd up a ditch cast by order of the heritor for preventing
any damnage to be done by water to the said James Lightons
lands. Whereupon the Baillie ordain'd the barly men adduced
for proveing the said damnage to compear, and they being
called accordingly compear'd, James Edward in Megray, and
Robert Edward in Mill of Cowie, who being on oath as sworn
barlymen, declair'd that the damnage done by the said Walter
to James Lightons land ammounted to a peck of corn with the
fodder yearly, at six shilling Scots the peck. All which being
considered by the said Baillie, he fyned and amerciat the said
William Kaird in the sum of three pound Scots mony to be
payed to the said fiscall for the heritors behoof, within term of
law, and grants precepts of poynding for that effect, and further
ordains the said William Kaird in time comeing to defend his
water furrs from doeing any further damnage to the said James
Lightons possession, and keep redd water furrs for that effect,
under pain of law. ALEXR. WALKER, *Baile.*
JOHN MAULE, *Clk.*

The said day anent a complaint given in by the said heritor

---

farm of Auquhirie by his son, John Walker (*b.* 1740: *d.* 1812), who was associated with Robert Barclay of Urie, son of the 'Robert Barclay, younger,' of the
text, in his attempts to introduce the principles of scientific farming into the
district. The Walkers were proprietors of the estate of Blairton in Aberdeenshire.

and fiscall that the tennents, subtennents, and others of the
Mains, Kirntoun, and Balnagight had contraveen'd the last act
relative to the selling of peats. But upon the tennents and
others forsaid enacting themselves to obey the act in time
comeing, the heritor and fiscall deserted the pursuit, and
therfor the saids haill tennents and others hereby enact themselves to obey the said act in time comeing, under the penaltys
and damnages therin contain'd, which they all did in face of
court, and to which the Baillie forsaid interpons his authority,
and subscrives for such as cannot write.

ALEXR. WALKER, *Baile*.

JOHN MAULE, *Clk*.

The said day compear'd the said Fiscall, and exhibite a complaint against Alexander Milne in Mill of Montqueich, for his
cruell beating, bruiseing, and blooding of Alexander Burnet,
weaver in Cowie, upon the   day of October last by past,
grapleing with him and throwing him to the ground, and
creaved that he might be fyn'd and amarciate therfor. Whereupon compear'd the said Alexander Milne, and being solemnly
sworn, depon'd and confess'd that he violently grapled with the
saids Alexander Burnet, but denys that [he] bled him or threw
him quite down to the ground. And that was the truth, as he
should answer to God.

ALEXR. MILNE.

ALEXR. WALKER, *Baile*.

JOHN MAULE, *Clk*.

In respect of the above deposition and confession the Baillie
fyns and amerciates the said Alexander Milne in the sum of
ten pound Scots, to be payed to the fiscall for the heritors
behoof, and ordains him to goe to prison till the same be
payed.

ALEXR. WALKER, *Baile*.

JOHN MAULE, *Clk*.

Barron Court of the lands and Barrony of Ury, pertaining
heritably to the honourable Robert Barclay, junior, of
Ury, holden at the Mannour place thereof the twelfth day
of June one thousand seven hundred and thirty nine,
in presence of the said heiritor, by Robert Wylie, in Pow-

bair, Balie of said Barony, John Gleny, Procurator
Fiscal to the said court, John Maule, nottar publick,
Clerk, William Thomson, officer, and   Demster
The suits called, and the court lawfully fenced and affirmed.

The which day, in presence forsaid, the said heritor represented that there had been several acts of Court made anent
preserving the mosses, muirs, meadow, and swaird grounds pertaining to said Barrony of Ury, and particularly to that act
made the twenty eight of July one thousand seven hundred
and thirty five, and another dated January 13th, 1738, and in
order to put the said acts in full execution, homologates,
aproves, and ratifies the same, and all former acts made, and in
preserving the said mosses, muirs, meadow, and suaird grounds,
and not only ordains the same to be keapt in full force in all time
comming, but also ordains the contraveeners of any particular
part thereof to be conveened before this court, and fine and
amertiate for such contraventione as has already happned, or
may hereafter happen, as the said act of Court and law fully
direct.   R. BARCLAY, Jr.   R. WYLIE, *balie.*
                                        JOHN MAULE, *Clk.*

The said day anent the complaint given in by the said procurator fiscal against James Cards, elder and younger in Woodhead, and William Card there, for their mutual beating,
bruising, and blooding one another, grapling with and throwing each other violently to the ground, upon the fourth day of
June currant, or upon one or other of the days of the said
month, and craving that the saids defenders might be fined
and amerciate in their persons, goods, and gear, as law directs.
And they being lawfully summoned for that effect, compeared
the said James Card, younger, and judicially confessed that he
grappled with and threw to the ground the said William Card,
and put his foot upon his belly, but denys that he blood him,
and declares he cannot write. Thereafter compeared the said
William Card, and being interrogate whither or not he beat,
blood, or bruised, or violently threw to the ground the persons
of saids James Cards, elder and younger, and the Fiscall offering to prove the same by the oath of the said William Card,

he refused to depon, and for which the Balie held him as confessed. In respect of which confession of the said James Card, younger, and the said William Card his refusing to depone, fines and amerciates the said James Card, younger, in the sum of ten pounds Scots, and the said William Card in the like sum of ten pound money forsaid, to be paid to the procurator fiscall for the heritors behoof, and ordains them to go to the ordinary prison of the barrony untill the same be paid.

Rot. Wyllie, balie.
John Maule, Clk.

Barron Court of the lands and Barrony of Ury pertaining heritably to the honourable Robert Barclay, junior, of Ury, holden at the Mannour place thereof the seventeenth day of January one thousand seven hundred and forty, in presence of the said heritor, by John Somervel, merchant in Aberdeen, Baillie of the said barrony, Robert Willie, Procurator Fiscal to the said court, John Glenny, Clerk, John Irvine, Officer, and   Demster.

The suits called, and the court lawfully fenced and affirmed.

The which day, in presence forsaid, and of Robert Barclay, elder of Ury, for his intrest, anent a complaint given in by the said heritor and fiscal against the hail tenants, subtenants, and inhabitants of the barrony for their contentious disobeying the laws and acts of courts relative to their selling of peats and turf, casting up of ground, wasting of their possessions, and the contraveening of other acts formerly made therefore, craving that the persons guilty may be ordined to pay the damnages to the heritor, with the penalties thereby incurred.

Jo. Somervel, Bailie.
John Glenny, Clerk.

January the 17th, presentia within Baillie, etc.

Accordingly compeared Robert Cruikshank, George Mouat, John Laurance, Alexander Youngson, and denied the lybal. Likewise compeared the tenants of Rothnick and Corsley, and likewise denied the lybal. The heritor and fiscal offers to prove.

Jo. Somervel, Bailie.
John Glenny, Clerk.

Barron Court of the lands and Barrony of Ury pertaining heritably to the honorable Robert Barclay of Ury, junior, holden att the Mannor Place thereof the second day of January one thousand seven hundred and forty one, in presence of the said heritor, by Robert Wylie in Poubare, Ballie of the said barrony, Joseph Mouat, Procurator Fiscall to the said Court, John Glenny, Clerk, John Irvine, Officer, and William White, Demster.
The suits called, and the court lawfully fenced and affirmed.

The which day, in presence of the heritor and baillie forsaid, complaints being given in by said fiscall thatt notwithstanding the many acts of court to hinder the wasting of mosses, muires, meadows, grass, and corn lands, woods, plantings, fishings, and wild fouls, and venison, continue little better then before, therefore craving that not only former acts thereanent be ratified, but new ones made in order the better to inforce the observance of the same for the future, and the persons guilty to be punished, and to pay damage in terms of law and former acts of court thereanent.   R. WYLLIE, *balie.*
J. GLENNY, *Clk.*

Which complent being considered by the Ballie, he, in presence of the hail tennants and subtennants within the barrony, statutes and ordains that in all time coming no peats shall be left in the mosses, nor no turfs upon the muirs, in any place whatsomever after the first day of September yearly, under the penalty of twenty pound Scots, to be paid to the heritor by every person for each time he shall be guilty of the same, besides the loss of such peats and turfs, which is to be forfeited to the heritor, who is hereby impoured to dispose of the same as he shall think proper. It is also further enacted by the forsaid Ballie, that no person whatsomever hunt fish or foul within the barrony, nor be found within any inclosure, without the heritors licience, under the penaltys prescribed by acts of parliament for such as shall be found to hunt fish or foul as abovesaid, and four pound Scots for each time they shall be found within park inclosure or planting in any place whatsomever. He also further ordains that no braes shall be

laboured but such as have been in use to be so, and they only
for three years, untill they be rested nine years each time
before they be taken in, and no brae to be laboured but such
as can be done without letting the ground fall to the foot of
the brae, under the penalty to be paid as above, and damages
likewise.   R. WYLLIE, *balie.*
                                             J. GLENNY, *Clk.*

Presentia forsaid eodem die.

The said Ballie likewise ordains that no ground be laboured
till five years rested if outfield, nor no ground to be watered till
past the fourth year, nor none to be laboured longer then four
years untill rested the said five years, under the within mentioned penalties and dammages, to be paid by each person
contraveening *toties quoties* as already directed.   And the
Ballie also further ordains all former acts of court relative to
mosses, muirs, meadows, suaird ground, bruntland, selling of
peats, to be punctuall observed, under the penalties and
dammages therein contained, to be duely observed in all time
coming by the hail tenants, subtennants, and others within the
barrony in the haill heads and clauses thereof, as if the same
were word for word herein expressed.
                                             R. WYLLIE, *balie.*
                                             J. GLENNY, *Clk.*

It is further enacted by the said Ballie that no ground be
cast up for any use whatsomever upon the lands of Glithnoe,
that the heritor shall think fit to be taken in out of the muirs
thereof, and so marked for that effect as probable to be taken
in for corn land, or shall be marked by [him] for the future for
said purpose, under the penalty of twenty pounds and damages,
to be paid *toties quoties* as already directed, which act shall
extend to the rest of the barrony.
                                             R. WYLLIE, *balie.*
                                             J. GLENNY, *Clk.*

The said day, on a complaint made by Robert Eduard in
Milne of Cowie, that severall persons neglect or refuse to assist
in bringing home of milne stones and mending the dam and

watergang of milne of Cowie, and performing other milne
services, it is enacted by the Ballie, that each deficient person,
where a horse shall be required, shall pay four pound Scots for
each time, and where a man is required, to pay two pounds Scots
for each time he shall be deficient after due requisition made
by the said Robert Edward his miller and his men or servants,
or any of them, who are hereby appointed officers for that
effect, and ordains them, and each one of them, to peind each
deficient the above sums in terms of law.

R. WYLLIE, *balie.*
J. GLENNY, *Clk.*

The said day Duncan Gordon and Alexander Burnet are
amerciate in ten pounds Scots by the Ballie, for their contumacy in absenting from the court, which they are hereby
ordained to pay to the fiscall for the behooff of the heritor
within term of law, and orders precepts of peinding to be
directed for that effect in form as effeirs.

R. WYLLIE, *bailie.*
J. GLENNY, *Clk.*

The said day Duncan Gordon and John Morton, with
Robert Crukshank, George Mouat, and John Lawrance, being
summoned to this court for selling of peats contrary to former
acts of court, and their own enacting to the contrary att the
said fiscall and heritors instance, craving the forenamed persons
may pay the penalties and damages appointed by former acts
of court, and otherways punished att the ballies discretion,
who accordingly appear'd and confest the libell; but except
the said Duncan Gordon, they all declared they could not write.

DUNCAN GORDON.
R. WYLLIE, *bailie.*
Jo. GLENNY, *Clk.*

Presentia forsaid eodem die.

The Ballie having considered the within judiciall confessions
of Duncan Gordon, John Morton, Robert Crukshank, George
Mouat, and John Lawrance, amerciates each one of them in
ten pounds Scots, to be paid to the Fiscall of court for the

heritors behoof, within term of law, and for that effect ordains precepts of peinding to be directed hereon in form as effeirs.

R. WYLLIE, bailie.
Jo. GLENNY, Clk.

The said day, anent a complaint given in by said heritor and fiscal, showing that by the late increase of houses, the mosses and grounds within the barrony are in danger of being wasted, particularly within the bounds of Burnhaugh and Trees. Which being considered by the said Ballie, he ordains that no houses be built but what were in old use and wont, and particularly orders that none but three houses for firing [1] be in Burnthaugh, and not above five houses for firing in Trees, under the penalty of twenty pound attour damages, to be paid by the contra-veeners <i>toties quoties</i> as formerly directed, and for that purpose the said tennants of Burnhaugh and Trees are required said day to take notice of said act by discharging all houses except-ing in the above terms.

R. WYLLIE, bailie.
Jo. GLENNY, Clerk.

Barron Court of the Barrony of Ury and lands of Matheris [2] pertaining heritably to the honourable Robert Barclay, junior, of Ury, holden att the Mannor place of Ury, the seventh day of June one thousand seven hundred and fourty six years, in presence of the said heritor, by David Barclay in the Manor place of Finlayston, Balie of the said barrony and lands, and Joseph Mouat in Rothnik, Procurator Fiscall of said court, John Glenny, Clerk, John Irvine, Officer, and William Caird, Dempster.

R. BARCLAY, Jr.

---

[1] <i>Houses for firing</i> seems here to be equivalent to <i>fire houses</i> in the next Minute of Court. <i>Fire houses</i> may be taken generally to mean dwelling-houses, though, strictly speaking, such a definition is not accurate. Many houses of the poorer people in the country had at one time no provision for firing, which, indeed, was looked upon as a luxury, and made subject to a tax called 'hearth-money.' In a return with reference to this tax, presented to Parliament by the sub-collector of Kincardine on 16th August 1704, the number of hearths in the county is reckoned at 3628.—<i>Acta Parl.</i> xi. p. 171.

[2] It is difficult to explain why the lands of Mathers are mentioned along with the Barony of Urie in this and the succeeding minute. David Barclay, an-cestor of the Barclays of Urie, sold the lands of Mathers, which had been in the possession of his family for three hundred years, in 1633.

The suits call'd, and the court lawfully fenced and affirmed.

The which day the hail tennants of said barrony and lands being conveened, it was enacted by the forsaid Bailie, for preventing the wasting of mosses, that the number of both tennants and subtennants fire houses shall not exceed six, in Crossley three, in milne of Montquhigh two, Burnhaugh three, and Trees four, and in case of contravention of this act, not only the tennant shall be obleidged who contraveens the same instantly to reduce the number of the above houses to the forsaid standard, but also to pay the damages occasioned thereby to the heritor, with ten pound Scots of penalty for each time this act shall be contraveened, to be paid within terms of law.

DA. BARCLAY, *balle.*
JOHN GLENNY, *Clk.*

June the 7th, presentia David Barclay, Bailie.

It is ordained by the Bailie that there be no casting of ground for firing upon the hill of the Walkmilne, except as allowed by the heritor, under the pain of the damages refounded, and ten pound Scots for each time this act is contraveened.

DA. BARCLAY, *Baillie.*
JOHN GLENNY, *Clk.*

The said day the heritor and whole tennants and others within the barrony of Ury and lands of Matheris agree to the apointing an aditional number of barlawmen within the said barrony and lands to the barlawmen formerly appointed, viz. : Alexander Milne in milne of Montquhigh, William Main in Jockys loch, Andrew Mason in Latch of Glithnoe, John Fothringham in Reedcloak, James Smith in nether Finlayston, and   , who all gave their oath *de fidele*, and to which the Bailie interpones his authoritie.

ALEXR. MILNE.
W. M.
ANDROW MEASON.
JOHN FODERINGEM.
JAMES SMITH.

DA. BARCLEY, *Ba.*
JOHN GLENNY, *Clk.*

June the 7th, Presentia David Barclay, Bailie.

The Bailie enacts that each barlawman shall receive of wages from those who employ them att the rate of twelve shillings Scots each time each person is called out, it being Scots mone, excepting in time of harvest, when the wages are to be one pound four shilling Scots for each time.

DA. BARCLAY, *Baille.*
JOHN GLENNY, *Clk.*

The said day David Williamson in Finlayston being summoned to this court for abstracted moulters by Robert Edward in Milne of Couie, and is found to be due to said Robert Edward by his oun confession one pound Scots, which the Bailie ordains to be paid, within terms of law, under pain of poinding, he being accordingly required att the Barr.

DA. BARCLAY, *Bailie.*
JOHN GLENNY, *Clk.*

The forsaid day, anent a difference betwixt John Mouat in Woodhead and William Caird there, concerning the run rigg'd land[1] presently posesed by James Caird, which is reserv'd out of William Caird's assidation thereupon, for which there is deduction of ten merks in the tack, which the heritor agreed to because William Caird asserted that to be the old price, and afterwards the said run rigg'd land was set to John Mouat for nine merks Scots by the heritor, who forgot the former price in William Caird's tack, because John Mouat asserted the price to be only nine merks, according to which the heritor would lose a mark yearly. To prevent which and in order to clear the same the Bailie and the said John Mouat and William Caird refer'd unanimously to the oath of Robert Youngson, who formerly lived in Woodhead, whether the merk in dispute should be paid by the said John Mouat or the said William Caird notwithstanding what is written in their respective assidations to the contrary. And accordingly the said Robert

---

[1] *Runrig lands* are lands where the alternate ridges of a field belong to different proprietors. It may also be applied to lands where the portions consist not of ridges only, but of alternate portions of several acres each.—Bell's *Law of Scotland*, p. 731.

Youngson, being solemnly sworn, purged of partiall councill, etc., interrogate, depones that the old price of the said runrigged land was ten merks Scots exactly, which is a truth, as he shall answer to God, and declares he cannot write.

Da. Barclay, *Baillie.*
John Glenny.

The Bailie having considered the above deposition, finds the true price of the above runrigg land to be ten merks Scots, and therefore ordains one merks Scots more then is contain'd in John Mouats assidation to his son Andrew to be paid by them to the said heritor, his heirs and assigneys, how soon ever the said John and Andrew Mouat, or either of them, posesses the said runrigg'd lands, which they are to pay to the heritor and his forsaids, always yearly and termly, along with the rent.

Da. Barclay, *Ba.*
John Glenny, *Clk.*

The forsaid day, *presentia* David Barclay, Bailie. Anent a Complaint of John Lyon in Burnhaugh, who alledged breach of Bargain in Alexander Meerns subtennant there, because he had sold him a stack of bear and fodder, which only delivered a part of, quhich being denied by said Meerns, the same was refer'd by the said Bailie to Alexander Meerns oath of verity, who depon'd negative. In respect whereof the Bailie asoilzied the said Alexander Meerns from the forsaid persuit.

Da. Barclay, *Baillie.*
John Glenny, *Clk.*

Barron Court of the Barony of Ury and lands of Matheris, pertaining heritably to the honurable Robert Barclay of Ury, holden att the Milne Toun of Cowie, the twenty fifth day of June seventeen hundred and fourty seven years, in presence of the said heritor, by George Edward in Upper Finlayston, Balie, John Glenny, Clerk, James Smith, Fiscall, and John Irvin, Officer, and , Dempster.   R. Barclay.

Sectis vocatis curia legitime affirmata.

The which day, in presence of the said heritor and Balie, the

hail tennants being conveen'd, it was enacted by the forsaid
Balie that in consideration the dam of Milne of Couie is presently out, therefore ordains that the whole sucken with men
and horses come in and work thereat till the same be sufficiently
mended, when required by Robert Edward, his millers or
servants, under the penalty of sixteen shillings Scots each
deficient man, and twenty shillings Scots for each deficient
horse. And the said Robert Edward, his miller, servants, or
ground officer for the time to point for the same, and ordains
the said Robert Edward and others impouered by him to warn
the sucken to begin regularly and go through the whole
sucken, always warning them, till the dam be compleatly
finished. And when any happens to be deficient, the said
Robert Edward must hire a man or horse, and repay himself
out of the said penalty. And as it may so fall out in this busy
time of the year that a man and horse cannot be got att the
ordinary wedges, and the work must not ly, in order to ingage
other men with horses to work the more readily, the said
Robert Edward is hereby empowered to give the full penalty
above enacted. And further, each man who labours his land
himself, or in neighbourhead with another, must always send,
when required as above, the half of the number of their horses.
And those who have their land laboured to them must always
serve as above, personally, as likewise all others, and the whole
inhabitants of the sucken must come every day when required,
with horses, preciesly att the miln dam att eight of the cloak
in morning, and work att least four hours before they go home,
with suitable instruments for working, with the said horses.
And when men are ordered to work without horses, then they
shall, each time they are required, be att the milne dam at
eight a clok in the morning, and work sufficiently till six a
clock afternoon, they always being obliedged to bring spades,
barrow, shovels, and other instruments as required. And in
regard there are not sufficient number of carts for this work,
therefore the whole tennants and inhabitants lyable in furnishing of horses hereby voluntarily obliedge themselves to pay to
the said Robert Edward fourteen shillings sterling, for which
he is hereby obliedged to furnish sufficient carts till the dam be
compleated, which they are to pay att the rate of a shilling

each plough, and the deficient person to be poinded by the ground officer. And likewise in regard there are not a sufficient number of barrows for this work, therefore all those who have their plough land ploughed to them do hereby voluntarly obliedge themselves each man to pay doun twelve pennies Scots to James Young, miller, who hereby obliedges himself for the same to furnish a sufficient number of barrows till the work is finished. And the deficient person or persons to be poinded by the said officer as above. And in respect it is enacted that the men who bring horses attend att the milne att eight a clok in the morning may sometimes occasion inconveniencys, therefore the said Robert Edward and forsaids are hereby empouered to warn the men and horses att any time betwixt sun and sun that he thinks proper, they being only to work four hours att each yoking, and the deficients lyable in the penaltys forsaid.   GEORGE EDVARD, *Ba.*
                                    JOHN GLENNY, *Clk.*

END OF THE BARRONY COURT BOOK.

APPENDIX

APPENDIX.

I.

THE RENTALL BUIK OFF THE BARONY OFF WRIE.

Banageithe ane Pluche.[1]

Iteme, Jhone Dunckane peyes ten bollis victuall, ane cus-tume[2] mart, ane vaddir,[3] ane dovssone of cappounes, ane dovssone off puttrie, with harrage, carrage within the maines,[4] togedder vith lang arrage.[5]

Cairntoune ane Pleuch.

Iteme, Robert Dunckane peyes tuentie bollis victuall, ane

---

[1] *Pluche, plewe,* or *plucht :* a plough. The term is sometimes used of the husbandman who is responsible for a plough's work, and sometimes, as in the text, of the *ploughgate, i.e.* the extent of land tilled by eight oxen, or 104 acres. —Innes's *Legal Antiquities*, p. 242.

[2] Besides giving *service*, which implied a great variety of duties, from that of *military service* downwards, the feudal tenant paid rent to his lord—(1) in money, known as *maill*; (2) in corn, or *ferme*; (3) in *customs*. Mr. Cosmo Innes enumerates some of the more ordinary custom-dues as follows :—' These are generally a *mart* or ox to be killed at Martinmas, two or three wedders or muttons, as many lambs, grice or young pigs, geese, capons, and poultry, chickens, eggs, and almost universally the ancient tax of a *reek-hen*, or a hen for every fire-house. A very little tallow is paid from the alehouse of the barony, and there are customs of butter and cheese in very small quantities. Besides these commodities for the kitchen, the low country farms often pay a few ells of cloth, not of wool, but linen cloth of three-quarters broad for my lady's napery.'—Innes's *Legal Antiquities*, p. 257.

[3] Wether.

[4] *Mainis :* the farm attached to the mansion-house on an estate, and in former times usually possessed by the proprietor.—*Jam.* Contraction of French *demesne.*

[5] *Arrage,* or *Harrage,* was the service due from a tenant to a landlord in men and horses. It is distinguishable from *carrage*, which implies the use of carts or waggons. *Long arrage* was such as required more than a day for its per-formance.—*Jam.*

M

custume mart, tua vaddiris, ane dovssone off cappounes, and dovsson off putrie, vith harrage, carrag, dov [1] seruice, as said is.

Glithnocht ane Pleuch.

Iteme, the Glithnothe peyes sax markes mell [2] at tua termes, to vit Vitsonday and Mertimes, tua vaddiris, sakis capones, ane dovsone of puttrie, with harrage, carrag vithin the maines.

Wodheid tua Plewes.

Iteme, Androv Dunckane and Villiame Duththe peyes betuix thaime tua, to vit, euerie ane off thaime ane chalder [3] meill, four bollis beir, ane mart, ane doussone off capounes, tua custoum vaddiris, ane dowssone off putrie, vith harrag, carrag vithin the grund.

Megra thrie Plewes.

Iteme, Alexander Dunckane peyes ane chaldir beir, ane chalder mill, tua dovson of capounes, tua vaddires. Iteme, Jhone Manecure peyes aucht bollis mill, aucht bollis beir, ane dovsson of capounes, ane vadder.

Powbair ane Pleuche vadsett. [4]

Iteme, Johne Movatt peyes ane chaldir of meill, four bollis beir, four capouns, sakkis puttrie.

The Croftis of Covy.

Iteme, James Mill peyes half chalder of beir. Iteme, Stephone Smythe, for the milne croft, halff chalder of beir. Iteme, Stephane Smythe, skipper, for his croft, xxvij s. viijd. [5]

Iteme, Alexander Tellzour, for his croft, xxvj s. viij d.

---

[1] Due.   [2] Maill.
[3] A measure consisting of sixteen bolls.
[4] Wadset: pledged, with power of redemption.
[5] 27s. 8d. Scots money, equal to a little over 2s. 3d. sterling. A pound sterling is equal in value to twelve pounds Scots.

II.

NOTES WRITTEN ON THE FLY-LEAF OF THE MS.

1.

These are to give notice that Barclay Fair, standing upon
the hill of Megray, nar Cowie, begining yearly upon the third
Tuesday of June ; as also Maithers Fair, standing in the same
place, and begining upon the second Tuesday of October,
yearly, both granted by act of parliament, and belonging
heritably to Robert Barclay of Ury, are both of them to continue always herafter for four days, to witt, Tuesday for sheep
of all sorts, Wedensday for all sort of timber in the morning,
and the rest of the day for all sorts of cloth and stockings,
and butter and cheese, with all sort of merchant ware, Thursday for all sort of nolt and cattel, and Friday for horse. All
buyers and sellers, merchants, and others, are expected to
attend ilk ane of these fairs with their comodities, where they
may expect good encouragement.

2.

Accompt of the Corne and Fodder receued from the tenents
of the Brea of Vrie, 1661.

	Boll	Fir.	Lip.		Boll.		
Imprimes from Jhon Erskine,	.	3	2	is	15	2	2
Item from William Wilsone,	.	1			4	3	3
Item from Allexander Falconar,					2		
Item from Andrew Moncure,	.	2		is	10	0	0
Item from Jhon Moncure,	.	.	2	2¾	is	13	2	0
Item from Jhon Duncan,	.		2	¼	is	9	2	3
Item from George Farfar,	.	1	1	3½	is	29	1	0

Item of Bear.

From William Wilsone.
From Allexander Falconar, .   . 1 : ½ pek : 2 l.   25   2   2

3.

I defend and forbid in his Majesty name and authorite, our

Soveraign Lord George the 2d, by the grace of God, King of Great Britain, France, and Ireland, Defender of the Faith, and in the name and authorite of Robert Barclay, heritable propriatar of the Barony of Ury and lands of Matheris, and George Edward in upper Finlayston, his Balie, that non molest the Court, under pain of law.

III.

CHRONOLOGICAL TABLE OF PRICES, CONVERTED
FERMES, CUSTOMS, ETC., EXTRACTED FROM THE
COURT BOOK.

	lb.	*s.*	*d.*
13 October 1604.			
Of everie hors carrige to Buchane,	05	00	00
Of everie fwit carrig to Buchane,	02	00	00
Of hors carrige to Aberdyne,	01	00	00
Of fwit carrag to Aberdeyn,	00	10	00
23 November 1614.			
Ane leitt of peittis,	16	00	00
A dour,	01	00	00
Ilk mert,	13	06	08
27 October 1615.			
Ane aix,	00	13	04
25 November 1615.			
Ilk mert,	13	06	08
12 May 1617.			
Ilk boll meill,	10	00	00
8 May 1618.			
Ane staine of talloun,	02	13	04
24 July 1618.			
Ane boll malt,	05	10	00
21 July 1620.			
Ane capon,	00	06	08
Ane custome wadder, wnder the woll,	03	06	08
Ane custome mert,	10	00	00
Ane pultrie foull,	00	03	04
Ilk dozen elnis of sarking lining clayth,	06	00	00
Ane pynt of oylie,	00	08	00
Ane staine of brew tallowne,	03	06	08
Ilk burding of peitts,	01	00	00
Ilk laid of peitts on hors with creillis,	02	00	00
Ilk kairt full of peitts,	03	00	00
16 June 1621.			
Ilk boll bear,	05	00	00
Ilk dozen pultrie foullis,	02	00	00
Ane dozen elnis of sufficient sarking lyning,	06	00	00

	lb.	s.	d.
7 November 1621.			
Ane eln brown fleming,	01	13	04
Ane eln bred lyning,	01	01	00
Ane eln thrie quarter bred,	00	18	00
Ane once edgit frenzies,	01	05	00
19 January 1622.			
To carye the lairdis letters to Slaines,	02	00	00
2 July 1622.			
The saill of a boit,	26	13	04
22 November 1622.			
Cairadge, ordinar,	01	00	00
5 December 1622.			
Ilk staine of brew talloun,	03	06	08
Ane boll meill,	10	00	00
Ane boll bear,	12	00	00
Ilk leitt peitts,	03	06	08
17 April 1623.			
Ane boll meill,	10	00	00
Ane boll bear,	10	00	00
Ane eln off sarking lyneing,	00	08	00
A milne swyne,	06	13	04
Ilk capoun,	00	06	08
25 August 1624.			
Ilk elne of lyning,	00	08	00
Ane boll malt,	10	00	00
25 May 1625.			
Ane pynt of oylie,	00	08	00
30 November 1625.			
Ilk elne of sarking lyneing,	00	06	08
Ilk staine of brew tallown,	03	06	08
Thrie capounes,	01	00	00
8 August 1626.			
Sex wedders,	18	00	00
Ilk ell lyning,	00	08	00
5 October 1626.			
Thrie pultrie,	00	10	00
Ilk mart,	10	00	00
17 Jully 1627.			
Ilk elne of lyning,	00	08	00
10 November 1627.			
Ilk mart,	10	00	00
Ane steane brew creische,	02	13	04

					lb.	*s.*	*d.*
7 May 1628.							
A wedder wnder woll,	.		.		03	00	00
30 January 1629.							
Ane custome mairte,	.	.	.	.	10	00	00
8 May 1629.							
Ilk boll meill,	.	.	.	.	12	00	00
Ilk boll bear,	.	.	.	.	12	00	00
11 November 1629.							
Halff ane leit of peits,	.		.		05	00	00
Ane half mairt,	.	.		.	05	00	00
Sex poultrie foullis,	.		.		01	00	00
Ane elne lyning,	.	.		.	00	08	00
16 June 1630.							
Ilk boll meill,	.				10	00	00
Ilk boll bear,	.				10	00	00
Ilk dussone caponis,			.		04	00	00
Ilk elne lyning clayth,	.		.		00	08	00
16 May 1632.							
Ilk boll meill,	.	.	.	.	10	00	00
Ilk boll bear,	.	.	.	.	10	00	00
Ilk elne lyning clayth,	.		.	.	00	08	00
Ane leit of peittis,	.	.	.	.	10	00	00
Ane kow,	.	.	.	.	.	10	00	00
8 January 1634.							
Ilk boll bear,	.	.	,	.	.	09	00	00
Ane custome mairt,	.	.	.	.	10	00	00
Tua custome wadders,	.	.	.	.	06	00	00
Ane boll bear (payable before 3rd May)	.	10	00	00
Ane boll meill (payable before 1st March),	.	09	00	00
26 February 1635.							
Ilk boll meill,	.	.	.	.	.	10	00	00
Ilk boll bear,	.	.	.	.	.	12	00	00
Ane boll meill (coft in Aberdeen),	.	.	08	00	00
9 January 1636.							
Ilk boll meill,	.	.	.	.	.	10	00	00
Ilk boll bear,	.	.	.	.	.	12	00	00
23 August 1672.							
Ilk boll beare,	.	.	.	.	.	06	13	06
Ilk boll meill,	.	.	.	.	.	06	00	00

							lb.	*s.*	*d.*
14 March 1679.									
Ilk wyise of strae,				.			00	00	12
9 February 1730.									
Ilk boll oats,	.	.	.	.	.		07	06	08
Ilk boll bear,	.	.	.	.	.		06	00	00
Ilk boll peas,	.	.	.	.	.		06	00	00
Ilk boll white,	.	.	.	.	.		09	00	00
Ilk boll rey,	.	.	.	.	.		05	00	00
4 November 1738.									
A peck of corn with the fodder,	.	.					00	06	00

IV.

THE LAIRDS OF URIE, 1430-1892.

I. SIR WILLIAM HAY OF ERROL, Hereditary Great Constable of Scotland, obtained a charter of the Barony of Cowie on resignation of Sir William Fraser of Philorth, great-grandson of Sir Alexander Fraser of Cowie, 14th May 1415.[1] He was appointed one of the Commissioners to treat with the English for the release of James I., and was knighted at his coronation. He died in 1436, having had issue—

    I. GILBERT, who predeceased his father, married Alice, daughter of Sir William Hay of Yester, by whom he had two sons—

        1. WILLIAM (see No. III. *infra*).

        2. GILBERT (see No. V. *infra*).

    II. WILLIAM of Urie.

II. WILLIAM HAY OF URIE, second son of Sir William Hay of Errol, obtained from his father the lands of Urie in the Barony of Cowie in 1430.[2] He received from his nephew, Sir William Hay of Errol, a charter of Cowie, dated 20th September 1447, and subsequently granted, *ad sustentationem unius capellani perpetui in Capella Virginis Marie et S. Nauthlani, prope villam de Cowy*, the following crofts within the Town—the Langcroft *alias* Brounisland, the Balehalch, Maldiscroft, the Smiddycroft, and the Abbottiscroft.[3] He resigned Urie in March 1453, confirming this resignation fourteen years later to his grand-nephew, Nicholas Hay of Errol. He had issue—

    I. THOMAS of Little Arnage.[4]

    II. ELIZABETH, who married James Douglas, was served heir to her father in the lands of Raustoun and Cragy in the sheriffdom of Aberdeen, 1st June 1493.[5]

III. SIR WILLIAM HAY OF ERROL succeeded his grandfather, Sir William Hay, in 1436. He was created Earl of Errol in 1453, and is so designed in an acceptance of a resignation of the lands of Urie from his uncle, William Hay, in March of that year. He married Beatrix Douglas, daughter of the third Lord Dalkeith. He died in 1460, and left male issue—

    I. NICHOLAS, his successor.

    II. WILLIAM, third Earl.

[1] *Reg. Mag. Sig.* (1424-1513), 158.
[2] Spalding Club *Miscellany*, vol. ii. p. 321.
[3] *Reg. Mag. Sig.* (1424-1513), 2681.
[4] New Spalding Club, *Rec. Marischal College*, p. 9.
[5] Retours, vol. ii. *Acta Dom. Auditor.*, p. 170.

IV. NICHOLAS, SECOND EARL OF ERROL, succeeded his father
in 1460. By a charter, dated 12th August 1467, he granted the
lands of Urie to Master Gilbert Hay, his uncle. He died in
1470, and was succeeded in the Earldom of Errol by his brother,
William.

V. MASTER GILBERT HAY, brother of William, first Earl of Errol,
who, as above stated, received a charter of the lands of Urie
in 1467, became thereby the founder of the family of 'Hay
of Urie.' Following the example of his uncle, William Hay of
Urie, he contributed to the endowment of the chaplaincy of Cowie,
by a grant of 40s. annual rent of the lands of Magray.[1] He was a
lawyer by profession, and his name frequently occurs in the legal
processes of the period.[2] He married in 1471 Beatrice Dunbar,
daughter and heiress of Sir John Dunbar of Crimond, through
whom he became possessed of various estates in the shires of Aberdeen and Elgin. Master Gilbert Hay acted as Constable-Depute
at a Parliament held at Edinburgh on 4th May 1480.[3] He died in
1487, and left issue—

    I. WILLIAM, his successor.
    II. GILBERT.[4]
    III. THOMAS.[5]

VI. WILLIAM HAY was still a minor when, on the death of his
father, he succeeded to the lands of Urie in 1487. He married
Katherine, daughter of Archibald Rate of Drumtochty,[6] and the
same year, 1487, obtained from his mother, Beatrice Dunbar—'of
my filial love and affection to my very dear son and heir-apparent'
—a resignation of the Barony of Crimond.[7] Crimond remained
throughout in the possession of this sept of the family of Hay,
who in consequence came to be indifferently described as 'of Urie'
and 'of Crimond.' William Hay confirmed the gifts of his father
and great-uncle to the chapel of Cowie. He died in 1513, and
left issue—

    ANDREW, his successor.

VII. ANDREW HAY was served heir to his father in an annual rent
of 40 merks from the Barony of Kilmalamak on 17th February
1513.[8] [He married a daughter of Barclay of Gartly] and,
dying in 1531, left issue—

    PATRICK, his successor.

---

[1] *Reg. Mag. Sig.*, (1424-1513), 2681.
[2] *Acta Dom. Auditor.*, pp. 47, 145, etc.
[3] *Acta Parl.*, vol. ii. p. 129.
[4] Spalding Club, *Familie of Innes*, p. 92.   [5] *Ibid.* p. 90.
[6] Spalding Club, *Antiquities of the Shires of Aberdeen and Banff*, vol. iv.
p. 632.
[7] *Ibid.* p. 80.   [8] *Familie of Innes*, p. 94.

VIII. PATRICK HAY, who succeeded his father in 1531, resigned the annual from Kilmalamak, above mentioned, to Robert Innes of Rothmakenzie. He granted a charter to Gilbert Brabner and his spouse of the lands of Over Cremond or Cremondgortht, which is confirmed at Edinburgh on 22d March 1544.[1] [He married a daughter of Comyn of Inverallochy.] He died in 1552, and left issue—

    I. ALEXANDER : was next in substitution to George sixth Earl of Errol in the charters of Errol, Slains, etc., in December 1541.[2] He died before his father, and left no issue.

    II. WILLIAM, his successor.

    III. ROBERT.[3]

IX. WILLIAM HAY succeeded his father in 1552, and died in 1588. He was appointed a member of Committee formed for the valuation of the lands of Kincardineshire in 1554,[4] on which Committee there served among others 'William, Earl Marischal, and David Barclay of Mathers, his Depute,' the latter being great-great-grandfather of Colonel Barclay of Urie (see No. XVII. infra). He was one of the signatories of the band of allegiance to James VI., entitled, 'Bond of the Barons of the North,' subscribed at Aberdeen on 2d September 1574.[5] Having subsequently become involved in the treasonable conspiracies of his chief, Francis, eighth Earl of Errol (see No. XII. infra), he, by charter dated 12th January 1588, resigned the lands of Urie to his grandson, William Hay, retaining for himself and for John Hay, his heir-apparent, who was also implicated in the doings of the Popish faction, the liferent of the same.[6] The possible forfeitures which this deed anticipated were happily avoided. He married Jonete Wood[7] [daughter of Wood of Balbegno], and had issue—

    I. JOHN, his successor.

    II. WILLIAM of Little Arnage held the rank of captain in the king's service.[8] He had issue—

---

[1] *Antiquities of the Shires of Aberdeen and Banff*, vol. iv. p. 634.

[2] *Reg. Mag. Sig.* (1513-46), 2517.　　[3] *Reg. of Privy Council*, vol. ii. p. 723.

[4] Retours, vol. ii. *Inquis. Valorum*, 2. This Committee returned the aggregate value of all the lands in the county at 445½ pounds. The following are among the separate returns—Barony of Cowie xx *lib.* land ; Lands of Logy-Cowie i *lib.* land ; Barony of Uras x *lib.* land ; Barony of Dunnottar v *lib.* land. As to the meaning and significance of these valuations, see Innes, *Legal Antiquities*, p. 275 *et seq.*　　[5] *Ibid.* vol. ii. p. 723.

[6] *Reg. Mag. Sig.* (1580-93) 1435. In the above charter the lands of *Auchorthies* are mentioned as forming part of the estate of Urie. They appear to have been alienated prior to 1604.

[7] *Ibid.* (1546-80), 2256.　　[8] *Reg. of Privy Council*, vol. vii. p. 682.

1. John of Crimondmogate appears in the minutes of the Court Book as bailie to Francis, Earl of Errol, and William Hay of Urie, see p. 30 *supra*.

III. ? James.[1]

IV. [Jean married James Lyall of Balmaledy.]

X. JOHN HAY, on whose behalf the first recorded meeting of the Baron Court is held, on 8th July 1604, succeeded his father in 1588.[2] It does not appear whether he actually took the field in the unsuccessful rising in which, in the following year, the Earl of Errol was engaged, but that he sympathised with the Popish party and did not hesitate to render them assistance is clearly proved. In 1592 he is fined 1000 merks for hearing Mass, and for 'resetting and intercommuning with Jesuits, priests, and papests.'[3] He married Elizabeth, daughter of Sir Alexander Irving of Drum, and died in 1607, leaving issue—

I. William, his successor.

II. Alexander of Logie.[4]

XI. WILLIAM HAY, last of the 'Hays of Urie,' was summoned under pain of rebellion to appear before the Lords of Council, on 2d June 1590, to answer 'concerning persute and invasion of his Majesteis declairit traitouris, rebellious and unnaturall subjectis, tressonnable practizaris and conspiratouris aganes the trew religioun presentlie professet within this realme, his Majesteis persone and estate, and libertie of this cuntrey.'[5] He succeeded his father in 1607, and married Margaret, daughter of Sir Alexander Fraser of Philorth. He sold the lands of Urie to Francis, Earl of Errol, in 1630, and died subsequent to 1634.

XII. FRANCIS, EIGHTH EARL OF ERROL, succeeded to the titles and estates of that earldom on the death of his father, in 1585. He was a staunch Roman Catholic, and became one of the leaders of the Popish faction who espoused the interests of Spain in 1588. He took part, along with the Earls of Crawford, Huntly, and Bothwell, in the attempted rising of 1589, and on its suppression was imprisoned and arraigned for treason. After suffering a few months' confinement, however, he was liberated on the occasion of the king's marriage. In July 1592, he was again arrested on a charge of 'papistry,' but was again released. He renewed his treasonable correspondence with the Spanish Court, and in February 1593 was formally declared 'rebel.' On 3d October 1594 was fought the battle of Glenlivat, where,

[1] New Spalding Club, *Miscellany*, vol. i. p. 145.

[2] *Acta Parl.*, C. 141, vol. iii. p. 615.

[3] *Reg. of Privy Council*, vol. v. pp. 54, 60-61, 78.

[4] See p. 16, *supra*.   [5] *Reg. of Privy Council*, vol. v. p. 146.

in conjunction with the Earl of Huntly, he defeated a royal
army of 7000 men under the leadership of Argyll. The king
advancing in person to oppose the insurgents, both leaders ulti-
mately surrendered. They obtained permission to go abroad,
where they remained in exile for two years. Errol subsequently
regained the royal favour, and was one of the Commissioners
nominated by Parliament to treat of a union with England,
11th July 1604. The remaining years of his life were spent in
the administration of his vast estates, and in the exercise of a
princely charity among the poor. As above stated, he acquired
the lands of Urie in 1630. He died on 16th July 1631, leaving
issue by his third wife, Elizabeth, daughter of the Earl of
Morton—

WILLIAM, his successor.

XIII. WILLIAM, NINTH EARL OF ERROL, was educated in the
Protestant religion. He was brought up at Court, and was in
high favour with King Charles I., at whose coronation his personal
expenditure as Constable was so great as to severely cripple the
resources of the earldom. He continued to live in a style of
lavish magnificence, which eventuated, in the first instance, in
the sale of the old family estate of Errol, in the Carse of Gowrie,
which had been in the possession of his ancestors from the time
of William the Lion. Nor was this sacrifice in itself sufficient
to relieve the pressure of his financial embarrassments. At his
death, which took place on 13th December 1636, it was found
that the affairs of the earldom were almost hopelessly involved.
He married Ann Lyon, daughter of Patrick, eleventh Lord
Glammis and first Earl of Kinghorn, by whom he had issue—

GILBERT, his successor.

XIV. GILBERT, TENTH EARL OF ERROL, was a mere child at the
date of his succession. During his minority various expedients
were resorted to by his curators to redeem the fortunes of the
house. To this end, portions of the estate of Urie were from
time to time disposed of, among which were the lands of Redcloak
and Finlayston, together with the greater part of the Over-
barony, or Monquich, which last became the property of George
Thomson, Clerk of the Sheriffdom of Kincardine.[1] The remain-

---

1 *Retours*, vol. i., *Kincardine*, 132. The portion of Monquich thus alienated
consisted of the lands of *Balnagubs, Sauchenshaw, Old Hillock, Craigwells*, and
Netherley. It appears to have remained in the possession of the heirs of George
Thomson till 1748, when it was sold by James Thomson of Portlethen, advocate
in Aberdeen, to William Chalmers, Commissary of His Majesty's stores at
Gibraltar. In 1754 it again changed hands, being purchased from William
Chalmers by Alexander Silver, a retired East India merchant, who built the
present mansion-house of Netherley. He died in 1797. His son, George

ing lands passed in wadset to John Forbes of Leslie, in whose possession they remained till 1647.[1] In that year it was found necessary still further to relieve the indebtedness of the earldom, and permission was obtained from Parliament to sell Urie, which was thereupon acquired by William, seventh Earl Marischal.[2] Gilbert, Earl of Errol, married Catherine, daughter of James, Earl of Southesk, and died without issue in 1674.

XV. JOHN FORBES, *wadsetter*, was second son of William Forbes of Monymusk and Lady Margaret Douglas, daughter of the ninth Earl of Angus. He had obtained the lands of Leslie in Aberdeenshire in 1620, and ten years later secured the proprietorship of the estate of Banchory, in the parish of Banchory-Devenick.[3] A Presbyterian and a zealous supporter of the Covenant, he drew down upon himself the vengeance of Montrose, who, in March 1645, having first sacked the town of Stonehaven, and spoiled the Earl Marischal's lands of Dunnottar and Fetteresso, plundered the whole lands of Urie, burning the ancient fortalice of the Hays, and utterly wasting all that it contained.[4] Forbes, whose wadset on the lands of Urie was redeemed by Earl Marischal in 1647, married Jean Leslie, sister of Patrick, second Lord Lindores. He died in 1663.[5]

XVI. WILLIAM SEVENTH EARL MARISCHAL, succeeded to the earldom on the death of his father in 1635. He was a Presbyterian, and adhered to the Covenanting party till the surrender of King Charles I. in 1646. Henceforward he became an ardent Royalist. Raising a troop of horse at his own expense, he marched with them into England in 1648, and was present at the battle of Preston, where he narrowly escaped being taken prisoner. He subsequently entertained Charles II. at Dunnottar Castle in 1650, and would have accompanied him to England, had he not been appointed, along with the Earls of Crawford and Glencairn, to remain at home in charge of the kingdom.

Silver, acquired from Robert Barclay Allardice of Urie (*see* No. XXII. *infra*), the remaining portion of Monquich, conform to a disposition dated 1st October 1816. He died in 1841, and was succeeded by his son, also named George, who was resident in Madeira. The latter dying without issue in 1844, his brother James, who succeeded, sold the estate nine years later to Horatio Ross of Rossie. Monquich, now known as Netherley, was purchased from Mr. Ross by William Nathaniel Forbes of Auchernach, the present proprietor, in 1863.— *Notes on the Titles of Netherley*, in the possession of W. N. Forbes, Esq.

[1] *Acta Parl.*, C. 85, vol. viii. p. 532.
[2] *Ibid.*, C. 339, vol. vii. p. 762.
[3] Henderson's *History of Banchory-Devenick*, p. 14.
[4] Spalding's *Memorialls of the Trubles in Scotland*, vol. ii. p. 460.
[5] Retours, vol. ii., *Inquis. Generales*, 4749.

After the defeat at Worcester, he was attainted by the Cromwellian Parliament, and having been surprised at Elliot, in
Angus, by a strong party of English horse, was conveyed to
London and imprisoned in the Tower. There he remained till
the Restoration. As above mentioned, Earl Marischal purchased Urie in 1647. In the following year he disposed of it
by sale, along with various lands in the parish of Dunnottar, to
Colonel David Barclay, son of David Barclay of Mearns and
Mathers.[1] In recompence for his great merits and suffer-
ings in the royal cause, he was appointed a Privy Councillor by
Charles II. in 1660, and shortly afterwards was made Lord Privy
Seal, which office he retained till his death in 1661. He had
married Elizabeth Seton, daughter of George, Earl of Winton,
but, having no male issue, was succeeded in the earldom of
Marischal by his brother.

XVII. COLONEL DAVID BARCLAY was born at Kirktonhill, in the
parish of Marykirk, in 1610, and married in 1647 Katherine,
daughter of Sir Robert Gordon of Gordonston, second son
of the Earl of Sutherland. In his youth he served under
Gustavus Adolphus, and was present at the battle of Lutzen
in November 1632. Returning to this country on the outbreak of the civil wars, he allied himself with the Covenanting
Party, and did good service in the field on its behalf. His
purchase of Urie in 1648 was so far unfortunate. Having failed
to complete his titles before the forfeiture of the Earl Marischal, he was denied admission to the lands on the plea that
they had fallen to the State. He thereupon applied himself
to obtain a seat in the Cromwellian Parliament as an only
means of vindicating his rights. He was elected member for
Sutherlandshire in 1653, and for the shires of Forfar and Kincardine in 1654, and again in 1656. In 1654 he was appointed
a Trustee on the Confiscated Estates in Scotland,[2] a distinction
for which he afterwards suffered at the hands of Charles II.
by imprisonment in Edinburgh Castle. It was while in prison
on this occasion that he was induced to embrace the doctrines
of the Society of Friends, through the influence of Judge
Swinton. Having obtained his freedom in 1666, he retired to
Urie, where he afterwards continued to reside. On 13th
August 1679 Colonel Barclay obtained from the king a formal
charter erecting his lands, which he had purchased from the
Earl Marischal twenty years previously, into 'ane haill and
free Barony, called the Barony of Urie.'[3] He built the 'Old

---

[1] Barclay's *Genealogical Account of the Barclays of Urie*, Ed. 1812, p. 20.
[2] *Acta Parl.* vol. vi. 2, p. 821 a.
[3] *Ibid.*, C. 85, vol. VIII. p. 531.

House of Urie ' (see Frontispiece), and dying on 12th October 1686, left issue—

    i. ROBERT, his successor.
    ii. JOHN, married in New Jersey, and had issue ; died in 1731.
    iii. DAVID, died unmarried in 1685.
    iv. LUCY, died unmarried.
    v. JEAN, married Sir Evan Cameron of Lochiel.

XVIII. ROBERT BARCLAY was born at Gordonston, in Morayshire, on 23d October 1648, and was educated at the Scots College, Paris, of which his uncle, Robert Barclay, was rector. He returned to Scotland in 1664, and three years later joined the Society of Friends, which found in him its most devoted champion and ablest advocate. He married in 1670 Christian (died February 1725), daughter of Gilbert Mollison, merchant in Aberdeen. In the same year appeared the first of his published works, a pamphlet in vindication of the religious tenets of the Quakers, entitled *Truth Cleared of Calumnies*. His famous *Apology for the Quakers* was published in Amsterdam in 1675. From November 1676 till April 1677 he was imprisoned in Aberdeen, at the instance of the clergy, during which time he occupied himself in the composition of his treatise on *Universal Love*, a remonstrance against the criminality of war. *A Vindication of the Apology* appeared in 1679, followed in the same year by *The Anarchy of the Ranters*, in which latter work he laboured to defend the Quakers from the charge of superstition on the one hand and fanaticism on the other.[1] In 1681 he became one of a syndicate for the purchase of the American Province New Caesarea or New Jersey, as it eventually came to be called, lying between the Delaware and the Hudson. A year later he was appointed nominal life-governor of the Province by the proprietors. The remainder of his life was chiefly spent in laborious efforts to further the interests of this Colony. He died on 3d October 1690, and left issue—

    i. ROBERT, his successor.
    ii. DAVID, settled in London. He married (1) Anne, daughter of James Taylor, draper in London, and (2) Priscilla, daughter of John Freame, banker. He entered the Mercantile Profession, and had the honour of entertaining the first three Hanoverian Monarchs on Lord Mayor's Day, at his residence in Cheapside.[2]

---

[1] For a complete list of the writings of Robert Barclay, the Apologist, see Anderson's *Scottish Nation*, vol. i. p. 245.
[2] David Barclay is ancestor of the present Robert Barclay, Esq., of Bury Hill, Dorking, in whose possession is the original MS. of the *Court Book of the*

III. John, resident in Dublin, married **Anne, daughter of** Amos Stretell, merchant.

IV. Patience, married Timothy **Forbes, son of Alexander** Forbes of Aquorthies.

V. Catherine, married James **Forbes, brother of the preceding.**

VI. Christian, married, in 1699, Alexander Jaffray of Kingswells, and died in 1751.

VII. Jean, **married Alexander Forbes, merchant, London.** son of John Forbes of Aquorthies.

XIX. ROBERT BARCLAY was born on 25th March 1672, and succeeded his father in 1690. He resigned the Dunnottar portions of the Barony to the Earl Marischal prior to 1715, and having acquired the lands of Finlayston and Redcloak, which had been alienated during the minority of Gilbert, Earl of Errol (see No. XIV. *supra*), he in 1722 executed a deed of entail over the estates. He published in 1740 *A Genealogical Account of the Barclays of Urie.* He died 27th March 1747. By his wife Elizabeth, daughter of James O'Brian, merchant in London, he left issue—

I. Robert, his successor.

II. David was born in 1728. He married Margaret, daughter of John Pardoe, merchant, Worcester, and died 30th May 1809.

III. John, died unmarried.

IV. Mollison, married John, son of John Doubleday of Alnwick Abbey, in Northumberland.

V. Elizabeth, married Sir William Ogilvy, Bart., of Barras.

VI. Catherine.

Barony of Urie, and to whose courtesy in permitting it to be printed the Society is indebted for this volume. Mr. Barclay is heir-male of the Barclays of Urie. The following is his descent—

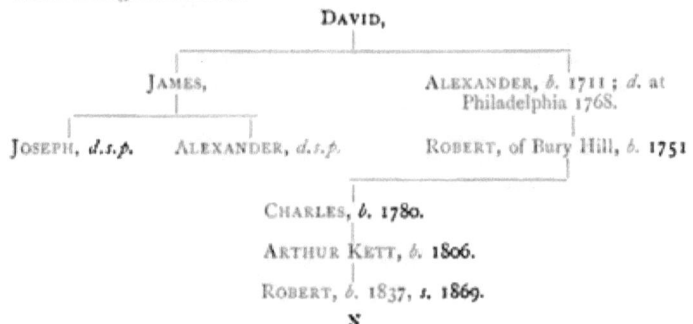

DAVID,

JAMES, ALEXANDER, *b.* 1711; *d.* at Philadelphia 1768.

JOSEPH, *d.s.p.* ALEXANDER, *d.s.p.* ROBERT, of Bury Hill, *b.* 1751

CHARLES, *b.* 1780.

ARTHUR KETT, *b.* 1806.

ROBERT, *b.* 1837, *s.* 1869.

XX. ROBERT BARCLAY, known as 'Robert the Strong,' was born 20th July 1699, succeeded his father in 1747, and died 10th October 1760. He is accredited with having had friendly leanings towards the Jacobites, but if so, was careful not to commit himself in '45. He married Une, daughter of Sir Evan Cameron of Lochiel, and had issue—

    i. ROBERT, his successor.

    ii. EVAN, unmarried.

    iii. ALEXANDER, unmarried.

    iv. DAVID, unmarried, killed at taking of Martinique in 1762.

    v. JANE, born in 1726, and died unmarried in 1750.

XXI. ROBERT BARCLAY-ALLARDICE, the distinguished agriculturist, was born in 1731, and died 7th April 1797. He was educated at the University of Aberdeen, and afterwards studied farming in Norfolkshire. He succeeded to the estates in 1760, and eight years later began his experiments in scientific farming.[1] In 1788 he was elected member of Parliament for Kincardineshire, and continued to represent the county till his death in 1797. The New Town of Stonehaven was founded by him in 1795, encouragement to build upon what was then known as the *Links of Arduthie*, being afforded in the granting of feu-charters on liberal terms. He married—

(1) Lucy, daughter of David Barclay, by whom he had issue—

    LUCY, married Samuel Galton of Duddeston House, Warwick.

(2) Sarah-Anne, only daughter and heiress of James Allardice of Allardice, who in 1785 was served nearest lawful heir-portioner of William, last Earl of Airth and Menteith, and had issue—

    i. ROBERT, his successor.

    ii. JAMES ALLARDICE, born in 1784, died at Ceylon, unmarried, in 1803.

    iii. DAVID STUART, born in 1786, was Major in the 28th Regiment of Foot, and died unmarried at Otranto, in Italy, in 1826.

    iv. RODNEY, born in 1782, and died unmarried in 1853.

    v. ANNE, born 13th September 1777, and died unmarried on 29th October 1782.

    vi. UNE CAMERON, born in 1778, married John Innes of Cowie, and died September 1809.

    vii. MARY, born in 1780, died unmarried in 1799.

    viii. MARGARET, married Hudson Gurney of Keswick.

---

[1] For particulars as to Mr. Barclay's agricultural improvements, see *British Biographical Dictionary*; old *Statistical Account*, vol. xii. p. 597; Pennant's *Tour in Scotland*, vol. iii. p. 148; Donaldson's *General View of the Agriculture of Kincardine*, p. 17.

XXII. CAPTAIN ROBERT BARCLAY-ALLARDICE was born in 1779, and was educated in England, studying for a time at the University of Cambridge. As heir-general and of line of William, first Earl of Airth, he unsuccessfully claimed the Earldoms of Strathearn, Menteith, and Airth. He entered the army and served, as aide-de-camp to the Marquis of Huntly, in the ill-fated Walcheren expedition, sent to the coast of the Netherlands in 1809, to aid Austria in her struggle against Napoleon I. Subsequently abandoning the military profession, he betook himself to farming and cattle-rearing. In 1822 was formed the once famous Urie Herd of Shorthorns, which did much to improve the breed of cattle in the district. He is now chiefly remembered for his pedestrian achievements. His great feat of walking 1000 miles in 1000 consecutive hours took place at Newmarket in June and July of 1809.[1] The deed of entail executed by his great-grandfather (see No. XIX. *supra*) having been proved faulty, he sold to George Silver of Netherley the lands of Monquich, etc., in 1816.[2] At his death, which happened in 1854, the remainder of the Barony of Urie passed from the family of Barclay, being purchased by Mr. Baird of Gartsherrie. Captain Barclay married in 1819 Mary Dalgarno, and had issue—

    I. MARGARET, who assumed by Royal Licence, 2d July 1883, for herself and her heirs, the surnames and arms of Barclay-Allardice. She married—

    (1) in 1840, Samuel Ritchie, by whom she had issue—

        1. ROBERT, her heir.

        2. SAMUEL FREDERICK, died unmarried in 1862.

        3. DAVID STUART, married in 1868 Fannie Foster, daughter of Edwin S. Elliott of West Brattleboro, Vermont, U.S., and has issue—

            1. ROBERT, *b.* 1869.

            2. ELLIOT RITCHIE, *b.* 1873.

            3. DAVID GRAHAM, *b.* 1877.

            4. CLINTON, *b.* 1882.

            5. MARGARET ANNA.

            6. AUGUSTA STANDISH.

            7. AMELIA.

        4. MARY HAY, died in 1849.

    (2) in 1854, James Tanner, and had issue—

        AUGUSTA GRAHAM, died, unmarried, in 1874.

XXIII. ALEXANDER BAIRD, a member of the celebrated firm of iron-masters, the Messrs. Baird of Gartsherrie, Lanarkshire, pur-

---

[1] See Thom's *Pedestrianism* (1813).
Notes on the Titles of Netherley.

chased the Barony of Urie, as above stated, on the death of Captain Barclay-Allardice in 1854. He built the present House of Urie in 1855, on the site of the old 'Manor Place' of the Barclays. He died without issue in 1862.

XXIV. JOHN BAIRD OF LOCHWOOD succeeded to the Barony of Urie on the death of his brother, Alexander Baird (see No. XXIII. *supra*) in 1862. He married Margaret, daughter of John Finlay of Springhill, and died in 1870, leaving issue—

    I. ALEXANDER, who succeeded to Urie.

    II. JOHN of Lochwood and Knoydart.

    III. JANET, married Colonel Chalmer.

XXV. ALEXANDER BAIRD OF URIE succeeded his father in 1870. He purchased the estate of Rickarton, which, previous to the forfeiture of George, tenth Earl Marischal, had formed part of the Barony of Fetteresso, on the death of Captain Rickart-Hepburn in 1874. Mr. Baird, who has travelled much, is an accomplished Oriental scholar, his acquirements in this respect being recognised by Sir Richard Burton, who, in dedicating to him the ninth volume of his *Thousand Nights and a Night*, says, 'Your long residence in Egypt, and your extensive acquaintance with its "politic," private and public, make you a thoroughly competent judge of the merits and demerits of this volume ; and encourage me to hope that in reading it you will take something of the pleasure I have had in writing it.' On the outbreak of famine in Upper Egypt in 1879, Mr. Baird, who was then resident in Cairo, was intrusted with the relief of the starving populations in the Provinces of Girgeh, Kenneh, and Esneh. In a report which he subsequently presented to the Egyptian Government, he contended that the distress under which the people suffered was 'a money famine,' due to over-taxation, and suggested various reforms in the interest of the *fellahs*, all of which have since been carried into effect. For his services in this crisis he received the thanks of the Egyptian Government, and was invested by the Khedive with the Order of the Osmanie. Mr. Baird succeeded the late Sir Thomas Gladstone, Bart., of Fasque, as Lord-Lieutenant of the County of Kincardine in 1890. He married in 1873, the Honourable Annette Maria (died 21st May 1884), elder daughter of Lawrence Vaughan Palk, first Lord Haldon, and has issue—

    I. JOHN LAWRENCE, his heir.   IV. NORAH.

    II. EVELYN.   V. NINA.

    III. ALEXANDER WALTER FREDERIC.   VI. MURIEL JANE.

GLOSSARY

ACT, *instrument.*
Allegance, Alledgeins, *allegation.*
Allenerlie, *only.*
Amerciament, *a fine.*
Amerciat, *to fine.*
Appone, *to appose.*
Assedatioun, *a lease.*
Assertaining, *fixing,* **apportioning.**
Assythment, *compensation.*
Astrickit, *bound, engaged.*
Attour, *beyond, in addition to.*

BANNOCK, *one of the duties exacted at a mill.*
Barley-men, *members of a* **Court** *of Burlaw.*
Bauk, *a ridge.*
Be others, *more than others.*
Beddell, *a bedeman, a beggar.*
Befor, *for.*
Beit, *to mend.*
Bestiall, *live stock.*
Beyndis, *boundaries.*
Bigging, *a house.*
Binty, *covered with bent grass.*
Birk, *the birch-tree.*
Boll, *a dry measure.*
Brack, *to fail, to break.*
Brew-lauche, *the privilege of brewing.*
Brosteris, *brewers.*
But, *without.*
Butt, *a small disjoined portion of land.*
Bygaine, *past.*
Byganes, *past offences.*
By past, *past.*
Byrune, *past.*
By which, *whereupon.*

CALSE, *causeway.*
Campesce, *to restrain.*
Cast, *to dig, to cut.*
Chapelandrie, *chapel* **lands.**
Clew, *a ball of thread.*
Coff, *to buy.*
Coft, *bought.*
Collis, *coals.*
Collude, *to have collusion with.*
Common, *to have dealings with.*
Compone, *to come to an agreement.*
Compryse, *to seize, to arrest.*
Concord, *to unite.*
Concurse, *concurrence, co-operation.*
Condescend, *to agree.*
Contravert, *to dispute.*
Contumassie, *contumacious.*
Cotter, *one who inhabits a* cot *or cottage.*
Cowmond, *common.*
Cowmountie, *a common.*
Creill, *a basket made of osiers.*
Creischie, cris, chreese, *tallow.*

DACKER, *to search for stolen goods.*
Daik, dyik, *a wall.*
Darseing, *sowing.*
Decerniture, *a decree of Court.*
Depoition, *deposition.*
Designe, *to mark out.*
Detfull, *due.*
Dilete, *to legally accuse.*
Dilict, *a misdemeanour, a petty crime.*
Ding, *to beat, to strike.*
Dischairging, *prohibiting.*
Dispached, *driven out of.*
Dispone, *to convey to another.*

Dittay, *an indictment.*

Dogg, *a lever used by blacksmiths in hooping cart wheels.*

Ducat, dowcat, *a dove-cot.*

Dust, *the beard of the grain produced by taking off the outer rind.*

EAR, *to plough, to till.*

Effeirs, *it behoves.*

Eldyng, *fuel of any kind.*

Ell, elne, *a Scotch measure containing thirty-seven inches.*

Entres, *interest, concern.*

Extend, *to assess, to value.*

FACE, *an edge.*

Failze, *failure, a penalty.*

Fair, *thorough, complete.*

Farres, *ridges.*

Feall, faill, *turf.*

Fermoreis, *payers of ferme, farmers.*

Fiar, *one who has the reversion of property.*

Firlot, *the fourth part of a boll.*

Flaughter-spade, *an instrument for casting turfs.*

Flit, *to remove from one's house.*

Fra, *from.*

Fremen, *fishermen.*

Frenzie, *a fringe.*

Froster, *a forester.*

Furr, *a furrow.*

Furth, furthe, *abroad, manifest.*

GAITING, *making one's way.*

Gaitte, *a road.*

Gatherings, *gleanings.*

Geir, geyr, *goods, effects.*

Girne, *a snare.*

Gowpin, *a handful; one of the duties exacted at a mill.*

Gradually, *proportionally.*

Greatt balzie, *chief bailie.*

Gresman, *the tenant of a cottage who has no land attached to it.*

Grinter-man, grintall-man, *the keeper of the laird's granary.*

Guidis, *live stock.*

Guidman, *a small proprietor.*

Guidsir, *a grandfather.*

Gyff, *if.*

HALUMES, *All-hallows.*

Handie-grips, *close grappling.*

Haining, *an enclosure which is neither cut nor pastured.*

Hedrowmis, *the outer boundaries of a feu or toft.*

Heirfor, *therefore, wherefore.*

Helping, *repairing.*

Hiecher, *higher.*

Hog, *a sheep of a year old.*

Holt, *oxen.*

Husbandman, *a farmer.*

Hwill, *a small skiff.*

Hyreman, *a male servant who works for wages.*

ILK, *each.*

Impasche, *to hinder.*

Inconsiderate, *of little consequence.*

Indweller, *a resident.*

Intent, *to prosecute.*

Intromett, *to intermeddle.*

Introvussion, *alienation.*

Instruct, *to prove clearly.*

Invade, *to attack.*

JOIS, *to possess.*

KAIL, keall, keyll, *colewort.*

Keains, *customs paid in poultry and eggs.*

Keilling, *a large codfish.*

Keip, *to heed, to watch.*

Keippeythe, *a boat's crew.*

Knawshipe, *one of the duties exacted at a mill.*

LAID, *a mill-race.*

Lairis, *places on which peats are spread to dry.*

Lambes, Lammas, *the first of August.*

Larache, *the site of a building.*

Latch, *a bog, a marsh.*

Laubor, *to till, to cultivate.*

Lauboring, *tillage, a farm.*

Laufull, *law-abiding.*

Lede, leyd, *to cart.*

Leitt, *a load.*

Lesum, *lawful.*

Lippie, *the fourth part of a peck.*

Loak, loke, *a handful; one of the duties exacted at a mill.*

Loip, *to overleap.*

Lykas, lykwayis, *likewise.*

Lyne-man, *a white fisher.*

MAINES, *the farm attached to a mansion-house.*

Maill, *rent.*

Maistlie, *especially.*

Malicious, *troublesome.*

Manse, *a manor house.*

Meaneis, *common lands.*

Meit, *meal.*

Mell, *to meddle.*

Merchand, *marketable.*

Merk, *a silver coin, equal in value to thirteen shillings and four-pence.*

Metteing, *measuring.*

Midding, *a dung-heap.*

Milne swyne, *swine fed on a mill.*

Moull, *the refuse of meal.*

Mouter, multer, *a fee for grinding corn.*

Mwir, *heath.*

Mureburn, *the act of burning heath.*

NANE, *no, none.*

Nor, *than.*

Notour, *well-known, notorious.*

OBLEIS, *to bind to engage.*

Obstraiking, *withdrawing.*

Of before, *formerly.*

Offend, *to injure.*

Onnawayis, *in no wise.*

Or, *before, ere.*

Otheris, *each other.*

Our, *over.*

Outbounds, *common pasturage.*

Outlabour, *to exhaust by too much tillage.*

Oylly, *oil.*

PAIRT, *to divide, to portion off.*

Pas, *to pace, to measure.*

Pasche, *Easter.*

Patent, *ready.*

Peck, *the fourth part of a firlot.*

Peckcaman, pekaman, pickie-man, *a miller's servant.*

Pendicul, *a small piece of ground either depending on a large farm, or let separately by the owner.*

Petitour, *one entitled to raise a petitory action.*

Petpotteis, *holes from which peats have been dug.*

Plaice, *a manor house.*

Plee, *a dispute.*

Posit, *interrogated.*

Pott, *a hole whence peats have been dug; to make peat-holes.*

Precept, *a summons.*

Prejugit, *injured, deprived.*

Preparative, *a precedent.*

Pretend, *to set forth, to state.*

Probablye, *clearly, certainly.*

Procuratour, *solicitor.*

Promit, *to promise.*

Possession, *a holding.*

Pundlar, *a distrainer.*

QUALIFYIT, *proven.*

Quhair, *since, whereas.*

Quhairanent, *concerning which.*

Quhill, *until.*

Quhyt, *wheat.*

REAPLIE, ripely, *fully.*

Recusantis, *refusing.*

Red, redd, *to put in order, to clear.*

Redigie, *to repair.*

Reist, restand, *that remained due*

Remanent, *other.*

Remeid, *to remedy.*

Rest, *to be indebted to any one; balance due.*

Ribb, *to half plough. To plough in such a way as to throw the earth turned over upon an equal quantity of surface which remains undisturbed.*

Roum, rowm, *a holding.*

Rountrie, *the mountain ash.*

Ruid-day, *the third of May, the day of the invention of the Cross.*

Ryot, *a depredation.*

Ryve out, *to plough lea land.*

Sarking, *shirting.*

Sauch, *a willow.*

Scair, *mishap.*

Schell, *to take off the husks of grain.*

Schilingis, *grain freed from the husk.*

Servitour, *a servant.*

Set, sett, *a lease.*

Sheir, *to reap corn.*

Sheep rive, *pasture for sheep.*

Sicht, *inspection; to inspect.*

Sicklyk, *similarly*

Sincerely, *honestly.*

Smeddie, *a smith's workshop.*

Smoutis, *salmon fry.*

Spilling, *destroying.*

Staig, *a young horse.*

Stamp, *a trap.*

Stouth, *theft.*

Stryp, *a long narrow plantation.*

Stuff, *grain of any kind.*

Subscryve, *to sign.*

Suckin, *the jurisdiction attached to a mill.*

Suffer, *to delay.*

Swa, *so.*

Tack, *a lease.*

Tallown, Tallowne, *tallow.*

Taxisman, tacksman, *a tenant.*

Tensell, *forfeiture.*

Tempper, *to adjust.*

Thankfull, *legally sufficient.*

The morne, *to-morrow.*

The piece, *each.*

Thirl, *to bind by the terms of a lease, or otherwise to grind at a certain mill.*

Thoill, *to bear, to undergo.*

Toft, *a portion of land sufficient for a house and garden, a feu or plot.*

Tollerans, *permission.*

Tor, *an eminence, a hill.*

Toume, *a place into which rubbish or manure is emptied.*

Towne, *a farm steading.*

Trawaill, *labour.*

Turris, *turf.*

Ulie, *oil.*

Underlie, *to be subjected to, to undergo.*

Unlaw, *a fine; to fine.*

Unlikely, *an offence.*

Veice, *stead.*

Visie, *to examine.*

Vistage, *remains, ruins.*

Wallour, *value.*

Walk, *to watch.*

Want, *to lack, to miss.*

Warn, *to summon.*

Wictuall, *grain of any kind.*

Win, wine, *to dry.*

Wmquhill, *late, deceased.*

Wyises, *trusses.*

Ward, *a small piece of enclosed pasture ground.*

Yaird, *a garden.*

INDEX

Printed by T. and A. CONSTABLE, Printers to Her Majesty, at the Edinburgh University Press.

Scottish History Society.

———◆———

LIST OF MEMBERS.

1890-91.

3

LIST OF MEMBERS.

ABERNETHY, JAMES, 11 Prince of Wales Terrace, Kensington, London, W.

Adam, Sir Charles E., Bart., Blair-Adam.

Adam, Robert, Brae-Moray, Gillsland Road, Edinburgh.

Adam, Thomas, Hazelbank, Uddingston.

Adams, William, 28 Ashton Terrace, Hillhead, Glasgow.

Agnew, Alex., Procurator-Fiscal, Court-House Buildings, Dundee.

Aikman, Andrew, 27 Buckingham Terrace, Edinburgh.

Airy, Osmund, The Laurels, Solihull, Birmingham.

Aitken, Dr. A. P., 57 Great King Street, Edinburgh.

10 Aitken, James H., Gartcows, Falkirk.

Alexander, William, M.D., Dundonald, Kilmarnock.

Allan, A. G., Blackfriars Haugh, Elgin.

Allan, George, Advocate, 56 Castle Street, Aberdeen.

Allan, Rev. William, Manse of Mochrum, Wigtownshire.

Allen, Lady Henrietta, Tusculum House, North Berwick.

Anderson, Archibald, 30 Oxford Square, London, W.

Anderson, Arthur, M.D., C.B., Sunny-Brae, Pitlochry.

Anderson, John, jun., Atlantic Mills, Bridgeton, Glasgow.

Andrew, Thomas, Doune, Perthshire.

20 Armstrong, Robert Bruce, 6 Coates Crescent, Edinburgh.

Arnot, James, M.A., 57 Leamington Terrace, Edinburgh.

Arrol, William A., 11 Lynedoch Place, Glasgow.

Baird, J. G. A., Wellwood, Muirkirk.

Balfour, Right Hon. J. B., Q.C., 6 Rothesay Terrace, Edinburgh.

Ballingall, Hugh, Dundee.

Barclay, George, 17 Coates Crescent, Edinburgh.

Barron, Rev. Douglas Gordon, Dunnottar Manse, Stonehaven.

Begg, Ferdinand Faithfull, 13 Earl's Court Square, London, S.W.

Bell, A. Beatson, Advocate, 2 Eglinton Crescent, Edinburgh.

30 Bell, Joseph, F.R.C.S., 2 Melville Crescent, Edinburgh.

Bell, Robert Fitzroy, Advocate, 42 Heriot Row, Edinburgh.

Bell, Russell, Advocate, Kildalloig, Campbeltown.

Beveridge, Erskine, St. Leonard's Hill, Dunfermline.

Black, James Tait, 29 Palace Court, Bayswater Hill, London, W.

Black, Rev. John S., 6 Oxford Terrace, Edinburgh.

Blaikie, Walter B., 22 Heriot Row, Edinburgh.

Blair, Patrick, Advocate, 4 Ardross Terrace, Inverness.

Bonar, Horatius, W.S., 15 Strathearn Place, Edinburgh.

Boyd, Sir Thomas J., 41 Moray Place, Edinburgh.

40 Brodie, Sir T. D., W.S., 5 Thistle Street, Edinburgh.

Brookman, James, W.S., 16 Ravelston Park, Edinburgh.

Broun-Morison, J. B., of Finderlie, The Old House, Harrow-on-the-Hill.

Brown, Professor Alex. Crum, 8 Belgrave Crescent, Edinburgh.

Brown, J. A. Harvie, Dunipace House, Larbert, Stirlingshire.

Brown, P. Hume, 25 Gillespie Crescent, Edinburgh.

Brown, Robert, Underwood Park, Paisley.

Brown, William, 26 Princes Street, Edinburgh.

Brownlie, James R., 10 Brandon Pl., West George St., Glasgow.

Bruce, Alex., 16 Royal Crescent, Crosshill, Glasgow.

50 Bruce, James, W.S., 23 St. Bernard's Crescent, Edinburgh.

Bruce, Hon. R. Preston, Broom Hall, Dunfermline.

Bryce, James, M.P., 54 Portland Place, London, W.

Bryce, William Moir, 5 Dick Place, Edinburgh.

Buchanan, T. D., M.D., 24 Westminster Terrace, West, Glasgow.

Burns, George Stewart, D.D., 3 Westbourne Terrace, Glasgow.

Burns, John William, Kilmahew, Cardross.

Burns, Rev. Thomas, 2 St. Margaret's Road, Edinburgh.

Bute, The Marquis of, Mountstuart, Isle of Bute.

CALDWELL, JAMES, Craigielea Place, Paisley.
60 Cameron, Dr. J. A., Elgin.
Cameron, Richard, 1 South St. David Street, Edinburgh.
Campbell, Rev. James, D.D., the Manse, Balmerino, Dundee.
Campbell, James A., Stracathro, Brechin.
Carne-Ross, Joseph, M.D., Parsonage Nook, Withington, Manchester.
Carrick, J. Stewart, 58 Renfield Street, Glasgow.
Chalmers, Mrs. Patrick H., 29 Albyn Place, Aberdeen.
Chambers, W. & R., 339 High Street, Edinburgh.
Chiene, Professor, 26 Charlotte Square, Edinburgh.
Christie, J., Breadalbane Estate Office, Kenmore, Aberfeldy.
70 Christie, Thomas Craig, of Bedlay, Chryston, Glasgow.
Clark, G. Bennet, W.S., 57 Queen Street, Edinburgh.
Clark, James, Advocate, 4 Drumsheugh Gardens, Edinburgh.
Clark, James T., Crear Villa, Ferry Road, Edinburgh.
Clark, Robert, 42 Hanover Street, Edinburgh.
Clark, Sir Thomas, Bart., 11 Melville Crescent, Edinburgh.
Clouston, T. S., M.D., Tipperlinn House, Morningside Place, Edinburgh.
Cochran-Patrick, R. W., LL.D., of Woodside, Beith, Ayrshire.
Coldstream, John P., W.S., 6 Buckingham Terrace, Edinburgh.
Constable, Archibald, 1 Nelson Street, Edinburgh.
80 Cowan, George, 1 Gillsland Road, Edinburgh.
Cowan, Hugh, St. Leonards, Ayr.
Cowan, J. J., 38 West Register Street, Edinburgh.
Cowan, John, W.S., St. Roque, Grange Loan, Edinburgh.
Cowan, John, Beeslack, Mid-Lothian.
Cowan, William, 2 Montpelier, Edinburgh.
Cox, Edward, Lyndhurst, Dundee.
Craik, James, W.S., 9 Eglinton Crescent, Edinburgh.
Crawford, Donald, M.P., 60 Pall Mall, London.
Crole, Gerard L., Advocate, 1 Royal Circus, Edinburgh.
90 Cunningham, Geo. Miller, C.E., 2 Ainslie Place, Edinburgh.
Cunynghame, R. J. Blair, M.D., 18 Rothesay Place, Edinburgh.
Currie, James, 16 Bernard Street, Leith.

Currie, Walter Thomson, Rankeillour, by Cupar-Fife.
Currie, W. R., 28 Holyrood Quadrant, Glasgow.
Cuthbert, Alex. A., 14 Newton Terrace, Glasgow.

DALGLEISH, JOHN J., of Ardnamurchan, 8 Atholl Cres., Edin.
Dalrymple, Hon. Hew, Lochinch, Castle Kennedy, Wigtown-
　　shire.
Davidson, Hugh, Braedale, Lanark.
Davidson, J., Solicitor, Kirriemuir.
100 Davidson, Thomas, 339 High Street, Edinburgh.
Davies, J. Mair, C.A., Sheiling, Pollokshields, Glasgow.
Dickson, Thomas, LL.D., Register House, Edinburgh.
Dickson, Dr. Walter G. W., 3 Royal Circus, Edinburgh.
Dickson, William K., Advocate, 19 Dundas Street, Edinburgh.
Dickson, Wm. Traquair, W.S., 11 Hill Street, Edinburgh.
Dixon, John H., Inveran, Poolewe, by Dingwall.
Doak, Rev. Andrew, M.A., Trinity Free Church, Aberdeen.
Dodds, Rev. James, D.D., The Manse, Corstorphine.
Dods, Colonel P., United Service Club, Edinburgh.
110 Donaldson, James, LL.D., Principal, St. Andrews University.
Donaldson, James, Sunnyside, Formby, Liverpool.
Douglas, Hon. and Right Rev. A. G., Bishop of Aberdeen and
　　Orkney, Aberdeen.
Douglas, David, 15A Castle Street, Edinburgh.
Dowden, Right Rev. John, D.D., Bishop of Edinburgh, Lynn
　　House, Gillsland Road, Edinburgh.
Duncan, J. Dalrymple, Meiklewood, Stirling.
Duncan, James Barker, W.S., 6 Hill Street, Edinburgh.
Duncan, John, National Bank, Haymarket, Edinburgh.
Dundas, Ralph, C.S., 28 Drumsheugh Gardens, Edinburgh.
Dunn, Robert Hunter, Belgian Consulate, Glasgow.

120 EASTON, WALTER, 125 Buchanan Street, Glasgow.
Ewart, Prof. Cossar, 2 Belford Park, Edinburgh.

FAULDS, A. WILSON, Knockbuckle, Beith, Ayrshire.
Ferguson, James, Advocate, 41 Manor Place, Edinburgh.

Ferguson, John, Town Clerk, Linlithgow.

Ferguson, Rev. John, Manse, Aberdalgie, **Perth.**

Findlay, J. Ritchie, 3 Rothesay **Terrace, Edinburgh.**

Findlay, Rev. Wm., The Manse, Saline, Fife.

Firth, Charles **Harding, 33 Norham Road, Oxford.**

Fleming, D. **Hay, 16 North** Bell Street, St. Andrews.

130 Fleming, J. S., 16 Grosvenor Crescent, Edinburgh.

Flint, Prof., D.D., LL.D., Johnstone Lodge, Craigmillar Park, **Edinburgh.**

Forrest, James R. P., 32 Broughton Place, Edinburgh.

Forrester, John, 29 Windsor Street, Edinburgh.

Foulis, James, M.D., 34 Heriot Row, Edinburgh.

Fraser, Professor A. Campbell, **D.C.L., LL.D.,** Gorton **House,** Hawthornden.

Fraser, W. N., S.S.C., 41 Albany **Street, Edinburgh.**

Gaedeke, **Dr.** Arnold, Professor of History, Polytechnikum, 3 Liebigstrasse, Dresden.

Gairdner, Charles, Broom, Newton-Mearns, Glasgow.

Galletly, Edwin **G., 22 Albany** Street, Edinburgh.

140 **Gardner, Alexander, 7 Gilmour Street, Paisley.**

Gartshore, Miss Murray, Ravelston, Blackhall, Edinburgh.

Geikie, Sir Archibald, LL.D., Geological **Survey, 28 Jermyn Street, London, S.W.**

Geikie, Prof. James, LL.D., 31 Merchiston Avenue, Edinburgh.

Gemmill, William, 150 Hope Street, Glasgow.

Gibson, Andrew, 3 Morrison Street, Govan.

Gibson, James T., LL.B., W.S., 28 St. Andrew Sq., Edinburgh.

Giles, Arthur, 107 Princes Street, Edinburgh.

Gillespie, **G. R., Advocate, 5 Darnaway Street, Edinburgh.**

Gillies, **Walter, M.A.,** The **Academy,** Perth.

150 Gordon, Rev. Robert, Mayfield Gardens, Edinburgh.

Goudie, Gilbert, F.S.A. Scot., 39 Northumberland Street, **Edinburgh.**

Goudie, James Tulloch, Oakleigh **Park,** Nithsdale Drive, **Pollokshields.**

Goudie, Robert, Commissary Clerk of Ayrshire, Ayr.

Gourlay, Robert, Bank of Scotland, Glasgow.

Gow, Leonard, Hayston, Kelvinside, Glasgow.

Graeme, Lieut.-Col., Naval and Military Club, 94 Piccadilly, London.

Grahame, James, 93 Hope Street, Glasgow.

Grant, William G. L., Woodside, East Newport, Fife.

Gray, George, Clerk of the Peace, Glasgow.

160 Greig, Andrew, 36 Belmont Gardens, Hillhead, Glasgow.

Grub, Prof. George, LL.D., University, Aberdeen.

Gunning, His Excellency Robert Haliday, M.D., 12 Addison Crescent, Kensington, London, W.

Guthrie, Charles J., Advocate, 13 Royal Circus, Edinburgh.

Guy, Robert, 120 West Regent Street, Glasgow.

HALKETT, MISS KATHERINE E., 2 Edinburgh Terrace, Kensington, London, W.

Hall, David, Elmbank House, Kilmarnock.

Hallen, Rev. A. W. Cornelius, The Parsonage, Alloa.

Hamilton, Hubert, Advocate, 55 Manor Place, Edinburgh.

Hamilton, Lord, of Dalzell, Motherwell.

170 Hamilton-Ogilvy, Henry T. N., Biel.

Harrison, John, 36 North Bridge, Edinburgh.

Hedderwick, A. W. H., 79 St. George's Place, Glasgow.

Henderson, J. G. B., Nether Parkley, Linlithgow.

Henderson, Joseph, 11 Blythswood Square, Glasgow.

Henry, David, 2 Lockhart Place, St. Andrews, Fife.

Hewison, Rev. J. King, The Manse, Rothesay.   .

Hill, William H., LL.D., Barlanark, Shettleston, Glasgow.

Hislop, Robert, Solicitor, Auchterarder.

Hogg, John, 66 Chancery Street, Boston, U.S.

180 Honeyman, John, A.R.S.A., 140 Bath Street, Glasgow.

Hope, Sir John David, Bart., Pinkie House, Musselburgh.

Howden, Charles R. A., Advocate, 25 Melville St., Edinburgh.

Hunt, John, Fingarry, Milton of Campsie, Glasgow.

Hunter, Colonel, F.R.S., of Plâs Côch, Anglesea.

Hutcheson, Alexander, Herschel House, Broughty Ferry.
Hutchison, John, D.D., Afton Lodge, Bonnington.
Hyslop, J. M., M.D., 22 Palmerston Place, Edinburgh.

Imrie, Rev. T. Nairne, Dunfermline.

Jameson, J. H., W.S., 3 Northumberland Street, Edinburgh.
190 Jamieson, George Auldjo, C.A., 37 Drumsheugh Gardens, Edinburgh.
Jamieson, J. Auldjo, W.S., 14 Buckingham Ter., Edinburgh.
Japp, William, Solicitor, Alyth.
Johnston, David, 24 Huntly Gardens, Kelvinside, Glasgow.
Johnston, George Harvey, 6 Osborne Terrace, Edinburgh.
Johnston, George P., 33 George Street, Edinburgh.
Johnston, T. Morton, Eskhill, Roslin.
Johnstone, James F. Kellas, 3 Broad Street Buildings, Liverpool Street, London.
Jonas, Alfred Charles, Poundfald, Penclawdd, Swansea.

Kemp, D. William, Ivy Lodge, Trinity, Edinburgh.
200 Kennedy, David H. C., 27 St. Vincent Place, Glasgow.
Kermack, John, W.S., 10 Atholl Crescent, Edinburgh.
Kincairney, The Hon. Lord, 6 Heriot Row, Edinburgh.
Kinnear, The Hon. Lord, 2 Moray Place, Edinburgh.
Kirkpatrick, Prof. John, LL.B., Advocate, 24 Alva Street, Edinburgh.
Kirkpatrick, Robert, 1 Queen Square, Strathbungo, Glasgow.

Laidlaw, David, jun., 6 Marlborough Ter., Kelvinside, Glasgow.
Laing, Alex., Norfolk House, St. Leonards, Sussex.
Lang, James, 9 Crown Gardens, Dowanhill, Glasgow.
Langwill, Robert B., Manse, Currie.
210 Laurie, Professor S. S., Nairne Lodge, Duddingston.
Law, James F., Seaview, Monifieth.
Law, Thomas Graves, Signet Library, Edinburgh, *Secretary*.
Leadbetter, Thomas, 122 George Street, Edinburgh.
Livingston, E. B., 9 Gracechurch Street, London, E.C
Lorimer, George, 2 Abbotsford Crescent, Edinburgh.

Macadam, W. Ivison, Slioch, Lady Road, Newington, Edinburgh.

Macandrew, Sir Henry C., Aisthorpe, Midmills Road, Inverness.

Macbrayne, David, Jun., 17 Royal Exchange Square, Glasgow.

M'Call, James, F.S.A., 6 St. John's Ter., Hillhead, Glasgow.

220 M'Candlish, John M., W.S. 27 Drumsheugh Gar., Edinburgh.

Macdonald, James, W.S., 4 Greenhill Park, Edinburgh.

Macdonald, W. Rae, 1 Forres Street, Edinburgh.

Macdougall, James Patten, Advocate, 16 Lynedoch Place, Edinburgh.

M'Ewen, W. C., W.S., 2 Rothesay Place, Edinburgh.

Macfarlane, George L., Advocate, 14 Moray Place, Edinburgh.

Macgeorge, B. B., 19 Woodside Crescent, Glasgow.

Macgregor, John, W.S., 10 Dundas Street, Edinburgh.

M'Grigor, Alexander, 172 St. Vincent Street, Glasgow.

Macintyre, P. M., Advocate, 12 India Street, Edinburgh.

230 Mackay, Æneas J. G., LL.D., 7 Albyn Place, Edinburgh.

Mackay, James F., W.S., Whitehouse, Cramond.

Mackay, Rev. G. S., M.A., Free Church Manse, Doune.

Mackay, James R., 37 St. Andrew Square, Edinburgh.

Mackay, John.

Mackay, Thomas, 14 Wetherby Place, South Kensington, London, S.W.

Mackay, Thomas A., 14 Henderson Row, Edinburgh.

Mackay, William, Solicitor, Inverness.

Mackenzie, A., St. Catherines, Paisley.

Mackenzie, David J., Sheriff-Substitute, Wick.

240 Mackenzie, Thomas, M.A., Sheriff-Substitute of Ross, Old Bank, Golspie.

Mackinlay, David, 6 Great Western Terrace, Glasgow.

Mackinnon, Professor, 1 Merchiston Place, Edinburgh.

Mackinnon, Sir W., Bart., 203 West George Street, Glasgow.

Mackinnon, William, 115 St. Vincent Street, Glasgow.

Mackintosh, Charles Fraser, 5 Clarges Street, London, W.

Mackintosh, W. F., 27 Commerce Street, Arbroath.

Maclachan, John, W.S., 12 Abercromby Place, Edinburgh.

Maclagan, Prof. Sir Douglas, M.D., 28 Heriot Row, Edinburgh.

Maclagan, Robert Craig, M.D., 5 Coates Crescent, Edinburgh.

250 Maclauchlan, John, Albert Institute, Dundee.

Maclean, Sir Andrew, Viewfield House, Balshagray, Partick, Glasgow.

Maclean, William C., F.R.G.S., 31 Camperdown Place, Great Yarmouth.

Maclehose, James J., 61 St. Vincent Street, Glasgow.

Macleod, Rev. Walter, 112 Thirlestane Road, Edinburgh.

Macniven, John, 138 Princes Street, Edinburgh.

M'Phee, Donald, Oakfield, Fort William.

Macray, Rev. W. D., Bodleian Library, Oxford.

Macritchie, David, 4 Archibald Place, Edinburgh.

Main, W. D., 128 St. Vincent Street, Glasgow.

260 Makellar, Rev. William, 8 Charlotte Square, Edinburgh.

Marshall, John, Caldergrove, Newton, Lanarkshire.

Martin, John, W.S., 19 Chester Street, Edinburgh.

Marwick, Sir J. D., LL.D., Killermont Ho., Maryhill, Glasgow.

Masson, Professor David, LL.D., 58 Gt. King St., Edinburgh.

Mathieson, Thomas A., 3 Grosvenor Terrace, Glasgow.

Maxwell, W. J., Terraughtie, Dumfries.

Millar, Alexander H., Rosslyn House, Clepington Road, Dundee.

Miller, P., 8 Bellevue Terrace, Edinburgh.

Milligan, John, W.S., 10 Carlton Terrace, Edinburgh.

270 Milne, A. & R., Union Street, Aberdeen.

Milne, Thomas, M.D., 17 Mar Street, Alloa.

Mitchell, James, 240 Darnley Street, Pollokshields, Glasgow.

Mitchell, Rev. Professor Alexander, D.D., University, St. Andrews.

Mitchell, Sir Arthur, K.C.B., M.D., LL.D., 34 Drummond Place, Edinburgh.

Moncrieff, W. G. Scott, Advocate, Weedingshall Ho., Polmont.

Moffatt, Alexander, 23 Abercromby Place, Edinburgh.

Moffatt, Alexander, jun., M.A., Advocate, 37 Northumberland Street, Edinburgh.

Morice, Arthur D., Fonthill Road, Aberdeen.

Morison, John, 11 Burnbank Gardens, Glasgow.
280 Morrison, Hew, 7 Hermitage Terrace, Morningside.
Morton, Charles, W.S., 11 Palmerston Road, Edinburgh.
Muir, James, 27 Huntly Gardens, Dowanhill, Glasgow.
Muirhead, James, 10 Doune Gardens, Kelvinside, Glasgow.
Murdoch, Rev. A. D., All Saints' Parsonage, Edinburgh.
Murdoch, J. B., of Capelrig, Mearns, Renfrewshire.
Murray, David, 169 West George Street, Glasgow.
Murray, Rev. Allan F., M.A., Free Church Manse, Torphichen, Bathgate.

NAPIER AND ETTRICK, LORD, Thirlestane, Selkirk.
Norfor, Robert T., C.A., 30 Morningside Drive, Edinburgh.

290 OLIVER, JAMES, Thornwood, Hawick.
Orrock, Archibald, 17 St. Catherine's Place, Edinburgh.

PANTON, GEORGE A., F.R.S.E., 73 Westfield Road, Edgbaston, Birmingham.
Paton, Allan Park, Greenock Library, Watt Monument, Greenock.
Paton, Henry, M.A., 15 Myrtle Terrace, Edinburgh.
Patrick, David, 339 High Street, Edinburgh.
Paul, J. Balfour, Advocate, Lyon King of Arms, 32 Great King Street, Edinburgh.
Paul, Rev. Robert, F.S.A. Scot., Dollar.
Pearson, David Ritchie, M.D., 23 Upper Phillimore Place, Kensington, London, W.
Pillans, Hugh H., 12 Dryden Place, Edinburgh.
300 Pollock, Hugh, 25 Carlton Place, Glasgow.
Prentice, A. R., 18 Kilblain Street, Greenock.
Pullar, Robert, Tayside, Perth.
Purves, A. P., W.S., Esk Tower, Lasswade.

RAMPINI, CHARLES, LL.D., Advocate, Springfield House, Elgin.
Rankine, John, Advocate, Professor of Scots Law, 23 Ainslie Place, Edinburgh.

Reichel, H. R., University College, Bangor, North Wales.
Reid, Alexander George, Solicitor, Auchterarder.
Reid, H. G., 11 Cromwell Cres., S. Kensington, London, S.W.
Reid, John Alexander, Advocate, 11 Royal Circus, Edinburgh
310 Renwick, Robert, Depute Town-Clerk, City Chambers, Glasgow.
Richardson, Ralph, W.S., Commissary Office, 2 Parliament
    Square, Edinburgh.
Ritchie, David, Hopeville, Dowanhill Gardens, Glasgow.
Ritchie, R. Peel, M.D., 1 Melville Crescent, Edinburgh.
Roberton, James D., 1 Park Terrace East, Glasgow,
Robertson, D. Argyll, M.D., 18 Charlotte Square, Edinburgh.
Robertson, J. Stewart, W.S., Edradynate, Ballinluig.
Robertson, John, Elmslea, Dundee.
Robson, William, Marchholm, Gillsland Road, Edinburgh.
Rogerson, John J., LL.B., Merchiston Castle, Edinburgh.
320 Rosebery, The Earl of, LL.D., Dalmeny Park, Linlithgowshire.
Ross, T. S., Balgillo Terrace, Broughty Ferry.
Ross, Rev. William, LL.D., 7 Grange Terrace, Edinburgh.
Roy, William G., S.S.C., 28 Broughton Place, Edinburgh.
Russell, John, 7 Seton Place, Edinburgh.

Scott, John, C.B., Seafield, Greenock.
Shaw, David, W.S., 1 Thistle Court, Edinburgh.
Scott, Rev. Archibald, D.D., 16 Rothesay Place, Edinburgh.
Shaw, Rev. R. D., B.D., Auchencairn Manse, Hamilton.
Shaw, Thomas, Advocate, 17 Abercromby Place, Edinburgh.
330 Shiell, John, 5 Bank Street, Dundee.
Simpson, Prof. A. R., 52 Queen Street, Edinburgh.
Simpson, Sir W. G., Bart., Stoneshiel Hall, Reston, Berwick-
    shire.
Simson, D. J., Advocate, 3 Glenfinlas Street, Edinburgh.
Sinclair, Alexander, Glasgow Herald Office, Glasgow.
Skelton, John, Advocate, C.B., LL.D., the Hermitage of
    Braid, Edinburgh.
Skene, W. F., D.C.L., LL.D., 27 Inverleith Row, Edinburgh.
Skinner, William, W.S., 35 George Square, Edinburgh.

Smart, William, M.A., Nunholm, Dowanhill, Glasgow.

Smith, G. Gregory, M.A., 9 Warrender Park Cres., Edinburgh.

340 Smith, Rev. G. Mure, 6 Clarendon Place, Stirling.

Smith, Rev. R. Nimmo, Manse of the First Charge, Haddington.

Smith, Robert, 24 Meadowside, Dundee.

Smythe, David M., Methven Castle, Perth.

Sprott, Rev. Dr., The Manse, North Berwick.

Stair, Earl of, Oxenfoord Castle, Dalkeith.

Steele, W. Cunninghame, Advocate, 33 Dublin St., Edinburgh.

Stevenson, J. H., Advocate, 10 Albyn Place, Edinburgh.

Stevenson, Rev. Robert, M.A., The Abbey, Dunfermline.

Stevenson, T. G., 22 Frederick Street, Edinburgh.

350 Stevenson, William, Towerbank, Lenzie, by Glasgow.

Stewart, Major-General Shaw, 61 Lancaster Gate, London, W.

Stewart, James R., 31 George Square, Edinburgh.

Stewart, R. K., Murdostoun Castle, Newmains, Lanarkshire.

Stewart, Prof. T. Grainger, M.D., 19 Charlotte Sq., Edinburgh.

Stirling, Major C. C. Graham, Craigbarnet, Haughhead of Campsie, Glasgow.

Strathallan, Lord, Carlton Club, Pall Mall, London, S.W.

Strathern, Robert, W.S., 12 South Charlotte St., Edinburgh.

Strathmore, Earl of, Glamis Castle, Glamis.

Stuart, Surgeon-Major G. B., 7 Carlton Street, Edinburgh.

360 Sturrock, James S., W.S., 110 George Street, Edinburgh.

Sutherland, James B., S.S.C., 10 Windsor Street, Edinburgh.

Taylor, Benjamin, 10 Derby Crescent, Kelvinside, Glasgow.

Taylor, Rev. Malcolm C., D.D., Professor of Church History, 6 Greenhill Park, Edinburgh.

Telford, Rev. W. H., Free Church Manse, Reston, Berwickshire.

Tennant, Sir Charles, Bart., The Glen, Innerleithen.

Thoms, George H. M., Advocate, 13 Charlotte Sq., Edinburgh.

Thomson, John Comrie, Advocate, 30 Moray Place, Edinburgh.

Thomson, Rev. John Henderson, Free Church Manse, Hightae, by Lockerbie.

Thomson, John Maitland, Advocate, 10 Wemyss Pl., Edinburgh.

370 Thomson, Lockhart, S.S.C., 114 George Street, Edinburgh.
Thorburn, Robert Macfie, Uddevalla, Sweden.
Trail, John A., W.S., 30 Drummond Place, Edinburgh.
Trayner, The Hon. Lord, 27 Moray Place, Edinburgh.
Tuke, John Batty, M.D., 20 Charlotte Square, Edinburgh.
Turnbull, John, W.S., 49 George Square, Edinburgh.
Tweedale, Mrs., Milton Hall, Milton, Cambridge.
Tweeddale, Marquis of, Yester, Gifford, Haddington.

Underhill, Charles E., M.D., 8 Coates Crescent, Edinburgh.

Veitch, Professor, LL.D., 4 The College, Glasgow.

380 Waddel, Alexander, Royal Bank, Calton, Glasgow.
Walker, Alexander, 64 Hamilton Place, Aberdeen.
Walker, James, Hanley Lodge, Corstorphine.
Walker, Robert, M.A., University Library, Aberdeen.
Wannop, Rev. Canon, Parsonage, Haddington.
Watson, D., Hillside Cottage, Hawick.
Watson, James, Myskyns, Ticehurst, Hawkhurst.
Waugh, Alexander, National Bank, Newton-Stewart, N.B.
Weld-French, A. D., Union Club, Boston, U.S.
Will, J. C. Ogilvie, M.D., 379 Union Street, Aberdeen.
390 Wilson, Rev. J. Skinner, 4 Duke Street, Edinburgh.
Wilson, John J., Clydesdale Bank, Penicuik.
Wilson, Robert, Procurator-Fiscal, County Buildings, Hamilton.
Wood, Mrs. Christina S., Woodburn, Galashiels.
Wood, Prof. J. P., W.S., 16 Buckingham Terrace, Edinburgh.
Wood, W. A., C.A., 11 Clarendon Crescent, Edinburgh.
Wordie, John, 49 West Nile Street, Glasgow.

Young, David, Town Clerk, Paisley.
Young, A. J., Advocate, 60 Great King Street, Edinburgh.
Young, J. W., W.S., 22 Royal Circus, Edinburgh.
400 Young, William Laurence, Solicitor, Auchterarder.

PUBLIC LIBRARIES.

Aberdeen Free Public Library.
Aberdeen University Library.
All Souls' College, Oxford.
Antiquaries, Society of, Edinburgh.
Baillie's Institution Free Library, 48 Miller St., Glasgow.
Berlin Royal Library.
Bodleian Library, Oxford.
Boston Athenæum.
Boston Public Library.
10 British Museum.
Cambridge University Library.
Copenhagen (Bibliothèque Royale).
Dollar Institution.
Dundee Free Library.
Edinburgh Public Library.
Edinburgh University Library.
Free Church College Library, Edinburgh.
Free Church College Library, Glasgow.
Glasgow University Library.
20 Gray's Inn, Hon. Society of, London.
Harvard College Library, Cambridge, Mass.
Leeds Subscription Library.
London Corporation Library, Guildhall.
London Library, 12 St. James Square.
Manchester Public Free Library.
Mitchell Library, Glasgow.
National Liberal Club, London.
National Library of Ireland.
Nottingham Free Public Library.
30 Ottawa Parliamentary Library.
Paisley Philosophical Institution.
Philosophical Institution, Edinburgh.
Procurators, Faculty of, Glasgow.
Royal College of Physicians, Edinburgh.
St. Andrews University Library.
Sheffield Free Public Library.
Signet Library, Edinburgh.
Solicitors, Society of, before the Supreme Court, Edinburgh.
Speculative Society, Edinburgh.
40 Stonyhurst College, Blackburn, Lancashire.
Sydney Free Library.
Vienna, Library of the R. I. University.

REPORT OF THE

FOURTH ANNUAL MEETING

OF THE

SCOTTISH HISTORY SOCIETY

———————◆———————

THE Fourth Annual Meeting of the Scottish History Society was held in Dowells' Rooms, Edinburgh, October 28, 1890—Professor Masson in the chair.

The Secretary submitted the report of the Council as follows :—

The Council has to announce with regret the death of ten members of the Society during the past twelve months. Among the deaths there should be specially mentioned that of Mr. J. J. Reid, the honorary treasurer of the Society ; and that of Mr. George Burnett, late Lyon King of Arms, a member of the Council. Seven members have resigned ; but, after filling up the vacancies, there still remain nineteen names on the list of applicants for admission. Mr. J. T. Clark has, on the invitation of the Council, kindly undertaken to act as interim honorary treasurer, in the place of the late Mr. Reid ; and the Council now proposes to the Society the ratification of his appointment to that office. It is also proposed to confirm the appointment of Mr. T. G. Murray, W.S., and Mr. James Ferguson, advocate, to the vacant places in the Council.

Three volumes have, within the past week, been issued to members. Of these, one only, *The Book of Glamis*, edited by Mr. A. H. Millar, properly belongs to the issue of the year 1889-90 ; for the second part of the *Register of the St. Andrews Kirk-Session* was due to the preceding year ; and *The List of Rebels* is an extra volume, a gift for which the Society has to thank Lord Rosebery, the president. The second volume promised for this year's issue, viz., Mr. Constable's translation of *Major's History*, is, however, completed, and a few sheets of the text have already been set in type ; but the work of revising and annotating this important volume, which will extend to about 500 pages, must proceed carefully and slowly.

But if the Council is behindhand with regard to this volume, the Society will take into account the fact that the executive has far exceeded its promise in the total quantity of matter issued during the past four years. The Council undertook at the outset to supply to members 640 printed pages annually. Actually the seven volumes already issued, excluding *The List of Rebels*, give 2865 pages, or 240 pages in excess of the stipulated amount. If we include *The List of Rebels*, we have had up to this date 680 pages, or roughly estimated the equivalent of two volumes over and above our bargain without reckoning *Major's History*, which is due.

Good progress has been made with several of the works in contemplation. It is proposed to issue in the course of next year, 1890-91, the first portion of the *Records of the Commission of the General Assembly*. Matter sufficient for one volume has already been transcribed by Mr. Henry Paton, and is ready to go to press. It will include the 'Acts and Proceedings of the Commission of the General Assembly holden in Edinburgh,' from June 1646 to August 1647. It will be edited by Dr. Christie, and furnished with a preface by Professor Mitchell of St. Andrews. The companion volume for the year, *The Diary of Sir John Clerk of Penicuik*, has also been transcribed, and is now in the hands of Mr. J. M. Gray, the editor. *The Diary of Mr. Andrew Hay*, 1659-60, to be edited by Mr. A. G. Reid of Auchterarder, is in an advanced state of preparation. *The Court Book of the Barony of Urie* is also transcribed. The titles of other works in progress will be found in the list of announcements printed at the end of *The Book of Glamis*.

It will be seen by a reference to the accompanying abstract of the interim-treasurer's accounts that the income for the year has been £475, 10s., and expenditure £336, 3s. 10d., leaving a balance in favour of the Society of £139, 6s. 2d. It is, however, to be noted that from this balance the cost of the production of *Major's History* falls to be deducted. With regard to the reserve fund agreed to at the meeting of the Society held last year, the Council, understanding that this fund was not meant to be cumulative, have considered it right that the interest accruing thereon should form part of the annual income, and that the sum in reserve should stand at £300.

The Chairman proposed a special vote of thanks to Lord Rosebery for his generous gift of the volume—*The List of Rebels*—a gift not only valuable on its own account, but valuable also as one more proof of the active interest which Lord Rosebery, as President of the Society, had taken from the first in its affairs and its objects. Mr. Traquair Dickson, W.S., seconded the motion.

The Chairman, in moving the adoption of the Report, mentioned that the Society had in prospect a gift by Sheriff Thoms of a volume of documents giving a complete history of the Scottish Lord High-Admirals and Vice-Admirals, and a history of the Admiralty Court generally, with an introduction by himself. Mr. Goudie, Treasurer of the Society of Antiquaries, seconded the motion, which was adopted.

[OVER

ABSTRACT OF THE TREASURER'S ACCOUNTS.

For Year to 1st November 1890.

CHARGE.

Balance from last year, ...	£320 13	1
Less credited in error, ...	1 1	0
	£319 12	1
400 Subscriptions for 1889-90 at £1, 1s., . .	420 0	0
36 Libraries at £1, 1s., ...	37 16	0
Copies of previous issues sold to new members, .	3 3	0
Interest on Bank Account and Deposit Receipts, .	14 18	5
Sum of Charge, .	£795 9	6

DISCHARGE.

I. *Incidental Expenses—*

Printing Circulars and Cards, .	£2 16 6	
„ Annual Report of Council,	1 6 6	
„ Report of Third Annual Meeting, . . .	1 13 6	
„ Rules, etc., . . .	1 16 0	
Stationery, ...	1 1 0	
Making-up and delivering copies,	10 0 0	
Postages of Secretary and Treasurer,	4 7 0	
Clerical work, ...	3 1 6	
Charges on Cheques, . . .	0 17 0	
Hire of Room for Meeting, . .	0 5 0	
		£27 4 0

II. *St. Andrews Register, Vol. II.—*

Composition, Presswork, and Paper, ...	£147 18 7	
Proofs and Corrections (including marginal and footnotes), .	37 12 0	
Copying MSS., Lithographing, and Engraving, ...	7 19 0	
Carry forward, £193 9 7		£27 4 0

	Brought forward,	£193	9	7	£27	4	0
Binding and Back-lettering,	.	18	2	3			
Transcribing,	. . .	.	28	0	0			
		£239	11	10			
Less paid to account 1889,	.	45	9	0			
					194	2	10

III. *Glamis Papers—*

Composition, Presswork, and							
Paper,	. . .	.	£58	15	9			
Proofs and Corrections,	.	.	6	12	0			
Collotype Reproductions,	.	.	9	15	0			
Binding and Back-lettering,	.	18	16	3			
					93	19	0

IV. *Barony Court Book of Urie—*

Transcribing and Examining Papers, . . 15 18 6

V. *Craig, De Unione—*

Transcribing, . 5 0 0

Total Expenditure, . £336 4 4

VI. *Balance to next Account—*

19 Subscriptions for 1889-90 in							
arrear,	. . .	.	£19	19	0			
Sum due by Bank of							
Scotland on Deposit							
Receipt,	.	. £300	0	0			
Sum due by Bank of							
Scotland on Cur-							
rent Account,	.	141	8	2			
					441	8	2
		£461	7	2			
Less 2 Subscriptions for 1890-91							
paid in advance, .	.	.	2	2	0			
					459	5	2

Sum of Discharge, . £795 9 6

EDINBURGH, 19*th November* 1890.—We have examined the
Accounts of the Treasurer of the Scottish History Society for the

6

year ending 1st November 1890, and having compared them with the vouchers, we find them to be correct, closing with a balance in the Bank of Scotland of Four hundred and forty-one pounds, Eight shillings, and Two pence, Sterling, whereof Two Guineas are subscriptions paid in advance.

(Signed)   { RALPH RICHARDSON.
                          { WM. TRAQUAIR DICKSON.

www.ingramcontent.com/pod-product-compliance
Lightning Source LLC
Chambersburg PA
CBHW020944120726
47905CB00008B/2671